SOLOMON'S
COMPASS

Enjoy!

Carol Kilgore

SOLOMON'S COMPASS

BY

CAROL KILGORE

18 17 16 15 14 13   10 9 8 7 6 5 4 3 2 1

Solomon's Compass

ISBN: 978-1-48185-014-8

ISBN-10: 1-48185-014-8

Copyright © 2013 by Carol Kilgore

For John,

my true north.

And to all Coast Guard veterans,

especially those who served during the Vietnam Era.

Thank you for your service.

Bangkok, Thailand—Summer, 1970

The Patpong bargirl tapped Jake Solomon's shoulder. "You go buy my friend drink." She pointed toward the other end of the noisy bar as she wrapped her other arm around Ham Norberg's neck and let her fingers play with the short hair at the back of his head.

Jake frowned at Ham. "You good with that?" The Rolling Stones blared from speakers at the back of the tiny go-go stage and prevented words from carrying farther than a couple of inches.

Hamblen Norberg was the most married man Jake had ever known. Here they were, on the other side of the damn world, two sailors free in Bangkok on R&R, and Ham hadn't even danced with anyone. Much less done anything else.

Ham looked up. "Yeah, I'm good. Stop halfway." He ordered a drink for the girl.

Jake nodded, moving several feet down and squeezing between two other Americans at the crowded bar. Near enough to reach Ham in seconds, if the need arose. The mamasan behind the bar motioned for the bargirl's friend to join him. He inched over to give her space on the side nearest Ham so he could see them both at the same time.

The first bargirl's dark head was bent close to Ham's blond one. Her lips were moving, and Ham nodded.

The friend-bargirl next to Jake tugged his shirt and mimed taking a drink. He waved bills in the air. A minute or two later, the barkeep brought him another beer and the expensive, watered-down fruit juice the bargirls drank.

Ham's bargirl raised her leg to his lap and removed a garter. She slid it up to his bicep and repeated the action with her other leg. After securing the second garter on Ham's muscled arm, she kissed his cheek, downed her drink, and left the bar. Ham knocked back the rest of his beer.

Jake left his bargirl to fend for herself. Back next to his buddy, he waited while Ham paid for a fresh beer. "What was the deal with the bargirl?"

Ham snapped the garter. "She asked me to hold these for her."

"How much did she want for you to keep them?"

"Nothing. She'll be back in an hour."

Three hours and many beers later, the bargirl hadn't returned.

"Gotta take a piss, man." Jake slid off the barstool. Had to stop drinking, too. The room spun like a merry-go-round.

"Same here."

They staggered through the open door into Patpong. More Americans on R&R like Ham and Jake roamed the street. Everyone wore civvies, as if that would keep them from being recognized. Bangkok touts and ladyboys did their best to lure them inside every open bar door. Jake glanced at his watch—two-thirty in the morning and the street was bright as day. Loud music ebbed and flowed as he stumbled over the cracked sidewalk, Ham at his side.

A few steps later, Jake spied the opening to an alley. "Let's go in here."

Ham turned to the wall on the right. Jake to the left. Over his own sounds, Jake heard scrapes coming from near a trash bin a few yards into the alley. "Hurry up. Someone's back there."

"Probably Army. Too cheap to get a hotel room."

They laughed. The noise came again, an arm or leg bumping against metal.

"Three hours, and she's a no-show. I'm done. We'll come back tomorrow."

"Mamasan let her leave and didn't get a girl to stop us. Maybe her kid's sick." The bumping sounded again, this time accompanied by a moan. Jake zipped up.

Ham faced the street. "Army's getting his rocks off. Let's give him some privacy."

A burst of metallic blows and a faint high-pitched scream split the air.

Jake ran toward the waste bin, Ham's footfalls behind him. "Jesus H." Jake dropped to one knee in the neon twilight.

The bargirl who had given Ham her garters lay on the ground, still banging her forehead against the bin.

Ham rushed to her shoulders, pulled her away from the side of the bin, and let her head rest against his broad chest. "Stop, baby. It's me, Ham. I have your—oh, Christ, no!"

Ham had seen what Jake saw from the beginning. The girl lay in a pool of blood and used her hands and arms to hold her belly closed.

Her head drooped to the side. Jake didn't know how she'd had the strength to raise it, much less use it to make enough noise to attract their attention. Her left hand slid down her side and landed palm up in her blood.

Ham felt for a pulse and shook his head. "I'm going to be sick."

Jake forced down the saliva trapped in his mouth and moved to the waste bin. It was smaller than the ones in the States, but the same shape. Patpong smells were bad enough, but the ones emanating from the bin were worse. He held his shirttail over his nose with one hand and dug through the garbage with the other. He pulled out a metal box, the size and shape of a small safe deposit box. Beneath it were two silk pouches with drawstring closures.

Ham approached as Jake pulled out the sacks. "What are you doing? Let's get out of here."

"She heard American voices. She wanted us to find something in here. I did."

"What?"

Jake held out the box and pouches. "Stick the bags in your pockets or inside your waistband. I'll do the same with this box.

My shirt's baggy enough no one will notice. When we get back to the hotel, we can look inside."

CHAPTER I

Taylor Campbell was on a quest. Not just any quest—a quest to unearth her uncle's buried treasure. Except she was a U.S. Coast Guard commander, the captain of a 270-foot cutter. Coast Guard commanders didn't go on quests to unearth buried treasure.

Oh, yeah. Taylor had one more minor glitch.

She was certain the buried treasure was all in Uncle Randy's dementia-riddled mind. The final words of his last email to her were *Tell no one.* She had promised to honor his wishes, and a promise was a promise. Even though Uncle Randy had been dead almost a full year.

She was so screwed.

Yet here she sat, in the D/FW departure gate, still experiencing the day from traveler's hell. Her first flight left late from Charleston, and the second had a long weather delay in Atlanta, complete with two hungry infants and the thunderous man who appeared to be calling everyone he'd ever known and telling them all his innermost secrets.

By the time they reached Dallas, Taylor had missed her connection to Corpus Christi. She would still arrive tonight, but by the time she checked in at the hotel in Rock Harbor, the witching hour would be closing in.

If only she were a witch. She could grab her broom and arrive at the coast with a wiggle of her nose.

"Hi. Mind if I sit here?"

Taylor left her fantasy and glanced up. "No, not at all."

When had the seats filled up? She moved her backpack from the one next to her and placed it between her feet.

The blonde woman sighed as she sat. "This flight better leave on time. I have a busy schedule tomorrow."

Taylor smiled. "What do you do?"

"Realtor. I come up here to shop, when I want to *really* shop. You know what I mean. Corpus gets me by in between, but there's nothing like a shopping weekend in Dallas."

The woman could have come straight from a photo shoot. Not a hair was out of place, no wrinkles in her dress, French-manicured nails. The only other person Taylor had ever seen layer on so much make-up was her mother. And two minutes walking in the woman's high-heeled sandals would make Taylor limp for a week.

"I'm not much of a shopper." She looked down at her jeans and flip-flops. Crap, she'd dropped mustard on her tee at lunch.

"Attention, ladies and gentlemen. We have a mechanical delay. The flight will be called to board in approximately one hour."

Taylor swore the gate attendant looked straight at her and said the last with a smile in his voice that meant one *long* hour. And only if she was lucky.

Her stomach churned. Just perfect.

Absolutely. Friggin'. Perfect.

CHAPTER 2

A large bird swooped low across the hood of Kelly's car just as she pulled to a stop. "Son of a bitch. That damn thing almost made me pi—"

"I get the picture. You always were a fraidy cat." Jake braced for the blow he knew his sister would deliver. She didn't disappoint.

"Ogre."

"Princess." Their name-calling had endured since childhood and always earned them a huge eye roll from their mother.

"Damn straight. And don't forget it."

He turned his head to smile so Kelly wouldn't see. She might have been the one to flinch, but the bird's close pass honed Jake Solomon's nerves to a fine edge. He pulled a flashlight from a small brown duffel on the floor. "The bird's a night heron. Heading to the bay for dinner. The first time I saw one in Colombia, I was lurking in a stand of reeds waiting for a band of FARC rebels to settle in for the night. I thought it was attacking me, and it was all I could do to stay calm until it passed."

Kelly turned off the engine and killed the lights. "Your voice is becoming more like Dad's. You haven't sounded so much like Brooklyn since high school. Even more after hearing those Texas accents at dinner."

"Sounding like Dad is my job. Remember?" Jake looked out the passenger window. "So this is Rankin's place."

Thanks to the information his dad had drilled into his head for months, he knew a frame house with a metal roof stood behind the row of live oaks at the street. To the right, the metal building of Rankin's Marine Salvage hulked in the deep twilight.

"Even in the dark, I see you changing into Dad. The way you hold the light. The angle of your head. You always resembled him, but now that you let your hair grow shaggy, you're doppelgängers. You're walking like him, too. Even the foot shuffle he does when he's tired. I have to remind myself it's you, not him."

"Sometimes I do a double-take if I catch myself in a mirror. I know it's unsettling, but I have to *be* him, Kel. I can't switch him on and off. I made videos of the way he moves. Talks. I played them twenty-four seven for weeks. And I *am* tired. I flew halfway around the world to get here." He had to nail the performance—physical, mental, and emotional. One incorrect quirk of an eyebrow could get him killed. He didn't want anyone giving his eulogy anytime soon.

"The move Dad does with his hand when he's making a decision. The action that always precedes him telling me no. Do you do that, too?"

Jake bounced his left wrist up and down—two clicks up, one down.

"Stop." Quiet but firm. No nonsense.

"No detail too small, Kelly Jane."

"Don't call me Kelly Jane." Her words came through clenched teeth.

"Dad would." And it gave him an excuse to get away with it.

"Get out."

He chuckled as he stepped onto the asphalt road and closed the door without a sound. Irritating his baby sister was fun, but they had work to do.

Kelly met him at the gate. "Shine the light on the lock."

He switched on the Maglite and zeroed in on the padlock hanging in the center of the gates. Kelly went to work with her pick and the padlock clicked open. "Follow me." She opened one side of the gate far enough for them to slip through before closing it.

"Not bad so far."

"Looks worse in daylight. Wait until your eyes feast on the luscious goodies inside. I'll show you the house first."

"At least the grass is cut."

"Commander Campbell arranged for an exterminator and general upkeep of the grounds. Almost three acres—the house, the business building and parking area, and an empty salvage yard."

U.S. Coast Guard Commander Taylor Ann Campbell. Randy Rankin's niece, and the primary purpose of his mission to Rock Harbor, Texas. Keep her safe. No matter the cost. Do not become involved with local law enforcement.

Not bodyguard protection—proactive protection. Keep the problem away from the subject, and keep the subject unaware. That meant identifying the problem and stopping it at its source. He and Kelly made a good team. Working together, proactive protection wouldn't be a problem. It was one of the services the family security business, Compass Points International, provided its clients.

Kelly led him across the lawn between the ancient trees by the road and the old house. They rounded the corner. She stopped, and he shined the beam through a salt-encrusted window. "Jesus H. This place needs to be bulldozed."

"You're creeping me out with Dad's words." She shivered. "I told you it was a rat's nest. Dad said Rankin was as squared away as they came. Even tried to be spit and polish out on the rivers in the jungle. Each one of his tools on the Point boat had a spot where it stayed unless he was using it. Rankin kept every area aboard that he was responsible for the same way. That sort of organization is missing here."

He angled his light through the window to reduce the glare. Engines, boat seats, boxes, and open bins of parts were stacked floor to ceiling. On a folding table, set after set of glassware stood in rows. Jake needed to understand this man, but the enlightenment wouldn't happen from rereading his dad's memories. Tonight was a start.

"Look at these." He ran the beam over the glasses.

Kelly leaned closer to the window. "Junk heaped in piles, and he sets up for a party."

"Strange." Something was off. He didn't know what, but he would. In time.

The next window provided a view into another bedroom. This one held a twin bed, carefully made up. Closed plastic boxes, three high, flanked a small dresser on the far wall. One box stood under each of the two windows.

"Crowded, but neat." Kelly slapped at a mosquito.

"Right. This looks more like the Randy Dad knew, except for the boxes." The glasses. The bed. The jumbled mess. Jake would let the pieces bump around in his head for a day or two.

They worked their way from window to window. The other rooms echoed the first, jumbled but with one neat item tucked in, like the glasses.

The house stood on pilings, taking it a few feet off the ground. Not enough to walk under. Jake put a knee down and bent to take a look. The Maglite beam revealed several tufts of weeds sprouting through a layer of oyster shells.

"Let's go over to the shop." He turned the flashlight off and strode beside Kelly. They crossed the shell driveway and stepped over a fallen fence separating home from business. Wooden shutters covered the windows of the shop. "You went inside?"

"It's worse than the house. No alarms in either place."

"I've seen enough." He could barely hold himself upright, much less concentrate, from lack of sleep—over the last thirty-six hours, only two short naps.

"Dad may be wrong about Rankin. Perhaps he did get lost in the fog the last few years."

"He says no. We have to trust him, Kel, and play by his rules."

"Not my strength."

Kelly had been the wild child. She flourished at the edge. The whole family did, himself included—Compass Points International was a family business, after all—but Kelly outshined him and their parents.

"Dad respects your independence. Look where that untamed streak has taken you." His sister was one of the top cyber security experts in the world.

She shrugged. "Whatever. I have two more spots to show you tonight."

"Tell me."

"Where Will Knox lives."

"He owns the boatyard across the street?"

"Bingo." She pointed to it as they walked to the car.

"I don't suppose you're going to provide any more clues?"

"You're a smart man. Form your own conclusions."

"And the other spot you want to show me?"

"You'll find out." Kelly's phone chirped. "Commander Campbell just checked in."

"Good."

Kelly kept her speed a mile or two under the limit and didn't run any yellow lights. They passed his hotel and turned onto Milam Beach Road, the same street they had taken to dinner earlier. Before reaching the restaurant, Kelly inched over to put the two right wheels on the tiny shoulder and turned on the flashers.

"Why didn't we stop here before?"

Kelly turned to him, eyebrows raised. "Traffic. Daylight."

"Hmm." He couldn't wait to get back to his hotel room and crash for a week.

Kelly tapped his arm. "Wake up. I know the trip from Helsinki was hard, but you've got to be more alert, more careful."

Christ, he'd actually thought he was awake and fairly alert. He needed sack time bad. "You're right."

"We'll be at your hotel in ten minutes or less. For now, suck it up. Look around. We're parked by a rickety pier that runs a hundred or more feet out into the bay. The middle of the pier is washed out."

He reached for his Maglite.

"Leave your flashlight on the floor. I know how you always want to see everything, but it's too dangerous for us if someone is watching."

He straightened and stared into blackness.

"Large rocks line the coastline. Between them and the water is a narrow beach."

"How narrow?"

"Three, four feet when the tide is all the way out. When it rolls in, it laps halfway up the rocks."

"This is where they found Rankin?"

"Right. Half under the pier. Face down. A bottle of Jack tucked up like a football."

An ounce or two of whiskey had remained in the bottle and had tested out as pure Jack Daniel's—no drugs or other extras. Jake and his dad disregarded the ruling of accidental death by drowning. The other evidence of murder was overwhelming when looking at the full picture. Randy Rankin was the most recent in a line of Compass Point deaths.

Jake's fingers curled into fists. It didn't matter that Rankin had been his dad's buddy, not his. He'd lost buddies in Iraq. More in Afghanistan. He forced himself to remain in the car, unable to see where land met ocean. He wanted to climb over the rocks, lie on the sand where Rankin had died, protect the man's memory. And he couldn't even see the place where his dad's friend had taken his last breath. *I'll be back, buddy.*

"How can I find this pier in the morning?" His voice sounded harsh to his own ears. He cleared his throat.

"One point eight miles this side of the parking lot at Flounder Bay, the restaurant where we had dinner." Her soft voice held respect.

On the other side of the road, the land rose up to a low hill topped by a small, unlit cottage. "What does that house look like?"

"Yellow with white shutters and trim."

"Is that where Will Knox lives?"

"No, but you're following the path. I wanted you to fix the location of the pier in your mind first." At the second street they climbed the hill and drove for two blocks. She turned left. "Third house down on the right."

"Go slow."

Lights from a white bungalow illuminated neatly trimmed shrubbery sheltered by an old live oak. A pickup stood in the driveway. By the side of the road, the eyes of a cat reflected the lights from Kelly's car.

"Would a murderer leave a body that close to home?" He knew the answer before he asked the question.

"Some bury victims in their own backyards."

He rotated his head, first in circles then from one side to the other, stressed-out muscles clicking with his movements. They needed to find Rankin's killer and learn why he'd killed the men of Solomon's Compass. All of the men but one. Jake's dad. The man who shared his name. The last surviving member of the original Compass Points.

But finding the killer wasn't enough for Jake. Six months earlier, two weeks after Thanksgiving, his dad got sick. And scared. Jake got sick and scared, too. Both for his dad's health and because his dad was troubled about something beyond his illness that he wouldn't talk about. Jake caught his worried looks, and once when he walked into the den, his dad shoved a folder into his desk drawer just a little too quickly.

While his dad was in the hospital for surgery, Jake found the file. He had to pick the lock on the drawer, but he was as good at that as Kelly. Their dad had taught them both. And he hadn't been surprised when Jake told him what he found. His dad was afraid he would die without knowing why the Compass Points were in the bull's eye—and who was targeting them.

With Jake's assurance of help laid out on the table, his dad opened up. And entrusted Jake to carry out his wishes. After keeping the details to himself for more than four decades, it took him several days to tell Jake the complete story. Although Jake was scared that he wouldn't be good enough to keep them from being killed, he had determination on his side. He and Kelly would succeed unharmed. He would not allow his dad to suffer another loss.

His dad was ill, but the illness didn't keep him from being a grueling taskmaster. Months of work and preparation followed. And months of convincing his dad to bring in Kelly. Six weeks ago, his dad agreed. Kelly found and sent reams of data based on the general information he gave her. His dad poured through it all, pulling out only what he deemed appropriate. And Kelly went back to work, digging deeper.

His dad might be the last man standing, but instead of being the winner, he was the target. With any luck the game would end in Rock Harbor, and Jake would live to tell about it.

As if reading his thoughts, Kelly sighed. "I won't let you down. You need rest, and so do I. We'll be at your hotel in two or three minutes, depending on the traffic light at the highway."

"You're sure you didn't leave a trail when you reserved our rooms and cars?"

She laughed. "Aces! Exactly like Dad. Nobody is ever as secure as they believe. Except maybe CPI, 'cause they've got me. And one or two government agencies. Why do you think Dad is choosy about what I do? And for whom?"

"You wouldn't be prejudiced."

"Stating a fact, bro."

Kelly was smart, and Jake was tough. Together they would be unbeatable because they were fighting for their dad.

Right now Jake's head pounded and his body ached. He needed sleep before jet lag kept him from being of use to anyone. Kelly dropped him off, and he watched as she pulled out. She waved back to him without turning around, knowing he would stand guard until she was out of sight, no matter how long it took. He'd been doing that all her life. When the taillights of her rented beige Ford rounded the curve, he followed the sidewalk around the side of the building toward the parking lot to make sure Commander Campbell was still in.

Kelly had given him the license plate number for the rental, and he spotted Taylor Campbell's rental car on the first row, but gave it no more than a casual glance. No shadows moved. No sounds broke through the hum of traffic.

He continued around the building to the front door, just a man getting in a short walk before returning to his room. Or so it would appear to anyone who didn't know him. He smiled at the male clerk behind the desk and strolled to the elevator.

Given that security was his business, he took extra care when he traveled. Three motion-activated cameras covered every inch of his room. One was obvious to anyone who knew what to search for. The second could be found by a diligent professional. The third camera would only be recognized by someone with a recent special ops background.

If the motion sensors had been triggered, his smartphone would've rung, enabling him to view the break-in in real time. If someone had tampered with the sensors or tried to destroy them—either physically or with a virus attack—Jake would've received an emergency text. No one had been inside his room. All the same, he checked each camera upon entering, then put them on snooze.

Nobody messed with Jake Solomon. Neither of the Jake Solomons. Or their family.

Tomorrow he would install cameras in Taylor Campbell's room and outside in the hall to watch her door. His dad had promised Randy Rankin that if anything should happen to him, he would keep an eye on his niece, Taylor Campbell. Jake promised his dad that if anyone tried to harm Taylor, they would have to go through him first.

And Jake Solomon, father or son, never broke a promise.

CHAPTER 3

Taylor had hoped for a bright, sunny Monday for her first visit to Randy's house. The Weather Mama had other plans.

Beneath low, leaden clouds, a beige something-or-other behind her had its signal on and turned to the right. A small midnight-blue SUV followed a block behind. She must have seen seven or eight dark-colored SUVs before she turned on Church Street—the uniform car of Rock Harbor, most of them more suitable in color for a funeral procession than life at the Texas coast.

They had been plentiful on her drive from Corpus last night, too. Before checking in at the hotel, she'd checked in with her GPS and found the white bungalow at 209 Amberjack. Even though it was midnight, she'd been prepared to dig. The steel gray pickup with fancy wheels and a vanity plate—WILL U—sitting in the driveway dissuaded her in a heartbeat.

She had come to Rock Harbor with two objectives. The first was to find or confirm the absence of her Uncle Randy's treasure and say a final goodbye.

Her second mission was to decide the disposition of her uncle's estate. Randall Dallis Rankin, owner of Rankin's Marine Salvage, had died last June with a gut full of bourbon and two lungs full of seawater, drowned in his own beloved Copano Bay.

He passed out on the meager beach and never knew when the tide came in.

Gusty winds twisted palm fronds this way and that, the same way dementia had twisted Randy's mind. If she made it inside his house before the storm arrived in full force she'd be happy.

Stilt houses thinned to a few scattered buildings, a church. After the American Legion Hall, Church Street curved to the right, and Oyster Bank Road teed into the middle of the curve on the left. The SUV turned into the American Legion lot. She turned onto Oyster Bank, and the bay appeared straight ahead, pale green against the stormy sky.

Oyster Bank was barely wide enough for two cars to pass. Rankin Marine Salvage and the asphalt parking lot were on the right. The old metal building, twenty years older since her last visit, had held up well, except for shrinking from the never-ending cavern of her memory to a structure measuring closer to twenty by forty feet.

She could still hear Uncle Randy telling her to get out of the salvage yard before she got hurt. The mountains of anchor chain, mounds of trawling nets, and a derelict boat or two had proved irresistible. She hadn't known what all the items were, but the salvage had sent her imagination spiraling.

Rain peppered down in fat drops as she followed the road to the right.

Randy's house faced the bay about fifty feet away from the shop building. The metal roof was rusty, and two screens on the side hung on by one clip. A chain-link fence separated the house from the shop and the empty salvage yard, but the back side of the fence lay mostly on the ground. Randy's lawyer said the inside would be worse. She would be in Rock Harbor for ten days, and probably all she'd have time for was compiling a comprehensive list of projects that needed doing and getting recommendations for the right people to do them.

A lock hung on the gate. Rather than getting soaked, she pulled to the shoulder beneath one of the big live oaks lining the road in front of the house and cut the engine to wait out the squall. She'd loved climbing these trees and tossing acorns to the seagulls, wondering with each toss why the seagulls never caught them. Randy had loved these old live oaks as if they were his children.

Across the street was a boatyard that hadn't been there twenty years ago—Copano Boat Works. Several boats in various stages of repair stood in travel lifts, nestled in blocks or on trailers. As boatyards went, it appeared neat and tidy. And busy. The owner must do good work.

Lightning flashed, and thunder followed an instant later, rumbling loud and deep. The hair on her forearms sprung out. Over the boom of thunder, Taylor heard a sharp crack and looked up. The moonroof framed a lightning bolt as it struck the massive oak limb and snaked down the tree. The edge of the limb ripped from the trunk. Shredded bark burst into the ozone-heavy air.

"Crap!" She unsnapped her seatbelt and flung open the door. Her feet hit the pavement at full speed. Midway across the road, leaves and branch tips fell against the backs of her legs. Metal screeched. She turned her head. The limb lay atop her rental, and the smashed roof was level with the hood.

Lightning flashed again, and Taylor counted all the way to one before thunder boomed. The gates to Copano Boat Works stood open, and she raced to the nearest building—a ships' store bulging with parts and accessories. She splayed her fingers across her chest in a futile effort to calm her pounding heart.

"May I help you?" The melody of Texas played in the female voice.

Taylor wiped the rain off her face and shook her arms and legs like a dog before running her fingers through her short hair—more to stop their trembling than to do anything about the inevitable frizzies. A woman in her early twenties with golden skin and black hair pulled into a sleek ponytail stood behind the counter at the back. Curiosity filled her almond-shaped brown eyes.

"Will you call somebody for me? My car's across the street—"

A man wearing a Cowboys ball cap burst through a door near the counter. "Hey, Trinh, call A.J. and tell him to get his wrecker over here. A limb blew down from one of Rankin's trees and smashed through the roof of some poor bastard's car. I'm going to see if I can help."

Trinh pointed at her while reaching for the phone.

Taylor produced a weak smile. "Thanks. That poor bastard would be me. I'm alone, but my stuff is inside the car."

He pulled a red shop rag from his back pocket and wiped his hands as he walked toward her. "Sorry. You all right? Need a doctor? I'll get you a chair."

"I don't need to sit. I'm fine. Lightning struck the limb. I got out before it landed." She shrugged. "I guess that's obvious."

He smelled of boats and the sea, oil and salt. Scents she lived with every day.

"Rankin loved those trees. Wouldn't trim them. Said as long as he lived, they'd grow as God intended. But he died last year. The property is just sitting here. Scuttlebutt says he left everything to some out-of-state relative. I can give you the lawyer's name."

"Not necessary. The owner would be me, too. Taylor Campbell. Randy Rankin was my uncle."

"Will Knox."

Trinh interrupted, "A.J. says if you'll adjust his prop tomorrow, he'll get right over here. Otherwise, he's going to haul in a paying customer from the highway. Three-car pile-up."

"Tell him it's a deal and to get himself over here. Let somebody else make the big bucks." He turned back to Taylor. "Sorry about your uncle. Are you here to inspect the place?"

"You might say that. I'll be around until next week."

"I liked Rankin, but his place is a pigsty. Be prepared."

"His attorney told me both the house and salvage shop are a mess, but I can take inventory of needed repairs, things like that."

Will's cell rang. "Excuse me."

She walked over to Trinh, her sandals squishing water with each step. "Thanks for calling a tow."

"No problem. A.J. will probably be here before it stops raining." Trinh pointed at her. "Love your shirt."

Taylor looked down. Today she'd worn Doc. Besides travel clothes, all she'd brought were work clothes—old shorts, a couple of even older Coast Guard tees, and a set of Snow White and the Seven Dwarfs tees she'd bought on a port call in San Juan several years before. Height appropriate, she thought. "Thanks. Makes me smile."

"Me, too." Trinh tilted her head. "You're calm for almost getting killed."

Taylor had trembled, but her training prepared her to perform under stress. Fear hadn't taken hold. "Anytime I don't have to worry about something ripping a gash in the hull and sinking us before everyone gets out, I'm good to go."

"You must work on the water."

"Coast Guard."

"They have a group in Aransas Pass. Are you going to be stationed there?"

"No. I'm on a cutter in Charleston. South Carolina."

"Too bad. They have boats around here. And helicopters. Do you do one of those?"

"Boats." Taylor grinned. "But my boat has a helicopter."

"Your boat?" Trinh's eyes widened. "Are you the captain?"

"I am."

"Cool." A big smile split Trinh's face, and her head bobbed up and down. "Will won't believe you. He can be old-fashioned. Especially about boats. He thinks they're totally a guy thing. No matter how much I tell him otherwise. My grandfather taught all of us how to operate a boat. He believed it was necessary since we live by the water."

"Good for your grandfather. It's not always easy being a woman."

"But it's fun."

They shared a laugh and became instant friends.

Trinh waved her arm behind her. "The boats in Aransas Pass are pretty big—about a hundred feet. Yours must be bigger."

"My cutter's almost three hundred feet."

Trinh's eyes grew large. "I thought only the Navy had ships."

"No one gives us a second thought." *Or remembers cutters.* "Besides, most of the Navy ships make even our large cutters look like bathtub toys."

"I can't wait to tell Will. Why do you call them cutters?"

"Way back when, the Coast Guard was called the Revenue Cutter Service."

"Oh." Trinh bobbed her head, then paused. "Mr. Rankin was your uncle, huh?"

"My mother's brother." From acting as her only male role model growing up, to becoming her life raft at the Academy, Randy had been the most real and normal person in her family until two years ago when his emails began making less and less sense.

"I remember your mother from his funeral. Black dress. Big black hat with a veil. And really high heels. I never saw her face."

Rest assured there were no tears beneath that veil. Taylor's mother was a train wreck camouflaged by a pretty smile. One of Taylor's jobs growing up had been to clean her mother's bedroom and closet. The woman didn't know a duster from a toilet brush, but she could spot Louboutins or Jimmy Choos from two blocks away. She cared more for shoes, bling, and herself than she did for anyone else. Including Randy and Taylor.

"That sounds like Mother. I was in the middle of the Atlantic."

The day the email from her mother arrived telling her of Randy's death, she'd been at sea, three days out from a port call at Copenhagen. She'd given the bridge to her executive officer and spent the day in her cabin, rereading the emails and letters she'd received, trying to make sense of his death. And nursing the empty place in her heart. Randy had taught her to take her job seriously. He would understand her being a year late to get to Rock Harbor to handle his affairs and say goodbye.

"I didn't know you existed. Your uncle seemed fine one day. But the next, one of his oars didn't quite reach the water. The last year or so, he stopped cutting the grass. Will cut it a few times. Rats and snakes can be a problem out here. I remember Mr. Rankin painting his house once when I was in high school. When it needed it again, he no longer cared."

"The last time I was here was spring break my last year in high school. That was in the early nineties. The house and shop still looked nice then. Randy was proud to have built a successful business from scratch. White paint, blue shutters. I used to play over here when I was little. Before the boatyard, this was sandy field with patches of grass between Uncle Randy's and the water. I fished from a pier down the road."

"The government settled my grandparents here from Vietnam after the war. Your uncle and my grandfather sometimes fished together."

"Randy loved to fish."

"I didn't know him real well, but I liked him. He always told me jokes and talked about Vietnam. He remembered a lot from the war. Did you join the Coast Guard because of his stories?"

Taylor held up her hands. "You got me. The summers I came here, we talked and fished. He loved people and Vietnamese food. He used to make rice or pasta with grilled fish or meat and fresh cucumbers and carrots. He probably fixed Minute Rice and ramen noodles, but he called it Vietnamese. We always ate with chopsticks."

Because of Randy, she had applied to the Academy all those years ago. She shared his obsession for doing the best job possible, and that would never change. No matter what duty she performed in the Coast Guard, bottom line her job—and the job of every Coastie—was to protect people on the sea and protect the country from threats delivered by sea. Coasties were adaptable and responsive. Plain and simple, she and the others were Always Ready. *Semper Paratus.*

Will came up and laid his Cowboys hat on the counter. His stubby strawberry-blond hair looked like the working side of a shoe brush.

"Ms. Campbell—"

"Taylor. Please call me Taylor. Both of you."

"All right. Taylor, I hope you'll forgive my bluntness earlier. It's just that Rankin never got the assistance he needed in the housekeeping department, and the mess grew."

She remembered Uncle Randy sweeping the kitchen and keeping the bathroom spotless. But people changed. "I understand. Apology accepted."

The door opened and a huge man entered. Tall, with a ruddy complexion. Graying blond hair receded from his high forehead and wicked eyebrows.

Will raised a hand in greeting. "Hey, Glen. What's up?"

He walked toward them. A Rock Harbor Police ID hung from a lanyard draped around the man's neck. He turned his blue stare to her, and his bushy brows squirmed. His expression was kind, but she'd seen eyes like his. They would freeze to ice if the need arose.

"Glen, this is Taylor Campbell—Rankin's niece. Taylor, Glen Upchurch. Rock Harbor's finest detective."

"That's me." Upchurch smiled. "Pleased to meet you. Sorry for your loss. I liked your uncle."

"Thanks. Good to meet you, too."

"That your car under the tree? Are you all right?"

Will answered for her. "She's fine. A.J.'s on his way. She'll need a report. Can you fix her up?"

"I'll call it in." He turned back to her. "The officer will ask you some questions and look at your license."

"Everything is in the car. I'll go out when the limb is off."

"While you're seeing to your vehicle, I'm going to help myself to some of Will's coffee and see how cheap he'll sell me a new Bimini top. As soon as I call the dispatcher." He walked toward the door.

The phone on the counter rang, and Trinh picked it up.

Will touched Taylor's elbow. "It's a pleasure to meet you. I've been thinking about making an offer on Rankin's place. Are you interested in selling?"

Selling? Sell her uncle's dreams? He'd been the one person in her life who'd kept her grounded. "No. Not at all."

"Will?" Trinh's voice shook, and so did the receiver in her hand. Her face had paled and her eyes were huge.

"What? Who is it?"

"I don't know, but they said we're going to die."

CHAPTER 4

Glen hurried to the counter, returning his phone to his pocket and pulling out a notebook. "Tell me exactly what the caller said."

Trinh licked her lips. "'If you help that woman, you'll die, too.' That was all. Whispered."

"Did you recognize the voice?"

"No. I couldn't even tell if it was a man or a woman."

"I was looking outside while I called in Ms. Campbell's accident. I didn't see anyone out there. Do you have caller ID?"

Trinh nodded. "Private Caller."

Will tugged his ball cap over his thick hair, scowling. "The caller could have driven past and then called. Taylor, does anyone know you're here?"

"No. Well, Randy's lawyer. And some service contractors."

"Word travels fast around here, Ms. Campbell. Where are you staying?" Glen's pencil hovered over the pad.

"The Waterfront. Call me Taylor, please."

"Taylor it is. Your hotel is reputable. How about back home? Any problems? And where is home?"

The cutter was her home, but she slept at a rented condo in the West Ashley area of town when the *Susquehanna* was in port. "No. No problems. I'm Coast Guard, stationed aboard a cutter homeported in Charleston, South Carolina."

Glen turned to Will. "How about you? Someone playing a joke?"

Will pulled off his cap, dragged his hand through his hair, and shoved the cap back on. "You know everyone I know. I wouldn't put it past any of them. If it was a bad joke, somebody will fess up in a day or two."

"Trinh." Glen's eyebrows hitched up in the middle.

They looked in Trinh's direction, but she'd vanished.

"Trinh!" Will stomped off toward the back as Trinh poked her head around the corner.

"I'm making coffee. Jesus, Will. Do some breathing exercises or something. Get a grip."

"How did that caller sound to you?"

"The words were scary, but—I don't know—it didn't hit me until after I hung up."

Glen's pencil hovered again. "Do you believe someone was playing a joke on you?"

Trinh shrugged. "Possibly."

Taylor paced the aisles past shelves filled with boating supplies. No one in Rock Harbor knew her. The people who knew she would be here didn't know she would be at Will's boatyard. Hell, she hadn't known the boatyard existed until a few minutes ago. Obviously, someone would confess over a beer to playing a joke on Will. She reached the counter.

Glen handed her his card. "If someone tells you they made this call, let me know. Best to use my cell. I already told Will and Trinh."

"Okay." A clap of thunder made her flinch. The rain no longer fell in torrents, and the sky had gone from charcoal to ash. Across the street, the back end of her rental poked out from beneath live oak branches. What a way to introduce herself to the neighbors.

A police cruiser rolled through the gate. "Here's the officer. Let me talk to him first." Glen strode toward the chandlery door.

Taylor leaned against the counter. The call was too bizarre to be real, but she couldn't stop thinking about it. No one had any reason to want to kill her. The only person she'd ever known here was dead.

The door opened, and a uniformed officer walked through. He put his hands on his hips and looked down at her. "That your car under the tree?"

"Rental, but I was the driver."

He nodded. "How'd it fall?"

"Only one large limb." She made a slicing motion. "Lightning."

"You were coming here?"

"No. I'm Randy Rankin's niece. I was going to see his . . . *my* property. Still having a hard time with that. The papers and keys are in the car." Flashing yellow lights reflected off the glass. Taylor pointed out the window at the arriving tow truck. "Trinh called someone named A.J. for a tow. After he gets the limb off, I'll show you everything."

The truck parked in front of her rental and a tall, slim figure jumped down from the cab. She'd expected a burly man with a scraggly ponytail and dressed in baggy clothes.

"A.J.'s fast. He'll do a good job."

"I'll go get the papers. No use both of us getting wet."

Without waiting for a response, she ran out—and stopped. Parked behind the covered work area across the driveway stood WILL-U. Will Knox. How messed up had Randy's head been? *Don't think about it now.*

She ran to the tow truck, and the driver turned.

"I'm Taylor Campbell. It's my rental hiding under the tree." Rain blew in her face, and she blinked it out of her eyes. It was slacking off, and the sky grew lighter by the second.

"August Janacek. Everyone calls me A.J." His neutral accent bounced off the local twang and pegged him as an outsider. Strands of gray ran through his hair, and his leathery skin showed his love of the outdoors.

"I need my things as soon as you get the limb off. An officer is waiting inside to make a report." *And I've got a full day planned.*

"Won't take but a minute." He pulled a pair of dirty leather gloves over long-fingered hands. She would've never pegged him as a tow truck driver.

"Have you lived here long?"

"About ten years. I'm a Colorado transplant. Moved to Austin for the climate and came here to fish. Gasoline went up, and I decided to move here full time. Have you known Will long?"

"Just met him." She inclined her head toward her uncle's. "I'm Randy Rankin's niece."

"I didn't know. Sorry for your loss." He looped chain around the limb in two places.

"It's okay. You did right to move to the place you love. Randy loved it here, too. "

From the control panel on the side of the truck, he maneuvered the boom and attached the ends of the chains to the hook. "Stand over in Will's driveway in case a chain snaps."

A.J. worked with the controls, and a minute later, the limb sat on the side of the road. The front third of the roof was smashed level with the hood, the windshield folded inside the car.

"Wow." The word came out unbidden. If she hadn't escaped, she would be dead. "Thank you. How much do I owe you?"

"Nothing. I'll collect from the rental company . . . and from Will."

"I'd say a prop adjustment is a good deal."

"You know about props?"

"A little." She raised her chin toward the car. "Will you get my things out?"

"Sure."

"Keys are in the ignition. My purse and a large envelope are on the seat. Rental papers in the glove box." She stood where she could watch. The rain had stopped. Randy had called these morning downpours tropical thunderstorms.

He popped the glove box with a crowbar. "Your uncle was a good man. We miss him."

A good man. Yes. Randy Rankin had been the rock in her life. As he pinned on her first set of shoulder boards when she graduated from the Coast Guard Academy, he reminded her about devotion to duty. Randy was an Old Guard Coastie and always told her *we have to go out, but we don't have to come back.* The political correctness of the twenty-first century had diluted that Old Guard motto, but for most Coasties, the passion remained. And it carried over into their lives outside and after the Guard.

She touched A.J.'s arm. "Thank you. I'm aware Randy lost it those last couple of years, so I appreciate your kindness."

A.J. shrugged. "You may hear all kinds of comments around. I wanted you to know that many people here cared about him."

"That means a lot. I haven't been here in years. The place probably didn't look so bad when he was alive." She hoped. Randy was a squared-away sailor. And the Randy she knew would have been embarrassed by the current state of disrepair. She still hurt when she thought about him.

"You may meet a few crawly critters in there." He nodded toward Randy's house.

"The exterminator has been out twice."

"That's good. Do you need a ride to the rental company?"

"Yes, but I may be a while. I need to go back and talk with the officer."

"Not a problem. If I get your car loaded before you're ready, I'll just check my email and the market." He pulled a smartphone an inch or two out of his shirt pocket and let it drop back in.

Taylor must be the only person left on the planet with a non-smartphone. Hers may be a three-year-old antique, but it didn't matter. It got the job done for her.

An SUV pulled to a stop next to them. The wine-red exterior was so dark it was almost black. The tinted passenger window slid down revealing the blonde from the airport behind the wheel. "A.J. What the hell happened here? Is everything all right?"

"Got it under control. Zia, this is Taylor Campbell, Rankin's niece. His place is hers now. Taylor, Zia Markham."

"We talked at the airport last night." Taylor stood up straighter.

Zia leaned toward her. "What a fiasco. Are you all right?"

"Fine." Taylor managed half a smile.

Zia passed her a card. "Call if I can help you while you're here. Or if you want to sell. I have to run. Showing a house down the way." The window slid up, and Zia drove off.

Taylor turned the card over. "Zia Grant Markham. ZGM Properties."

"Don't mind Zia." A.J. rubbed a stray drop of rain from his cheek with a knuckle. "She's hot and cold. Her brain is always on business. If you break through, she's a hundred percent with you, but keeping her there is on you."

"High maintenance."

"And then some. But very successful." A.J. started hooking up the rental. "Tell Will if he wants some firewood, he better get here with his saw before I bring my boat over tomorrow."

"Got it. Thanks."

Inside the chandlery, Glen and the officer stood at the counter talking with Trinh. Taylor held out the rental papers to the officer. "Here you go. One second, and I'll get my ID."

She removed her driver's license and Coast Guard ID from her wallet, placed them on the counter, and turned to Trinh. "A.J. said he's taking the limb for firewood tomorrow if Will doesn't get it before then."

"He's gassing up the chainsaw now."

The officer picked up her ID. "You're Coast Guard?"

She lifted her chin. "Right. Here on leave. I have a copy of my orders in the envelope."

"Not necessary. I'll be back. I'm going out to look at your car before A.J. loads it."

Glen looked at her ID, too. "What do you do in the Coast Guard?"

She smiled. "I'm CO of the *Susquehanna* out of Charleston."

"My nephew enlisted a few years ago. He's an avionics guy."

Will came through the door and went into the back room.

"Great field. Where's he stationed?"

Will returned and joined them.

"At the air station on Cape Cod."

"Always hectic up there." To say the least. Cape Cod was the only Air Station in First District, and its units were responsible for all the waters from New Jersey to the Canadian border. They had to be ready to go within thirty minutes 24/7, so equipment and replacements always had to be in working order and good repair.

"He loves it."

"I understand. I do, too."

Will kicked the tile with the heel of his work boot. "You inherited Randy's business. Isn't that a conflict of interest or something, a marine salvage business run by someone in the Coast Guard?"

"No conflict—there is no more business."

Trinh pushed Will's arm. "Don't mess with her. She's captain of a ship."

His eyebrows drew together. "You're a busy woman. If you decide you want to sell, let me know."

"You and Zia. Don't hold your breath."

The officer returned, gave her information about accessing the report online, and said goodbye. Taylor gathered her belongings. "Thanks for everything. I'll be around. Right now A.J. is taking me to get a replacement car."

She walked out by herself. Will, Trinh, and Glen were friendly enough, but Taylor was happy to be back in the rain-freshened air, even if would be a sauna in about three minutes.

A.J. spotted her and waved. He slipped his phone in his pocket. "Ready?"

"You bet." She pulled herself into his truck.

He turned the key. "You did that like a pro."

"I learned early how to get myself into and out of places. Nothing is designed for those of us who are vertically challenged."

A.J. laughed. "How challenged are you?"

"About four or five inches at minimum. I'm five-one. Almost. With shoes."

CHAPTER 5

Instead of staying at a hotel, Kelly had rented a small pink cabin by the water. Jake stretched out on the sofa, willing his body to settle into local time, while she started to work.

She had taken photos of everyone Taylor Campbell met at the boatyard through a long-lens camera. He had kept track of their plate numbers through binoculars. After the tree branch fell, it was all he could do to keep his hands steady. His mission to keep Taylor safe almost ended before it began.

A series of beeps came from Kelly's laptop.

He opened one eyelid. "Are you secure?"

"I have a new facial recognition program. It's damn good—better than the FBI uses. The photos are transferring while I'm looking up plate numbers. Make sure everyone matches up."

"That's not what I asked you." Now both his eyes were open.

She hadn't looked up. "Absolutely. Encrypted mobile broadband to tap into a secure line from your hotel with code buried in the reservations system. I used the masked encrypted line to activate a line with double encryption for Compass Points Secure. Everything is backfilled, flagged, and double-trapped."

"How can you be secure if you tapped in?"

Her computer beeped again. She turned around. "Don't ask questions you wouldn't understand the answer to."

He sat up. "What about the beeps?"

Kelly crossed her eyes and stuck out her tongue. "The facial recognition software beeps on acquisition and completion. I can change the sound. You want a gorilla roar or horn honk? Or I can mute it."

"Not necessary. I just worry that the men in black suits get a signal each time you do, and I don't want them to come calling."

"They're minor league."

"Says she with spiky purple hair."

"My hair was only purple for a few weeks. Simon said it looked bruised."

Until yesterday, he hadn't seen Kelly since Thanksgiving. Her purple hair and the black leather suit she'd worn for the family dinner had fired his dad right up, which had been her intent. Their work usually sent them in different directions. Each time he saw her, he never knew what her hair and eye color would be.

"I like the red. Goes well with your real eye color." He was grateful she'd ditched the yellow cat's-eye contacts she once favored.

"It's not red. Honey blonde with copper. Says so on the boxes."

"Looks rusty. How's Simon?" His sister had unique tastes, none more so than her genius husband, Simon Wetmore, who kept himself cocooned in an MIT physics lab.

She flashed a brilliant smile. "Working on some tunneling issues."

Simon lived in a tunnel of his own, but he and Kelly understood each other and she was happy. That's what mattered.

"We're trying to get pregnant."

Jake didn't want that image in his head. "Good luck."

Kelly turned back to her laptop and entered more data. "Simon says we have a ninety-five point nine two chance of succeeding within six months."

The day Simon could calculate creation, Jake would eat his skivvies. "How long before we have names for these people?"

"Results are coming in now."

"I thought I had time for a nap." Six hours of sleep hadn't cut it. If he could get to bed by ten tonight, he should be a new man tomorrow.

"No way, bro."

He yawned on his way to the table she'd turned into desk space. "Who's who?"

"I'm waiting for one more. If we were in my office, I'd have additional monitors. I don't want to minimize the window just yet."

Her computer chimed.

"Okay. Ready." She tapped some keys. The screen went black. Taylor Campbell's photo came up and filled the space. Kelly had caught her looking back at the fallen limb. Kelly hit the spacebar. The photo narrowed to the left side of the monitor. Information filled the right.

"The real Taylor Campbell. I have all you've sent on her, so no need to linger here."

Jake didn't want Taylor's photo to linger on the monitor. He liked the fire dancing from her eyes. When lightning struck and the limb fell, his gut had turned to mush. He yelled at Kelly to go so they could rescue her, but Taylor was running before Kelly put down her camera. Her rapid reflexes saved her life, and he'd been awestruck. He couldn't be awestruck and do his job properly without risking her safety. And his. He needed objectivity. And distance.

The screen filled with a second photo—a young Asian woman inside the chandlery. The information came up. "Trinh Le. We presumed she's an employee. Can you check?"

Kelly scrolled down. "Seven years. Since high school. Rock Harbor native. Married to a local police officer. No children. More?"

"Not now. What's your program comparing the photos to?"

"Every concern that issues a photo ID has cloud storage. My program mines the cloud first. That's as deep as it needed to go for these." The next photo came up. "Will Knox."

"Right. Next."

The large man appeared.

Kelly pointed. "Love his eyebrows."

The data came up. "Glen Upchurch. Detective. Rock Harbor Police Department. We guessed two for two."

The next photo. "Would you guess this guy drives a tow truck? He's so slender, like Simon. August Janacek."

"Not typical." Jake perused the information that followed. "The truck is registered to A.J.'s Towing."

The last image was the woman in the SUV who stopped to chat with Taylor and Janacek for a few minutes.

"There's a snazzy blonde for you, bro."

"Ball breaker."

Kelly laughed.

The data appeared. "Zia Grant Markham. Owner of ZGM Properties. I was right—she's a Realtor. Definitely a ball breaker." He didn't want a woman in his life right now. Especially not one who would demand things her way twenty-four/seven.

"You want me to dig deeper on any of these, keep them on warm, or what?"

"Just addresses for now, but keep them warm."

Kelly's phone rang. "It's Mom."

He headed for the sofa. "Say hi for me."

"Hi, Mom. What's up?"

Jake closed his eyes. Maybe he could sleep for five minutes.

"Is he all right?"

Jake shivered, wide awake. *Dad.*

"Don't be silly. Dad is more important. He needs all of us." Kelly rubbed her forehead.

Jake got up and went to her side. She put her arm around his waist.

"Okay. I understand. Jake will, too."

He gave her a questioning look, and she held up her index finger.

"Probably not until tonight since it'll be a connecting flight. Do you want me to bring you anything?" Kelly tilted her head back and stared at the ceiling while their mother talked. "Okay. I'll call you."

Jake waited for her to punch the end button before he spoke. "What happened to Dad? Is he okay?"

She tapped some keys before looking at him. "Dad started running a high fever. Mom called Doc Grady, and he met them at the hospital. Dad's in ICU. I'm the only one going back."

"Like hell!" Jake stormed to the window.

"I'm checking flights while you have your tantrum. Dad was emphatic you stay here."

"It's the fever talking. He'd want both of us there." Jake's stomach knotted with fear and resentment made worse by jet lag and his lack of sleep.

"No. Mom said under no conditions are you to come home while this mess is going down. It's up to you to fulfill Dad's promise."

"Son of a bitch." Outside a lawn mower started. His dad was dying and somebody was cutting grass. He squeezed his head. Life went on. He plopped into an ancient recliner.

"You can't go, Jake."

"I know. Doesn't mean I have to like it."

"If Dad gets worse, I'll book you a flight myself without telling anyone."

They had always looked out for one another. "Dad's going to pull out of this."

Kelly nodded. "Let me run your addresses and get my flights. Then I'll pack."

His dad would be all right. He would. Kelly and their mother would see to it. Without him. At times, the damned Solomon Honor System sucked.

CHAPTER 6

Taylor hated cemeteries in general, and the complete silence surrounding Randy's grave haunted her. Not one chirp from a sparrow or one call from a gull. Not one butterfly. Not one breath of breeze.

She laid the stems of red carnations, white gladiolas, and blue asters, still in their waxy green wrapper, across Randy's flat granite headstone and rubbed her arms to ward off the heebie-jeebies. Worse than the silence was the location. The cemetery was inland, with no view of the bay he loved. He would never have agreed to this desolate plot of earth. Taylor's mother had never approved of his lifestyle and must have chosen the spot out of spite.

She'd planned to sit and talk to him, show him the flowers. Tell him she followed his coordinates, planned to dig for the treasure he wrote about. But Randy wasn't here. She stayed only long enough to touch his gravestone and pull the grass from its edges. Her heart said she'd never return, so she said a short prayer before leaving.

"Love you, Uncle Randy. Can you even hear me in this place?"

She drove north to the old fishing pier where police discovered his body. She owed Randy the honor of seeing where he died, but she didn't look forward to the visit. She'd steeled herself against the horror since learning of his death.

Randy loved saltwater. Ocean, gulf, bay—as long as it was open water and not a lake or river, he was happy. He sold his sportfisher, *Renegade*, not long before his decline began. After he started going downhill, she wondered if he'd known something was wrong earlier than the symptoms began. With no boat, he'd contented himself with beaches and piers.

She counted to the third pier after the picnic area—the one her mother told her—and parked on the shoulder with her flashers on. Her fears vanished. This was Randy's kind of place. If he had to die, at least it happened in the water he loved.

On a knoll across the road from the pier, a sunny yellow and white house overlooked the scene, completely out of sync with death. The private pier had a locked gate about ten feet from the narrow road to secure access from the land side. The center section was washed out, but the end, a T-head, stood about a hundred yards into Copano Bay.

The dilapidated pier looked more like death, yet she felt Randy's presence more here than at the cemetery and wished she'd brought the flowers to scatter on the water. *No worries.* She shivered at the sound of his voice in her mind, but it banished her fear.

Taylor got out of the car and took in the area around the pier to ground herself before stepping onto the salt-encrusted boards. The tide was in, and the water lapping against the rocks a few feet below obscured the beach from her view. Thousands of sun diamonds sparkled on the blue-green water, and puffs of bright white clouds floated here and there leaving shadows across the bay. She tested the gate before leaning against it and resting her chin on her hands. If Randy's spirit hung around, it would be somewhere on the bay he loved.

Closing her eyes, she let the breeze blow in her face and the memories play in her mind. Her heart ached knowing she'd never again see Randy's crooked grin or hear his deadpan delivery of a really dumb joke. The little things. His salute after he'd pinned on her shoulder boards. The stories about his Coast Guard friends—the

Compass Points. What good care he'd taken of his Solomon's Compass belt. The belt was the only thing she wanted from his house.

Below her, waves lapped against slick rocks in the soothing ebb and flow lullaby of the sea. "Talk to me, Uncle Randy. Coastie to Coastie. I'm listening."

After several minutes the kinks in her stomach relaxed. She took a deep breath of salty air. A year had passed since Randy's death, and while she didn't like it any better, she finally accepted he was gone.

The past few years, Randy had declined from an active older man, healthy both mentally and physically, into a state of paranoid dementia. In every phone call, every email, he talked about someone trying to kill him. In his last email, he said the next time she came to visit they'd go treasure hunting. He listed a set of map coordinates. Map coordinates! From someone with dementia. He said the treasure would be their secret—his instructions to tell no one of his hidden buried treasure, a sad product of his decaying mind.

She left the pier and turned at the next street to go back to the highway. A cold chill ran up her spine. *What the hell?* At the second street, she turned left and stopped in front of the third house on the right—209 Amberjack. Will Knox's house.

In the daylight, she saw recently cut grass and neatly trimmed hedges. Begonias and flowers she didn't recognize bloomed everywhere. She hadn't realized he lived so close to where Randy died.

Taylor squeezed her head in her hands. Something didn't feel right, but she couldn't identify what felt off. What did it mean that Randy buried his supposed treasure in Will's backyard and chose a tiny beach so far from his home, yet so close to Will's, to spend what turned out to be his last evening?

After concentrating a few minutes, she was left with nothing. It would come to her. She just needed to give it time.

On her way back to Randy's, mesquite smoke coming from a large pit next to a ramshackle building made her mouth water.

She parked in a crowded lot anchored by a red neon BBQ sign. Not much tasted better than Texas barbeque—in Charleston she got sweet pork. She stood in line, then took her food to a counter against the wall. The smoked brisket melted in her mouth. If she hadn't been here to attend to Randy's affairs, she would gain ten pounds by binging on her favorite foods. But on this trip, she would work off the extra calories and more.

After dumping her trash, she fished out her keys. With them in one hand and her iced tea in the other, she threaded through a knot of people at the door. One man turned as she passed, his fingers raking her keys to the floor.

"Sorry. I'll grab them." The streets of New York came alive with his voice. Not just New York, but Brooklyn. Like Mark's voice.

The man rose up, holding out her keys with a smile. "Here you go, good as new. I dusted them off." He gave them a shake, his mischievous green eyes sparkling under shaggy silver hair. It would be impossible to stay upset at him.

She could see the taxis, hear the horns, and smell the exhaust just by listening to his voice. And she could see Mark's face. She blinked to make it go away.

This man was no Mark Vitulli. He was older, maybe by ten or fifteen years. It was difficult to guess. His tanned, trim body belied his rugged face and silver hair.

She laughed in spite of herself and took her keys. "Thanks."

The word got tangled up, and she spat it out before fleeing to the safety of her car. His fingers had brushed her wrist, making her mouth go dry and her pulse quicken. Her belly still fluttered. But she couldn't stop thinking about him, and it wasn't because his voice was like Mark's. Something inside her responded to him as if he'd always been a part of her life. It scared the crap out of her, and she didn't even know his name

She shook her head to rid it of such crazy thoughts. He probably had a wife, three kids, and a dog. And she had work to do.

Jake's morning hadn't gone well. When Kelly left for the airport, he'd followed her to the highway and turned in the opposite direction to get an eyes-on of Will Knox's house in the daylight. Clean and neat, like Copano Boat Works. A lot of landscaping.

The pier was next, and he turned onto the shore road. The door of a silver Chevrolet parked at the pier opened, and Taylor Campbell emerged.

Although he'd planned to stop, his orders were to watch and not become involved until the time was right. He noted her new plate number, kept driving, and stopped at a picnic area several hundred yards away. He pulled out his binoculars.

Clearly grieving for her uncle, Taylor reminded him of a lost kitten. He wanted to console her. Hell, who was he kidding? He wanted to touch her, look into her eyes and tell her he would slay the monster. But he couldn't. Jake was obligated to the mission. The time would come for him to tell her the story of the Compass Points, the almost certainty that Rankin's death was not accidental. That her own life was at risk. He would follow his dad's plan. And allow Taylor another day or two of freedom from the knowledge that some sick bastard murdered her uncle in cold blood.

When Taylor returned to her car, he stowed the binoculars and put the car in drive. She drove to Will Knox's house and stopped. Then straight back to the pier. She made the connection, but how did she know where Knox lived? He needed to find out. And find out what it meant.

She continued toward Rankin's but stopped at a barbeque place. He waited for several minutes. Two other people went inside after she did and came out carrying bags, so he ventured inside through a haze of wood smoke.

The place was packed, but he spotted her right away, eating alone at a counter. He understood eating alone, and he didn't wish that for her, but he couldn't meet her yet. On a professional level, he needed to see if anyone appeared interested in her. Or himself. Personally, he needed more emotional distance after watching her escape death just hours earlier.

He waited near the door, blending into group after group that came and went. After several minutes, she picked up her tray, and he moved to the corner of the entrance area next to the door.

Seconds later one group of people entered just as another group was leaving. He worked his way through them. Taylor stood two feet away. He turned toward her. Despite knowing it was too early, he couldn't stop himself from reaching out to touch her, pulling her keys from her fingers as an excuse.

Her touch propelled a burst of heat through his body. To keep his emotions at bay, he ducked to retrieve her keys and get himself under control. From Kelly's photos, he hadn't been able to see the way freckles covered her skin or the way her hair curled around her ear. Or maybe it was the Doc T-shirt. He was near enough to touch her, and his mission changed to personal in a heartbeat.

Jake waited for Taylor to reach her car before he left the restaurant. After their encounter, she drove straight to Rankin's. Now she pulled into the driveway and got out. Jake put his car in gear and drove off.

He didn't drive far.

Ahead on the right, a Bud sign called his name. His body was adjusting to the time change, and tomorrow he should be a hundred percent, but today it was halfway on Helsinki time. Which would put him around . . . Buenos Aires or Rio time. Perfect for a drink. He parked in the shade of a massive tree. Kelly should be in Houston waiting for her connecting flight. Since he hadn't heard from her or his mom, his dad must be holding his own.

Jake cut the engine. The frame building looked different from taverns in Brooklyn, and certainly different from those in Helsinki, but beer signs were the same the world over. And his dad had told him about Lulu's.

He glanced over his shoulder. Rankin's place stood across two empty fields, and Taylor sat in a swing on the back porch, keeping it in motion with her foot. Jake walked into the roadhouse, his smile growing. He'd expected a minimum of two televisions mounted at each end of the bar and loud country music from a jukebox. Instead, one large flat screen stared out from above a pool table, and opera flowed from hidden speakers.

Behind the bar, a mountain of a woman towered at least six feet. Her bright red Hawaiian muumuu didn't camouflage much of her three hundred or so pounds. "Whatcha havin', hon?" Her gravelly voice told of years of smoke, either first- or second-hand.

"Bud's fine. Bottle. I'll open it."

She nodded and set the bottle atop a napkin on the polished bar. "You want a tab?"

He handed her a ten. "No, but I'll take another one in a few."

"Thanks." She pressed a key on an antique cash register that sat on the back counter and placed the bill inside the drawer. A thick gray braid traveled the length of her spine.

"Are you Lulu?" He twisted off the cap.

She held out her arms. "Every last bit of me." She laid his change on the counter in front of him.

"Pleasure to meet you. I'm Jake."

"New York?"

He nodded. "You a native here?"

"Born and bred. Lotsa bread." She laughed and patted her stomach.

"I'll bet you knew Randy Rankin."

Lulu crossed her arms, and they rested on her breasts. "Did you?"

"We served in Nam together."

She pulled up a pair of glasses he hadn't noticed hanging from a gold chain around her neck. After setting them on her nose, she focused on his face. This was do-or-die time. If he couldn't sell the charade to Lulu, he'd have to fess up and toss his dad's plan out the window.

"You don't look old enough to have been in Vietnam. Your hair's silver as moonlight, but your face, eyes? No."

"I was seventeen."

"Oh, hell. You were a damn baby." She removed the glasses.

"Not after growing up on the streets of Brooklyn." He held his breath.

"Your eyes tell me you don't take crap from anybody, but I wouldn't peg you earlier than Desert Storm."

He slugged half the beer. He'd been at Annapolis in Desert Storm.

"Except for the beer. I haven't seen that in a long time. In the future, I'll try to remember not to open them for you, but you've no worries here. I keep a safe bar."

His dad said the beer would cement the deal. Back then, water was bad, liquor was worse, and there was no way to tell what would be in a beer bottle if it came to you open. "Good to know. Randy told me he used to come over here every day for beer and nachos. Extra jalapeños and pico. Said yours were the best in town."

"Closest, anyway. He was a steady customer right up to the end."

"I know he had some trouble, but he didn't say how bad. Said he could handle it."

Lulu lowered her head and moved it from side to side. "One day the same old Randy trotted through that door. The next, paranoia dragged him around by the short hairs. He thought somebody was out to kill him. I never saw anything like it."

"Told me much the same. Said it was a Charlie Foxtrot, and he couldn't even trust the police. I guess he trusted you."

She shrugged. "We thought he'd floated 'round the bend—all he could talk about was somebody trying to kill him. And there's no need to be politically correct on my account. If I'd never heard of a clusterfuck by now, it's high time I did."

Jake downed a swig of beer. "The police ruled his death accidental."

Lulu rolled her eyes. "You don't believe that any more than I do."

"Randy talk about who he thought might want him dead?"

Lulu shook her head. "He suspected everyone he knew and everyone he met. The sad part is we didn't help him. I'll always regret not helping him." Pain glittered in her eyes.

"He was a proud son of a bitch. He wouldn't have let you help."

"You got that right."

"I like you, Lulu. You appreciate where I'm coming from. And where I've been."

"I like you, too. As long as you pay."

He held his beer in both hands. "Money always talks."

CHAPTER 7

Taylor climbed the three steps to Randy's back porch. No one ever used the front door, and now she'd never know why. Her hand shook as she inserted the key. "Okay, Randy. Ready or not, here I come."

She turned the key and pushed open the back door. A wave of heat washed over her, and sweat popped out on her forehead. She didn't believe the sight before her. "Holy Mother of God."

From one side of the room to the other, the room was covered—on the kitchen table, on chairs, counters, floor—in junk. Rusty tools, a generator, life vests, a row of blenders. Non-marine items she couldn't identify. She craned her neck to the left to peer down the hall. Everywhere. Piled high. Her heart sank. Ten days wasn't enough time to get through the house, much less the shop. What had Randy been thinking? Had he been thinking?

The air stunk. "It must be a hundred degrees in here." She used a box to prop open the door.

Randy had installed a central air system after a storm wrecked his window units. She dropped her tote by the door, followed a narrow trail to the hall, and pushed the thermostat to the bottom. Nothing happened.

"Shit!"

The electric company had assured her the power would be on. The breakers must be off. The box was in the kitchen. She'd gotten in trouble more than once for playing with the switches. Now a pyramid of rusty metal and plastic hid it from view.

A couple of crew members would come in handy right about now, but wishing wouldn't get the job done. She took a deep breath of stuffy air and slid a stack of life rings over the threshold to the porch. After ten minutes of moving items to the porch, she climbed over the remaining pile to reach the panel.

"You better be wired up, you bastard." She flipped every switch. The air conditioner came on, and from somewhere a radio played George Strait singing about his exes in Texas.

Her phone rang. The Bixby people—her trash bin would arrive the following morning instead of this afternoon due to trouble with the truck. Wonderful. Just frigging wonderful. Her insides knotted up. What else could happen? She went to the porch, closing the door behind her to let the house cool, and plopped into the old swing. *Please God, don't let the wood be rotten.*

The movement of the swing and the breeze it created soothed her frazzled nerves. She leaned back and closed her eyes. With all the junk inside the house, she couldn't finish the job this trip. One day wouldn't make a difference. She'd fill up one bin and call it quits. Clean and paint empty rooms. Finish the house on her next leave. Tackle the first of the salvage shop on a later trip. Not her first choice, but it was the best she could do. Closure would have to wait.

The *creech* of chain against the swing's hinges continued to soothe her. A plan. A different plan from the one she'd arrived with, but a solid plan, nonetheless. Not one foot inside the shop on this trip. Otherwise she'd make herself sick over what she couldn't accomplish.

Her chin bounced against her chest, and she jerked upright. Soothing nerves was good. Taking a nap was out of the question. Besides, she needed to find Randy's belt and put it in her tote before it got mixed in with everything else. She jumped up and went inside.

Another George Strait song came on—this time he wanted to dance with her. At least she had music.

Jake left Lulu's, confirmed Taylor's car was still at Rankin's, and returned to the hotel. In his room he grabbed cameras from his portable equipment locker and the key card Kelly had provided. Taylor's room was located diagonally across the hall from his, and he was back in his room less than five minutes after leaving it. Her room was now equipped with the same camera setup as his own. He didn't enjoy invading her privacy, but she was his mission. In this case, the end definitely justified the means.

He settled in to reread the information Kelly had sent during the few weeks she'd been involved in the operation. In addition to background items and interviews, she'd provided every evaluation Taylor received during her seventeen-year Coast Guard career. He hadn't asked how she managed those.

Jake believed in preparation. Because anything could happen on an op, it was important to have as much raw intel as possible. The more he knew, the better he could do his job. Learning about the asset—in this case Taylor—was the best way to predict her reactions both to everyday and unexpected situations.

As an ensign, Taylor had overstepped her bounds left and right, resulting in fitness reports lower than they would have been otherwise. His had been the same way. Over the next few years, she mellowed a little. It had taken him more than half his career to reach that point. With her second marking period after graduate school, she began to shine. He didn't know what motivated her, but she would make captain and be a good one, despite her early aggressiveness. Her eyes said she hadn't conquered all her demons yet. Most likely, she slayed a new one with each promotion. He could relate to that.

His eyelids kept closing. He stretched and did a few sets of crunches. Anything to stay awake. No nap. Tonight he'd go to bed early and make the final push into Texas time.

Next came his notes on the murders of his father's friends. He scanned through details he'd previously highlighted. Almost twenty years earlier, the first Compass Point died—Ham Norberg hanged himself. Eight years later, the second—Kyle Easley—was murdered. His dad hadn't been suspicious or connected their deaths. He'd just mourned the losses of the men, two of his Coast Guard friends from Vietnam.

Five more years passed before the next murder—Ed Wharton. Ed's murder tripped his dad's alarm bells. He reviewed the details of the first two deaths and became convinced a killer was stalking the Compass Points. He'd warned Randy Rankin, but it hadn't done any good. In his usual way, his dad tried to do everything himself, trusting no one and nothing except his gut. Three years after Ed Wharton was shot and killed, Randy Rankin was dead.

His phone rang—Kelly. "You must be over the Mississippi about now."

"I don't know. My so-called great flight out of Houston got canceled. I sprung for a private one."

"Good decision. You'll get to the hospital quicker in the long run."

"Good chance. Anyway, I've been working."

"How are you secure at thirty thousand feet?"

"You have zero faith. I'm hitching a ride on an über-secure Feddie satellite."

"Jesus H." He bounded out of the chair. "Dad will have your ass and mine, too, if—"

"Zero. Faith. Trust me, bro. I designed and wrote the code. I left myself a way in and a way out. You know why I love working with you?"

"Because I'm your big brother, and I'm a laugh a minute." He didn't crack a smile.

"Well, there is that. No, it's because you're not afraid to jump in. And no matter how insecure you are about my security precautions, you're not afraid to let *me* jump in."

"Ha. Ha."

"Dad thinks all I can do is geeky computer work. Never mind how much my side of the business brings into the company in direct dollars, referrals, and goodwill."

"It's growing. Last figure I saw was forty-one percent." Jake sat back down.

"Exactly. It's not a side business any longer. He likes to forget I worked for the FBI out of college and can handle myself in the world. I think he calls your side of the business *the boys* just to piss me off."

"He doesn't want you to get hurt."

"I've never told him about clients who gave me bare bones information, and when I told them what they wanted might be dangerous, they didn't care. The hell with my safety, just deliver."

"You were smart not to tell him." Any company was foolish to try stunts like that, especially with Compass Points. Kelly was nervous. Otherwise she would never have told him this.

"Hell, yeah. Anyway, that's why I like working with you."

"I like working with you, too." Or told him this. Not having their dad at the helm of the family ship was taking a toll on each of them. "Tell me what you found out."

"Right. Will Knox. Once upon a time a problem child of the first order."

"Christ." Jake ran his fingers through his hair.

"All is well. Detox, rehab, and a will of iron have kept him clean for better than a decade."

He relaxed by about half a point.

"Divorced. One daughter. The women in the area use the phrase Will's Drill. For what that's worth."

"Fits with his license plate. Remember?

"WILL U. Who could forget? He and Zia Grant Markham have a long-standing friends-with-benefits arrangement. Neither is looking for more."

"Must be nice." He couldn't imagine how she found that out. Probably somebody's blog.

"Back to Zia. Zia Markham *is* ZGM Properties. It used to be Markham Real Estate, run by Ross and Zia Markham. Husband and wife. Ross died almost eleven years ago. Their office was on the road your hotel is on."

"Zia took over?"

"Took over. Changed the name. Expanded with the boom, and didn't crash with the bust."

"Good business intuition."

"During the boom, she sold the former location and bought a block of land in town on the water. She tore down several old buildings and built new ones. Shops run along the ground floor, including the ZGM Properties office. Two condo units make up the upstairs space. She lives in the one over her offices and beyond. The other is unfinished space."

"The entire block?"

"One side of the street, yes. It's a short block, and the building isn't as deep as some."

"We're talking serious cash, though. Even for Podunk."

"Yes. Moving on. Trinh Le. Oops. Mom's calling."

She hung up before he could say goodbye.

Taylor still hadn't returned. If she wasn't back by seven, he would go to Rankin's. So far the killer hadn't struck in daylight, but that didn't mean much. Each victim had been killed in a different way and in their hometowns. Taylor may or may not be a target, but Jake was here for her. He would honor his dad's promise and keep her safe.

Jake's dad suspected the death of Kyle Easley's daughter had also been a murder—the case remained active. He conveyed his concern to Rankin, and Rankin believed his niece would become a target after his death. The killer wasn't Jake's primary mission. But he planned to root the son of a bitch out whether or not he showed up for Taylor. The more he learned, the easier the sick bastard would be to find. Otherwise, his dad would become the next victim. If the cancer didn't kill him first.

It was bad enough for the killer to target men who had served together in war. Worse to set his sights on a woman. If the killer turned the crosshairs on Jake, the joke would be on him. Twenty years as a Navy SEAL had given Jake the tools he needed to stay alive. And to kill.

CHAPTER 8

Randy kept his Solomon's Compass belt in a loose coil on the top of the chest of drawers in his bedroom. He said seeing the belt twice a day and touching the embossed words kept him grounded. The summer Taylor was six, she saw the belt and touched the blue stone in the buckle. Randy saw how she admired it and told her about the men of Solomon's Compass.

Taylor squeezed through the path down the hallway and turned into Randy's bedroom. No belt rested on the top of the chest—the chest could be the only surface in the entire house that was bare. He hadn't been wearing a belt when he died; as far as she knew, he only wore the belt on special occasions. He must have moved it to a drawer or his closet.

Once a month, he cleaned and conditioned the leather and polished the buckle. Randy said he used the time to remember the war and his friends. He talked about them so much, she felt as if she knew them, too.

She opened the first drawer—paired socks on one side, folded tighty-whities on the other. The second drawer held folded tees with pockets on the left. White on one side, colors on the other. All in neat stacks.

Taylor frowned at the tidy drawers. Randy must have organized them before his dementia took over. Maybe during his decline, he stopped using the dresser. The closet probably held a pile of mixed clean and dirty clothing. She opened the third drawer. Shorts—khaki and denim. Folded. Khaki on one side and denim on the other. Taylor shook her head. "Randy, I'm so sorry I didn't get here in time to help you." She might not have made any difference, but at least he would have had company.

The bottom drawer squeaked. Two stacks of folded pullover cotton sweaters, all white, lay inside. No belt.

Taylor leaned against the chest, having a hard time wrapping her mind around the items in the drawers. She looked around. Eight royal blue plastic bins were stacked along the walls. His neatly made bed was a military model. This was the only tidy room in his home.

She looked under the bed, under the pillow, and between the mattress and spring. No belt.

The scent of leather drifted out of the closet when Taylor opened the door. Several pairs of jeans and a few slacks hung next to mostly short-sleeve shirts with two long-sleeve dress shirts at the end of the row. On the other side of the jeans hung a few windbreakers, a winter jacket with a zip-out lining, and a full-length slicker. She ran her hands over each item. No belt. On the floor, two pairs of boots, a pair of dress shoes, and several flip-flops.

Taylor went for the boots, but neither pair held the belt. She pulled over one of the boxes to stand on to see the shelf. Bare.

"Crap!" Where was Randy's belt?

She sat on his bed and put her head in her hands. If she could get into his frame of mind, she could figure out where he put the one item he valued more than anything else. Besides, she needed a break before she searched the boxes.

Randy loved the soft, black leather belt with *Solomon's Compass* embossed across the back. He would never throw it away or sell it. Even if the belt fell apart, he'd keep the pieces. It represented a special time in his life. And special people. Ham Norberg was the oldest, followed by Randy. Married, Ham's wife gave birth while they were in Vietnam. Ed Wharton and Kyle Easley were younger and single. The youngest was Jake Solomon, yet Randy said he was the glue that held their group together.

Jake Solomon and Ham Norberg went to Bangkok on R&R. On Coast Guard Day a few weeks later, they gave out the Solomon's Compass belts to the other three. Randy and the others had been surprised by the embossing. They'd always called themselves the Compass Points—their last names began with N, E, S, and W.

That first time Randy told her the story about the belt, he taught her about compasses and directions. He drew a rough picture of a compass on the back of an envelope—two crossed lines with N, S, E, W at the ends. She kept it in her scrapbook. Randy called the directions the four winds, and she'd giggled.

Taylor hadn't seen her uncle's name anyplace and asked him why. Randy had been so patient. He drew a circle around the lines and letters.

"See this?" He pointed to the circle and everything inside it with his pencil.

Taylor nodded.

"A drawing of the four winds and where they meet at the center, like petals on a flower, is called a compass rose. This is simple, but on some maps and compasses they're fancy and show all the points in between."

"And your name begins with R, for rose."

"That's right. You're a very smart young lady. I think that calls for ice cream."

After that summer, he filled in more details from time to time. Once he'd shown her photos of each of the Compass Points. She hadn't found those either. It was time to search the boxes.

Jake finally gave in and allowed himself a ten-minute nap. When the alarm went off, he took a cold shower and rejoined the living. Still no Taylor. He checked the time. "Jesus H. It's only four-thirty."

He had to get out of the room or he'd be mush again in two minutes. After setting the camera alerts to his phone, Jake headed outside. The sea breeze here blew almost continually, and he took a few deep breaths of salt-laden air while reconning the area. No one lurked. He wasn't surprised. Both the temperature and the humidity hovered in the nineties, and the combination made sweat break out along his hairline.

Across the street, a grassy area separated the sidewalk from an inlet off the bay. He set out. If Kelly were here, they'd bounce ideas off one another. He bounced plenty around with himself, but it wasn't the same without a team. Even if the team consisted of only two members. Unlike his dad, Jake was a team player, and his Navy SEAL training had only reinforced his natural tendencies. He rarely worked alone, even at CPI.

Jake walked for an hour—at the water, behind the hotel, several blocks in all directions—feeling the heartbeat of the town. He went into a used bookshop. His mother loved to read and collected early twentieth-century editions by American novelists. He poked around for twenty minutes with no success.

One more hour. If Taylor hadn't returned, he'd go find her.

The first three boxes contained old records from the salvage shop. The three boxes on the other side of the chest contained family relics. Taylor's mother hadn't wanted any of her parents' belongings after their deaths. *Surprise, surprise.*

The family wasn't wealthy. Most items in the boxes possessed only sentimental value. One box held quilts sewn by Taylor's grandmother. A dried stem of the lavender she'd loved lay across the top, its scent faint in the fabric. Another, some old Fiesta serving pieces and other kitchen items. The third held her grandfather's barber tools and the sign from his shop. She would keep these boxes.

She was definitely on the right track. Randy kept his personal possessions here. In one room. The belt and photos would be in one of the two remaining boxes.

Inside the next box, she found a shoe box with his tax returns from the last several years. And several more shoe boxes filled with what appeared to be every letter and postcard she'd ever mailed him. Her eyes burned and she blinked hard. She kept Randy's letters in the old wicker picnic basket he'd given her for her seashells when she was ten.

Taylor huffed out a breath. Only one box left. She licked her lips. The belt and photos and other information about Randy's time in the Coast Guard lay in the box at her feet. She both wanted to open the box and keep it closed. In one way she felt like an intruder. No. Randy would want her to see how the Coast Guard had changed and how *Always Ready* remained the same.

She knelt. "Okay, Taylor. Dig in." The lid popped when she opened it.

The box was empty.

"What the. . . ." The answer dawned on her as she spoke. The Coast Guard items were Randy's treasure. He meant them only for her.

CHAPTER 9

After a quick shower, Taylor opened her laptop and pressed the on button. Before she left to try again for Randy's buried box, she wanted to search for information on the people she'd met and check her email for an update on the status of the *Susquehanna's* turbine repair.

She pushed the button again. Nothing. She hadn't used it for long last night; the battery should be fine. All she got for her trouble was grinding and a click. "Son of a bitching piece of useless shit!" She yanked the plug from the wall.

The prime specimen of electronic crap was less than a year old and had been in for repair twice. Never again. The day she got back to Charleston, she was trading her old phone for a smartphone with every bell and whistle available—computer, camera, and phone all in one. The perfect solution.

Tomorrow she would make progress. She *would*. Her grand plans for the day had died belly up, but she had made new ones. Better ones. Maybe during the night someone with a truck would take the junk she left on Randy's porch and think she was the fool. She smiled.

It never paid to dwell on events over which she had no control. Except for one—it was enough. Her brief encounter with Mr. Brooklyn today at the barbeque restaurant had brought the memories back full force.

She'd been dwelling on Mark Vitulli for seventeen years. His fatal accident had opened the door for her career, her current life. She wondered how their lives would have been if he hadn't died. If they would have lasted as a couple, had children.

She ran her fingers through her hair, adding some extra lift as it dried. Mark and Mr. Brooklyn would have to wait. She grabbed her keys and her tote. Time for dinner and some exploring until it got dark enough to go after Randy's treasure.

After a taqueria dinner, she drove back past her hotel intending to return to Randy's. Maybe climb a tree and take in the end of the day looking over the bay in the same way she'd done as a child. A few blocks down from the light, a brightly colored strip of shops shimmered in the golden glow from the setting sun. She pulled to the curb and parked. The bay would wait.

The developed area spanned three blocks. In the first two, shops and galleries inhabited an old gas station and a variety of other buildings. People walked and laughed, enjoying the end of the day. In the next block on the other side of the street, the buildings resembled Hollywood's version of a Caribbean shopping district with masses of flowers in planters near the street and more in galvanized tubs flanking each door.

Zia's real estate office anchored the first corner Taylor came to. Next to ZGM Properties was Bravo, a gallery. Followed by Juliet's Tango, a tearoom with white plantation shutters covering the windows. She passed Echoes, an antique shop with a small sign at the bottom of the window that read *Dan's Designs*.

Taylor stopped short. Her brain filled with the phonetic alphabet she had learned as a first-year cadet. Alpha through Zulu, one word and one flag for each letter. She forced herself to walk.

Mike's Golf Shop. What was going on? The next shop, Elements, was filled with contemporary accent pieces—the kind of shop she loved. She continued to the corner and into the Rock Salt Ice Cream Company.

Bravo, Echo, Golf, Juliet, Mike, Tango. No need to write them down. She would never forget them. She used those words every day. The military used them for clarity, to avoid mistaking a spoken B for a V, and so on. If she needed Form CG-1650, she asked for Charlie Golf 1650.

The words stood out in the shop names, clear and obvious to Taylor, but the letters they corresponded with didn't spell anything. Was it a code or a signal? How could she find out? Had she missed others? She left the ice cream shop without ordering.

She crossed to the other side of the street for her return trip. Names of the shops she'd passed would be easier to spot from this side. She paid attention to each shop she passed, but found no more alpha-code words.

As she stepped off the curb, the hairs on the back of her neck prickled. Someone was watching her. She spun around, but no one raised her suspicion. *Get a grip, Taylor, or you'll grow as paranoid as Randy.*

Jake, with a ball cap pulled over his forehead, tracked Taylor from shop to shop, taking care to keep well back and on the opposite side of the street. Groups of laughing, squealing kids made hiding easy.

She made the alphabet connection as fast as he did. When the words clicked, Taylor stopped on the spot in the middle of a busy sidewalk. Her pause gave her away. A second or two later, she continued. After a quick trip into the ice cream shop, she came back and checked again. Persistent and determined. Only a fool wouldn't see that.

He took in the surroundings while he kept an eye on her. Evenly spaced concrete planters shaped like huge seashells stood along the street edge of the clean sidewalk, one in front of each shop. They provided a decorative touch, but he knew their true purpose—to prevent vehicles from ramming the large bay windows.

While he watched he sat on a bench in front of the ZGM office. Only top shelf properties were advertised in the window, both sale and vacation rentals. The bread and butter would be in a drawer and on the MLS.

He counted shops. Seven, including ZGM Properties on one corner and Rock Salt Ice Cream Company on the other. He'd return another time to try a cone. In between, an art gallery, a tearoom, golf shop, an antique shop, and a shop with accent pieces called Elements.

Taylor marched back in his direction, and he followed the sidewalk around the corner until she passed.

She might be the tiniest wisp of a woman, but her mind raced faster than a computer. In front of the tearoom, she even stopped to admire the flowers before squaring her shoulders and continuing to the corner. He smiled. "Go, Taylor."

In the glow of streetlights, Taylor slid behind the wheel. A mosquito had dined on her ankle, and she scratched the bite with her toe. She drove past her hotel and followed the same route she'd taken the night before to find Randy's treasure.

WILL U was in the driveway of the white bungalow. She continued to the corner without slowing. The dashboard clock read 8:29. She punched on the radio—Rihanna sang her heart out about finding love. Instead of heading toward the hotel, Taylor turned right and drove north, crossing a long bridge over the bay. On the opposite side, she turned around at the first opportunity and made the return trip. She'd been keeping an eye on the mirrors. No one followed.

Back in Rock Harbor, she drove up and down several side streets on the other side of the highway from Will's. At nine-thirty, she turned off the radio and crossed the highway.

Will's truck hadn't moved. One light shone from the back of the house near the corner. She drove on.

Accomplishments for the day: Naught, nada, and nothing.

Jake popped a peanut butter cracker in his mouth with one hand and thumbed the channel button on the remote with the other.

After the shops, Taylor had gone to Knox's house, passing without even slowing. Most likely because his truck stood in the driveway. She'd driven north, crossed the bay, turned around. And never spotted him. The side streets had made staying unnoticed difficult, but not impossible. Thanks to many hours of surveillance training.

He passed her on the highway and parked down the street from Knox's house. Sure enough, she followed several minutes later, her frustration evident in the set of her jaw and hunched shoulders. She wanted something from Knox's house. Was she planning to break in? He could help, but only as lookout or clean-up to keep her out of trouble. Wouldn't be the first time he'd assumed the role of troubleshooter.

He piled some peanut butter on another cracker and took a bite. No one had called him yet about his dad. He turned off the ten o'clock news and picked up his phone.

CHAPTER 10

"Good morning!" Will Knox walked up Randy's driveway.

"I was prepared for a mess, not a nightmare. All this"—Taylor spread her arms—"porch and grass, is from the kitchen. I haven't touched the cabinets or any other room. The rest of the house is packed as tight or tighter." Except for Randy's bedroom.

"I came to help, so what can I do? My time is yours until this afternoon."

She shook her head at the junk. No need to piss and moan. Time was ticking by, and she needed all the help she could get. It was barely ten, and her clothes were drenched with sweat. "I brought trash bags and rigged up this stand to keep them open and upright. Help me search for broken items, obvious trash, things like that."

Will rubbed his hands together. "Yes, ma'am."

She snickered. "No lollygagging either, mister. I've rented a commercial trash bin, and it's supposed to arrive today. If you're here, you can help me start loading that up, too."

"Got it." He pulled a pair of work gloves from his back pocket and moved toward the far corner of the lawn and a stack of oars.

She started to work on the porch. Gulls swooped above her in the hot, unmoving air, their calls urging her to *look, look, look.*

Until she dug up Randy's treasure, she would look through every single container before tossing it. If Randy hadn't said his treasure was a secret, she would ask Will if she could dig a big gaping hole in his pristine backyard. And promise to fix it. But until her options ran out, she would keep Randy's treasure their secret.

After pulling a frayed length of yellow nylon rope from a small anchor, she wound it into a coil out of habit to keep it under control until she reached the trash bag. Shells crunched in the driveway, and she turned, looping the rope over her shoulder.

A forest-green SUV rolled to a stop. Will worked a good thirty feet away, bellowing "Margaritaville" at the top of his lungs.

The car door slammed and Will's singing stopped. He raised his hand. "Hey, Dan. What are you doing out here?" Both men walked toward her.

"A.J., Zia, and every busybody in town told me about Randy's niece. I came to meet her and introduce myself."

Taylor's head swiveled toward the man from the SUV, Dan, climbing the steps in khaki shorts, tucked-in plaid shirt, and boat shoes with no socks. A huge Rolex adorned his left wrist.

She smiled. "Here I am."

Will stood on the bottom step. "Taylor, this guy is Dan Blair. He owns a couple of shops in town."

Taylor held out her hand before seeing how dirty it was. "I'd shake, but you don't want to come within ten feet of this." She flashed her palm at him.

Dan touched her arm in greeting. "No problem. I may look neat and tidy now, but getting dirty is my business."

Her next door neighbor in Charleston was a toucher. He was gay. Was Dan?

"I own an antique shop and an art gallery. To Will they're the same since they have nothing to do with boats."

Dan's Designs—the card in the antique shop—Echoes. The gallery—Bravo. If she got to know him, she'd ask about the shop names.

"Hey! I like stuff besides boats." Will gave him a mock frown.

Dan turned back to her. "I'm so happy to finally meet you, Taylor. Your uncle and I bid against each other for a lot of the pieces he has here."

"You must have outbid him on the best items. Why would you be at the same auction?"

"Auctions around here are pretty much a mixed bag—one-stop shopping."

The picture came into clearer focus. "Randy went to regular auctions? Estate sales?"

"Right. Until the last couple of years, he stuck to boat and nautical items and the marine-only auctions in Corpus. Of course sometimes he'd purchase kitchen—excuse me—galley gear and other odd items even at those."

Will shook his head. "You wouldn't know a scupper from a rub rail, Danny Boy."

"Rub rails sound intriguing."

They continued to banter. She paid more attention to their actions than their words. Maybe Randy had suffered a minor stroke. That might explain the short circuit that caused him to hoard all the junk in the house.

"So anyway, Taylor, I want to invite you to my gallery. We're opening a new exhibit this weekend. Everyone's invited, even Will and tourists. I hope you'll come."

"Thank you, but I need to keep working here. And I didn't bring appropriate clothing for an event." She held out the tail of her Sneezy tee.

"It's not fancy. I hope you'll reconsider. I also want to make you an offer."

"What kind of offer?" Did he want to buy the property, too? Like Will? And Zia?

"I've got work to do." Will left them alone.

"I'd like the opportunity to be the first to view everything. To make that prospect more appealing, I'm prepared to help you go through all of it."

"You can't imagine how much stuff is inside."

"I'm in the antique biz, remember?"

She waved her arm to include the lawn and porch. "All of this came from just the kitchen. The entire house is packed, and I hear the salvage shop is worse."

"Randy was my friend. He spent his life building this business, and just because his brain decided to take a trip using a different travel agent doesn't mean I stopped being his friend." He smiled. "Actually, this is my chance to repay him in a small way for being my friend when I needed one."

Dan's expression said he'd been dismayed by Randy's death. It brought her own feelings to the surface. These two weeks were going to be harder than she'd anticipated. "I'm sure Randy would thank you. I do, too. But I want to take time to see if there's anything I want to keep. I found some of my grandparents' belongings in his bedroom. Besides, you have your shop and gallery to look after."

"I have people who do that. I'm out and about every day."

"We don't have time to go through everything. I'm flying back to Charleston a week from Thursday."

"Oh, sweetie, you really do need me." He grabbed her hands. "We'll get through all of it, and you can keep what you want. We'll toss the trash, and I'll put you in contact with dealers who'll buy the rest in bulk. You'll get much more with a touch of effort up front. I'll give you a fair price on the items that make my heart flutter, and you can check with another dealer or online to confirm my prices."

Concern filled Dan's deep brown eyes. Knowing he was Randy's friend made getting a grip on her emotions easier to say than do. "You're welcome to see what's here, but I really want my own eyes-on."

"Do you want to spend the rest of your life going through nuts and bolts, bent propellers, and tangled fishing line? Together we can sort the diamonds from the rhinestones in no time flat. I promise."

"It is a fair offer."

"Well?" He was intent as a cat watching a bird. But she wasn't a sparrow.

If she agreed, she would still search for the belt and photos. "I need some time to think about it."

"Do you have a plan?"

"I'm going to clear the house and clean it first. A trash bin is on the way, and I'm having the trash guys haul off the fridge and whatever's inside. I'm not even opening the door—the power's been off for over a year."

"If I missed a prize—if I let you miss a prize—I'd just be sick. I know Randy was your uncle, but I once watched him freeze his favorite lure in a margarine container filled with water so no one would find it. This happened before he rounded the bend, so there's no telling what's inside that refrigerator. But I'll wait until after they bring it out before I venture in. It's the least I can do for you. Especially if you decide not to let me help."

"I'd hate to deny you such a privilege." But she wasn't cleaning up the mess if he tossed his cookies all over his shoes.

He shuffled his feet and pumped a raised fist in the air. "Yes! I keep gloves and masks in my car. In the antique business, priceless jewels often show up in the damndest places."

Will returned to the porch. "Your bin is rolling up the road. The rain is supposed to hold off for a few days, so things will be all right sitting out until you can move them back. This time of year, it's probably safer weather-wise to do one room at a time if you decide not to take Dan up on his offer."

"Two bits of good news. I'll take what I can get." She wanted to know more about Randy's decline, but no time had seemed right to ask those who'd known him.

"I have a wagon and a couple of dollies across the street. They'll make this job a lot easier. I'll be back."

Dan watched him walk away. "He's got the cutest ass, don't you think?"

His comment didn't come as a surprise. She followed the progress of Will's ass down the driveway. It was all right, but it didn't do anything for her. Not like Mr. Brooklyn. "Not bad. You have a good eye."

CHAPTER 11

J ake hadn't eaten a burger like Lulu's in years. She told him the cook ground fresh beef every morning and mixed in her own blend of seasonings. Since it was morning, he opted for coffee instead of beer. After he finished eating, he and Lulu talked for a long time—mostly about the Vietnam Era. Again, he was thankful for his dad's memories.

Lulu sprinkled her recollections with stories about Rankin. People missed him. He'd been a cut-up and a devoted volunteer. Each summer he'd funded day camp for two at-risk kids. Information Jake already knew.

During his meal and the conversation with Lulu, Jake took periodic breaks, getting up to check the front window every ten minutes. Lulu presumed his actions were part of an old habit, and he said nothing to dispute her belief. People who had been through war had quirks; they believed those eccentricities had kept them alive.

Taylor had moved odds and ends out of the house for an hour before Will Knox showed up. Not long after, a small SUV pulled into her driveway and a man who looked dressed for golf got out.

Jake had stayed at Lulu's long enough. Any longer, and he might raise suspicion. He paid and told Lulu she hadn't seen the last of him. He walked out with her laughter ringing in his ears.

From his car, he snapped images of the man and his license plate, and sent them to Kelly.

He drove to Church Street and parked in the same place Kelly had parked the day before. This time, he pulled more powerful binoculars from the duffel on the floor. Several minutes passed with no significant activity.

A rumbling grew behind him. A truck passed so close Jake could have reached out and lost an arm. It carried a large waste bin and backed into Rankin's drive, accompanied by loud beeps.

His phone rang.

"Mr. Solomon, this is the general manager at The Waterford. I'm sorry to bother you, but this morning someone broke into three of our rooms—three that we know of. We're asking guests who are out of their rooms to check as soon as possible to make sure nothing is missing."

Jake's camera alert hadn't sounded. Neither had the alert for Taylor's room.

"Were the break-ins on my floor?"

"Yes, sir. An alert housekeeper saw the man come out of the room next to yours and move to the room directly across the hall."

Taylor's room. His antenna stood straight up.

"The housekeeper sent security a 911 beep, and the thief was apprehended before entering that room."

If the hotel knew Taylor's room was secure, she wouldn't receive a call. Jake would draw attention to himself by not returning within a reasonable time. "I'm just sitting down to an early lunch. I'll be there as soon as I finish."

"Thank you, sir. That will be fine. Again, I'm sorry to interrupt your plans, and I apologize for the inconvenience."

Jake's dad had a suspect in mind for the murders, but no proof, only a feeling—a master of disguise who could change his identity at will—Oliver Fallon. His dad had shown him two old photos of Fallon, and the images hadn't looked like the same man. He focused his binoculars and zoomed in on Will Knox, then moved to the new man. Knox and the other man were both younger than

Fallon. But if Jake could pose as his dad, it was entirely possible his dad's nemesis employed plastic surgery to pose as a younger man.

Neither man wore the black stainless bracelet his dad said Fallon never removed. Nor did either possess the burn scar that ran from Fallon's lower left jaw to his left elbow. The scar caused when the vial of acid was the only weapon his dad possessed.

Kelly said Knox was local, and his parents before him, so he posed little worry. Jake wasn't as convinced the other man was safe, but Knox knew him and appeared at ease.

This looked like a first meeting, with Knox introducing the man to Taylor. Odds were that if this was the case—and if the man was the killer—the other man would have either gone into action almost immediately or not at all, there only to gain Taylor's confidence. Jake watched for a good twenty minutes before he felt comfortable enough to leave. He would entrust Taylor to Knox's care for the short amount of time he would be gone.

The screen door banged against the side of the house, and the refrigerator came through the door. Dan followed two seconds later, mask and gloves in place.

Will came up the driveway pulling the dollies with one hand and the wagon with the other. People were so willing to help. Somewhat like the Coast Guard, where everyone aboard a unit worked together as a team to accomplish a task. "These are great, Will. Thanks for the loan."

Dan jogged toward them, the mask flapping around his neck. "Randy cleaned out the fridge. Musty, but it's empty."

A chill ran up Taylor's spine. Had Randy known he was going to die? He'd cleaned his refrigerator, and if she made the assumption he buried his Solomon's Compass treasures, it certainly looked that way. Had her uncle committed suicide?

Will scratched his head and frowned. "Crazy."

"Some people have death premonitions." Dan pulled off his gloves.

"I'm going to tackle the cabinets." She climbed the steps. Randy became more of an enigma by the moment.

Taylor worked hard for a half hour before taking a break, drinking a bottle of water in two long swallows. The cabinets were emptied and wiped down, the contents tossed in the trash. Will brought over a set of wooden steps he used for climbing into boats to make it easier for her to lift bags into the bin when she worked alone.

Soon she'd be back to the world she knew on the *Susquehanna*. She couldn't wait. Being among people Randy had known was difficult. Everyone here seemed to place her under a microscope, and she didn't like having her wings spread and a pin stuck through her heart.

She finished her water on the porch. Several yards away, Dan walked among the junk holding a clipboard.

Will came around the corner of the house pocketing his phone. "A Stiletto catamaran was coming in for repair tonight, but it's been bumped up to late afternoon. I'll need to head back across the road sooner than I thought. More like three instead of five, so I'll have enough time to read through the most recent repair and prepare myself to deal with the owner."

"They want their babies fixed yesterday. I know the drill. Stiletto's a good product."

"Beautiful thirty-footer, and Nate Brady treats her like she's a piece of shit." He puffed his cheeks and blew out air. "Tears her up on a regular basis."

"People are like that. On the water and off. I meet them every day, one way or another." She pointed toward the yard. "What is Dan doing?"

"Taking inventory, I guess. He didn't say."

She shook her head. What could she say so he understood she meant to do this herself? "I'm going back inside to finish in the kitchen and start in the bathroom. If you could move the items in the hall between the kitchen and bath, and those in the bathroom, I can get to the cabinets."

"Sure. I'll grab a dolly and be right in." His phone rang. "As soon as I finish here."

He answered on his way down the steps.

She stood in the center of the kitchen and turned in a circle. Before she arrived, her mind was filled with grand visions. In person, they evaporated into pipe dreams. Next summer she could add two coats of white paint to the walls and cabinets and have the floors tiled. The space the fridge had occupied was nasty. Behind the stove would be the same or worse. She would need to move the stove forward to clean behind it.

At times like this, she hated being short. Her arms weren't long enough for good leverage. She grabbed the back of the stove, and searing pain shot through her hands.

She yanked her arms away. Blood dripped from both hands across the tile counter and into the sink. She turned on the faucet with her right wrist. Cool water washed the blood away and her panic ebbed. Deep cuts sliced midway between the last knuckle and tip of the first three fingers of her left hand. The cuts didn't reach the bone, but they needed stitches. On her right, a shallow cut crossed her palm beneath her first and second fingers. It would be sore, but her right fingers were unharmed.

"I'm ready to—what the hell happened?" Dan ran the last few feet to her side.

"Something on the back of the stove. It's so old. Probably no one gave a thought to sharp edges back then. I should've had Bixby haul it away along with the fridge. Hand me some paper towels from one of the bags by the door so I can apply pressure."

Dan threw items from one bag after another until he found the roll and ripped off a strip. He ran back, thrusting them at her, and zoomed to the door again. "Will! Get in here! Hurry!"

She held her arms above her head and pushed her left fingers against her right palm. "Dan, my purse is with the bags by the door. Will you drive me to the ER? I need a few stitches."

He scooped her purse under his arm and held the door for her.

Will came bounding up the steps. "What's going on?"

"I cut myself. Dan's going to drive me to the ER for stitches."

"I'll take you."

"No. You have a catamaran coming in. Take care of your customer. I'll be fine."

"But—"

"Dan will take me. Go."

Dan placed his hand at the small of her back to guide her down the steps. "Are you sure you're going to be all right?"

"Of course." They reached the ground. "Hey . . . my purse matches your shirt."

Dan stepped back, eyes round and mouth open. "How can you make jokes? You're bleeding."

Taylor kept walking.

"Don't walk too fast, or your hands will bleed more."

"No they won't. They're above my heart. I'll be fine."

"Shock. You must be in shock." He opened the passenger door, his face pale. "You're entirely too calm."

"I command a cutter. I deal with things like this and more every day. I know what to do. Now, snap my seatbelt and shut the door."

The physician's assistant in the emergency medical clinic deadened her fingers and hand, cleaned the cuts, and glued them back together after putting two tiny stitches inside one finger. One tetanus shot later she was free to go.

Dan's color had returned. He fastened her seatbelt. "You gave me such a scare. I'm glad you're okay."

"Told you." A grin tugged at the corner of her mouth, and she fought to stop it from spreading. She liked Dan, and she didn't want to hurt his feelings.

"I should've listened instead of working myself up. I do that, but it comes without thinking. I called Will and told him you were all right."

"Thanks." She reclined her head against the seat. Dan was more emotional than a teenage girl. She had been the same, once upon a time. Before Mark Vitulli. Before Mark died.

For her own peace of mind, and because she always needed to see the whole picture to feel in control, she needed to look at the back of the stove to see what had cut her. She'd ask Will to move it out.

Two cars waited in her driveway—Zia's SUV and a plain black Charger. Dan parked on the street and freed her from the seatbelt.

On the back porch, Zia leaned against the wall reading a joke from her phone to Glen. She wore a pair of jean shorts and a yellow and white striped knit top with skinny straps.

Zia rushed down the steps and hugged her. "Oh my God, Taylor. Are you all right? Dan called me. Then he called Trinh to watch your place, and she called me, too."

"No need for flowers. They said I'll live. If I wasn't on leave, I wouldn't even get light duty. The PA at the emergency clinic glued the cuts together."

"I'm going to finish cleaning for you." Zia patted Taylor's shoulders.

Taylor opened her mouth.

"Don't say no. Dan said someone needed to clean and paint in here and you wouldn't be able to do it. I have people."

Glen squeezed Taylor's shoulder. "I'm glad you're good. Tell me what happened."

She retold the story.

"You don't know what you cut them on?"

"Jagged metal. The backing of the stove must be rusted or pried loose." Maybe Randy had stashed something inside. "Did Dan call you, too?"

He chuckled. "Trinh. Let's go look at your stove."

All four of them trooped inside.

Dan and Upchurch held the front of the stove and walked it out of its space inch by inch. Her blood stained the razor blades duct taped to the edges of the rear panel. The cuts hadn't been an accident. Someone didn't want her here. Or maybe not just her. Maybe the blades were meant to deter anyone from moving the stove.

The sight of her own blood made her head light and her stomach woozy, but she met the detective's questioning look. "Is there a way to tell if these are newly placed or if they've been here for a while?"

"We don't have funds for the testing needed to confirm that." He pulled on a pair of clear PVC gloves. "Before elaborate forensic evidence was required, we did it ourselves. See the dust back here?"

He loosened an edge and pulled off a piece of duct tape. The razor blades and dust from the back of the range stayed attached to the tape. Where the blade had been, dust remained on the metal. "They're new."

A knot tightened in her stomach. Yesterday's phone call had niggled, but not enough to raise her level of concern. Had the call been directed at her after all? It looked that way. Razor blades attached to the back of the stove wouldn't kill her, and they might scare off some people. Whoever was responsible didn't know her. USCG CDR Taylor A. Campbell kept a healthy respect for danger, but she didn't frighten easily. In fact, like most Coast Guard members she was trained to meet problems head on and deal with them.

Upchurch ripped off the other blade and ran his light over the rest of the rear plate. "I'll take these. We might get a partial off of them, but I doubt it."

Someone wanted something inside the house. Anyone could have a key; but they hadn't found what they were looking for. She shook her head. Maybe Randy had treasure beyond the Solomon's Compass keepsakes.

"Thanks for coming out."

"My job. You gonna be okay?"

She'd have to be. "Things will move on a slower bell, that's all." And no digging for a few days. That was the worst part.

"Walk out with me." Glen held the door for her but didn't speak until they reached his car. "Have you received any phone calls like the one Trinh answered? Anyone suspicious come out here?"

"No. And only the people you see here."

He opened the driver's door. "Better get on back in there before Dan busts a gut trying to hear what we're saying."

She smiled. Barely.

Zia sat in the porch swing talking on her phone. Inside, Dan was wiping her blood off the top of the stove and the counter.

"Thank you, but you didn't need to do that."

"Yes, I did. You can't even feel your fingers." He finished and tossed the wet paper towel into an open trash bag. "I *will* be here in the morning. I'll do the heavy lifting. You will supervise and make the decisions."

She shook her head.

Dan bowed with a sweeping flourish. "I will be your humble servant."

Taylor laughed. "How can I refuse a humble servant?"

He placed his hands on her shoulders. "You can't. Now that I've gotten a better look at what's here, I know what you're up against. Together, we can clear this house in a couple of days."

"No way."

"Oh, yes, way." He walked around the room gesturing to match his words. "We'll move things around in the salvage shop so items we move from the house will fit. When your hands are better, you can clean, paint, whatever you need to do in here. Then you can determine if you want to tackle the shop on this visit."

Unbidden, she teared up and bit down on her lips. She looked toward the porch so Dan wouldn't see. Her plans for her time here were being shanghaied from every direction. She wouldn't be able to finish inside the house without help. Who could have guessed she would pull out the stove? She hadn't known herself until she tried.

After several quick blinks, she turned back. "I appreciate the offer, and I accept."

"Good. You didn't really have a choice. I'm persistent as hell." He grinned.

The screen door slammed, and Zia came in. "I was on the phone with my office. My housecleaner is on the way. I'll do what she says, which will be to hand her things, and say I helped. A painter who owes me a favor will be here at eight in the morning to paint."

"You don't need to—"

"Nonsense. You'll be back to speed next week. In the meantime, go sit in the swing. They made room." Zia put one hand on her hip and pointed toward the door with the other. "Go. Now. Let me get to work. When Paulette gets here, we'll let you say what to keep from the bathroom, we'll clean it, and the painter will paint. Now scoot."

Taylor had held command positions for years. Relinquishing control to someone else wasn't easy. She knew in her mind the cleanup and paint job were gifts of kindness from Zia. But in her heart, Taylor felt as if she was losing part of herself by not participating in the process.

CHAPTER 12

The manager of The Waterfront met Jake in the lobby and escorted him upstairs, filling him in on details he should have kept private. He did have the decency to wait in the hallway while Jake went inside and looked around. The housekeeper hadn't reached his room yet, and he added a twenty to the few dollars he'd placed on the table before he left. He found a notepad and wrote *Thanks for being alert*. More than likely she wouldn't receive any extra from the hotel.

His computer sat on the desk. His clothes were in his bag. His toothbrush and shaving gear stood by the lavatory. He traveled light. Except for the bag of tools locked in the trunk of his rental.

In order not to raise suspicion, he waited three more minutes before opening the door. "Everything accounted for."

Relief washed over the manager's face. "Very good."

"Do you need me for anything else?"

"Yes, as a matter of fact. I need you to sign an insurance release that nothing was stolen from you. And a Rock Harbor police detective would like to meet with you. He promised it would take only a few minutes of your time."

Inside, Jake groaned. *Police* and *a few minutes* never went together in the same sentence. Another reason his dad didn't like for anyone to cozy up to local law enforcement. Signing the form wasn't quick and easy either. The manager hadn't expected him to read it first. Ten minutes later, the manager took him to the open door of a small meeting room and left. Inside was the same detective that stopped at the boatyard yesterday morning. Up something-or-other. With the eyebrows.

The detective stood. "Come in, come in. You're in room—?"

"Jake Solomon." He gave the detective his room number.

"Have a seat. I'm Detective Upchurch. Let me find you on the list. Here you are." He ran his finger across the page. "You checked in Sunday. Correct?"

Jake sat. "Yes. For two weeks." Purposely longer than Taylor would be here, so as not to show an overt connection.

The detective went on, confirming his address, phone, and email. He asked for a photo ID. Jake complied and pitied the thief during his interrogation. It would last a while, even though he was caught in the act. "May I ask you something?"

"Sure."

"I understand you arrested the suspect?"

"Yes."

"Did he have any distinctive scars or was he wearing any distinctive jewelry?"

"How distinctive?"

"I'm not at liberty to say."

Upchurch leaned back. "Are you an investigator?"

Jesus H. He should've never brought it up. He pulled a card from his carrying case and pushed it across the table. Then he mixed up a smidgen of truth to hide his lie. "We're a global security firm. I'm not here on business, but sometimes the business thinks otherwise. If you get my drift."

Upchurch nodded. "I do, indeed. I can't give you particulars, but there were no identifying scars. The only jewelry was a sleeve of gang tats. Or maybe that falls under scars."

Jake returned the detective's smile. "Perhaps. But it's not what I was looking for."

The detective turned into a proud travel guide until his phone rang. "I hate to cut this short, but business calls. Pleasure talking to you."

An hour after arriving, Jake walked out of the hotel and waved goodbye to Glen Upchurch.

While he was in town he decided to top off the gas tank—all part of being prepared. Before he reached the station, Kelly called. He pulled over.

"What's the latest with Dad?"

"No change. Still running a high fever and being pumped full of IV antibiotics. I can only use my laptop by dropping the security a couple of levels. Mom is home now. When she comes back, I'll go. Then I'll see if syncing to my home computer through a secure satellite will work."

"I don't expect you to work while you're with Dad."

"Please. I'm as invested as you are. Visiting hours are for ten minutes every four hours. What else am I going to do? I've already read three books and called Simon so often he told me he had work to do."

That was Kelly—Type A personality and workaholic. "Thanks, sis. I wish I was there."

They talked for several minutes, and Kelly was in a better mood by the time they hung up. He finally reached his surveillance location two hours after he left. Zia Markham had arrived. Jake pulled the binoculars to his eyes.

Taylor sat in the swing on the back porch, keeping it in motion with her foot. Her head lay against the back and her eyelashes fanned over her cheeks. The exposed curves of her neck invited him to linger. His forty-some-year-old penis jerked to life.

Down, bozo. Jake shifted in his seat and cleared his throat. He was here to protect Taylor, not get lucky.

The binoculars trailed down her body to her hands in her lap. His gut clenched.

What the fuck?

Gauze wrapping covered one of her hands.

He zoomed in for a closer look.

The fingers of her left hand sported large Band-Aids. On the right, her fingers were exposed, but gauze padded her palm and extended to her wrist.

A sick feeling rose in his throat, and he sucked in air through his teeth. He loosened his grip on the binoculars but kept them to his eyes for several seconds until he was satisfied the regular rise and fall of Taylor's chest was real and not his imagination.

Jake had followed his dad's wishes and kept his distance. If Oliver Fallon was the killer, he would kill Jake at first glance. So far he'd played by his dad's rules. Now he would play by his. No one harmed those he cared for. No one.

CHAPTER 13

Words failed Taylor as she walked through the kitchen and bathroom after Zia and Paulette, her housecleaner, had gone on their way. The fresh orange scent replaced years of dust, grime, and grease and made her smile. The windows were clean and streak free. The painter would be here in the morning.

Taylor crossed the street to the boatyard. She'd seen each item taken out of the bathroom, and Randy's belt and photos hadn't been included. A half hour ago, the tips of her cut fingers had started to throb, but the numbness lingered in her palm. Several pickups were parked in front of the boatyard, and the chandlery was filled with customers, so she didn't disturb Trinh. In the work area, Will waved to her from under a bow rider. From time to time he scooted fore to aft and back again—either a bottom job or damage repair.

After a few minutes, he crawled out. "How are you?"

"Better, thanks." She wiggled her fingers a tiny bit and set off a new wave of throbbing. "The numbness is fading. Do you mind if I hang out over here until I can drive? Trinh's busy, or I would've chatted with her."

"You can wait in my office." He pointed toward a door between two large windows. "It's not locked."

"Thanks. I need to walk around. You don't need to entertain me."

He waved his arm. "What's mine is yours."

She headed down the quay, heat from the sun beating on her tight back muscles and finally loosening them. Will ran a good boatyard. She'd never owned a boat, but she was in and out of boatyards and shipyards regularly. Neatness counted. Not only for appearance but for safety.

Several yards out in the bay, a catamaran limped along parallel to the shore. It had to be the one Will expected. The hulls, jib, and mainsail were red. She turned back toward the office. Will was nowhere in sight, so she went inside. From the edge of a window, she watched the cat turn into the channel.

Will was right. The Stiletto had the bones of a beautiful craft. The boater was clueless about how to handle her. He tugged and shoved and jerked instead of applying simple, smooth motions. Had the wind been stronger than the light breeze that swept across the bay, he would have slammed into the quay. The resultant damage would have served him right.

Will entered her field of vision, and he didn't look happy. He stood with both hands on his hips, shoulders squared, and chin up, ready for a fight. She opened the door a crack to listen to their conversation. After all Will had told her, she wanted the rest of the story. Or at least the story the cat's owner decided to tell.

The *Red Witch* floated to the quay no more than thirty feet in front of her, and she had a perfect view. The owner, Nate Brady, towered over the hulls, and cussed up a blue streak, as Randy would've said. Will was right about him having no respect for the boat.

"You think it'll take the full three weeks?" Brady stepped onto the quay and hitched up his shorts.

"Probably." Will removed his ball cap and ran his hand through his hair before he tugged it back on. "She's listing like a drunk whore. What'd you do, run into a buoy?"

"None of your damn business." Sunglasses hid Brady's eyes, but his words and the quick snap of his head said *go to hell*.

"We'll lift her out tomorrow and get an eyes-on."

"I want this fixed right, Knox." He waved a finger at Will.

"If you don't stop trying to sail her as though she's indestructible, one day I won't be able to put her back in shape. It's been less than a year since you had her in here for work."

"Last July. You let me worry about that. I'm flying to the Panhandle tomorrow. The Gulf Spirit Regatta is in five weeks, but I'll be back in three to put her through her paces. Have her ready."

"We'll do our best."

"If she's not waiting and in the water, I won't bring her here again."

"Take her elsewhere if you don't think we can do the job." Will's hands returned to his hips. "Right now."

Brady took off his sunglasses and revealed hard little pig eyes trapped by extra folds of skin, like a double eyelid. "Don't get pissy with me, Knox. Don't think I wouldn't, except my ride's waiting for me out front."

He slammed his sunglasses back on and strode toward the entrance with a long gait.

Who in the world would give him a ride? Too bad a window didn't overlook the street side so she could find out.

She shivered. Someone like Nate Brady could make threatening phone calls. And tape razor blades to the back of a stove.

Will was checking the lines. When he finished he'd probably head in here. She gently closed the door before choosing an overstuffed arm chair in the corner and leaning back. It wouldn't do if he thought she'd eavesdropped on his business.

If she caught one of her officers or crew listening to what she presumed to be a private conversation, she would issue a verbal reprimand to the offender and instruct her XO to hold sessions for officers and enlisted on the rights and responsibilities of privacy. *Do as I say, not as I do.* How many times had she heard that growing up? Christ, she was turning into her mother.

A few minutes later, Will walked through the door and tossed his hat to his desk.

"All done?"

He jumped. "Sumbitch! I forgot you were here."

"Soaking up the free air conditioning."

He laughed. "Go for it. I'm finishing an order before I head out. You're welcome to stay until then."

"Can you chat and work?"

"Sure. What's up?" He focused on the computer screen and didn't look at her.

"I just wondered if I needed to be quiet. Do you have a boat?"

"Not now. Everybody else does, so it's not like I never go out. I'll probably break down one of these days, though. How about you?"

"I like to sail, but I don't own a boat either. Ones I can afford seem pretty small after the *Susquehanna*."

"How long is she?"

"Two hundred seventy feet. Thirty-eight-foot beam."

He whistled through his teeth.

"Looks like a rubber ducky next to an aircraft carrier. Size is relative."

"Only in some things." He raised his head and wiggled his eyebrows.

"You're not old enough to be a dirty old man. How did it go with the catamaran?"

"One of these days Brady's going to break the *Red Witch* in half, and when he does, I wonder if he'll have enough courage to hang on."

"I know the type. We rescue them all the time, or find their swamped boats."

He pushed away from the computer and leaned back in his chair. "None of the other yards will deal with him. Rumor is he likes to gamble, and if he loses, he pays the debt by running drugs. I've never seen evidence firsthand, but I always expect the task force to show up when he brings her in. His other boat never has a problem, but it's engine driven, not sail."

"Go-fast boat?"

"No. Similar to your uncle's sportfisher but not as nice."

Lots of room to stash a payload of drugs in a sportfisher. But no need to share her Coast Guard thoughts with Will. "Some people are born to sail, and some aren't."

Will stretched his arms and moved his neck around. "I often wonder, though, who'd ever expect a catamaran to be a drug boat? Especially one operated by an inept sailor."

"Maybe that's what Nate wants them to think, so the focus is on the cat."

Nate Brady could take the sportfisher out anytime, throw out lines, and no one would be the wiser.

CHAPTER 14

At the same café where she'd eaten dinner the night before, Taylor lingered over a second cup of strong black coffee and practiced her fractured Spanish with the server. It was barely dawn, and she'd been the only customer; but as they talked, the taqueria came to life. She paid her bill and went across the street to a drugstore. Inside the door, she stopped. Her eyes widened, and her skin tingled. A few feet away, Mr. Brooklyn browsed through a large rack of postcards.

A smile grew on her face as she walked toward him. She had a new understanding of why women were attracted to older men. He was sexy as hell. "Good morning. We really need to stop meeting this way."

He looked up.

Oh crap. He didn't even remember her. Her smile vanished. She was being too silly—like a teenager. "From the—"

"What happened to your hands?"

He reached out and held her wrists in his palms, his touch as gentle as the breath of air she couldn't seem to catch.

"I thought you didn't remember me." *Shut up, Taylor.*

He explored her face, and she thought her heart might explode. "I could never forget you."

Heat rose to her cheeks, but she didn't break the connection. "I just, well, I. . . ." *You wanted to talk, Taylor. Spit it out.*

Those green eyes stirred feelings absent from her life for years. She took a deep breath. "I thought I'd never see you again, and here you are."

He smiled, but the caring in his eyes never wavered. "Your hands?"

Oh. "Yesterday afternoon. Cleaning. I sliced them on some sharp metal."

Even though her heart beat like a drum roll in her ears, she wasn't about to go into details with a stranger. That's what he was, even if she did want to jump his bones. Oh, Lord, where the hell had that come from? It was the truth.

"Did you go to the doctor?"

"The PA at the clinic glued the cuts closed. Four fingers and a short slash across my palm." She wiggled her cut fingers. "In a few days, I'll be good as new."

"I'm glad."

He kept hold of her wrists. Or she didn't move them. Neither of them broke eye contact.

Except her heart ran the New York Marathon in those few seconds while she explored the depths of his intoxicating eyes. Her skin sang. He cupped her hands with his, his fingers barely touching her wrists. The skin-to-skin contact ignited a fire that burned from deep inside.

If she didn't move, she would go crazy. "I, uh, came in to get some padding and a couple pair of thick rubber gloves."

He released her wrists. "More cleaning?"

"More than you could ever imagine."

"Guess I'll see you around."

That was all? Of course. His wife, kids, and the dog waited at home. He might feel an attraction to her, but he wouldn't act. Even though his expression held a hint of wistfulness. Neither would she. It was probably her imagination.

"Given our track record, you probably will." She waved goodbye and went about her shopping.

After talking with the pharmacy clerk, she walked out with a box of PVC gloves, two pair of bright yellow rubber gloves, and a bag filled with gauze pads and cotton balls to stuff inside them to keep her cuts snug and dry. She didn't spot Mr. Brooklyn anyplace.

The smile on her face drooped. Only after she sat behind the wheel of her car did she realize she'd forgotten to ask him his name.

By the time she reached Randy's, Dan waited in the swing. "Morning, girlfriend. How are your hands?"

"Stiff and sore, but I've been moving them a lot and the glue is wonderful." She held up the bag. "I stopped for gloves and padding, so I can pitch in. No lifting or moving yet, but plenty good for sorting."

"Don't push it. Any problem, you stop. Deal?"

She reached the porch and unlocked the door. "Deal. We need a plan of the day."

"Let's take a peek inside the salvage shop and strategize."

"I'll glove up."

A few minutes later, they walked the short distance to the salvage shop, and because she couldn't feel the key through the gloves and padding, Dan performed the honors.

When he pulled open the door, a wave of heat rolled over her. "Search for the thermostat and turn on the air."

"Found it." He shoved items away from the wall, and the blower came on seconds later. "Now I know you're a military officer. That was an order if I ever heard one."

"Sorry, habit. Happens when I'm stressed."

"No problem. Let's go back to the house. This overstuffed cavern will take an hour or two to cool."

She stared at the mess, her shoulders slumped in defeat. Junk. Everywhere.

"Don't worry, Taylor. We'll clear the house room by room. Wherever we are after an hour, we stop and come back here."

"Maybe we'll have half a room clear in an hour."

He raised her chin with a finger. "Oh, ye of little faith. Follow my lead. We'll come out here and first clear this fairly open space at the front. The aisle to the back is already clear. We'll start in the back corners and work forward. I'll show you what to do. Trust me."

She gnawed at her lower lip. The clutter-filled area in front was as wide as the entire shop and about ten feet deep.

Dan pulled the door closed, and they started back to the house. "By doing it this way, we make room to move things straight here without doing double work. Your house will be clear, and we'll take the shop a step at a time."

She stepped over the downed chain links. "If you think we can get it done, I'm for it."

He smiled. "Faith, Taylor. It will happen. If it's all right with you, I'm going to get Will to cut this portion of fence out."

"Please. Before someone gets hurt. It's useless and dangerous."

"The last time I talked to Randy was out here." Dan pointed to the big oak in the backyard. "The day before they found his body."

His last day alive. A tiny chill passed through her. "I wish I'd been here for him. He was already buried before I learned he was dead."

"My God! What happened?"

Taylor turned away. She really shouldn't vent to Dan. Or badmouth her mother. Even if she had notified Taylor immediately, attending the funeral wouldn't have been possible.

"Oh, I'll bet you were out on the ocean someplace."

"When I received the email from my mother, we were in the North Atlantic, three days out from Copenhagen. The email arrived the day after Randy was buried."

Dan wrapped his arms around her in the sweetest hug she'd received in a long time. She returned it. After several seconds, he stepped back. "Don't you worry one bit about missing Randy's funeral. He loved and respected the Coast Guard. And he loved and respected you. He was so proud of you. He would have wanted you there, I'm sure, but he would have loved and respected you even more for doing your duty. That's the way Randy was. So stop feeling guilty about that."

Taylor nodded and blinked away the sting in her eyes. "I know that, logically. But it's hard to accept in my heart."

"You'll always love him, but the pain will lessen. I promise. On that last day, we sat under the tree and drank a beer. For the first time in a long time, he seemed like the same old Randy. He said he was sure going to miss this place when he was gone. I asked him where he was going." Dan took a few more steps in silence.

"What did he say?"

Dan glanced at her. "He winked at me and said I had to live in this town after he was gone, and the less I knew, the safer I'd be."

A chill spread through her, and she shivered in the muggy heat.

"He'd been so paranoid—I remember thinking his words were just more of the same. Then I thought maybe he was moving. After seeing his refrigerator, I really do believe he had a premonition."

"Thanks for sharing with me.

He ran his hand over his hair. "You're his kin. You deserve to know."

Jake's day had been busy. Overnight he placed a tracking device on Taylor's car enabling him to record her location on his phone—a Class A misdemeanor in Texas. He'd gone in the drugstore while she had breakfast to pick up toothpaste and some protein bars. Taylor surprised him by walking in, sexy as hell and wearing another dwarf tee. Grumpy—bah. Anything but. He wondered if his face had registered the same shock as hers.

After the drugstore, she drove to Rankin's, stayed all day, stopped at the same taqueria on the way home. The device only provided the location of her car, but with Kelly back in New York, it was the best of his choices.

Jake had his own work to do following up on leads Kelly left for him. So far, what he'd learned didn't point a finger at anyone, but instead became more pieces of the puzzle—Dan Blair's entanglements, Zia Markham's affairs, Will Knox's women.

The only person he could firmly mark off his list of suspects was the fishing guide in Port Aransas who had purchased Rankin's boat. The guide had shown him proof that during the week of Randy's murder, the boat had been getting a bottom job in Ingleside, and he himself had been in the hospital for back surgery.

Full from another burger at Lulu's, Jake went back to town for a stroll down to the water. Gentle waves lapped at rocks and boulders lining this stretch of shoreline. He'd walked beside the sea in countless spots around the world. Copano Bay was better than some, not as good as others. Kelly called as a line of pelicans hunted for dinner.

"How's Dad?"

"Still in ICU. They expected different results on some tests, and they want to keep a close watch for at least forty-eight hours." She sighed.

"Hang in there. Go pick on an intern when you feel helpless, and don't worry about Rock Harbor. I'm getting a good overview and some insight on Rankin."

Kelly sighed again. "There seems to be a disagreement between doctors, and they're running more tests. Simon's checking with some oncology specialist he knows."

"Good. That will keep everyone honest. Knowledge is power. Maybe I should sling some around down here. See who pays attention." A sand crab crawled to the top of a large black rock and stared at him. Like Kelly watching over their dad, scurrying here and there.

"You better behave yourself. Dad told you to observe only. I can't come down and post bail."

"Would I—"

"You have. I don't want to hear it."

Finally. A trace of his real sister had returned to her voice. "What can I do to help you, Kel?"

"Nothing I can think of. All I've done is visit him every four hours and run errands in between. Mom is holding up. We should be half as strong. This afternoon I rode up in the elevator with one of Dad's doctors, and she talked to me after she checked on him. The doctor confirmed what I read on Dad's official record."

Of course Kelly tapped into the hospital's medical records. He hadn't expected less. "Take care of yourself, give Mom a kiss, and tell Dad I'm doing everything *exactly* the way he would."

Jake smiled at Kelly's laughter. Since childhood, whenever their dad taught them something new, he always said, "Do *exactly* what I tell you." They never did, and he always responded with, "If you'd done it the way I showed you…."

"Thanks, Jake. I needed that."

"Catch me up when you can, and call if you need me. I'll find you if I need anything urgent."

They hung up, and he walked back to the street. Midway down the block, he found an empty bench and blended into the shadows. Like the previous evenings, people filled the sidewalks. No one stood out, he didn't spot a black stainless bracelet, so he took a few minutes to answer a text from the man who took his place in Helsinki. While he reread his response, Zia Markham stepped onto the sidewalk and walked toward the ice cream shop. For the polished, blonde type, she was a good-looking woman. A woman who knew how to work it, as Kelly would say.

He sent the message and followed the same direction Zia had taken, except he stopped in front of the golf shop. After a few minutes, Zia came out of the ice cream shop with a to-go bag. When they were six feet apart, she made eye contact and rearranged her lips into a seductive smile filled with the promise of sin.

"Evening." He inclined his head.

"Do I know you from someplace? You look …" Her inspection of him trailed down his body and back up. "… familiar."

"I'm here on vacation. Nice town."

Kelly said Zia had been involved with one man after another since her husband died. The two names she had were Nate Brady and Will Knox, neither one exclusive on Zia's side. Kelly said she liked one-night wonder boys. She hadn't looked into Brady yet.

She tilted her head. "New York, right?"

He turned on a bright smile. "Decided to check out someplace new."

"We're pretty quiet. Family or friends here?"

"A colleague from another lifetime."

"What do you do in this lifetime, Mr. . . ."

Such fishing techniques came straight from Sales 101, but he admired her technique. Had he been willing, he could have shared her ice cream later in the evening. He gave her a grin. "Some of this, some of that. Not as much of anything as I used to."

"I'm Zia Markham—ZGM Properties down on the corner." Her voice lost its warmth and turned businesslike. "Come see me if you decide to stay a while."

She was good. Hard to pass up the implied meaning in her words, especially since her nails trailed along his palm when she handed him her card. He turned his wrist as if checking the time. "I'm late for an appointment. Pleasure meeting you." He walked away, not waiting for her to respond.

Behind the wheel, he risked a glance along the sidewalk, but she was gone. He'd wanted a closer look, and it had given him enough information. Her directness and confidence told him Zia liked to play with the big boys, but she put herself first and always would.

He followed the beach road north and parked two lots down from Will Knox's house. Knox wasn't home, so he'd arrived in plenty of time. He pulled a beat-to-hell paperback from the glove box and opened it to a dog-eared page.

The book was his dad's. Like the beer, it was a tool meant to nail his impersonation. Since the day his dad left for Vietnam back on October 4, 1969, *You Only Live Twice* had been with him. The torn cover, with part of the skull balloon missing, greeted

Jake like an old friend because it had always been on his dad's desk, his security blanket. Inside, James Bond lurked half a step away from becoming an alcoholic.

Jake's father, Jacob Daniel Solomon, was a Coast Guard gunner's mate in Vietnam. A damn good one. He roamed the rivers on an eighty-two-foot Point boat, the *Point Whitebanks*. Jake thought he embellished his stories until he did his own research. Prowling rivers and deltas in an eighty-two-footer was one thing. Going it in a thirteen-foot Boston Whaler was a whole other ballgame. Bond and Tiger Tanaka had kept him company. And according to his dad, kept him safe.

Jake stared unseeing at the print. Waiting for Knox to show was nothing like scanning the horizon for the tiniest movement. People who moved silently in the night were the most deadly kind. Like his dad. Like him.

Now he was performing due diligence on the locals who had made Taylor part of their circle. Looking for underlying reasons. Seeing if anyone had a motive for killing Rankin.

Ten minutes later, Knox's truck turned into the driveway. Jake left the book on the seat and closed his door without a sound. An old habit. In less than a minute, he rang Knox's doorbell.

"Hold your horses, I'm coming," came from inside. Followed by footsteps across a hard surface floor.

The porch light glowed, and the door swung wide. "May I help you?"

Knox stood open to the world, one hand on the door, the other on the frame—barring entrance but showing he had nothing to hide.

Jake gave him a quick smile. "You don't know me. My name's Jake Solomon, and I'm a former shipmate of Randy Rankin. I'd like to talk to you for a few minutes."

Knox stared at him a second. "C'mon in. His niece is in town now, too. Do you know her?"

He ignored the question. "You shouldn't invite strangers into your home. Likewise, I'd be more comfortable talking to you out here."

Knox shrugged. "You're not from around here. Texas is different, but I can take the heat and mosquitoes if you can." He stepped outside and pulled the door closed.

Jake doubted Texas was much different, not in ways that counted. "Thanks. Old habits die hard."

"How'd you know Randy?"

"We were stationed together in Nam. Got into a lot of shit. Bound a lot of us together for a long time."

"He served in the Coast Guard. You?"

"Same. Never thought when I joined I'd find my ass in Vietnam. Thought I'd be out on the Sound, rescuing damsels in distress."

"No damsels?" One corner of Knox's mouth hiked up in a semi-grin.

"They were around, but they sure as hell didn't need rescuing. I got to Nam and thought I'd be a big hotshot. Win the war single-handed. I learned real quick that the Coast Guard's not a place for divas and rock stars. He tell you about his time over there?"

"Bits and pieces. Usually over a beer or two. Sometimes his stories made sense, sometimes not." Knox picked at his thumb nail.

"He ever tell you about any R&R trips?"

"No." Knox frowned. "Told me about getting shot at."

"A time or two."

"He was closer with my dad, Vernon Knox. Dad said Randy was the one person in town he could always depend on to do what he said."

"Randy was like that." Time to get down to business. Jake pulled out an old photo of his dad and the man his dad suspected of Rankin's murder. The photo had been taken sometime in the seventies on the Spanish Steps in Rome. "Ever seen this man around? The one on the left? Anytime, recent or a while back."

Knox took the photo and stepped back into the light. He studied the photo for close to a minute before handing it back. "Not that I recall."

"Was Randy involved with a woman? Or anyone who might have been involved in iffy business?"

"No women since his mind went. And never anyone iffy." Knox frowned. "He'd been seeing this woman named Jill for a while—year or so. They broke it off—but now I think about it, they broke up a while before Randy started looking under rocks and behind doors. She was the last one I know about."

"She live here? Got a last name?"

He shrugged. "Randy didn't share much personal stuff with me. I can barely keep track of the women I date, much less any others."

"Women always want something. Starts small, then they want the moon." Except for Taylor Campbell. All she wanted was to make captain. "That happen to you?"

"I'm divorced. Got a beautiful daughter. I never plan to go down that path again. Rock Harbor has a good supply of women—vacationing women. Know what I mean?"

Jake knew.

"Everybody gets what they want. And nobody gets tied down."

Jake nodded. "None of them want anything? None of them ever asked about Randy Rankin?"

"All they want is a good time. Same as me." As Jake's words sank in, Knox tilted his head and gave Jake a hard look. "You think Randy's death might not have been an accident?"

"I don't like loose ends. That's all. If you remember anything I might like to know, here's my card. My cell's on it. Thanks for talking to me."

CHAPTER 15

Every muscle in Taylor's back ached, making getting out of bed when her alarm went off an exercise in patience and pain. At least her room hadn't been one of the ones broken into yesterday. A moment of panic had made her heart race when the manager called with the news. Not that her room contained anything valuable—even her laptop was worthless—but one extra second of turmoil may have sent her over the edge. She had enough to worry about.

Yesterday's progress amazed her. She and Dan had settled into a routine. While she sorted through the mess, pulling out broken items and trash, he went behind her and pulled out more scrap for the trash bin. He moved what remained to the salvage shop. Dan knew what would sell and what would be worthless clutter that would drive the lot price downward. And he was fast. Taylor hustled to stay ahead, even though he performed the heavy lifting.

The best part of cleaning out this way was she got to search through the whole lot. If Randy's belt or the Compass Point photos were in the house, she would find them.

Taylor met Dan on the porch. "Coffee! You're a lifesaver. I had one small cup at the hotel. And yogurt. If I eat another breakfast taco, I'll have to get my uniform altered." She took the tall cup from him.

"It's my own cruel curse. Without my coffee, I simply can't function."

"Sorry I can't offer any breakfast. I should have grabbed a taco for you."

"I had oatmeal." He grimaced. "Cholesterol."

She nodded. So far she'd been fortunate, but her XO already took meds to lower his.

She unlocked the door and they went inside. Randy's kitchen table and chairs occupied their space in the kitchen. His headboard, bed frame, and chest remained in his bedroom. And the three boxes of family belongings were in his closet. Her uncle's home was starting to look the way she remembered. As long as she didn't look in the living room.

"The tight line down the center of your forehead is missing this morning." Dan followed her inside.

"Sleep works wonders."

They chatted over their coffees and got to work in the living room. She used extra padding to wrap her hands and lifted a box or two with no problem. *Yay, glue.* She'd be able to dig for Randy's treasure before she had to return to Charleston, and she was now convinced he really had buried something. Most likely the belt and photos.

Dan kept the mood light, filling her in on the happenings in Rock Harbor. She had mental images of a lot of people she'd never meet. And knew who was sleeping with whom.

"Will and Zia? You're sure?"

"They don't try to keep it secret. Everyone knows. They've been friends for years, but only lovers if neither one is involved with someone else. An open friendship."

Taylor suddenly felt very old. Or maybe it was old-fashioned. "I guess if that's what they want." She was a one-man woman. And there hadn't been that many men. The past few years, especially, she'd been almost exclusively career focused. But she couldn't imagine such an arrangement with Mark or Mr. Brooklyn. *Stop it, Taylor. Remember . . . wife, kids, dog.*

"Will has his pick of women. And no strings is exactly what Zia wants. I guess she never got over it when Ross died. She's been different since then."

"Was Ross her husband?"

"Yes. And then there was Nate Brady."

"Nate Brady! You know him?"

Dan stopped moving. "Do you?"

She shook her head. "I overheard him talking to Will about his catamaran. Do they know about each other?"

"Will knows about Nate. From all I know about Mr. Brady, Will would no longer be among the living if Nate knew about him."

Dan's opinion of Nate Brady matched hers. "How well do you know him? Brady, I mean."

"I've met him briefly a time or two. If he's been out here, you need to armor up. I gather he's a real slick bastard. Some people think he runs drugs." Dan sucked on his bottom lip. "I'm not willing to put that label on anyone I haven't met."

Taylor hadn't quite expected his answer. Dan was the first one to tease and share gossip, but as she thought back, his stories were about people he knew. And they were funny, not harmful. He cared about people. She liked that.

They went back to work, and by noon they'd cleared the back row of tables in the salvage shop and made room for the rest of the items from the house.

Dan flopped onto a kitchen chair. "Lady, you're a real worker. I haven't moved this fast in years."

"Cholesterol. Exercise is good for you."

He roared. "You're too much. If I wasn't gay, I'd so make a play for you."

"If you weren't gay, you wouldn't even notice me."

"I beg to differ. I like frou-frou on things in my antique shop, not on people. You're cute, smart, and down to earth. If you come to the opening tomorrow, you'll see for yourself. You are coming, aren't you?"

"If I can find a dress. I brought jeans, shorts, and shirts. Mostly these."

"It's dressy casual, but a teensy bit dressier than Bashful there. I'd offer to go shopping with you, but my schedule is full all day." He wagged a finger. "No frou-frou."

She grinned. Dan was the sister she never had. "Not a problem."

"Are you up for tackling the shop on Monday?"

"I'm going to enjoy the whole weekend. My hand and fingers should be good to go by Monday. Every bit we finish means less I'll have to do when I come back again. What are you doing for lunch?"

"Meeting the electrician. The fixtures I ordered came in, and I want to make sure they go in the right places."

"I passed this place over on the old highway called Lulu's. Supposed to have burgers."

"The best in town. You'll love Lulu, too. Go eat a burger and drink a beer."

"Want me to bring you one?"

"I'm having a salad. With grilled chicken. It's in the fridge at the gallery."

"Cholesterol." They said the word in unison.

"The doctor said if I can lower it with diet and exercise he won't put me on meds. After lunch, you and I will reorganize and tackle the living room."

He hugged her and kissed the air somewhere near her right ear before he let himself out.

Taylor's phone jingled with a *Private* call. Probably someone on the *Susquehanna*.

"Commander Campbell."

"What did you think of my warning?"

Warning? Taylor's stomach dropped—the razor blades. "Listen, you sick sonofa—"

Eerie whispered laughter cut off her rant. Then a click.

"Go to hell!"

Someone knocked on her door.

"Come in."

Will opened the door. "I hope you weren't talking to me."

Taylor ordered herself to relax. "I just had a call."

Will frowned. "A call? You mean a call like Trinh had? What did they say?"

"'What do you think of my warning?'"

Will sunk into a chair. "Bastard. Call Glen."

"I will."

"Now."

"You don't give me orders. I said I'll call him, and I will. I need to think about the voice first."

"Sorry." He looked around the room and down the empty hall. "I'm impressed. Rankin would be proud."

"You think?"

"I think." He set a paper bag on the table. "Almost forgot. I brought you some homemade tamales for lunch."

She gawked at him. "*You* made tamales?"

"No, no. Not me. My neighbor. She usually makes them only at the holidays, but her daughter works in London and is coming home for a visit. They're what she wanted, so Mama and her sisters made them and shared."

"I don't want to take your lunch."

"I have several dozen. I brought you six. Plus some fresh salsa I *did* make."

"Well, thank you. My mouth's watering."

"Enjoy. I have to get back to work." He stood and walked to the door. "Call Glen."

"After lunch."

The tamales tasted like her childhood. She ate four before sitting back and putting her feet on the seat of another chair. She found her phone and Glen's card, and entered his number.

"How can I help you?"

She told him about the call. "Will knows. And probably Trinh by now."

"I suggest you pay close attention to your surroundings from here on out. And try not to be alone."

She eyed the room. Fat chance of that.

"I'm going to put more pressure on County to see if they can find any prints on the tape and blades. Stay in touch with me, and I'll keep you informed."

Right before she hung up, a car door slammed and the chirp of Dan's lock sounded. She swung her feet to the floor just as the back door opened.

He assumed his regular seat at Lulu's bar.

"Whatcha having today, Jake?"

"A beer. I'll order food later. Someone's meeting me."

"Coming right up."

Before his dad got sick, he and Jake had talked about the need for another remote Compass Points location. Having the capability to meet certain clients or hide them away was imperative. CPI had the safe room in the Jersey offices, and a cabin in upper Michigan. Even so, they continued to keep an eye for other locations. Rock Harbor would be perfect.

Lulu set his unopened beer in front of him, and he moved to a nearby table so he could watch the door. He toyed with the bottle until Zia Markham arrived, her presence changing the atmosphere of the room as much as a ballerina's would in the center of a football huddle.

She walked toward him, and he stood. "Thanks for meeting me."

She gave him a big smile. "I love having lunch with a handsome man, Mr. Solomon. And I'm glad to finally learn your name."

With her flirty reply, he half ducked his head, keeping his attention all on her. "Call me Jake. In my younger days, I wouldn't have realized you were hitting on me. By the time I figured out how women operate, I was too old for the knowledge to do me any good. But I enjoy being able to play along." He pulled out a chair for her.

After he sat, she reached across the table and placed her hand on top of his. The scent of jasmine overcame the seared beef and onions aroma of the bar. He leaned back in his chair to keep away from the sweetness of Zia's perfume. Beer and burgers were the best part of being his dad. He would go back to his regular diet and exercise routine when he returned to New York, or he'd be too out of shape to work.

Zia's French-manicured nails kneaded his skin. "I'll see what I can do about your playing along after lunch."

"Maybe you should wait until you hear me out before you decide."

She pulled her hand away and clasped it with the other. "What's that supposed to mean?"

He winked. "It means I'm flattered. What man wouldn't be? But I'm also interested in purchasing a small piece of Rock Harbor. I like this area."

She licked her lips. "Real estate?"

"Right. I don't want a place with major upkeep. Probably a condo, but I don't want a hundred neighbors. I could stay on the Jersey shore and have that. Got anything for me?"

Lulu shuffled over. Zia huffed. He wasn't sure what that was about. But if he had to guess, he'd say Zia was snorting her superiority.

"What can I get you two?" Lulu flashed her pearly whites at Zia and waited. Score one for Lulu.

"A small salad. Oil and vinegar. Water with lemon."

Lulu turned back to Jake, and it was all he could do not to laugh out loud, much less smile. Her expression left no doubt she thought Zia made a wrong turn someplace.

"Burger and another beer for me." He tilted his bottle toward her.

"Coming up." She walked away.

Jake sipped his beer. Zia took a small bottle of hand sanitizer from her bag, rubbed some on her hands, and put the bottle back. She finally glanced at him and pulled a smile into place.

He set his beer back on the table. "So . . . got what I'm looking for?"

She cleared her throat. "What's your price range?"

"As close to five as possible. That seems fair for what I'm looking for based on prices I've seen in the paper and in your window. I'm willing to pay more if I find exactly what I envision. Unblocked water view."

"What else?"

"Needs to be spacious but not obviously so. I don't want the house that stands out on the block. So large rooms more than large house. Couple bedrooms. Up to date, either new or renovated. Unfurnished. Ample balcony or patio. High-quality amenities."

"What about a house with a maintenance agreement?"

"Sure, as long as it doesn't go into the rental pool and is taken care of when I'm not here."

"A few locations come to mind. Let me call my service and have them set up appointments for after lunch. Soon enough?"

He raised his beer in a toast. "Perfect."

Zia had wanted him to ride with her, but that would've been foolish on every level—riding with a stranger to an unknown destination, for starters. At his refusal the smile vanished from her face. The first property was a definite no—he didn't step foot out of his car. The location presented a security nightmare with an exposed electricity connection and a stucco wall that could conceal one intruder or an entire army.

Zia's expression indicated she thought of him less as a potential wonder boy and more as an irritating gnat. The next two houses had kick-ass views, but one needed major renovation and the other had a bad layout. He hadn't seen any he would drop half a million on.

He followed her back to town and into the ZGM lot.

She bounced out of her car with a huge smile on her face. "I know the perfect property for you."

"Why didn't you show it to me?" He put a little extra New York attitude in his voice.

She waved her hand back and forth. "The property isn't built out yet, but I can show you what it could look like."

"Interesting. Tell me more." This must be the empty condo space next to hers—the one he'd hoped to see. The one he couldn't let her think he knew about. Then again, maybe she was cunning enough to have scripted this out.

"It's in town. Convenient."

Yes. Finally. He locked his car.

"Not on the water, but with a solid water view. Brand new. Interior build-out to your specs. The complex is small, so cash or private financing only. Can't get around the mortgage laws."

"How small?"

"Four units total. Two are built. The other two will be within five years. Assessed taxable value last year on the occupied unit was high six figures, and the base price for this one before build-out is in your range."

"I think I'm interested." So far Zia's description fell in line with what Kelly told him last night.

"With what you save on waterfront maintenance, you can cover the cost of the build-out in no time."

"Good sales pitch. What about condo fees?"

The amount was reasonable. "Covers property and liability insurance—wind and flood included—plus a healthy reserve for maintenance, adjusted annually. You'd be responsible for your utilities and insurance on personal property. The only drawback is there isn't a pool or any type of recreation or fitness facility. There is, however, a wonderful gym two blocks away."

"Let's go look." He unlocked his car.

"That's what I like." She favored him with a huge smile. "We're here."

"Excuse me?"

"I own this block of buildings. The second floor is divided into two living spaces with a solid firewall between."

"What about the other two condos? Where will they be built?"

"I own the other side of the street, too—the downturn in the economy set everyone back. I have the plans, but I held off on construction."

"Can you get me current demographics on Rock Harbor?" Kelly was checking classified databases for more specific, sensitive information. If the numbers didn't work, the deal was dead. He beeped the lock again.

She nodded. "Absolutely. Come up and look at mine so you can envision the possibilities and the views. Then I'll show you the before version. The tax records are in my office. If you're interested after looking at the space, we'll discuss details."

As Zia talked, he could tell she'd forgotten about him as a man. He became a mark, a potential buyer. Her skills focused solely on his needs, and on how to pitch the properties she had available to those needs. Her language could have come straight from a marketing brochure.

They entered her space through a canopied area that resembled a sidewalk café. "Do you ever sit here?"

She gave him a puzzled look. "On the street? No. A small balcony up faces the street as well. In the back, a covered terrace runs the length of the building and overlooks the bay."

He wasn't surprised she didn't sit at street level, but he was surprised she hadn't erected a living wall—a row of large potted plants or vine-covered lattice. A security camera was attached above her door so she could view anyone who rang the bell. It should be adjustable to pan the entire area. Whether it was, he couldn't tell. It could just as easily be a fake. Without a closer inspection, they all looked alike.

"Are both units connected through the terrace?" That would be a deal killer, too.

"No. The brick firewall extends through the roof and through the terraces, making each unit totally private. A fire barrier also separates each floor. You can go to the city offices and read the inspection reports. It's not shoddy construction."

He'd stirred her pot. She knew her stuff and strutted it with confidence. All the same, he'd ask Kelly to send him copies of what she found on file. A few minutes' work from her would save him a day-long trip to city hall.

They walked into an amazing entry no larger than ten by twelve. Zia closed the door, and the street sounds vanished. No windows. Recessed can lights in the tall ceiling. Bold greens and blues on the walls. Two wooden benches painted bright coral. Large canvases filled with color hung above the benches. On the third wall, a wide stairway curved upward. On the fourth, three doors. He inclined his head in that direction. "Closets?"

"One closet. One opens into my private office at ZGM. The third leads to a double garage."

The woman was all about convenience. "Let's go up."

The stairs led to a large open space with white marble floors. On the street side was a dining area and kitchen. Black granite counters with blue, green, and gold glass tiles on the backsplash. On the island a wide, shallow fishbowl brimmed with blue and green sea glass. Several decorative jars and containers massed in a corner. He'd be surprised if she cooked.

On the bay side, the living area. Black leather furniture, soft gray walls. Accessories in coral, green, and blue reflected the colors in the entry and the colors of the bay and stopped short of looking cluttered.

"Nice."

"Thank you. My decorator is top-notch."

"The entire living area is spacious. How many bedrooms?"

"Two bedroom suites, each with its own bath. A powder room in the hall for visitors. An office. Nothing is cramped. I don't like tight places. Follow me."

She led the way down a wide hall. No one would feel the walls closing in. He peeked into the powder room, paced off a large office with built-in cabinetry and French doors, and praised the guest suite before coming to the master.

He stopped at the threshold to take it in. The master bath angled off to the side, and all he could see was a darker gray wall and the corner of a green rug. The bedroom colors were the same as those in the living area. Black silk drapes hung at the sides of the large back window, tied back with wide black bands. A smaller bowl of sea glass sat on her black dresser—its only adornment.

If he'd ever had any doubt, he now knew for a fact he would never want to get to know Zia on a more personal level. At heart she was precision and hard edges, stark and unyielding. Not his type.

Zia touched his arm, her nails trailing lightly for an inch or so. A cat testing her boundaries. "What do you think?" Her voice purred.

"It has the space I need. Plus a kick-ass view. I'd probably change the configuration—my needs are different. Let's look at the unfinished side before we talk."

He walked the empty space, and jotted some thoughts about the safe room. After a quick survey of the terrace, they went to Zia's office. The only architectural features he wouldn't be able to change were the windows already in place on the street side. He closed the folder she prepared for him. "Let me think about it. I want to talk to some people about a build-out, get some figures. Digest the information. I'll be in touch before I leave."

Zia smiled. "I understand. If your people have questions, ask them to call me. Anytime. I'd be pleased to have you for a neighbor, even part-time."

He returned her smile. "You have my card. Call if anyone comes around asking about the space. I don't want it stolen out from under my nose without an opportunity to make a fair offer."

They parted with a handshake.

After starting his car, he jotted a few more notes. Zia had shown off her space as he'd hoped. A few layout ideas flashed through his mind, and he drew two separate floor plans while putting together a mental list—architect, contractor, designer, color consultant, probably the same ones they had used for the Michigan cabin. Security was paramount.

He put the car in gear. He'd talked with Will Knox and Zia Grant-Markham. Next on the list was Dan Blair.

CHAPTER 16

Friday morning after breakfast, Taylor came back to her room with a tall cup of coffee. She had a lot to do, none of which involved working at Randy's. Thank God. She needed a break. She rummaged in her purse for Zia's card and punched in her number.

"Hi, Zia. This is Taylor Campbell."

"Taylor! I'm so glad you called. How are your hands? What can I do for you?"

Zia was perky for early morning. "Much better. Healing. I wanted to thank you again for your help at Randy's."

"I know what it's like to pick up the pieces after someone you love dies. You would've done the same."

"It's difficult." Taylor took a deep breath. "I'm also calling because I'd like to hire your painter. He did such a great job in the kitchen and bath that I want to talk to him about finishing the job. All I know is his name is Bodie. If you'll give me his name and number, I'll call him from Charleston."

"You can't be finished already?"

"In the house. Dan is a jewel. We finished yesterday afternoon, but we have most of the shop to sort through. At least the only thing left to move is trash out to the bin."

"He must have worked you like a race horse."

Taylor laughed. "He might say it was the other way around."

"Let me find the painter's number." Zia came back on the line almost as soon as she put her on hold.

Taylor wrote down his name and two phone numbers. "Thanks. I also need another favor."

"Name it."

"Dan's invited me to his opening tonight, so I thought I'd go. He's so excited."

"Like a mama-to-be. He can't wait to give birth and show off his babies."

Taylor frowned at the mental image Zia's words created. "The problem is I only brought work clothes with me. I need some advice on where to shop."

"Rock Harbor has a few shops. It'll be dressy casual."

The same wording Dan had used. What was dressy casual? The only events Taylor attended either didn't have a dress code or were Coast Guard functions where her uniform served as dress of the day. She'd need to depend on a sales clerk.

Zia continued, obviously excited to talk shopping. "Go to Azul first. They usually have a better selection. Lotus is good. And Off Ocean. All are in strip centers on the way to the bay bridge, within a few blocks of each other."

Taylor made notes. "Thanks. Just what I needed." An all-day shopping trip. *Ugh.*

"I have another call coming in I need to take." Zia's voice changed to business. "I'll see you tonight."

At Azul, Taylor found three dresses that fit, but one stood out. The lightweight white silk fell from a halter top to a few inches above her knees. Clear beads caught the tiniest ray of light and outlined hibiscus blooms dotting the skirt in a random pattern. She loved it.

Instead of earrings, she purchased a white silk hibiscus on a clip to wear in her hair. Strappy silver sandals and a white satin clutch with a beaded clip completed her purchase. The dress cost more than she would've liked, especially since she'd probably never wear it again, but it made her feel sexy. Maybe she would make an occasion to wear it. She hummed on the way to her car. A woman needed to splurge every now and then.

Taylor hadn't brought any make-up with her, either, so she spent the better part of an hour in the drugstore purchasing lighter and darker colors because she wasn't sure which matched the shades she usually wore. Resembling a clown or a ghost was not an option.

By early afternoon she returned to her room. She needed a manicure, so she hunted for the emery board she kept in her purse and shaped her nails with no pain, only soreness. The natural look would have to do—she hadn't remembered to buy polish.

The entire process was going to take her longer, especially applying her makeup. And if she had to remove it and start over, what usually took her fifteen minutes could drag out to an hour. *Patience, Taylor.*

She wasn't accustomed to having extra time and didn't know what to do. For her entire career, she'd used every spare minute to push ahead in some way—volunteer work, time with her crew or peers, studying. She focused her energy on achieving her next rank, on being the best she could be, on not letting down the Coast Guard. On not letting Mark's death be in vain.

Now here she was with nothing to do. It was too early to get ready for the opening, even if it took her an hour to put on her make-up. She'd forgotten to bring a book, so she clicked on the television.

After rounding the limited channels twice, she chose a Food Network show.

She awoke with a start. When she'd started watching, the chef was female. Now a male chef was signing off. Crap. How long had she slept? She never napped.

A quick glance at the time told her she'd been out almost an hour. The good news was she could start getting ready. Every step of the process took longer than usual. Finally she clipped the silk flower behind her left ear.

Taylor barely recognized the woman staring back at her in the mirror. *Damn.* How had sexy happened? Because she was wearing the dress. That's how.

Cars lined both sides of the street in front of Dan's gallery. Two blocks away, she edged her rental to the curb in front of a kite shop. Thankfully, she'd come to her senses and chosen flat sandals over the drop-dead-gorgeous heels she'd clutched to her chest in Azul.

She passed Mike's Golf Shop, and the alphabet code flashed in her mind. She'd forgotten about it. Too much happening and too many distractions. She would trust her subconscious to figure out any secret meaning and supply the answer unless she remembered to ask someone.

Lights hidden in the planters flooded the entrance to Bravo. Inside, a silver tray holding flutes of champagne sat on a table to the left of the door. Two stacks of glossy brochures stood next to the tray. Taylor chose a glass, picked up a brochure, and followed the flat gray panels guiding the flow of art lovers into the heart of the gallery.

She stopped. What the hell?

Images of Zia stared at her from every wall. She stepped to the side and checked the brochure. Yep—*Zia Grant Markham, a Perspective*, by August Janacek. She didn't know who amazed her most, the subject or the artist. No wonder she hadn't thought of him as a typical tow truck driver.

Dan approached, wearing a huge smile. "I'm so glad you came. If you hadn't, I would've dragged you up here Monday morning kicking and screaming."

She laughed. "I told you I'd be here. This is exciting. I didn't expect Rock Harbor to have such drama."

"A.J. has put us on the art world map. Many of these pieces sold sight unseen long before tonight. Most of the rest sold during the private opening this afternoon."

"Wow. We're talking the same A.J., right? Drives a tow truck? Likes to fish?"

Dan laughed, and his eyes sparkled. "He says those activities recharge his batteries. You missed the most important detail."

"He paints?"

Dan waved the word away. "Besides that."

She shrugged.

"Sleeps with me."

For a second she just stared at him until a small smile formed. "I had *no* idea." For sure. A gay A.J. hadn't crossed her mind.

"You should have. I told you I don't like my people frou-frou. Speaking of which, you look fantastic. Turn around, let me see all of you."

She turned.

"Perfect for you and perfect for tonight. Love your bare back. I won't be the only man who feels that way, though for entirely different reasons. You don't need my guidance in the style area of your life at all."

"We should have a long talk. You'd be surprised what I need help with."

"I'd love that, but not now. Enjoy yourself. Don't think about buying any of A.J.'s work. You can't afford them on a Coast Guard salary." Dan bit his lip. "I'm giving away a secret, but A.J. put a painting aside for you. We chose it together. It reminds both of us of you."

"But these are of Zia." How could a painting of Zia remind them of her?

"You'll see why later. It's not hung here."

What Taylor knew about art fit into one brain cell, but she followed the maze of panels, each with a separate Zia, until she reached the back wall. In the center of a two-foot band of white paint at the ceiling, black disconnected cursive letters spelled out Bravo. A painted Bravo flag—solid red with a v-shaped cutout opening to the right—flanked the name of the gallery on each side.

The Bravo flag signified dangerous cargo. Zia might be classed as dangerous cargo in some circles, but Dan's gallery had been here before this exhibition. She would ask him about the name on Monday if she hadn't figured it out.

Her attention turned back to the wall. A two-inch black bar separated the band of white from the rest of the wall, which was painted bright red. Several large black-and-white photos of Zia stretched across canvases of various shapes, from stars to dialogue clouds like those in comic strips.

In a nook, out of the main traffic flow, a tall, narrow canvas stood out. Half of Zia's body appeared, with her right hand at a top corner, her left foot at the opposite bottom one. Nude, she stood mostly in shadow on a stark white background. A discreet sold card, the same as others she'd noticed, filled a slot on the wall to the right of the piece.

The maze led her toward the front and a table filled with finger foods. Several people milled about. She hadn't seen Zia, but that didn't mean she wasn't here. After downing the last of her champagne, she set the glass on a tray with other empties.

The different appetizers made her mouth water, but she'd be better off stopping at the market for a salad when she left. She didn't quite trust her fingers and palm to carry her through such a ritual. She hadn't worn even one Band-Aid.

"May I help?"

The deep voice startled her—Mr. Brooklyn smiled down at her and turned her knees to mush.

"You looked as if you were trying to decipher a problem, and I thought I might be of assistance. Besides, I can never resist talking to a beautiful woman. How are your hands?"

The laughter and vitality that lit his green eyes defied the silver of his hair.

"My palm has been itching all day and now one of my fingers, too. I'm definitely on the mend, but I'm not sure I can manage my bag, a fork, and a plate at the same time. Those shrimp are calling my name."

"I'll be happy to hold a plate for you."

"Are you sure?"

He picked up a clear glass plate. "Load it up."

"I'd almost decided on fast food in my room. Thanks for saving me."

She grabbed a fork wrapped inside a black paper napkin and chose peeled boiled shrimp, cocktail sauce, Kalamata olives, two different cheeses, a few crackers.

"Let's move over here out of the way." He touched her elbow and the same sizzle she experienced at the barbecue market sped along her skin. She let him lead the way to the side of a tall table near the wall. He set her plate in front of her. "By the way, I'm Jake Solomon."

"Jake Solomon?" Taylor didn't bother hiding her surprise. The youngest member of the Compass Points! Right here.

He faced her with his eyebrows drawn together in a frown. "Is there a problem?"

"No." Taylor didn't know whether to smile, give him a hug, or what. "I know you."

"You *know* me?" The frown changed to puzzlement.

"I'm Taylor Campbell. Randy Rankin's niece." Unable to decipher his expression, she forked a shrimp into her mouth.

"Randy talked about me?"

She swallowed. "All the time. You, Kyle Easley, Ed Wharton, and Ham Bone. I feel like I know all of you."

"What did he talk about?"

"Your times in Vietnam. He loved all of you like brothers."

"All of us felt the same way. I can't believe he told you about us. Then again, you were like a daughter to him. I shouldn't be surprised."

"He didn't talk about you so much after I got older, but when I was a young girl, he wove the most romantic tales about your exploits on the rivers, in the beer hall, on the beach. And he had photos of all of you. I haven't seen them in more than twenty years, so I couldn't have told you what any of you looked like."

Jake nodded off and on as she spoke. "We shared a special bond."

"You came to visit him once before. I remember when he told me because it was right after his cat died. For a long time I thought that was why you visited."

"Old Solomon."

"A very wise cat. Randy told me he named him after you because you were a very wise man."

Jake shook his head. "Not so wise. I just know how to put on a good show."

Taylor smiled and popped an olive into her mouth. Will came through the door, spied her. His glance shifted to Jake, and his smile changed to a questioning look. Did Will know Jake?

Will came straight to her. "I'm glad you decided to come."

"I'm glad I did, too. Will, this is Jake Solomon. He was kind enough to help me with my plate. The shrimp are perfect. Jake, Will Knox. He owns Copano Boat Works."

They nodded at each other, like two bull elephants on Nat-Geo. Will spoke first. "If you want to explore, I can keep Taylor company."

"I took the tour. Go ahead. We'll be here."

Will scowled. "I'll be back."

What was his problem? He acted as if he were jealous, but that was crazy. Will hadn't shown an interest in her, nor she in him. Except for noticing his cute butt, which didn't count. And Jake, choosing to stay with her. Not sure what to make of that, Taylor shoved her questions in a corner and enjoyed the last olive. But her curiosity wouldn't turn loose.

After swallowing, she looked at Jake. "You know Will?"

"We met the other day. I think he's jealous."

"Isn't that how he's acting? But I don't live here—I arrived Sunday afternoon, and I'm going home next week. I met him on Monday." *And you, too.* She needed to get her act together and take it back out to sea.

Jake looked uncomfortable. "I heard about your uncle—I'm sorry. Is your family here?"

"No. My mother is usually off one place or another. Randy was really the only family I had. He left me his place. This is the first opportunity I've had to return since his death. Before Sunday, I hadn't been here since high school."

Applause erupted near the door, and she and Jake both turned. Zia made her entrance. She wore an electric-blue satin cocktail dress with a plunging neckline and pencil skirt, diamond drop earrings, and matching satin sandals with the highest heels Taylor had ever seen.

Maybe one day she'd have nerve enough to wear such a dress. And shoes. Both would certainly stand out in her closet full of uniforms. She turned back to fork another shrimp. Jake's attention was focused solely on her. "What?"

"I like the flower in your hair. Enchanting."

Her stomach rode a rollercoaster. Zia was polished to a high gloss, probably closer to Jake's age, and the subject of all the paintings on display. Yet Jake's attention remained on her. How old he was he, anyway? The youngest of Solomon's Compass. If he'd been seventeen then, he'd be close to sixty. Hell, she was close to forty. What was twenty years?

She didn't want her voice to come out shaky, so she smiled to boost her confidence. "Thanks. I couldn't resist when I went shopping today. All I brought with me were work clothes. Not even make-up. I needed everything."

"You would've been the loveliest woman here if you'd come without make-up wearing cut-offs and a Seven Dwarfs tee."

"You're a silver-tongued devil, I think." She might not be completely socially attuned, but even she could hang her laundry on that line.

His eyes sparkled. "Guilty—at least of the devil part. But not now. I've seen you like that, so I know. You shine from within, and the glow surrounds you."

"I don't imagine Mrs. Solomon appreciates you paying such compliments to other women."

The magnetism between them ratcheted up to a new high. Taylor couldn't turn away.

"The only Mrs. Solomon I know is my mother. If and when there's another in my life, she won't ever need to worry about me looking for those attributes in other women."

Intense energy rolled off him in waves. If she hadn't been standing against the wall, she might have fallen over. Or grabbed onto him to stay upright. He hadn't said so, but his words held the strength of a promise. A vow.

Her hands shook and she was no longer interested in the few shrimp remaining on the plate. His focus remained solely on her, and it was her turn to respond.

She placed her fork on the plate, and it barely clattered. "She will be a fortunate woman."

"No." He set the plate on the table. "I will be the luckiest man in the universe."

CHAPTER 17

J ake hadn't meant to say any of those words to Taylor, especially after learning she knew him by name. Correction—knew his dad by name. But passion had erupted, and his words flowed of their own accord. He had not been able to stay in character as his dad and say he was married. As long as the stray bit of truth didn't impair or corrupt the mission, he could deal with other consequences.

"Tell me about yourself, Taylor Campbell. Where's home?" He wanted to hear her story in her own words.

"Right now Charleston, but I'm from Dallas. Do you still live in New York?"

"I do." A server passed. He snagged two glasses of champagne from the tray and handed one to Taylor. "To an exciting evening."

"With a new friend." She clinked her glass against his.

When Taylor said she knew him, he had to remind himself to breathe. He, his dad, and Kelly had discussed the possibility that Taylor would recognize his name. His dad dismissed it early on. She and Rankin often went years without seeing each other, and any stories he told her would have been general and in passing. So much for his dad's theory on that one.

Jake's SEAL training kicked in, and he formulated an instant plan. A plan he hoped didn't lead to disaster.

No woman had ever attracted him the way Taylor did. Most were out to impress him, and their efforts failed. He just had to take it slow and stay alert. After shadowing her morning shopping expedition, he'd scoured the newspaper and Internet to learn what was going on tonight. The opening at Bravo was the only event he found that would have necessitated her shopping trip. And it presented the perfect opportunity for him to meet Dan Blair.

He showed up early to talk to Blair, but he wasn't the only premature arrival. Blair was on top of the opening and whirled from place to place and guest to guest welcoming each new arrival. Jake's minute of chitchat combined with being able to observe made for a good first meeting. He'd been in the gallery for about a half hour when Taylor arrived, and he hadn't realized he'd been coiled like a cobra until she walked through the door and a huge smile split his face. Without Kelly here, trusting Taylor to electronic surveillance was the best he could do much of the time. He didn't like it, but he had to face reality.

Another round of applause broke out, interrupting his thoughts.

"There's A.J." Taylor nodded toward the door.

The crowd thinned to reveal a tall, slim man dressed all in black with slicked-back dark hair streaked with strands of gray. Long hands, slender fingers. High cheekbones and a patrician nose. Every inch screamed artist.

"You'd never think he drives a tow truck."

He kept his face composed. "You're kidding."

"A tree fell on my rental, and he towed it. Smart guy. And Dan's partner."

"He has part ownership here?"

"No. Or, rather, I don't know. I meant partner as in significant other."

"Ah. Okay." He tipped his glass, allowing a sip of cool bubbly to slide down his throat. He would pass the information along to Kelly.

Blair joined A.J. and Zia. "Everybody . . . I'm Daniel Blair, owner of Bravo."

A smattering of applause and one loud *Yeah!*

Dan dipped his head. "Our stars of the evening. Zia Grant Markham."

More applause.

"A.J.—August Janacek—the wonderful artist who created these beautiful paintings and photographs." More applause. After it died down, Dan spread his arms. "Enjoy yourselves. Mix and mingle. If you fall in love with one of A.J.'s brilliant creations, come talk to me. Now, have fun."

A couple Jake's parents' age latched onto Dan as soon as he moved away from his two stars. Taylor waved at A.J., and he strode toward them.

"Dan told me about your hands. How are they?"

"I'm fine. Thanks for asking. I had no idea you had such talent."

"Beats sitting behind a desk." A.J. shrugged. "I would've come out to help, but Dan's kept me too busy. I meet my shadow going and coming most days."

Jake held out his hand. "Jake Solomon. What made you choose to paint Zia?"

A.J. chuckled. "The question I usually get is 'How did you get Zia to pose for you?'"

"I enjoy being different."

"Excellent. So do I. Zia has an interesting face. On the surface she's symmetrical, and her features are balanced and pleasing to the eye. So I skew her perfection. She sometimes makes off-the-wall comments that make it easier. Here, I'll show you."

He led them to a painting of Zia's face. "One day she came to pose and two kids playing on the sidewalk started fighting, bickering really. Young kids, maybe three or four. She said she believed it took a village to raise a child, and it made her want to set her hair on fire because she had no authority to discipline them. This is the result."

Jake studied the portrait for a few seconds. He enjoyed contemporary art, and in his view A.J. had considerable talent. "Flames for hair and fire engine eyes all wrapped in a firefighter's turnout coat. Good work."

"Thanks. I better go mingle—keep Dan happy."

Jake followed A.J.'s progress over to Dan and the older couple before turning back to Taylor. "You're awfully quiet. Don't you appreciate his work?"

"I think I'm too practical. I liked one of the photographs a lot, but abstract art has always been beyond my comprehension."

He could teach her, if she'd let him. "I learned. You can, too."

"I'd rather learn how to operate the fire engines."

He laughed at her unexpected words. "Learning about art is stimulating, but in truth, I think fire engines would be more fun."

"What would be more fun?" Zia came up in a cloud of spicy perfume with Will Knox in tow.

"Driving a fire truck."

Zia's heavily made-up eyes glazed over. She touched his arm. "There's a photograph I want to show you."

Jake stepped back and took Taylor's elbow. "Lead the way."

Zia's eyes turned hard, telling him she didn't condone such a rebuff. She spun around, hips swaying, and moved to lead them through the crowd, one hand straying to Knox's neck, her fingers playing in his hair.

In the back, she stopped by the section of photographs. He'd viewed them earlier, but took them in again, wondering which one had caught Taylor's eye.

Zia walked to one and turned around, all smiles. "This is the one I wanted you to see."

In the starburst-shaped photograph, Zia sat on a white shag rug, nude, legs pulled up to her chin, hands clasped around her ankles. Her chin rested on her knees, and she stared at the camera, the tip of her tongue barely visible through parted lips.

He could say with absolute certainty it was not the photograph Taylor had in mind.

Bubbles of champagne tickled Taylor's nose. Zia was a huge player. She was using poor Will to make Jake jealous, but Will didn't seem to mind. He laced his fingers with Zia's, oblivious to her unwavering attention to Jake. Or maybe excited by it.

Jake took a firmer hold on Taylor's elbow. "It's a winner, Zia. How long did it take for A.J. to complete all this?"

"We started last fall and finished around Easter. I think Dan got jealous of the time we spent together."

Taylor slugged the last of her champagne—the flutes had been only half full. Zia reminded her of her mother. One man after another. Never satisfied. The older her mother got, the quicker she went through men. Taylor never wanted to be that way.

Jake smiled. "I've enjoyed the exhibition. A talented artist and a beautiful model. Who could ask for more?"

If Zia had been a cat, she would have stretched, purred, and licked her damn butt to point the way. Taylor had witnessed the same behavior from Dear Mom.

The room floated a bit from the bubbles in Taylor's head. She touched Jake's arm. "I enjoyed talking to you, but I need to go. Tomorrow will be busy." *And I need fresh air. Now.*

"I'll walk you out."

On the way to the door, she smiled and nodded to other guests, but outside she took a couple of deep breaths. Fresh air. That's what she needed. It was good she had a couple of blocks to walk so her head could clear.

Jake took her arm. "Zia Grant Markham is something else."

"She is that." The fresh air and change in atmosphere were clearing the fog.

He lifted her chin. "I could see your reaction to her."

She reacted? All she did was gulp her champagne. A tiny reaction.

"No worries, Taylor. She'll soon be out of our lives."

Our lives. Our lives? Those words cleared her head faster than the fresh air. "I didn't realize we had an *our lives*." Her voice came out a little prickly.

He smiled. "Your life, my life. I like you, but we need time to get to know one another."

Okay, better.

His crooked grin morphed into a pained expression.

She stopped. "What? Your face doesn't quite match your words."

He kicked at the seam in the sidewalk. "I'm an old guy. You know? Friends with your uncle. You're young and lovely." His voice turned rough, and he cleared his throat.

She touched his cheek. Her breath caught at the electric charge that flowed through her. "You're not *that* old—you were the youngest Compass Point. And I'm not that young. I want to know you better, too."

His face lit up with a real smile. "All right. Which way to your car? I'll make sure you get there safe and sound."

She laughed. With an increase in weekend visitors, the sidewalks were more crowded than she'd seen them since her arrival. She took a step toward her car. "This way. And thank you for looking after my safety."

He dropped his arm across her shoulders. "My pleasure. I mean that."

They reached her car before she was ready to part from him. She opened the door. "Thanks for walking with me."

"Any time."

Her entire body tingled, and not from the salt-filled breeze.

He touched the flower behind her ear, and his fingers lingered. "I really do like this."

The tingles sped up. She could power Rock Harbor with the sexual energy speeding around her body. "It's just a piece of silk."

"Doesn't matter." He kissed her forehead.

Oh. She caught her breath. "But it won't ever wilt."

He smiled before kissing the tip of her nose. His hand moved from the flower and cupped the back of her head.

He moved closer, and his lips met hers. Taylor didn't care if Jake Solomon was a hundred and sixty.

Heat roared through her. She wrapped her arms around his waist and returned his kiss. His hands moved on her bare back and her knees turned to mush. She craved his touch, his skin against hers. If they hadn't been standing in the street, she would've ripped off his shirt.

She moved her hands up his muscled back to pull him closer. He made a quiet growling sound and deepened his kiss. The heat spreading through her body raged into an inferno, and she wanted the flames to keep burning.

His soap and water scent filled her senses, and her mind could no longer form a thought. All she wanted was touch. Pleasure. Maybe she moaned. She wasn't sure. But the sound brought her back to reality. In the street.

Jake must have had the same thought because he pulled away. With his breath coming as hard as hers, his hands cupped her face. "Meet me for lunch tomorrow?"

She nodded. "Where?"

"Lulu's. You know where it is?"

"I do. Noon?"

"Perfect." He kissed her again.

CHAPTER 18

Taylor lay in her bed staring at the ceiling. Outside, the wind had picked up, whistling at the window. Rain would arrive during the night.

The taste of Jake still lingered on her tongue. His scent on her skin. She sighed. She was thirty-eight years old, and no man had ever made her tingle all the way to her toes. Not even Mark.

She'd met Mark when they were both eighteen. Classmates, then friends, and finally lovers. Their emotions took root, grew, and eventually blossomed into a fragrant flower during their four years at the Coast Guard Academy.

Not four days in Rock Harbor, Texas.

Had it been only four days? She counted them out on her fingers, like a kindergartener, before pulling the covers over her head to hide from the truth.

Rain pattering against the window woke her just after dawn. Taylor peeked out on low gray clouds scuttling in from the water. Soft thunder rumbled from a distance. The weather blowing in would probably blow out before noon, the same way it had on Monday. She stretched and smiled, remembering last night.

She touched her fingers—tender, and now they all itched. The cut on her palm really itched. She could hoist a shovel. Whoever was attempting to scare her off didn't know her very well. She'd do everything to protect herself, but she wouldn't run.

She dressed and grabbed her purse. Right now she needed caffeine. Serious caffeine. And a donut. Chocolate.

By the time she reached Randy's with a tall to-go cup of black coffee, the rain had stopped and only a few clouds remained. Sun diamonds sparkled on the green water of the bay.

She had planned to drive to Padre Island and walk along the beach, but she was filled with energy. Pulling out trash for a few hours today would give her and Dan a huge boost on Monday. Dan said the shop would go quicker than the house. They would move plenty of items to the trash bin, but they didn't have to move the keepers out of the shop. She'd been surprised to learn they really had done the hardest work first.

Still, the sight of the mess in the salvage shop made her cringe. Jake had occupied most of her thoughts since waking, but now she pushed him away. Before Monday morning when Dan returned, she wanted to ferret out the obvious trash. With so much work ahead, she couldn't keep dreaming of last night's kiss.

Taylor went to the house, put on gloves, inserted the padding, and grabbed the trash bags. In the shop, she started in the back where Dan left off and worked outward. Newspapers and ripped magazines. Tangled fishing line. Crushed paper towels. Broken plastic items—cups, glasses, plates, even toys. The dreck and debris were easy to identify and needed to go.

She worked out her frustrations across one row of tables and the spaces underneath. At the last table, the cover from a Merc 150 outboard lay on its side stuffed with a stack of *People* magazines. The rest of the outboard lay in pieces on top of the table surrounded by an empty gas can and two wiring harnesses. Over it all was a web of fishing line tangled with several tools and propellers. Two shafts lay on the floor beneath the table along with a pile of boat bumpers.

Her phone rang. It was Glen Upchurch. "Checking to see how your fingers are doing."

"Healing. Itching like mad. Next week, they'll be fine." *And I'll be able to unearth Randy's treasure.*

"Any more calls?"

"No, but I've been thinking. I'm pretty sure the caller used a voice changer."

"Possible."

"Probable. The words were too perfect. None of them tagged onto the previous or next word. Each was distinct and separate."

"I'll add your observations to my notes."

They said goodbye, but before Taylor could return the phone to her pocket, it rang again. Glen must have forgotten a question he meant to ask. "Yes?"

"You didn't take my hint. Leave. Or you'll end up like your uncle."

"You don't scare me, you bastard. The police know you're calling. They'll find you."

A wheezy laugh followed. Then the wavering end tone.

Taylor called Glen.

"Did you remember something?"

She told him about the call. "The voice was identical—the same disconnected words. The same laugh. If they want me gone, they must want something in the house." Or in the buried box. She opened and closed the fingers of her right hand to stretch the skin on her palm.

"You sure you've seen nothing of interest?"

"Positive."

"Dan?"

"He has pieces picked out, but nothing vital or priceless, I assure you. You're welcome to come look. We've finished the house. The items Dan wants are together at the front of the shop."

"Tomorrow. I have baseball and softball games to attend today. In the meantime, I'm going to request Rankin's be put on drive-by rotation. You put my cell on speed dial."

"Okay."

"I'm going to pull the records for the drowning investigation and reread them, along with the autopsy report. The M.E. ruled the death accidental, but I don't recall any details. In light of the threats against you and Will, I need to revisit those findings. I'm dealing with the hotel break-ins, too, but I'll get it done."

"You don't think the break-ins are connected, do you?" She hadn't put Randy's possible murder and the hotel break-ins together until Glen mentioned both cases back to back.

"The thought crossed my mind, but so far I haven't seen any indication."

They hung up for the second time, and Taylor stared at the wall. She hadn't dwelled on the call to Will. When the first one had come to her, a tiny tickle at the back of her mind raised the possibility that Randy might have been murdered. She had ignored it. This call moved that tickle toward the front, flipping the odds. One thing Taylor knew for sure—the caller was desperate to acquire at least one of Randy's former possessions.

If the break-ins were connected, the burglar wouldn't have found what he was looking for in her room. Whether it was the belt, or the photographs, or something else entirely, Taylor knew without a doubt that whatever it was, she would find it buried in Will Knox's backyard.

She went back to clearing tables, her mind on the call and on Randy. Her energy had dropped, and it took her longer than it should have to remove the fishing line around the outboard motor parts. At the next table, more line stretched from one end to the other, around, under and over items, encircling a coffeemaker. A bored kid must've been in here with his dad. She found the scissors Dan had brought out from the house and went to work.

Thirty minutes later, she stepped back and surveyed her progress. She'd cleared a fourth of the table. She pushed on. An hour later, she neared the far end. She understood how moving things on the table could've caused the line to tangle. The longer she worked, the more she doubted her theory of a bored child. Every inch of the shop was trashed, but this table was the worst. What if Randy had sabotaged it in some way? She started looking for booby traps.

A folded tarp—or maybe it was a small sail—lay atop the line. She moved it and found two dozen mugs in blue and white in the bottom of an old cardboard box. The mugs were set up like a checkerboard, alternating blue and white. In a white one lay an old watch.

She picked it up, her energy level zooming. "Wow!"

As beautiful as the curved art deco watch on the front was, her focus returned to the two blue stones tethered at the ends of the rectangular timepiece with thin copper wire. She rubbed them against her cheek and inhaled the familiar scent of the leather band. Finally she found an item she wanted. The last time she saw the lapis lazuli stone, it had been in one piece instead of two and set in the center of Randy's belt buckle. The compass rose.

Taylor brought the band to her nose and inhaled again. Her nose hadn't lied. She would never forget the scent of the cream Randy used on the belt. Memories flooded back. Driving his boat. Their conspiracies against her mother. Playing dominoes. She sighed. She still had trouble believing Randy was gone.

After pressing the band against her cheek, she held it out for inspection. The leather was the right thickness, but held no embossed letters. If it was his Solomon's Compass belt, why had he cut it up? She didn't know. But maybe she could find out if she could figure out the right questions to ask those who knew him.

She set the time on the watch and wound it, but the second hand didn't move. Oh, well. She could have it repaired. The bulky one-piece band dangled from her wrist, so she shoved it to her elbow to keep it snug.

By the time she finished the table, she'd filled six trash bags, three on the first row and three at the last table alone. Dan might throw away more, but his discards would be items he recognized as having no value. She took the bags to the trash bin and checked the time on her phone. It was almost noon—time to head to Lulu's. And Jake.

She locked up and started to her car. Will was crossing the road and waved.

He waited by her car door. "What are you doing tomorrow afternoon?"

"No plans. Maybe work here."

"I'm taking the *Red Witch* out for trials. Want to come along?"

"Are you kidding? Sure! Not many people can say they've participated in sea trials on a catamaran. You finished the repair already?" Taylor would welcome a day on the water and away from Randy's mess.

He laughed. "Turned out to be less of job than I thought. I still have to clean, prep, and paint both hulls so they match. I thought you might like to get out on the bay. Be here around noon and we'll head out."

Will turned back toward the boatyard, and Taylor backed down the driveway. At the corner she stopped and removed the watch. Might not be a good idea to show the world what she'd found.

At Lulu's, a Bud sign blinked in a small window, and several newer cars and pickups filled the parking lot. Taylor wondered which was Jake's. Inside the door, she took several seconds while removing her sunglasses to scan the room for him.

Two large windows in the rear overlooked a shady patio. The outside tables were empty—no one wanted to eat outside when the temperature hovered near a hundred degrees. A silent baseball game took place on the television and music from *Aida* played in the background.

Not finding Jake, Taylor clambered atop a stool to wait for the large woman working at the other end. Carved names and messages covered the old mahogany bar. None of the names were familiar to her, and she wondered if Randy had etched his mark onto the bar.

"Whatcha want, honey?"

Taylor met the woman's solid gray stare. "Are you Lulu?"

She nodded. "All my life."

"Hey, Lulu," a man called from the far end, "we need another round over here."

"Menu's up on the blackboard, hon. Be right back to take your order." She grabbed a fresh pot of coffee as she went.

Taylor was busy trying to decipher some of the words on the bar when someone sat on the stool to her right. Without looking, she sensed Jake's presence. Warmth spread through her.

"Fancy meeting you here."

She smiled at the Brooklyn accent. "Small town. Have you seen these messages?"

"You presume I've been in here that much?"

She cocked her head at him. "Well?"

He smiled. "Guilty as charged."

Lulu returned. "Okay, hon."

"I understand your burgers are the best in town. I'll have a cheeseburger and a Shiner Bock."

Lulu looked at Jake. "You want your regular?"

He nodded and winked at her. "You know I'm in love with you."

Lulu turned away without a word.

Taylor punched his arm. "Boy, she's got your number."

"Everybody's got my number. How are your hands doing today?"

"Healing." She held them out. "My palm itches like crazy and the soreness has gone. The fingers all itch and are pretty sensitive."

"Tell me again how it happened."

"I didn't tell you the first time. I was cleaning my uncle's house, and a couple of razor blades got in the way."

"They make holders for them to keep your fingers safe."

He was fishing, but she wasn't sharing.

Lulu arrived with their beers. "Won't be long—burgers are on the grill. You need to watch out for him, hon. God blessed him with a smooth gift of gab, and the devil made him a rogue. Twenty years younger, and I'd make a play for him myself."

Jake leaned over the bar and kissed her. "I can die happy having met my match."

"Hey, Lulu," came from the far end. She took off with the grace of a herd of gazelle.

Taylor sipped her beer. "I like her. Randy did, too, I imagine. Sometime when there aren't so many cars in the lot, I'll stop and talk to her about him."

"She'll like meeting you."

"Were you on the Point boat with him? I don't remember the boats each of you rode."

"I was on a different one—the *Point Whitebanks*. Same division."

"Were you keeping in touch all these years?" A new idea winked to life, and she turned it this way and that.

Jake held his hand above the bar, palm down, raising one side then the other. "Phone calls every now and then. You knew I came here once, and he dragged himself out of Texas once to visit me."

"About fifteen years ago?"

"Seventeen."

Exactly. "He pinned on my shoulder boards when I graduated from the Academy."

"I knew a woman had to be involved."

They both laughed.

Lulu roared through the swinging doors. "Burgers!"

Jake made a show of rubbing his hands and licking his lips in anticipation.

She slid the plates in front of them. "Y'all enjoy."

The burgers were huge and came with giant homemade onion rings. Jake dug right in. She cut hers in half. The aroma made her mouth water, and she savored the first bite.

"Now I know why the parking lot's full. This is wonderful."

Jake uttered an agreeable but unintelligible sound and raised the thumb of his left hand.

Taylor was ravenous, and Jake ate as if he'd been stranded for days on a desert island with nothing but coconuts. They didn't talk, and the silence allowed her time to form her thoughts into questions for Jake. When she finally pushed her plate away, all the rings and three-quarters of the burger were gone. Jake's was empty except for ketchup smudges. He downed the last of his beer.

She took another drink of hers. "What brought you to Rock Harbor?"

"My company is looking for a few corporate condos in separate locations around the country. I remembered my visit here, did some checking to see how Rock Harbor had grown into the twenty-first century, and here I am."

"Great place for fishing and getting away from the hustle and bustle."

"Exactly."

"Have you found the perfect place?"

"Maybe. I sent the details back to New York. I'm waiting to hear from different people, get some firm numbers, things like that. I'd like to wrap it up before I leave next weekend."

"That's how you know Zia."

"She showed me around town."

I'll just bet. Taylor would have bought into his story if he hadn't started picking at the label on his beer bottle as they talked. Everything he told her was probably true simply because in this small a town she could check it out. But it probably wasn't the full story.

She finished her beer and was about to ask Jake about the last time he talked to Randy when he interrupted her thoughts.

"Look at the back of my belt."

"What?"

He held out his hand. "Hop down and look at the back of my belt."

She swung off her stool, knowing what she would see. But why had Jake brought his Solomon's Compass belt along on a business trip? This was part of what he hadn't told her about his visit to Rock Harbor.

His yellow golf shirt was tucked neatly into his jeans. She had to move closer to read the almost smooth letters embossed across the old black leather. Jake's scent filled her head, as the scent of Randy's belt had. But the memories were totally different. She allowed them to linger for a moment.

"Solomon's Compass. Like Randy's."

He turned and faced her. A blue stone, matching the ones on her watchband only larger, adorned the belt buckle framed by his hands.

"The stone on Randy's belt was in the center for the compass rose. Yours is on the bottom. Solomon. *S* for south."

"Yes. I didn't know if you knew about his belt or not."

"Randy loved his belt. He always showed it to me, let me hold it. Because it was so special to him, I liked it, too. He took good care of it and only wore it on special occasions."

"I think all of us felt that way."

So lunch with her was a special occasion for Jake, too. "I want to show you what I found this morning, but I don't want to show you here. Will you follow me to Randy's?"

Jake handed her his card. "Call my cell after you get there, and I'll leave here and meet you then. We're less likely to raise eyebrows if we leave separately."

CHAPTER 19

Taylor sped back to Randy's and into the kitchen.

She removed the watch from her pocket and studied the band more closely. After seeing Jake's belt, she was more convinced than ever the band came from Randy's belt. The underside of the band was also black, but a closer inspection showed the color was different, as if someone had stained the leather with shoe polish or a black marker.

No words or markings spoiled the surface. Her rush of adrenaline faded, and she frowned. As much as Randy loved his belt, she couldn't believe he didn't leave some sort of identifier to connect this small piece of leather to it.

She laid the watch flat and examined the underside of the band with the mini-light on her key ring, but its beam didn't make a difference. She saw nothing on the ends connected to the timepiece. The underside appeared as smooth as the outside. She closed her eyes and ran her fingers across the leather. The smooth, cool finish on the outer band didn't carry over to the reverse. The under surface was rough and filled with tiny bumps and depressions.

She carried it to Randy's bedroom window. Bright sunlight streamed through, and she turned the band every which way. "Why can't I figure this out?"

After a minute or so of staring at the watch and band, turning them aimlessly in her hands and letting her mind wander, she placed the band on the sill and knelt to peer across it. The indentations her fingers had identified finally came into view, but they spread across the leather without a discernible pattern. Finding this much was a start. She scooped up the watch, returned to the kitchen, and laid it on the counter.

For the past week, she'd stopped every morning to buy a cup of coffee. The clerk stuck two bags of sugar, one bag of artificial sweetener, and one container of liquid non-dairy creamer in the bag every time. She'd given up telling them she didn't need the packets, and instead dumped them in the drawer next to the kitchen sink once she arrived at Randy's. Now she plucked the sugar packets out and tossed them on the counter.

She sprinkled the contents of three bags over the inside of the watchband. Then she tore off a length of gauze and used the ends like a feather to carefully brush away the excess sugar.

The indentations were so faint they appeared to have been scratched in with a needle or a small nail. The sugar didn't fill all of them, but it filled enough for her to read the words.

Solomon's Compass.

Sweet.

Three minutes later, Jake walked through Taylor's door.

A tingle spread outward from her belly. She licked her lips and hoped she didn't appear as nervous over seeing him alone in Randy's house as the tingle in her belly and her shaky legs said she was.

"Got here as quick as I could. Didn't want that smile to fade from Happy's face." He inclined his head at her tee.

Taylor shook her head. "Any quicker and they'd call it time travel. Come on in."

Jake ran his palm over the smooth top of the kitchen table. "You did a good job cleaning. Randy would smile."

"I never thought I'd be here cleaning his house." *Or that someone might have killed him.* Her voice cracked, and with no warning, tears stung her eyes. She tried to blink them away.

Jake gathered her close. "We're always shocked when life plays wicked jokes."

She sniffed. "Thanks. I'm not usually quite so wimpy, but Randy was about ninety percent of my entire family."

"You were a hundred and ten percent of his, so you made a good match." He tilted her chin and gave her a searching look. "Better?"

The steady beat of his heart and solid strength of his arms kept her from wailing like a baby. She nodded and took a few steps away.

"He took great pride in you and your accomplishments, Taylor."

"He was the reason I joined the Coast Guard. I was proud of him, too."

"He knew you loved him."

She sniffed again. "Come look." She led Jake to the counter.

"What have we here?"

"I think it's part of Randy's belt."

Jake bent over the watch. "Solomon's Compass. What is this? Sugar?"

"The belt was Randy's baby. I looked through everything in the house. The belt wasn't here. Neither were the photos he had of the Compass Points. If you're finished looking at the back, shake that sugar out over the sink and turn the watch over."

Jake cupped the band in one large hand.

"I believed he would mark the watch in some way if it was part of his belt. I was right. The words are barely there. I can't imagine what he used to make them."

"Probably a pocket knife."

"Wouldn't the cuts be deeper?"

"Not necessarily. Consider how you score meat to cook. You can barely make an indention or slice completely through. Same with leather." He rubbed his thumb over the edge of the band. "The leather is the same thickness as my belt. In my view, the carving wasn't meant to be deep."

"Why would he go to the trouble of carving it halfway?"

"To keep it safe for the only the person who knew what to look for and understood the meaning. For you." His eyes searched hers, but she couldn't read the question she saw in them. "No one else would even suspect the words were there. Even if someone discovered them, they wouldn't make sense."

"I can't imagine what possessed him to cut up the belt he loved more than anything except for you and the other Compass Points."

"He loved you more than any of us. And more than the belt."

Her emotions threatened to erupt again, and she took a couple of deep breaths, counting to work through her grief and focus her mind elsewhere.

Jake was rubbing his thumb over the lapis stones. "Randy's stone was the largest. Each of these pieces is almost as large as the stone in my belt. He didn't send you a letter? Leave a message for you with his lawyer?"

The buried box. A clue about the watch must be inside. She couldn't tell Jake about the box. Randy said to tell no one. She raised her chin. "I didn't find the watch with Randy's things. Not his personal belongings, I mean, in the house."

"Where did you find it?"

"Out in the shop."

"Show me."

They started across the yard, and Jake stopped at the bin. "Did all this trash come out of the house?"

"Most. Some came from the shop. We haven't finished going through it yet."

"Who's we?"

"Dan Blair. From the gallery. He also owns an antique shop in the same area. Echoes."

"Bravo. Echo."

She snapped around to face him. "You get it, too."

He raised his eyebrows.

"Also Mike's Golf and Juliet's Tango."

"Bravo, Echo, Golf, Juliet, Mike, and Tango." He counted them off on his fingers.

"The letters don't spell anything. And the flag meanings don't make any sense if they're combined. I presume the letters and flags have a meaning, but Dan and I have been so busy I keep forgetting to ask him about it."

"Dan has been helping you go through everything?"

"Yes. He was here when I sliced my fingers and took me to the emergency clinic."

Jake frowned.

"What?"

"Awfully convenient, don't you think?"

Taylor bristled. "Convenient? For me. Dan's a total sweetheart. He wouldn't harm anyone for any reason."

Jake stopped her. "Taylor. Look at me."

She turned her head. Jake's green eyes held tenderness and concern. "I'm not assessing blame."

"No?"

"No." He caressed her cheek. "I'm exploring avenues. Sorting through possibilities. However you cut your hands, it wasn't an accident, was it?"

Damn him.

"Taylor?"

She sucked in a big breath. "No. But the police are looking into it."

Jake nodded. "Okay, then. Forgive me?"

His attention focused solely on her. No one had ever looked at her the way Jake did. She smiled. "Of course."

"Good. Let's go see where you found the watch."

Taylor took a step and tripped over a rock, thinking more about Jake's eyes than where her feet landed.

Jake caught her elbow. "Okay?"

"Fine. Thanks for keeping me off my face." His touch sent heat rushing up her spine, for all the good it would do. Sexy women didn't go around tripping on rocks.

Sexy? Where had that come from? For starters, she wasn't sexy. Mark had always made her feel sexy, but that was because they'd been in love. Yesterday's dress didn't count.

She pushed sexy aside, and they continued to the shop. Jake held the door open while she flicked on the light.

"Jesus H." He planted his hands on his hips while he surveyed the mayhem.

"Ha. Looks good now. Over here are the items Dan wants. Everything in the back right quarter came out of the house— what didn't go straight to the trash bin. We haven't gone through the rest of what's in here."

"You said you found the watch here? In this mess?"

"This morning I came out to remove more trash. I started at the back on the first full row of tables."

Jake rubbed his neck. "Randy was a squared-away sailor. Neat, even in the jungle. The one time I came here to visit, he kept his house as clean as an old spinster's. What the hell went wrong?"

She shook her head, unable to fathom her uncle hoarding a building full of junk. "I wish I knew the answer. I remember the neat-freak Randy, too. His shop had more actual marine gear. A lot of parts. Maybe he detoured into the junk business and couldn't find his way back."

Jake scooped a handful of tiny shells from a bowl and let them trickle back through his fingers. "Show me where you found the watch."

She led him to the table from hell. "Here. This is the last one I cleared. You have to visualize the table. See how the others are toward the front? Old magazines, papers, and fishing line everywhere?"

He nodded.

"Compared to how this one looked, those are tidy. I'm wondering if he made this table chaotic on purpose."

"Why?" The word was clipped, more an order than a question.

The expression in his eyes changed. Her words had brought an idea into focus for him, and he jumped all over it.

"Two reasons. One, if someone came in here hunting, to the untrained eye everything is rubbish. Nothing else. Two, if someone knew the watchband was here, they might have gone straight to that table because it looked the worst. Pages torn from magazines and crumbled into balls. Paper towels, newspapers—you name it. Fishing line"—she traced a large circle with her arm—"wound around items, and in one place even wound around the table."

"Like tying up a package with a bow. Any pattern?"

She shook her head. "Not that I could tell."

Jake nodded.

"I started looking for booby traps after a while. The band lay in the bottom of a mug. I didn't know what it was until I picked it up." She pointed to the checkerboard grouping.

"Which mug?"

She touched the rim of the white mug in the middle of the box.

"In the center—like the lapis stone on his buckle."

"I can't figure out why he cut up his belt."

"Let's go inside. We need to get comfortable. I'm going to tell you a long story."

When she turned from locking the door, Will strode toward them. He nodded in Jake's direction but stopped in front of her. "I just got another phone call."

CHAPTER 20

Taylor shoved her hands into the pockets of her shorts and balled them into loose fists to keep from pulling out her own phone to check for a missed call. And worked to wipe the frown from her face. Damn if she'd let the caller see her nervous, because gunnels to gangways he was watching from someplace he felt safe—with a pair of high-powered binoculars. "What did he say? Did you recognize the voice?"

"No." Will ran his hand through his hair. "Whispers. Like Trinh said. Man? Woman? No way to tell."

Jake interrupted. "What's this about *another* call? Is there some sort of threat?"

Will's nostrils flared. "It doesn't concern you."

"It does if it concerns Taylor."

Men. She shook her head and placed her palm on Jake's arm. "I'll fill you in later."

Will kicked at a large shell near the edge of the driveway. The muscles in his jaw clenched and unclenched. "You think that's a good idea? What if he made the calls?"

Her hands bolted into the air. "Will. Jake's been with me for the past ten minutes or so. More like fifteen. What did the caller say?"

He shot a glance at Jake before answering. "Trinh went to the back for an odd-size filter. I picked up. The person said, 'You're next,' and hung up.

Taylor pulled her phone from her pocket and punched in Glen's speed dial number. Screw the caller, watching or not. Will didn't know about her last phone call. She wouldn't be responsible for him ending up like Randy.

"Up—"

"It's Taylor Campbell. I'm at Randy's. Will just came over."

Jake cocked his head.

"He got another call."

"Put him on."

She held the phone out to Will. "Detective Upchurch."

Out of the corner of her eye, Taylor saw Jake nod. He'd be happy knowing she hadn't lied about the police involvement.

"Hi, Glen. . . . Right, like the voice Trinh described. . . . 'You're next'. . . . No, nothing else. . . . Not since the other one. . . . Not a clue. . . . Okay, here she is." He handed her phone back.

"Me again." A bee buzzed her head, and she ducked.

Jake's fingers touched her arm—she guessed to make sure she didn't lose her balance. The electricity between them still flowed.

"You did right to call me. Do it anytime. I'll see you sometime tomorrow."

"Oh, I'm going sailing with Will in the afternoon."

"Keep your eyes open."

They said goodbye, and she hung up.

"Does he have any idea who's been calling me?" Will's hands rested on his hips. "Does he think the calls are related to your uncle?"

She shook her head. "He didn't say."

"I'm going to contact the phone company Monday. Tell them to do something. This is crazy. I've got a business to run." He touched her arm and inclined his chin toward Jake. "You gonna be okay?"

She smothered a smile. She'd be better with Jake than with anyone else. "I'll be fine. You?"

"If I find out who's making the calls, I'm gonna make him wish he'd never seen a phone. Otherwise, yeah. *Hasta mañana.*"

Jake watched Will until he was out of sight in the boatyard. Next to him, he sensed Taylor's tenseness by the way she barely moved and the slight throaty sounds when she exhaled.

He turned to her. "What are you doing tomorrow?"

A frown crossed her forehead. "Will repaired a catamaran, and he's taking her out for a run. He asked if I wanted to hitch a ride. Who could resist sea trials on a cat?" Her frown changed into a smile as she talked.

He understood her love of the sea. It didn't change the problem of watching out for her safety. "When are you going?"

"Noon. I'm guessing right out in the bay. He'll want to get her up to speed, challenge her integrity. The hulls were messed up pretty bad."

If the cat kept to the bay, he could deal with that. "Tell me about the phone calls."

She squeezed her hands together, but stayed silent.

"You've received them, too, haven't you?"

She nodded.

The time had come for him to fill Taylor in on part of the story. "I'd like to hear about them. Randy talked about you a lot. He said his will left everything to you, and that if something happened to him, I should keep an eye out."

The heel of her right foot tapped a fast beat on the shell drive. "If something happened? Had Randy been receiving phone calls, too?"

"Not that I know about. Randy also said you were focused, and if anybody could make heads or tails of what happened to him, it would be you."

Taylor faced Jake full on. "What do you mean by *what happened to him*? When did he tell you this? Have you been following me since he died?"

Jake rubbed his knuckles over his chin. "I've kept track of you since he died. His death may not have been an accident. I'll go into when we shared that particular conversation later."

"Convenient."

"Actually, yes. It's my story."

Taylor bumped her forehead with the heels of her hands. She didn't like not being in command. His lips twitched, but smiling might not be a good idea if he wanted to come away bruise-free. Even though she was tiny.

"I'll tell you all I know, but it's too hot out here. How about we go inside."

He stopped just inside the door. "Let's get something on the table. Life's too damn short to play games. I have no right to come sniffing around, but I like you. I meant that last night, and I mean it right now. Whatever you want to do . . . the ball's in your court."

"I appreciate the attention. I do. You're the first man I've been attracted to in a long time. But I don't partake in vacation flings, and I'm not interested in a relationship with anyone right now. Your home is in New York. I'm going back to Charleston in less than a week. I'll make captain soon, and move a couple more times. I might stick around and give admiral a shot. I don't have time for a personal life."

"Up close and personal is where life is, Taylor. Don't let it pass you by."

"Nothing's passing me by. This is my choice."

Her sharp tone wasn't lost on him. He'd been the same way—a Type A go-getter. He'd hit a nerve, and he took it as a good sign. Somewhere along the way she'd been hurt, and right now she was reliving it. The pain in her eyes squeezed his heart.

"Can I help?" His voice softened.

She blinked and returned from wherever she'd been. "What? Oh. I'm okay." The last word trailed off.

The lady harbored deep secrets—secrets that didn't stand out in her file. Jake planned to learn what they were. They'd been talking about relationships. Taylor's involvements had been either short or lasted a year or two, and there hadn't been that many. All had ended by mutual agreement.

Kelly had made a note about a fling with an Academy classmate, but that was almost twenty years ago. He'd ask her to dig deeper. Something unusual had caused Taylor's strong reaction.

If Jake found the bastard who had hurt her, he'd teach him a lesson. "I'm here, but I won't ever force anything. You have my word."

She stepped forward and rested her forehead against his sternum. "You're a good man, Jake Solomon. I like you, too. More than I should, since we only met yesterday. Officially." She stood on tiptoe and kissed the side of his chin.

His arms ached to hold her, but he kept them at his sides. "I always fall for the tough ones. Never fails. Sit down and tell me about the phone calls, and I'll share what I know."

Taylor talked and Jake listened, making a mental note to ask Kelly to find answers. As soon as he figured out the right questions.

She sat forward and leaned her elbows on the table. "I thought the first call was a joke on Will. Or a prank. I knew different when I received a call, but I told myself not to worry. Maybe something important or valuable was mixed in with Randy's junk and the caller wanted me gone. The third call implied that Randy's death wasn't an accident. I think whoever is making the calls might have killed Randy."

Jake wasn't ready to talk about Rankin's murder just yet. "Maybe Randy trusted someone here and that person is protecting his trust because they believe you're the threat."

Taylor shot from her chair and held out her hands. "That's crazy. No one would do this to protect a man who's dead."

Taylor's phone rang, and both she and Jake flinched. Of all times—just when she was going to learn more about Randy. "Excuse me. I have to answer."

She pressed the connection key. "Hello, Mother." Her mother possessed a knack for calling at inopportune moments, and she would talk until she finished what she had to say. No matter what.

Jake smiled.

She stuck out her tongue.

"Must you always answer that way, Taylor? Whatever happened to a civil hello?"

"It's good to talk to you, too."

"I don't have much time. We're leaving here a few days early, and the plane is ready to board. We'll stay longer in Buenos Aires."

Jake stood and motioned he'd be outside. She waved him back to the chair and made a yakking motion with her fingers.

"You didn't like skiing?" All her mother had talked about for weeks was skiing in Chile.

"One or two days is enough. You know I'm a city woman."

Taylor shook her head. "You're bored already. How long will this marriage last?"

"None of your business, Taylor Anne. How much longer are you going to be on that boat? A lot of nice southern men live in Charleston. Wealthy southern men."

"Come find one for yourself after you get rid of what's-his-name." As if her mother would ever appear on her doorstep. They didn't engage in many face-to-face meetings. When they did meet, it occurred on neutral ground. She glanced up, pressing her lips together and biting down to keep from laughing at Jake's expression and raised eyebrows.

"*Tsk.* You could do worse, Taylor. Much worse. Believe me, I know."

"I'm sure you do." She'd encountered a couple of her mother's lovers.

"They're calling our flight. Ciao."

"Goodbye, Mother." She said the words to dead air.

Jake reached across and covered her hand. "A lot of love in that call."

She sighed. "I do love her. She's my mother, but we've never been friends. We don't think alike, and our priorities are totally different."

"I understand that. My old man and I . . . well, I'm just a wannabe."

"Tell me your story." Since they met she'd yearned to understand what gave this man the drive and energy that swirled around him. Maybe his relationship with his father.

"The full version is boring. Let me start with the short take. It will be plenty long, believe me. Feel free to ask questions."

"Go for it." Maybe one day she'd get all the details.

He pulled a leather case from his shirt pocket and handed her a card. "I gave you my personal card earlier. This is who I am to the rest of the world."

She read it aloud. "Compass Points International. Jacob P. Solomon, President. Ooh, Fifth Avenue. Your accent is Brooklyn."

"I'm *from* Brooklyn. How did you learn to recognize a Brooklyn accent?"

She hadn't meant to let him know she recognized it. Her comment slipped out when she read *Fifth Avenue*. "It's stronger than a regular New York accent. That's all. Compass Points . . . you named your company for your Coast Guard friends."

He studied her face before nodding. As direct as he was, an undercurrent of secrecy ran beneath his words. She sensed the secrets would be the details that would make the story of his life exciting.

"What does Compass Points do?"

"We take care of business."

Oh, yeah. "Such as?"

Jake leaned back and steepled his fingers. "I joined the Coast Guard at seventeen, fresh out of high school. My senior year, I'd gotten mixed up with a rough crowd, almost failed two finals. My SATs sank to the bottom of the harbor. Mom knew I'd end up in prison. Pop could've cared less. When the recruiter came on campus, I signed up. Pop had to sign, too, since I was only seventeen, but he was happy for me to go. The recruiter told me I had to pass a test or I'd have to take my chances with the draft. I think he was surprised I passed."

"The ASVAB." She went to the counter and grabbed two bottles of water.

"Right. So I went to boot camp down in Jersey, then to gunner's mate A School."

"Randy was a boatswain." She handed a bottle to Jake and uncapped hers.

He nodded. "Thanks. I was a crack shot. Never flinched under pressure. Flaunted all the medals, and earned myself an instant winner ticket to Nam before I graduated boot camp."

"Where you connected with Randy."

"Five of us in our division of Point boats used to hang out, go on liberty together. Sometimes we'd all be at the beer hall or wherever, sometimes only two or three of us."

"Randy told me about going ashore at a couple of different places." Shipmates often remained lifelong friends. The dynamics of war forged those bonds into hardened steel. Taylor had created a few friendships with former shipmates. Randy would've shouldered the world for any of his Nam buddies.

Jake drank some water, the muscles in his neck working as he swallowed. They looked as strong as those in his arms. Warmth spread through her. She fought her desire to touch them. With a sigh she looked away to clear the image—along with her thoughts.

He went on with the story. "We were in the boonies. Just the beer hall, usually. Or another boat. Sometimes we'd come off a patrol and barely have time to sleep before they sent us out again."

She fumbled with the cap on her bottle. "Did you and Randy go over at the same time?"

"He'd been in country a while. When they handed over his boat to the South Vietnamese, he went back stateside."

"What about you?"

"The *Point Whitebanks* was one of the last Point boats we transferred. I hadn't been in country for the full tour, so they sent me to one of the large cutters with big guns. Got to fire the five-inch thirty-eights."

She laughed. Coast Guard and big guns didn't belong to-gether in the same sentence. "If you liked big guns, you should've joined the Navy. They had some sixteens."

"I did better with the smaller ones. That's one of the reasons I got tapped."

"Tapped for what?"

"Special Forces."

CHAPTER 21

How many times had his dad told him this story? Hundreds. At least. And made him tell it the same way? A thousand. At least. Three months straight, every day, ten to twenty times a day. Always tweaking, planning ahead for any questions Taylor might ask.

Jake wasn't sure if Taylor knew the full story about Bangkok. In a way he hoped she did, so he wouldn't be the one to tell her. But in his heart, he knew she didn't. She was open and direct. She would have mentioned the horror of that night before now.

During all the tweaking, and learning to fully express the deep emotion his dad felt, Jake even relived the events in his dreams as if they were real. Combined with his own SEAL experience, the scene unfolded before him now as he spoke. As if he had lived it himself.

"I told the sons of bitches I wanted no part of Special Forces. All I wanted was to hang out and do my regular enlistment time before I went home to school. Hell, I wanted to live to see twenty-one, not get my body blown apart in the jungle."

"So what happened?" Taylor sipped her water more like a genteel lady than commander of a hundred-person crew. He wanted to get to know her in person, not just on paper. Explore her complexities. But not now.

"The *Whitebanks* worked with a number of SEAL teams, putting them in, extracting them. A couple of times under fire.

We laid down cover fire as best we could with fifty calibers. Some missions got tricky. The suits said I came highly qualified and recommended."

"I'm not surprised."

"Hell, I just did my job. I told them no thanks."

"Let me guess—wrong answer."

"Completely unacceptable. They knew about the cluster fuck in Bangkok."

She frowned. "I'm not connecting."

Taylor's frown broke his heart. She didn't know. He sighed. "R&R. I went with—"

"Ham Bone? Is this when you bought the belts?"

"Yes. There's more."

She sat at full attention. Jake had never wanted a woman as much as he wanted Taylor. His mouth went dry, and he filled it with water. A few seconds passed before he continued with his story.

"Hamblen Norberg was older, ex-Navy, with a pregnant wife stateside. Ham and Randy were on the same boat. I'd been on the *Whitebanks* maybe four or five months. We were tied up for a couple weeks with engine problems."

"I won't ask what you did in Bangkok because I've heard stories from some Old Guard Coasties."

She hadn't heard his, and he wished he didn't have to tell her. "We didn't miss much—*Ham and Jake Do Bangkok* would have been the movie title. Up and down Patpong 1 and Patpong 2. One night a bargirl got Ham to buy her a drink. Instead of taking him upstairs, she asked him to watch something for her for a few minutes." The cigarette smoke, stale beer, heavy cheap perfume, fish all came back from his own visits to Patpong a quarter-century after his dad's.

"He agreed, of course." Taylor sat forward, engaged by the story.

"Right. The bargirl reached under her miniskirt and removed a garter from each leg. We'd encountered a few ladyboys, but she was all woman. She slipped a garter on each of Ham's arms, and he kept on drinking."

"I can see this. Some big bruiser of a Thai pimp came after the garters."

"No one came, not even the girl. It was our favorite bar, and we'd seen her before. We were sure we'd see her the next time we were there."

Taylor's focus rested totally on him. He'd rather take her in his arms and make love to her right here on the kitchen table than tell her this story. But he didn't have that choice. Or that right.

"As many times as I rehashed all that happened, I'm certain we wouldn't have done anything differently. Until that point, nothing had raised an alarm. A couple of beers later, we walked outside to an alley several doors down. Both of us had to take a leak. We heard a noise—a moan."

"A trap."

Taylor's liquid eyes drank in every word. He had to take his feelings for her out of the equation. This mission held as much risk as any he went on as a SEAL. Taylor believed he was his father. *Keep remembering that, Jake. There will be hell to pay if she learns the truth.*

"We were too green to think that. We were full of piss and vinegar."

"And beer."

He grinned. "Exactly. We thought we ruled the world."

"You survived."

Others hadn't. He downed a slug of water. "We heard more noises. Then we heard a scream and loud banging. The bargirl lay partially behind a couple of trash cans. She'd left a trail of blood from farther up the alley. Someone had gone after her with a knife, and she was bleeding out. Barely conscious. She held her stomach together with her hands and banged the trash bin with her head until she died."

"Oh, no." Taylor's hand covered her mouth. Her eyes filled with pain.

Jake Solomon, you are the meanest son of a bitch in the fucking valley. "Ham and I eyeballed each other. I'm sure I looked as scared as he did. We sobered up damn quick."

"I know you didn't go to the police." She placed both hands palm down on the table top, ready to deal with facts, every inch the Coast Guard officer his dad sent him to protect.

"We'd have been dead before dawn. No, we gathered she wanted us to look in the trash can. The aroma of Bangkok. . . ." He shook his head.

"I've heard others talk about that. The sewer runs under the sidewalks."

"Most of the sidewalks were broken or boarded over. The trash can magnified the entire experience. Under some fish bones, egg shells, vomit, and who knows what else, we found two silk bags and a locked metal box."

He should have given a less graphic description of the experience. The muscles in Taylor's neck and jaw worked overtime until she swallowed.

If he hadn't promised his dad, he would stop this charade right now, lay out the facts for Taylor without the dramatics, and beg her forgiveness.

She drank some water. "You took them."

"And ran. Ham ripped off the garters and shoved them in his pocket. We each put one of the bags under our waistbands. The box presented a problem." According to his dad, they'd stood in the mouth of the alley looking at each other, neither able to think.

"How large was it?"

"Like a small safe deposit box, not as long. I gave Ham my bag and he put both bags under his waistband. I shoved the box under mine. I was skinny, and we wore civvies. I had to suck in my gut and pull out my shirttail as well as undo the button and loosen my belt. We reached the hotel without a problem."

"What did you find inside?"

"Jewels in the bags—sapphires and rubies."

"What about the box?"

"Locked. Finally we examined the garters. The bar girl, or someone, had sewn tiny pockets behind the elastic. We found a key in one of them."

"How about the other pockets?"

"This was the height of the Cold War, remember. Most contained tiny tubes, a bit like a flatter forty-five casing. About an inch long."

"What were they?"

"Message containers. One held a map. One a message written in Thai. The others were empty."

"And the key?"

He liked how Taylor sorted through his story. She might have been born with some of those skills, but the military had sharpened them. Just as it had honed his. Kelly would like her, too. *Forget it, Jake. You'll never bring her home to meet the parents.*

"Ah, yes. The key fit the box. Did I mention we didn't sleep that night? The box held lapis lazuli rocks and cash. A lot of cash."

"How much?"

"Two million."

"Damn!" Her eyes grew wide.

"We figured the bills were Russian counterfeit, so we split it to take it home with us. In the states, we'd find out if we could cash it in."

"How did two million dollars fit into a small box?"

"The bills were the kind banks used to use to transfer funds from one bank to another. Or so they told me later—ten-thousand-dollar bills."

"Damn. The money was real?"

"Yeah."

"This is a hell of a story." She gulped some water. "Did you find out about the bar girl?"

"We stayed in Bangkok for three more days, and nights—kept away from Patpong, changed hotels—before going back to Nam, and we didn't ask questions."

Taylor opened her mouth to say something, but stopped, apparently not pleased at his non-answer. He wanted to kiss away her annoyance. Make her smile. Instead, he'd get to the rest of the story in his own time, just as his dad had coached him. The good and the bad.

"Old Ham Bone took everything personally. He felt guilty for profiting from the girl's death. I told him she's the one who trusted him and who practically rammed the trash can down our throats."

"Ham was older. Perhaps he possessed a more fully developed sense of responsibility."

Jake shrugged. "We had the jewels, but people in Bangkok traded sapphires and rubies on the streets. And the lapis lazuli? Hell, we thought they were just pretty blue rocks."

"Pricey blue rocks, I think."

"Not so much. The lapis rocks in the box ranged from tiny to fist size, and in all shapes. We agreed to have belts and belt buckles made for the gang, and the next day we chose the five smallest rocks to put on the buckles."

"That's when you decided on Solomon's Compass."

She leaned forward, inches away from him. His breath came fast, and he mustered every ounce of reserve he had not to touch her. He forced his thoughts to anything but her—blaring horns in Brooklyn, Kelly's purple hair, his mother.

When he could control his breathing, he gave her a smile. "Not exactly. We'd decided to put Compass Points on the belts."

"I'm lost again." Taylor stood and moved about the kitchen.

"I took charge of getting the buckles, and Ham agreed to get the belts made. On the way to the leather shop he decided to use my name because he said Solomon knew everything. In reality, he wanted any flak to come my way, not his. I was surprised he even used Compass."

Her lopsided half-smile told him she thought as much about Ham's assertion as he did. "I imagine he denied that."

"Of course. When I had the buckles made at the street market, the guy in the stall took the stones and mounted them while I watched—no big deal. Bangkok continued to surprise me."

"Like the ladyboys."

The corners of his mouth twitched. "Yeah. Most of the buckle choices looked like ones you'd win at a rodeo, but I liked these square brushed metal ones. After I got home I learned the lapis is high quality."

"What makes it different?"

"The gold veins." He held the top and bottom of the buckle with his left hand and used his right thumb to trace the lines in the stone.

"Randy's stone looked like gold lightning against a stormy blue sky. Yours does, too."

"That's gold pyrite. Less gold pyrite or more white calcite equals a less expensive piece of lapis. Even high-quality lapis isn't as expensive as sapphire."

She went to the window. "I'm trying to take all this in. It's quite a story you tell, Jake Solomon."

"All true." True story, but not *his* story as Taylor thought. He had to get her out of his head. "Cross my heart."

She turned around. "I believe you. It's just so out of the norm. Out of my norm, anyway."

"Out of ours, too."

"Okay, so you found the girl and her treasures. Did you presume she was a spy or a conduit?"

"Right. Involved in espionage. Probably a courier."

She stopped for a moment before ticking off items on her fingers. "You thought the money was counterfeit. You had belts made for your buddies. You had lapis lazuli stones mounted on belt buckles. What about the sapphires and rubies?" With each point, Taylor made a circle of her thumb and fingers.

"We kept them safe, thinking they were the most valuable of the lot."

She started to the table, but stopped. "What did you do with the map? And the note? The Cold War was going on, your buddies were in Vietnam, and you and Ham were headed back."

He downed some more water. "The map looked like Vietnam, but it was drawn out freehand, so we weren't certain."

"Roads? Cities? Rivers?"

Taylor worked with neatly charted navigational maps, not raw intel from the field. "No. Letters, symbols, numbers at various points. We tried to figure it out, but we didn't know where either one came from or where they were supposed to go. Ham said if we sent it to the American embassy, someone would run with it."

"Why didn't you just take the map to the embassy your-selves?"

"We had the stones and the money, and we didn't want to give them up. More important, we didn't want to be blamed for the woman's death. Both of us agreed staying anonymous was best. After we found the address for the American Embassy, we addressed an envelope to the Security Attaché. We figured it would get someone's attention."

"I'm sure you were right."

"We wrote out the lyrics for 'We Gotta Get Out of This Place' and put them into the envelope with the map and the page written in Thai. We sent it from the main post office."

"No other details?"

"That was enough."

"Why the lyrics?"

"Oh, baby, that was *the* song. All of us wanted to go home." His dad had played the old Animals song as many times as he'd told him the story. Now the music and lyrics played in his mind. Every note. Every word.

She shook her head. "I don't understand. Why not just the title?"

"We thought by including the lyrics, they'd understand an American soldier sent the map. And by extension, they'd realize something happened to the girl—if they knew about the girl—but we'd stay in the clear with the money and stones."

Taylor bounced her bottle against her palm. Either she didn't approve of the way they handled the situation or she was putting the story together in her head trying to make sense of it.

"After we did everything we could think of, we had one more night in Bangkok."

She returned to the table. "Please tell me you didn't go back to that same bar."

"No. We'd been having only a few drinks at the hotel bar, but that night after a few extra beers, caution became way over-rated. We were invincible. Beer cost more in the hotel than it did stateside. Local Bangkok bars charged like a quarter. We'd just be extra careful and observant. If anyone showed any interest in us, we'd come straight back to the hotel. We also decided to stay on the main streets, and not go into Patpong."

Taylor shook her head as he spoke, and he knew she thought Ham and his dad were fools.

"We drank too much beer and made the rounds. And didn't stay on the main streets like we'd planned. On our way back to the hotel, congratulating ourselves on having such a fun time, two thugs came up behind us with pipes."

"Oh, crap." Her eyes widened to whiskey suns.

"Ham told them to take it easy, we'd give them our cash."

"Please don't tell me you had all the money with you?"

He laughed, but only for a second. "Of course we did. The jewels, too. Everything would've been gone if we'd left it in the room. Thai hotel workers back then would steal you blind while you watched, much less after you left. Remember the time pe-riod—early seventies. We suspected the money was counterfeit, but we weren't taking a chance."

"What about the belts and buckles?"

"Ham and I wore ours. We put the other buckles into the bags with the jewels, but we rolled up the belts in our duffels. No one bothered with them."

"What happened that night?" She leaned forward, her knuckles white on her water bottle. He ran his thumb over them, and her breath caught in a gasp. For an instant, he couldn't move.

He cleared his throat. "We'd divided the cash into four rolls, two for each of us to carry. Ham took a roll from his pocket, thinking he'd give it to them and keep the other one and the real money in his wallet safe. They looked at the money, had a few Thai words between them, and threw it on the street."

"They didn't think it was real, either."

"Ham picked it up, nodded and smiled, held it out. For his trouble, one of them whacked him on the back with the pipe." He shook his head. "The guy shouldn't have done that."

Taylor covered her eyes with a hand. "Oh, no."

"Ham had a short fuse. Mixed with too many beers, the combination turned lethal. He lost control, yanked the pipe out of the guy's hand, and hammered him with it." The sounds of a different, but equally severe, beating played in his head. One administered by thugs in an Iraqi prison. No one could ever forget the sounds of heavy blows to a man's body.

She gasped. Her water bottle crinkled.

"The other man tried to crack his knees, but Ham's reflexes took over. He went after the second guy with the pipe. Both of the Thais lay on the ground, bleeding." His dad said the scene had been worse than seeing the bar girl die.

"My God." Taylor's eyes grew even wider.

Every Coastie learned Coast Guard history and heard sea stories, but what he'd told her presented a different, stranger, and most unofficial scenario.

"I tried to pull Ham off, but I wanted to stay out of the way of the pipe and the blood. He wouldn't have realized it was me and not another thug. I picked up Ham's money roll and checked for a pulse on the second guy." He rolled the bottle between his palms.

"Was he alive?"

"No. Ham tossed the pipe and started kicking the first man in the side, yelling for him to get up. He was dead. It took a while for that to sink in. For both of us."

Her hand covered his with warmth and concern.

"I picked up the pipe he'd used. All the time I kept telling him to come on. We had to leave. The police would show up. We were far from a main street, but it wouldn't stay quiet long. Nothing in Bangkok ever did. I said whatever I could think of to get him moving. I'd have been guilty, too, if we'd been taken in."

"So you fled?"

"Finally. I all but dragged him along with me. Two blocks away I found some old rags and wiped off the pipe and most of the blood from Ham. I carried the pipe in one hand and held on to Ham with the other."

"You didn't take it to the hotel?" Her fingers slid between his.

"No. Somewhere along the way, I dropped it and the rags into a sewage ditch. The next day, Ham and I boarded an Air Force plane back to Vietnam."

But that was only the beginning of the story.

CHAPTER 22

Taylor let out a breath she hadn't been aware she held. Nor did she remember her fingers entwining with Jake's. She didn't pull away from the warmth of his touch. "What a frightening experience. How did it change the relationship between you and Ham? Did you even have one after that? You were seventeen?"

"I'd turned eighteen by this time. Neither one of us wanted to talk about what had happened. Ham didn't say much. The flight back to Nam lasted a couple of hours. When we landed, four soldiers we didn't know greeted us like long-lost friends. They took us to a row of offices on the air base, and stuck us in separate rooms. I waited hours—much longer than the flight lasted—before someone came in. When he did, he went straight to business. They'd started tailing us from the post office when we mailed the letter to the embassy. He knew everything."

"I'm not surprised by any of this. This kind of . . . recruiting still happens today, though perhaps not to the same extent of extortion." Although she wouldn't bet on it. Sealed orders sometimes asked for strange things—once a request for anyone in her crew who was conversant in French and had ever run a marathon. No one had fit the profile. "Needs of the service."

"Back then, our military moved in and out of Thailand with ease, especially Air Force and Navy. Single guys loved Bangkok for R&R, and it was popular as an information exchange. Because of all that, those with a need to stay on top of things did a good job."

"CIA." She let go of Jake's hand and stood again to loosen muscles tensing in anger at men who were probably now dead.

Jake nodded. "And their counterparts. They said they spotted us at the post office, intercepted our letter, and followed us afterward." His shoulders sagged.

She'd learned about the Cold War in history and more at grad school. "Were they following you the night you were attacked?"

"Oh, yeah."

"They didn't step in?"

"Why foil a perfect setup?"

The all-important case. Today Feddie investigators strove for barrels of evidence. Prosecutors wanted to have enough left for a conviction after a sharp defense attorney dismantled piece after piece as inadmissible or tainted evidence and dismissed witnesses with a sneer and a seed of doubt. Investigators and prosecutors alike also wanted to see if more information would lead them to conspirators at a higher level.

Jake leaned back in his chair, his concentration not leaving Taylor. "They wanted to see how much we knew."

"About the dead girl?"

"The girl, her actions, her contacts. Whether or not we were a part of her world. Anything they could learn. Then, as now, things weren't always what they seemed. They said they had my file. They also had our duffels. Ham had refused to carry any of our bounty in his. The belts, buckles, cash, jewels, and lapis rocks were in mine."

"Surprise, surprise."

He gave her a quick nod. "If I agreed to work for them, they wouldn't charge me with accessory to murder or turn me over to the Thai authorities."

She stopped short. "That's absurd!"

"Remember . . . I was eighteen with a fair share of Brooklyn street smarts, but I was halfway around the world and didn't know shit about the way the big leagues operated."

She started pacing again. "They wanted you. They liked that you remained composed under pressure, thought on your feet, and they used the incident against you to force you to sign up. I know how that works—probe for the weakest point and use it. They might have been watching your progress since boot and A-school. Or followed you since your arrival and waited for you to screw up. Or maybe they set you up."

"It was a war."

"Doesn't matter. In your case, they took advantage of your youth and innocence." Look at him now. He might be almost twice her age, but he sat at the table cool and sexy as nobody's business. His demeanor calmed her. She could fall hard, and those green eyes didn't make her resolve any easier.

"I signed a paper, and they said they'd be in touch. They sent me to my unit alone."

She sat back down. The bastards had put him through the wringer. "What about Ham?" She needed to concentrate on the subject. Not think about the earlier heat from his fingers.

"His boat was on the river when I got back. I didn't see him again until a month or so later on Coast Guard Day. All the boats were in."

"We still celebrate."

He grinned. "Used to piss off the Navy pukes."

Laughter swelled from inside her. "Nothing's changed. I love August fourth."

Jake walked to the door and back. "All the Compass Points met at the beer hall cookout. Ham pulled me aside and asked what happened. We exchanged stories, only I didn't tell him about having to sign up. He didn't mention anything either about signing up. He went straight to his boat and out on patrol. When his boat came back in, he had a letter from home."

"From his wife?"

"A baby boy. With photos. He showed them to me. Turns out this was his third kid. He was freaking, thought they'd keep him in country and he wouldn't get to go home or ever see his family again. All he wanted was to go home and make more babies. He had a couple of beers and said he had one hell of a story to tell everybody about Bangkok."

Taylor knew people like Ham. One drink and they aired all their dirty laundry. "I hope you could keep him quiet."

"Not a chance. I did suggest we go over and sit in the shade on the other side of the beer hall. His tale was confined to the Compass Points. Randy told me he asked Ham later if he'd told anyone else about Bangkok, and Ham said no."

"Small miracles."

"Exactly. We tried to calm him down, but Ham kept talking about those two Thai thugs and saying he should've handled the situation better."

"PTSD. He would have handled himself differently if he hadn't been drunk, and those men might have killed the two of you." She shivered inside.

He leaned back against the sink. "That's what Randy tried to tell him. Even told him it might not have been about the cash, that they may have come to kill us instead of rob us. Ham wouldn't shut up. I gave out the belts—I still had all of them."

"What about the cash and the jewels?"

"Confiscated. They didn't question the belts, so I guess they figured either those pieces of lapis were bought and paid for along with the belts or they'd throw them in as part of the deal."

"So did they ever approach you and Ham?"

"If they contacted Ham, he never told me. He got out not long after, so maybe they left him alone. I told you I left for a large cutter after the *Whitebanks*. They yanked me off after two months and sent me stateside to sniper school."

"Did you stay in touch with any of the Compass Points besides Randy?"

"We all stayed in loose touch. More so for a while after Ham hanged himself."

Only an insensitive son of a bitch wouldn't ache at the pain on Taylor's face. She squeezed her eyes shut and rubbed her forehead, and the craving to take her in his arms and make her grief go away gnawed at him. His dad had said the job wouldn't be easy. He was right.

Jake blew out a breath. "Ham's suicide didn't happen for a long while. I stayed in service for a total of eight years. When I got to sniper school, I had to sign another paper agreeing to an additional four on top of my original enlistment, but I'm a quick study. I bargained for guaranteed acceptance at a university of my choice—I chose Columbia—and a full ride for a master's. If they wanted me to kill people for them, I had a hunch it'd be a piece of cake for them to pull off my education."

"Did they? They had a good pick of Special Forces types back then." She got up and paced again, questioning him.

"Without so much as a haggle." He took a deep breath. "They weren't looking for team players. I became a chess piece. Over the years, I bumped into others. Each of us had figured out a piece of the puzzle, and eventually we started putting the picture together."

"So . . . you were independent operatives?"

He didn't answer.

"Were you attached to CIA or State?"

"Off the books. I imagine our salaries and training were paid for out of a contingency fund, or perhaps privately underwritten. Or maybe buried deep in State or CIA. I never knew."

"You had to fit in someplace."

"I can't tell you who we worked for."

"Bullshit." She stopped pacing.

His dad said people would have a hard time believing the way things were.

"This was in the Nixon administration. At least one of my cohorts had been around since Kennedy. Not long before I got out, I met a newbie who came in under Carter. Whatever agency or group paid and directed us had been around at least since the early sixties. And was still in operation in the late seventies. That's all I know, and I haven't tried to find out more. Too high-level for my blood."

"You were smart not to try to find out, I think."

"I can tell you no one ever burned any of us for our acts. We did things that had to be done. Sometimes they looked like accidents, sometimes not. Sometimes we got others to do the job. Not all our acts were bad. Rarely did our results make the news. We knew our actions changed the landscape for those in power. But most of the time we never saw the big picture. We followed orders, all of it blessed at the highest levels, no matter who held the office. Some things are better left alone."

"Does the group exist now?"

"I can't answer that either." His dad hadn't answered the question for him.

"Do you stay in contact with any of those men?"

He grinned. "A few work for me."

Her eyes widened. "You're kidding."

"No. Flawless setup—nobody suspects an old guy. It's a great cover."

Taylor laughed. "Unbelievable. I need a minute to take this in. Do you realize how much ground you've covered? Vietnam, Bangkok, murder, suicide, and now international intrigue." She held her head between her hands.

"It's a lot."

She nodded and closed her eyes. "I need processing time. Otherwise I can't find my way back to the original discussion."

"Follow the breadcrumbs."

"What?"

"That's what they taught us. If the trail got cold, we followed the breadcrumbs. Sometimes the breadcrumbs were drugs or murders. Or minor wars. Most of the time we followed the money."

Her eyes popped open. "Follow the money. Should we follow the money to find out who killed Randy—if he was killed?"

"You inherited, but you didn't kill him. We have to find different breadcrumbs."

"Let's go back. You chose Columbia. I understand why—it's back in New York. Plus some prestige, good contacts. What were the Compass Points doing during the time you toured the world and went to school?"

"Basically, everybody went to school or went to work. Got married. Started or expanded families."

She'd been regathering herself in ways she probably wasn't aware of, fidgeting a bit, touching her hair, making sure her personal world still functioned. Her eyes had gone from wild to concerned. Now she quieted. "What about your family?"

The question he'd dreaded she would ask. He pushed the palms of his hands together. "Not me. I married several years later, but it didn't last. Compass Points became my reason for living."

He'd uttered the first lie. Not counting the big one he'd lived since meeting her. The Big Lie was mission truth. And his dad's truth. It was his responsibility to stick to it. But the Little Lie turned his gut sour. If he were a kid, his dad would tan his hide. He couldn't tell her the truth about his parents. Not now. He'd already told her he was single. That truth was his real fuck-up.

She started pacing again. The worn floor creaked under her slight weight. "So what do you do? What does Compass Points do?"

He shrugged. "Growing up, besides wanting to be a fireman and a cowboy, no one ever encouraged me in any direction other than to finish high school and get a job. During sophomore year at Columbia, I started by providing secure messengering services in the boroughs. Extremely secure. I relied on my experience. The more I learned about how to run a company, the more I expanded my services. I moved on to corporate security, executive security, anti-kidnapping training. Things I knew about."

"You had street cred."

"So-so. The phrase *military security* opens a lot of doors most people don't know exist. I knew what a lot of people had done wrong. I also have an office in Jersey staffed with geeks doing the same sort of security on the electronic end. If they didn't work for me, they'd be hackers. In fact, all but a few started out that way. They get the job done." Kelly took excellent care of that.

"I'm guessing your clients pay somewhat more than the government." Light from the window lit her face and the hollow of her neck. Christ, he could barely concentrate.

He smiled. "Certain areas of the government contract us from time to time."

"Good for you. So when did things start going south with Ham?"

Jake massaged his forehead over his eyes where a headache was forming. "He had problems from the beginning. His wife said he'd gone to the VA, a private shrink, a church-sponsored group. They gave him a lot of different drugs, a lot of talk—nothing helped. He'd been back from Nam for several years by this time. The night before he committed suicide, he told his wife about Bangkok. The incident still roosted in his head. She thought he experienced a breakthrough and was getting well. When she came home from work, she found him in the garage." The phone call had shaken his dad to the core. He was different when he talked about it. "Ham used the Solomon's Compass belt."

She shuddered and wrapped her arms around him. "I know how much that hurt you."

A good wind could blow her away. But she was a rock of solid support, and her touch set him on fire. He returned her hug and moved back a step. "There's more. Since Ham died, all the Compass Points have been killed."

She stiffened. "Before Randy?"

He nodded. "Randy was the most recent. Ten years after Ham committed suicide, Kyle Easley was murdered. Six years later, Ed Wharton. Three more, Randy Rankin."

"This is why you're certain Randy was murdered."

"Yes. I'm next, unless I find the bastard first."

"You're not looking by yourself. I'm helping. He killed Randy and is trying to get rid of me. I tried to ignore the clues. Even this." Taylor held out her hands. "I won't now."

"This is my fight, Taylor, not yours."

"Like hell. Randy's death grieves me, but I won't open old wounds. He wouldn't like that." She squared her shoulders. "I'll do everything I can to help find his killer. That's what he would like. Tell me what you know."

He tipped an imaginary hat in her direction for her let's-do-it attitude. "If I'd made the connection with Kyle Easley, maybe I could've prevented the rest. But what's the connection between a suicide and a murder hundreds of miles and ten years apart? The wheels turned with Ed Wharton."

"What have the police said?"

Jake studied his feet before looking at her. "I talked to people I know. They put the word out about a possible connection. I understand someone at the FBI has the case information and possibilities. Everyone's busy, no one has enough personnel."

"Glen Upchurch is revisiting Randy's file. I'm sure he'll get the case re-opened. If you get with him—"

"Out of the question."

"You have to tell local law enforcement what you know."

"I can't tell them without revealing what occurred in Bangkok, which will lead to more questions and put other lives at risk. I shouldn't have told you. And I'm not about to talk to a local cop."

"Your opting out doesn't help Randy."

"I called him as soon as I learned of Wharton's murder."

"You gave Randy a heads-up. That's why he became so paranoid." Taylor pinched her nose.

Jake could almost hear her mind working. "I'd imagine that's the reason, yes."

"How often did you talk? Did you share what you learned?"

Taylor wasn't going to like what he had to say. He took a deep breath. "I was out of the country most of the time."

"What?" Taylor's hands moved to her hips, and she leaned forward from her waist, her feet planted firmly on the kitchen floor. "Are you insane? You left your friend to face death alone?"

He took her verbal assault in silence, waiting until she was spent. "Business, Taylor. It couldn't be helped."

"You own the company. Someone else could have gone. You could have been here for Randy."

"Randy knew I would be gone and would be in touch when I could. I loved your uncle and the other Compass Points like brothers. As far as sending someone else, I honor my obligations. I went because I was the one with the right contacts and background and knowledge. I was the one who knew the territory and the hidden pitfalls. I wouldn't place one of my people in a situation that would likely get them killed."

"You're impossible."

"I've been accused of worse. Perhaps I could have saved Randy's life had I remained stateside. Perhaps not. But because of the road I traveled, I know I saved a few hundred American lives—innocents like Randy. Does that make it fair? No. But I don't doubt my actions."

"Did you at least call him to say hi every once in a while?" Sarcasm dripped from every word.

"I stayed in touch when I could. In various ways. As the months and years went on, Randy became more vague and preoccupied. He often told me he was trying to root out the killer and everyone thought he was crazy."

"You saw his shop. Maybe he was."

"More than once he said, 'I don't know who I am anymore.'"

Taylor nodded. "I can believe that."

"I'm sorry I couldn't prevent Randy's murder. I'm convinced it's tied to Bangkok. Of everyone I know who could have a reason for killing the Compass Points, I've verified all but one were elsewhere on the dates and times of the murders. And on the date of Ham's death, in the event it wasn't suicide."

"Who's unaccounted for?"

"A man sometimes known as Oliver Fallon. Is the name familiar?"

"No."

"He's still active and can change identities at will. It's possible he knows about Bangkok. He may be innocent, but I can't verify his whereabouts on any of those three dates. Or on the date of Randy's death."

She dug the heels of her palms into her forehead. "I'm calling Detective Upchurch."

He stopped her hand on its way to her pocket. "This goes beyond police, Taylor. If this man's the killer, the only way to stop him is for him to locate me or me to find him first."

"Are you here because he's here?" She shivered.

"You have a keen sense of how these pieces fit together." Her insight had come as an unexpected surprise. "My first priority is to keep my promise to Randy by protecting you. My second is to draw the killer out, confront him on my terms, not his. It could be the killer is not Fallon but someone else. Perhaps you can find something I missed."

"I'm out of my element. And I don't have much to offer except my perceptions."

"Small and seemingly insignificant details often expose secrets. Something I've seen and dismissed because it was too common to me in my former life might shout to you." If Kelly were here, she could get right on any new ideas from Taylor and check them out. But their dad came first.

"Why would the killer want me out of the way?"

"I can't say. All I know for sure is each of the men still had their belts, but after their murders, the belts were gone. I told Randy that."

"Now I know why Randy cut up the one thing he valued above everything else."

"Any ideas where the rest of the belt or the buckle could be?"

Taylor shook her head. "It could turn up in the shop. You saw—there's no telling what's in there."

CHAPTER 23

Taylor told Jake Randy's belt might be in the shop, but her gut feeling was stronger than ever. Randy had not only destroyed his favorite treasure, but he buried it someplace no one would think about. She fought the urge to tell Jake about the box—and let him do the digging. But Randy's note had been clear—tell no one of his secret buried treasure. If he'd wanted Jake to know, he would have sent him coordinates, too. All the same, it wasn't easy keeping quiet.

Jake picked up his empty water bottle. "I'm glad we finally had this chance to talk. Think about all I've said. Something new may come."

"Right now I'm empty."

"You have my cell number. I'm not going anywhere."

"I'm going to town for ice cream. Maybe Dan will be around, and I can ask about Bravo and Echoes. Want to come along?"

Jake moved his hands to her shoulders. "Let's make a deal." His eyes sparkled with laughter.

She'd already fallen for him a little, despite her best intentions to remain uninvolved. If she wasn't careful, she would fall hard enough to skin her soul. Sheer willpower kept her arms at her sides instead of around his waist. "What kind of deal?"

"Keep going to town to daylight hours, and I won't tag along behind you. Promise to call me about anything. Any time."

Warmth spread throughout her body. She had to get a grip on her emotions. To even consider becoming involved with him was madness. They were both married to their careers and too old to change. And they were targets of a killer who had already murdered three men. All the same, she wanted to taste him, relish his touch, indulge herself in his scent. Maybe she was going mad.

Taylor forced a smile and raised her hands. "I give up. Promise. But since the sun is shining, I'm going for ice cream. And maybe window shopping. You're welcome to come along. I need some outdoor time to prepare myself for cooped-up salvage shop time next week."

"I don't think so." He lowered his head until his lips were by her ear. "Be careful." His words were a whisper, his breath barely a breeze.

She didn't trust herself to speak, so nodded her acknowledgment.

He moved his lips across her cheek until they found hers. His kiss was gentle, but it ignited her passion. She stepped into his embrace, and his arms tightened around her. He tasted of peppermint, and she wished she'd grabbed a mint from Lulu's, too, to dilute the remnants of her beer and burger lunch.

Whatever hints of flavor remained on her tongue didn't seem to bother him. He held the back of her head in one hand while his tongue delved and probed. Her legs turned to pudding, but for some reason held her upright. She returned his kiss, her tongue dancing with his time and time again.

He nibbled her lips. "You taste good." His voice sounded rough.

"I taste like lunch."

He chuckled. "I liked lunch."

She nuzzled his chest. "Good."

His fingers tangled in her hair, and as she relaxed, a black spot appeared in the corner of her mind. She shooed the smudge away, but the blackness grew and wouldn't let go.

"Jake?"

"Hmm?"

"Did Compass Points search for the killer?"

He didn't move. She hadn't been aware of any motion before, but now she couldn't even detect his breathing.

"No."

"Why not? Your people sound as if they'd be the perfect investigators."

"The killings were personal, Taylor. Compass Points is business."

She pushed away and walked to the end of the room before turning to face him. "So you let Randy die—be *killed* in cold blood—because it's *personal?*"

Damn it to hell. Tears streamed down her face as she walked into the empty living room. She couldn't even look at him. Who could do something so awful? He was as guilty as the bastard who killed his friends. Her shoulders shook, and she clamped her hands over her mouth to stay silent, thankful she hadn't told Jake Solomon about Randy's treasure.

Jake let himself out and slammed his sunglasses on against the bright afternoon light.

He'd hoped Taylor wouldn't reach this conclusion; but she was sharp, and he'd known in his heart it was only a matter of time. As his dad had known with him.

It still hurt. He knew how betrayed Taylor felt because he'd felt the same way. He'd gone out for a drink and wound up being dumped in a taxi by an unknown angel for the ride home at the end of the night. The following morning he learned his toilet's name was Clyde.

His dad pounded on the door just when he and Clyde were getting cozy. If Jake hadn't let him in the doorman would have. While Jake showered, his dad whipped up some godawful concoction with the kick-ass flavor of bug spray and fish scales. Whatever was in it worked. Half an hour later, his stomach no longer rolled, his head no longer throbbed, and his sluggishness had vanished. His dad sat him down and told him the rest of the story.

Telling him the Compass Points resources weren't used and waiting to tell him why gave Jake time to blow off steam and come to grips with the reality. When his dad filled him in on the reasons behind his decision, he was able to accept them. He hadn't agreed, but he understood. If he'd been in his dad's position, he would likely have reached the same outcome.

He didn't think Taylor would end up in a ditch, but she might eat a quart of chocolate ice cream all by herself. He would lurk in the shadows and keep the bogeyman away. After she had time to calm down, he'd talk to her. Tell her the rest of the story, like his dad had done with him.

And sink into the earth for being the biggest, vilest son of a bitch in the world.

"A double scoop of chocolate fudge on a chocolate cone."

Taylor paid and savored the first lick. How had she been so damn stupid? She'd kicked herself in the butt all the way to town. What a fool. Thinking Jake Solomon was like Mark was the worst.

She finished her ice cream cone in no time flat. At Mike's Golf Shop, she purchased a Rock Harbor golf towel for her executive officer. She hoped Dan was in Bravo getting ready for tonight. She headed in that direction, but spotted him coming out of Echoes with two large gold bags dangling from each hand. "You're not supposed to shop in your own place."

"Hey, Taylor." He raised the bags a few inches. "I'm renting pieces to a wedding reception at the country club. This is the last of the third load. The florist is *the* bitch from hell. I told her I'd be happy to help her, but she huffed all in my ear as if she's the Rose Queen or something and I'm the Black Thumb Ogre. She can just wait two extra minutes."

"I'll let you arrange flowers at my wedding. If I ever get married. How's that?"

"Perfect."

"Don't hold your breath."

He dropped the bags and hugged her. "You are entirely too hard on yourself, Taylor. You just need someone strong enough to let you shine. Which brings me to why I'm so glad to see you here. I meant to call you earlier, but I haven't had one frigging minute of peace and quiet all day."

"What's up?"

"A.J. and I want you to come over for drinks and munchies tomorrow evening. He wants to give you the painting."

"Should I dress up?"

"You can wear Happy if you want." Dan waved at her shirt. "Zia will be there, too. She's not thrilled about not getting a say in which painting we chose, so if she's a little Oscar-y that's why. Her pout isn't about you."

"Sounds like fun."

He wrote the address and directions on the back of his card and handed it to her. "See you at seven. Now I need to run. Half the town will be at this wedding. Will's cousin is the bride, so it'll be a big blowout. Then I have to hustle back to the gallery for another night of fun."

Will would be out for the night? She waved goodbye to Dan and started planning as soon as she took the first step to her car. The timing couldn't be more perfect. Will would be at the wedding and reception. She would be retrieving Randy Rankin's buried treasure.

And Jake Solomon could take a good long hike to hell.

CHAPTER 24

Taylor took a roundabout route to Will's before her treasure hunt. In the thickening twilight, she wasn't sure if anyone followed her, so several blocks from his house, she circled yet another block and cruised a parking lot.

She turned onto Amberjack and parked on the street between the house for sale and its next-door neighbor. Near the corner, a couple of teenagers shot hoops in a driveway. She decided to give them a few minutes to see if the mosquitoes would drive them inside.

While she waited, she stuffed toilet paper in the fingers of the left glove, wrapped toilet paper and gauze around her right hand over the bandages she'd taped in place, and pulled on latex gloves. Next came the thick yellow rubber gloves. This had to work.

The kids down the way showed no sign of going inside, but they appeared totally engrossed in one-upping each other. With a smidgen of good luck, they wouldn't notice her.

She turned off the interior light, opened the door, and retrieved her tote. Chirping crickets were the only alarm she heard in the thick air as she walked to Will's backyard. Good thing, too. Her story of returning his folding shovel wouldn't have held up in a strong breeze.

With a determined tug, she strapped on a head lamp and focused the LED light on Randy's last letter to see the coordinates.

As if you don't know them by heart, Taylor. Check and double check. A fraction of a degree off here in Will's backyard wouldn't make much difference, but Taylor had learned to navigate oceans before GPS systems were the norm. A fraction of a degree off could mean the land lights ahead were in Miami instead of Charleston. Or islands popping up where they weren't supposed to be.

She keyed in the coordinates and stepped this way and that, careful to keep the GPS out of the direct path of her head lamp. With each footfall she sank into lush St. Augustine. The tough grass tickled her ankles. One more step to the right. The GPS beeped and a red *X* marked the spot—inches from the edge of a freeform bed outlined in black monkey grass. She punched the button and dropped the GPS into her large shoulder tote.

Finding the general coordinates on Google Maps had been easy, but standing on them made her lightheaded. She was about to dig a hole. Trespassing and destruction of property. *Good, Taylor. Get your ass in a crack and lose your Coast Guard bennies to boot.* What the hell had Randy been thinking?

Taylor wiped the sweat from her forehead with the tail of her shirt before the mosquito repellant rolled into her eyes. A mockingbird started singing. Randy had told her the only mockingbirds that sang at night were young males that hadn't yet found a mate. *Good luck, buddy.*

She set her tote on the ground and removed a folding shovel followed by a large trash bag. She unfolded the bag on the ground about two feet from her then tugged on a pair of thick leather work gloves.

"Okay, Randy. Let's get this grass up and start digging."

With the shovel, she scored a patch of sod about eighteen inches square and scooped it out, turning it upside down next to the trash bag. The square of sod would be noticeable enough without a telltale patch of dirt in the lawn.

She licked her lips and tasted the salt in the air, almost like standing on the deck of the *Susquehanna*. After taking a deep breath, she plunged the shovel into the ground. Sandy soil greeted her beneath the sod layer, and she dumped the first shovelful on the trash bag. After five shovels she stopped. The usual evening breeze blew off the bay, but the high humidity zapped her energy. She wiped her face with her shirttail.

The skin surrounding the cut on her palm burned and stretched. Tomorrow she'd probably have blisters, but she could live with them.

After five more shovels, she stopped again. The hole was barely a foot deep, and as she dug, grains of sand scurried down the sides. She got half a shovelful with each jab. Her hands were holding out, so she was pleased. She went back for five more.

Half an hour later, the hole had grown to eighteen inches deep. The sand on the trash bag mounded to a peak. If she didn't find the box within the next thirty minutes, she needed to call it a night in order not to be up to her tush in Will's backyard when he returned. Her fingers were all right, but her hand throbbed. Thirty more minutes, or until her hand couldn't take any more.

One shovel load. Two. She wiped her forehead. The next time she drove the shovel in, the blade clinked.

"Yes!" She waved her right hand in a victory salute and danced in place, hoping the clink hadn't announced a water or sewer pipe.

She dropped to her knees and cleared away loose sand with her hands. Her head lamp illuminated the flat gray top of an ammo box with a collapsible handle in the center. Now she knew what she had. A military ammunition box was twelve inches in length, six inches across, and seven inches deep.

From the street a dog growled. A bored voice replied, "Come on, Thor. You can't go back there."

Crap. Don't move. Don't think. Don't panic. Her heartbeat took off like a runaway train.

Thor barked.

"I said *no*."

Taylor's nose itched, but she didn't move to rub it. Thor's bark was deep; he was large. She closed her eyes. *Don't move. Don't think. Don't panic.*

Thor whined.

"Leave it."

She moved enough to rub her forearm against the side of her nose and take a breath.

"Good boy. Wanna run? Come on. Let's go." The slap of shoes on the asphalt followed and grew fainter as she listened.

Thank God the dog owner had been authoritative instead of curious. She took a deep breath and waited for her heart to stop pounding before she clawed at the sides of the box. A tiny bit of space appeared on each side, and she clawed some more, enough to wedge the tip of the shovel under the bottom of the box. She used the shovel as a lever. With the box tilted upward, she knelt again and grabbed the handle, pushing the box from side to side to loosen it.

"Get out of there, you bastard." The words, whispered through her teeth, didn't budge the ammo can.

Taylor pulled again, landing on her ass when the box came free. "All right!"

Her hand throbbed, but the pain didn't stop her. She grabbed the shovel and loaded sand into the hole. Every so often she stepped in and tamped it down before continuing. Even with the sand back in the hole, the space slumped several inches lower than the surrounding area—a predicament she'd anticipated. She drew a small bag of potting soil from her tote, emptied it into the hole, and tamped it down. Perfect.

She retrieved the sod, laid it in place, and tamped it down as she'd done with the sand and potting soil. If Will returned this instant, she'd scoop everything into her tote, grab the ammo can, and run like hell. But she still had work to do.

A cat howled nearby, and she jumped. Christ, it was Animal Planet around here. She wouldn't need cardio for a week. After gulping some fresh air, she shook the trash bag and stuffed it into her tote along with the leather gloves.

From a small pocket on the side, she took out some folded paper towels. In the center lay another item purchased at the golf shop—a divot tool—grabbed from a rack at the register. Mark had been a golfer. Divots were chunks of sod and earth golfers often gouged out when making long driving shots. The tool wove the edges of sod from the fairway and the divot together.

Sitting on the ground, Taylor pushed and tugged the sod from both sides all the way around the square. The work was more difficult than she remembered, but this tough St. Augustine wasn't fairway grass. The head lamp showcased an imperfect outcome. After spending more minutes on a corner that didn't please her, she nodded approval. Will would have to crawl over his lawn on hands and knees to spot where the hole had been. As long as the square she scooped out didn't die. If he did find it, he wouldn't know what had transpired.

She pulled a liter bottle of water from her tote and took a long swig. Sweat soaked her clothes and tickled her back, but she was almost finished. She watered the edges of the square of sod first, then the center. And packed her tote. The ammo box went in first, followed by everything else, including the empty water bottle.

One more task and she'd be ready to go—she used the paper towels to blot any excess water that might sparkle in Will's headlights.

Now she could leave. She hefted the tote to her shoulder. At the corner of the house, she turned—the lawn appeared undisturbed. She hoped it held up as well under the hot Texas sun.

Jake followed Taylor to Knox's house, arriving at the end of the street in time to watch her walk to the backyard carrying a large tote. No fences divided the properties. He jogged to the street behind Knox's, thankful he'd changed out of his boots and jeans into shorts and sport shoes. No lights shone at the fifth and sixth houses. He snuggled between two tall bushes in the backyard and brought night vision binoculars to his eyes.

He was two houses away from Knox's property. Toward the back of the lot, large shrubs intermingled with a few trees. Several feet toward the house, a bed of flowers occupied a large space. Taylor stood near the flowers on the house side with a shovel in her hands.

Randy must have buried something here—possibly his belt—and told her where. It was all that made sense, but why would he have come here to bury anything? Why not on his own property where he would see if anyone came looking? Jake had the urge to go take the shovel from her and dig, but doing so would cause a scene. Not what she wanted, for sure, or she wouldn't be digging by the light of the moon when Knox wasn't around.

She scooped off a square of sod and went balls to the wall on the hole. Every once in a while she stopped for a minute or so before attacking it again. *Clink*. He heard the sound all the way across the lawns that separated them.

On her knees, Taylor focused on retrieving her goal, digging with her hands to loosen it. She pried it up with the shovel. There—an old ammo can. She held it at eye level then set it aside. Good. She needed to cover her tracks and leave while he stood guard.

Damn! She even brought extra dirt to fill in the hole. A divot tool! Wait until he told his dad. She could be a pro. If he didn't know her Coast Guard connections, he would've wondered.

He covered his mouth with his hand so no sound would escape and caught himself in time. His body shook with laughter while she watered the damn grass. He guessed so it wouldn't wilt. She even survived a barking dog and howling cat. That was his woman!

No, she wasn't his woman. She was mad as hell at him, and he didn't blame her. To make matters worse, she didn't know who he really was, and he couldn't tell her.

While she loaded her tote, he moved through the shrubbery to stay closer to her. Coming onto the street would present an excellent opportunity for an ambush, especially if the killer knew or suspected what the ammo can held. Jake was prepared, staying no more than twenty feet behind and in the shadows.

A big yellow tabby lay in the center of the street. As Taylor drew closer, the tip of his tail nodded to her in greeting. She walked past the cat and leaned her tote against the car.

Jake moved up to the massive trunk of an old tree with branches that spread over the front yard of the house next to Will's. Music played inside the house, and bits of the melody escaped into the night. As long as no one turned on a floodlight or opened the front blinds, he was fine.

Taylor was walking back toward the cat, talking to him. "Are you the one who howled?"

Come on, Taylor. Get a move on. It could be dangerous for you out here.

She crouched next to the cat. "I'll bet you are, and you're laughing over giving me a good scare."

Jake assessed the surroundings the same as if he were on a SEAL mission. Nothing raised an alarm. Nothing seemed added, missing, or disordered—just a quiet small-town street.

The only noise besides the music were Taylor's words to the cat as she scratched his ears. "You're an old softy."

One huge tree limb curved down and toward the street. He followed it, keeping the limb between himself and Taylor. Movement. At the corner. Jake froze. He inched his head far enough to see a dark SUV turning the corner. No headlights.

Jake dropped to a crouch and ducked under the limb to the other side. The SUV was gaining speed.

The cat bolted toward him as he ran toward Taylor. The rumble of a car engine grew louder. Taylor raised her head.

He was two steps away. Close enough to see the fear on her face at the sight of the SUV. Jake reached her as she turned away to dive in front of her car.

He wrapped one arm around Taylor and the other over her mouth to keep her from screaming. Lifting her off the ground, he spun them in front of her car just as the SUV roared past.

Taylor struggled against him, kicked his shins. He dropped his forehead against the top of her head and breathed in the scent of her shampoo. "Taylor. It's me. Jake. You're all right. Don't scream. Okay?"

She didn't move.

"Okay?"

She nodded, and he removed his hand from her mouth.

"Put me down."

Jake set her feet on the ground.

Her hands shook. "Where the hell did you come from?"

CHAPTER 25

"I'm doing my job. That's all." Only Jake knew he didn't have a choice. He'd died inside seeing the car speeding toward Taylor. Fear propelled him forward, faster than he should have been able to move.

Taylor's hands shook. The yellow gloves magnified the movement. "The headlights on that car were off."

"I know." He wanted to hold her. *Go for it, fool.* She would probably smack him.

"Did you see the driver?"

"No. I kept my eye on the ball. You were the ball."

"All I saw was a hat—like a fisherman's cap. I didn't think to look at the license plate. What kind of witness am I?"

"A living one." Thank God.

Taylor paced and kneaded her forehead with the heels of her palms. "I hate being jerked around by someone else."

She returned and stood in front of him. "Thank you for saving my life. I froze when I saw the car."

Jake shook his head. "You were up and in dive mode to reach the side of the street. You would have made it. I just got you there quicker. And kept you from breaking an arm or collarbone."

"I don't think so. At a minimum, I owe you a thanks for no broken bones." She slumped against him, her arms wrapping around his waist.

Jake held her close.

"I was terrified. And helpless. And angry. All at once. And at the same time I kept thinking I couldn't die that way."

He didn't want to turn loose of her, but they couldn't continue standing here in the street. The driver might return at any moment, and they might not be so fortunate next time.

He stepped back and placed his hands on Taylor's shoulders. "We need to move. Get in, open the trunk. I'll put your tote inside. Then drive me to my car. I'll follow you to your hotel."

Taylor nodded and unlocked her door.

Jake had her drive a random pattern around the surrounding blocks, but neither of them saw a lurking dark SUV. The adrenaline was leaving. Along with it, the strong emotions he'd experienced earlier.

A few minutes later, Taylor stopped next to his car. "I'm not going straight to the hotel."

"We're fine. No one will follow you. Except me."

She shook her head. "No. I have a bit of business down by the water. It won't take long." She pointed ahead.

"I'll be right behind you. Take your time."

Taylor barely made it to the pier where Randy's body had been found before her shoulders shook with huge sobs. Fear, sorrow. She'd never been so close to major injury or death. Through her tears, she tracked Jake's headlights. He pulled off behind her, leaving enough room he could pull out without her car moving. If necessary.

With the car in park, she pulled off both pairs of gloves and the smushed, sweat-wet gauze and toilet paper that had been around her hand. She'd finally stopped shaking. Another bottle of water would've been nice.

She faced the bay. "I've found your cache, Uncle Randy. I wish you had shared your problems, but I understand you tried to protect me. Thing is, I might have been able to protect you."

She was silent for a minute or two, just remembering all the good times.

Finally she sighed and put her hands on the steering wheel. "Now that I have your treasure, I hope I know what the hell to do with it."

A few minutes after leaving the pier, Jake pulled into the lot behind Taylor, parked next to her, and waited at the back of her car.

"I'm glad you followed me here. You know there are a lot of dark-colored cars in this town?" She opened her trunk and removed her tote.

Jake slipped the tote from her fingers before she could protest and closed the lid. "It was a small SUV. So that only rules out about half of the vehicles we saw heading here."

"You don't have to come in."

"Yes, I do."

"Whatever. But thanks for carrying my tote."

The desk clerk was busy with a late check-in. They reached the elevator, and Jake let Taylor push the button for her floor. He followed her to her door.

Her right hand gripped her room key card. She slipped it in the slot, removed it, and pushed open her door. "I appreciate your being my bodyguard."

"Wait here. Let me check your room." He went in, set the tote next to the television, and made the usual rounds while she watched. It wasn't necessary, because none of the cameras had been tripped, but it's what he would have done without cameras in place.

When he came out of the bathroom, Taylor stood on the other side of the small table and chairs, giving him plenty of room to open the door and leave without coming close to her. Her eyes were wide with fear, and he knew at least some of that fear was because of him.

Jake slid the table in front of the door. The chairs followed.

"What the hell are you doing?"

"Making sure you don't try to run away."

"Why would I do that?"

"Because you're afraid."

"I am not scared." Her voice wavered. She frowned and tucked her chin. "Especially not of you."

He grinned and raised an eyebrow, a trick of his dad's he'd worked for months to master. "You should be."

"After all you've told me, yes I should."

"I'm trained to kill. But I would never hurt you, Taylor. Not ever. You have my word."

Taylor's gaze flicked on and off of his, and she gave a curt nod. He walked around the room turning on lights: the bedside lamps, the vanity area, the bathroom, never taking his eyes off Taylor.

He returned to her and moved the tote to the table. "Okay. You do the honors."

She turned on him, standing tall and squaring her shoulders, every inch a Coast Guard officer. Except for her haunted eyes. "How did you follow me?" Her accusing tone said she meant business.

"I learned vehicle surveillance a long time ago. You did a good job on checking for a tail."

"At first I could see cars and colors. I was very careful, and I would have sworn no one followed me."

"You were careful. The double-back through the parking lot was a smart move. I have more training. That's all." *And your car has a tracking device.*

"How did you do it? You're one person, not a team. What should I watch for?"

"Practice. You didn't make any wrong moves. I'm more qualified in security is all, but I couldn't command a cutter."

"No, you couldn't."

Her shoulders relaxed a little, and she no longer looked like a wounded animal.

"You could've helped me dig. And saved my hand." She held it out, palm up.

"Aw, Christ." He winced. The swollen pink area around the cut hurt to look at. "Come in here."

He grabbed her wrist and pulled her to the lavatory. "Hold your hand under cold running water while I fix a compress."

She yanked her wrist away. "I can take care of myself."

"Jesus H. Let somebody help you for a change."

A few cooperative minutes later they stood at the table, Taylor's hand wrapped in two cold wet washcloths held in place by a dry hand towel. Three folded towels waited on the table for her to prop her hand on after she sat.

He pulled the ammo can from her tote. "For the record, I didn't know about this. Or that you were headed to dig it up. Can you open this thing one-handed?"

"If you'll hold the box, I'll open it."

CHAPTER 26

The ammo can opened by a flat latch on the front that lifted up and out. Taylor pulled the top of the box open. On top of the contents, lay the rest of Randy's belt proudly proclaiming the words *Solomon's Compass*.

The buckle clanked against the metal box as she brought the belt to her cheek. "I so wish I wasn't doing this." The familiar scent increased the longing for her uncle.

All she wanted was for Randy to walk through the door and give her a big bear hug. Jake draped his arm around her shoulders, letting her lean against him. She hated herself. She didn't want to lean on anyone, especially not on Jake Solomon, the bastard. He did save her life, even if he hadn't saved Randy's. As soon as she convinced herself not to bawl like a baby, she stepped away.

"I want—" She cleared her throat and blinked hard. "I want to remember the exact order of contents in the ammo can. It might be important. There's a notebook and pencil in the nightstand drawer over against the wall. Will you keep a list?"

"Good idea." He reached the nightstand in only a few steps. Her pulse quickened watching his body move. She hated that he still turned her on, so she sank into the chair, propping her hand on the towels. Jake pulled his chair next to hers and flipped to a blank page without stopping at the others. Not that it mattered. Her notes all pertained to the *Susquehanna*. On the top line he wrote *Randy's SC belt w/empty buckle* in a firm, quick hand.

Taylor! Stop thinking about Jake. She huffed.

"What's the matter? Is it your hand?"

Don't think about his damn instant concern either. "Nothing. This is more emotional than I thought."

"Take your time. How did you know about the ammo can?"

"Randy sent me a letter, mailed on the day he died. Or was killed. Let's go on. I'm good."

Jake ran his fingers over the face of the buckle. "Not even a tiny scratch. It's smoother than mine. Look how carefully he removed the lapis lazuli. He moved the mounting prongs just enough to remove the stone."

"I had to look hard to tell they'd been moved. Such care is directly opposite from the panic and paranoia in the rest of his life." She sighed and rested her head in her good hand. How would she ever figure this out? Randy had more faith in her than she did. She'd try not to let him down.

"What's next?" Jake's voice was soft.

She placed the belt on the table and removed an unsealed envelope, the kind that held a greeting card. She pulled out a small stack of old square photos, their colors no longer sharp. "Randy's photos! I knew they would be with his belt. He did bury his treasures."

"Good call."

She held out the thin stack. "I don't remember what any of you looked like in these photos. Except for Randy. There's a separate photo of each Compass Point. On the backs are each person's name and his compass position. All in print so I could read them before I learned cursive." She turned Randy's snapshot over—*Randall Rankin/Rose*—and handed it to Jake.

The next photo showed a big man with broad shoulders and blond hair.

Jake tapped it with his thumb. "Ham Bone."

"I'd forgotten how broad his shoulders were. No wonder he was lethal with the pipe." She turned it over. *Hamblen "Ham Bone" Norberg/North.* She passed it over.

Red hair topped the next man's round face and blue eyes. Looking at him made her smile. She imagined he'd had a great sense of humor, and she regretted not knowing him. *Kyle Easley/ East.*

"Easley never forgot anything. And he was a storyteller. He became a history professor." Jake took the photo she held out.

"Was Kyle Easley the one whose girlfriend became a movie star while he was gone?"

Jake laughed "Is that what Randy told you?"

"Maybe I remember wrong. Whoever it was, Randy said he didn't remember her name."

"No, you have the right Compass Point. She became a movie star all right, but adult movies. Porn."

"Ah. No wonder he wouldn't tell me her name."

The next man appeared nondescript, average height and weight, his face waiting for an artist to add character. Brownish hair and eyes—but with the old technology, she couldn't tell the color for sure. *Ed Wharton/West.*

"I always thought he looked like a pastor. I don't know why."

"Ed was pretty wild. He would have had a lot of stories to build sermons around. After he got out of the Coast Guard, he joined the fire department. Earned a medal for saving a few lives in some big fire." Jake's voice was a monotone. Just-the-facts, no nonsense.

A good man's life ended by a madman. She wanted to rant and scream at the injustice.

The last photo was Jake, without a doubt, except younger and with black hair. *Jake Solomon/South.* Like the others, he wore dungarees and a light blue work shirt.

The photos of these men were here in Randy's treasure box. But Randy's real treasure had been the Compass Points themselves. The men who made up Solomon's Compass. Now he had joined all of them—except one.

"So young. And now they're all gone. What a waste." He still spoke with the same colorless voice as he slipped the photos back into the envelope.

"You're here."

He added *Envelope w/photos of Compass Points* to the list. "Hmph. Debatable."

"Add the order the photos were in."

He just looked at her.

"Damn it. Give me the notebook. I'll keep my own list."

"Settle down. I was thinking how thorough you are. Not too many people are these days."

"The Coast Guard trained me as well as you." One minute she wanted to kill him, the next push him onto the king-size bed not two feet from where she sat. The bed she was struggling to ignore. She sat back in the chair. Her emotions were already awash in a stormy sea, and looking at Randy's treasures from the ammo can made the rolls she took faster and steeper.

But she needed to carry on with his wishes.

"Everyone is listed. In order. Next?"

She pulled out a rolled shirt.

Jake pushed the ammo can back. "Unroll it on the table in case something's inside."

Nothing fell out. She pushed at the shirt with her hand. "What the hell? Why would he put in an old fishing shirt?"

Jake turned it over. The logo of a local tournament filled the flap on the back. The date was five years earlier. He let the shirt drop to the table and added the information to the list.

She smoothed the fabric and refolded one side.

"Wait." He finished writing.

He stuck his fingers in the pocket, felt every seam, every hem.

"What are you looking for?"

"Whatever I find."

Infuriating.

His fingers continued the inspection. Both plackets, each button. The collar. He stayed with the collar the longest.

"Anything?"

"It has to be the shirt. He showed us he had the belt and the pictures of the Compass Points. Next, a ragged fishing shirt.

That tells us the shirt has to do with the deaths." He scratched his head.

"Maybe we just thought he was careful, and this box is as scattered as the rest of his life had become. Milestones in his life, happy memories."

The palm of Jake's hand came down hard on the table. "No. I don't believe that. I *won't* believe it. *Scattered* doesn't explain why he made the watch."

Taylor clenched her jaw. "Damn. It's frustrating, and it makes me crazy. I hate this."

"Take a minute. It's hard. He was your uncle, and you loved him."

"I know." She picked at the towel around her palm. "My hand's freezing. I need to take this off."

"Let me." Jake untied the outer towel and removed the washcloths. "Much better. The angry color is gone. Do you have some antibiotic cream?"

She took the towels to the bathroom and came back with a tube of ointment. "Monday I'll call the Chamber of Commerce and find out who to contact about the fishing tournament. Maybe Randy won."

Jake stared into space, tapping the eraser end of the pencil against the table. She finished applying the antibiotic and re-capped the tube. "I'll be good as new tomorrow."

"Huh? Sorry. I was thinking about something else."

As if that hadn't been evident. She held out her hand, and Jake flexed her fingers. "Good. Are you ready to look at the next item?"

"Not much is left. The shirt took up most of the space." She pulled out an old metal peanut can. "The shirt kept this from banging against the sides. Put that on the list, too."

"Yes, ma'am."

She opened the lid. "Bubble wrap. Oh."

"What?"

"Belt buckles. Like yours and Randy's."

"Let's see." He spread them out.

Three. The empty lapis mountings were at the top and sides—north, east, and west.

"Someone else removed these stones. Look at your uncle's belt."

"I don't need to. These buckles aren't just scratched, they're gouged. And the prongs have been pried wide. The ones on Ham's buckle are flat against the surface, and the others are almost as bad."

Jake rubbed his cheek. "One person removed all the stones except for Randy's. I wonder how Randy came into possession of them?" He sat still for a while staring into the distance.

She rewrapped the buckles in the bubble wrap, returned them to the can, and closed the lid. By the time she finished, Jake was adding it to the list.

She pulled out a business-size envelope. "This is the last thing."

"Open it."

Inside was a letter, several pages long, in Randy's normal handwriting before he fell victim to the stress near the end of his life. Though she wanted to devour it, her hands shook, and the pages trembled like leaves in a breeze.

CHAPTER 27

Taylor let the pages drop to the table. "I'm exhausted. Can we wait before I read this? I need a minute."

Jake stood and kneaded her shoulders. "This has been a trying day for you. The reason I didn't help you dig was that I feared you might beat me with the shovel."

She smiled to herself. "Smart man." His hands worked magic on her muscles.

"You were smart to choose a night when neither Knox nor his neighbors appeared to be home."

She tensed.

"What?" His thumbs made tight circles where the new knots had formed.

"How did you know that was Will's house? Who, by the way, is at his cousin's wedding."

"Do you really need to ask? It's my job."

"Mmm. Rub my neck." His hands moved. Fingers on her neck, palms on her shoulders. She rotated her head. This was heaven. She stopped. This was Jake. She sat up straight.

"What now?"

"Get your hands off me."

He did as she asked.

She stared at her hand. The cold compress had reduced the swelling and the redness was gone. She stretched and flexed it with no problem. The workout had been good for her.

Jake returned to his chair. "Do you want to talk about what's really bothering you?"

Hell no. I might strangle you with my bare hands. "Nothing is bothering me. I'm tired."

"Just asking."

"Actually, I do want to know something. When you were telling me about your clandestine work . . . I've been thinking about events that happened back then. My master's is in International Affairs."

"I know. George Washington University."

She shook her head. "Of course you do. Were you involved in Nixon's trip to China?"

He raised that damn eyebrow. "I've been to China."

"You're impossible. And I suppose you've visited Chile? Never mind Pinochet's coup took place during that time."

"As a matter of fact, I've skied in Chile. Like your mother."

"For God's sake, leave her out of this. I get enough of her without you bringing her up."

He shook his head. "Listen, Taylor, you know about nondisclosure agreements. I can't give you details. I trained as a sniper. I used the skill in my job. More than once. I created accidents and natural deaths. *In. My. Job.* I also saved people, prevented people from being killed by someone like me. I rescued people from both political and natural disasters. I located and re-kidnapped abducted children. Twice I delivered a baby. Those babies were the highest highs I've ever experienced. I won't provide details about those babies or anything else to anyone. Not even you."

For the first time since he began to speak she looked at him and found a depth of emotion in his eyes she'd never seen before. Gone was his general expression of amusement and mischief. He cared.

"You did all that, yet you let Randy die because you wouldn't use your resources to save him. I don't understand you."

"Follow the money."

"Money has nothing to do with it."

"You're wrong. Money has everything to do with it. People can be bought."

"Not everyone. You vet those who work for you."

"I do. Basically I trust each and every one of them. But everyone has a price. Even you."

"No."

"It's a matter of finding the price. Our government bought me for the price of keeping my friend out of prison. My life and education were secondary. None of us knows what our price is until it's offered."

His words stung. What if something happened to her mother? If she were caught up in a terror kidnapping? As much as they fought, Taylor would do anything to obtain her mother's freedom, including breaking laws.

"The same with those who work for me. All it would take is for the Compass Points killer to find one of them and discover his weakness. Or hers. It might be money. It might be family. It might be something else. Had I asked others to help, I would have knowingly placed them and their families at risk. We do so for clients every day, but I won't ask for personal benefit."

"Their help wouldn't have been for you. It would have been for your friends. That's a cop-out."

"You're wrong. I wasn't the first Compass Point killed. That meant the killer wanted me to agonize over their deaths. A child of one of the Compass Points has also died. It's inconclusive if the death was a homicide. The case remains open. Though it was beyond my control and not my desire, our belts say *Solomon's Compass*. My name, my responsibility."

"You could have used a team. Two teams. Three. You could have found the killer and stopped him."

"The man I believe to be responsible—Fallon—is a chameleon. I searched for him under rocks. I baited traps. He's the best in the business, and he has strong motivation."

"Still . . ."

"The mother of his unborn child got in the way on one of my operations. The outcome was fatal. He swore he would even the score. He tried once before. This is his style. It doesn't get any more personal."

"These men were your friends. That's personal, too."

"Taylor, I knew Fallon. I know what he's capable of. I also know I'm smarter. I didn't realize he was more cunning. He may kill more Compass Point family members before he comes for me. I shared that insight with Randy, along with some physical details, which is why he asked me to protect you."

"I think it's time you shared those physical details with me."

Jake got up and moved around. "You're right. And I should have shared them with you earlier. Like I said, the man is a master at changing his appearance and identification. He has a burn scar on his left arm that runs from his left elbow up to his lower left jaw. With the advances in medicine, it's possible the scar no longer exists. He also wears a black stainless bracelet. It's a cuff style, eighteen millimeters in width. This item is personal to him. He never removes it. Those are the only details I have about him that are permanent."

"I haven't noticed either of those. But I'll stay alert."

"Looking back, I might have made the wrong decision about not hiring CPI to identify and locate the killer. But I made the best decision I could make at the time. I stand by it. At least my employees and their families are not at extraordinary risk. The killing will stop with me."

His eyes pleaded with her to understand. She studied her hands. If she asked him to leave, he would go. He would keep watch over her, but he would go. She didn't want him to go. Jake understood her, and she understood him.

She reached for the letter Randy left and unfolded the dampish sheets of paper. "I know you wish the results were different. So do I. But I also know the difficulty of making a command decision. I should have let you explain before. At times it's necessary to put good lives at risk."

He struggled to smile. "You still don't agree."

She got up and walked back and forth. "Not true. I see your point. You traded Randy's life for those of the employees you would've pulled in to help you find the killer. Perhaps they would have located him before he killed Randy. Perhaps not. You went with the less risky choice. As we're taught. And you did warn Randy. I don't know if I could have made that decision—played God and balanced life against life—when all the lives were friends or family."

"A lot of things in this world are hard to come to grips with. You're a straight-arrow Coast Guard officer. Faced with the same choices, you would make the same decision. The important choices are never easy."

Boy, did he ever have that one right. She returned to the chair. "I'm glad you told me all this. I think you would have rather not shared, but I'm glad you trusted me enough. I'm ready to read Randy's letter now. How about you?"

He kept staring at the smoke detector. After a second or two, he glanced her way. "Go for it."

"It's dated the week before he died." She swallowed a lump in her throat.

"Hi Taylor—

"I hoped you'd never be reading this. Since you are, I guess the worst has happened, and I'm trying to trade St. Peter a couple of used boat motors for a ticket inside the Pearly Gates."

Jake bolted upright. "That doesn't sound like a man who's a delusional mess."

She nodded. He looked again at the smoke detector. What was going on?

"Do you remember old Solomon, the big yellow cat I had when you came to visit me as a little girl? I named him after a Coastie I served with over in Nam—Jake Solomon."

She glanced at Jake as a big smile spread across his face.

"Jake was one of the Compass Points we always talked about. I showed you their photos. Jake, Kyle, Ed, Ham, and me."

The letter went on several pages while Randy related a condensed version of the story Jake told her. Jake interrupted once to clarify a point before Randy moved on to things new to her.

"After Jake told me he and I were the only ones left, I thought if I acted as if I was going crazy—what do us old folks get? Alzheimer's, yeah—whoever was after me would leave me alone. So I pretended I couldn't remember shit. I spent a whole weekend trashing the shop. As I bought new things, I loaded them in the house and left it a mess. Sorry you found the place that way."

She put the letter down to keep from tearing up. "Damn it!"

Jake reached for her and held her close. Putting down the letter didn't work. Both her cheeks and Jake's were wet, and she didn't know if the tears were all hers.

She allowed herself the luxury. All the sorrow and loss she'd been unable to express when she learned of Uncle Randy's death poured out, and the emptiness in her heart spilled over into her whole being except for where her body touched Jake's. That part burned white hot. Jake's scent, his muscles, each breath he took intruded on her grief and replaced the emptiness with longing.

She raised her head. "I need some tissues."

Jake got up without a word and brought her several from the vanity dispenser.

She used them all to blow her nose and wipe her eyes. "I've got to find some grit and hold it together."

"You're doing fine." He ran his fingers through her hair. "Randy would be proud of you."

She picked up the letter again.

"I couldn't tell if anyone had taken an interest in me or not. Everything seemed normal, yet my gut told me different. So I started acting real paranoid around these people I've known for years. Hell, some I've known all my life. I was a real ass. Asked them straight out crazy questions. Were they trying to kill me? Did they hire a hit man? Did they know so-and-so was trying to kill me? Never asked the same question twice to any of them, but over the months, I asked everybody all the questions I knew to ask. I asked new people in town, too. Even the cops and the sheriff. And I watched when they answered."

She smiled. "I can see him doing this."

Jake nodded.

"*I keep asking, but now most people avoid me. Dan Blair comes around—thinks he can buy me out on the cheap and I won't notice or care. And Will across the street—I don't suspect him. He's good people. That's one of the reasons I'm burying this in his backyard. He was messed up with drugs a while back, but since he got clean, he gardens when he's feeling stress. If he needs to work off energy, he moves whole beds around in his yard. Damndest thing I ever saw. His yard's a sight to behold.*

"*I'm going to plant this box under a rose bush, but no telling what you found when you dug it up. If for some reason Will finds it first, I trust him almost as much as I trust you and Jake Solomon. Almost.*

"*Ground's sandy here, though, so the digging isn't too hard. I'll send you a letter with instructions as soon as I have coordinates. Oh, hell. I guess you got it, since you're reading this.*"

"Crap."

Jake took her hand in both of his while she blinked away more tears. She wouldn't cry again.

She cocked her head. "Do you think Randy's killer became friendly enough with him here to realize how close he and Will were? If so, the location of Randy's murder could have been chosen to cast suspicion on Will."

Jake shrugged. "Or perhaps the killer didn't like Will. Or planned to buy him out if he developed legal problems. Or the nearness could be coincidence."

She sighed. "Too many questions."

"*The buckles came in the mail last week with no return address, postmarked from Denver. None of the Compass Points lived in Denver. I don't know anyone there. I left a message for Solomon to call me, but I haven't heard from him. That was last week, the day I received them.*"

"Why didn't you talk to him?"

"I was unreachable. That's all you need to know. It was business."

"Bullshit. You knew if he left a message for you it was urgent."

"Unreachable, Taylor. On a job in a country where I was not welcome and did not enter legally. And working in an area with no electricity or cell towers. Unreachable. Randy knew the situation. He left a message; I called as soon as I could."

She had no argument to present to his words. It no longer mattered for Randy that no one was available for him when he needed them. Yet he seemed fine with fighting his battle alone. Anything she said would be futile, so she continued reading.

"The buckles must have come from the killer, and he must have the belts, too. Maybe the belts and buckles are why he's killing us. That doesn't make any sense to me, but I cut my belt apart and removed the stone in case he wants it intact. I put what was left in here.

"Lapis lazuli is a pretty stone, but it's not pricey. I've looked for people wearing it, but I haven't seen any. In the shop, three tables from the back on the left hand side, look under an old sail. You'll find some blue and white mugs. A piece of my belt and the stone are in there. You can keep them close to you."

"The watch." Tears rolled out before she could stop them. Jake wiped them away as she blinked. "I'm okay now."

"This morning I found the shirt hanging on the front doorknob. I don't know if it's a threat, a warning, or if somebody just forgot it. I do know I feel a need to get this in the ground without waiting any longer."

"I wonder how the old fox was able to bury the box without his killer knowing?" Jake massaged his neck. "He may have suspected someone and kept tabs on him."

"But not been sure enough to leave a name here. Or any hint that I see." Taylor riffled back through the pages.

"Finish reading. Think about it overnight and let your subconscious work on it."

"That's about all, Taylor. If you're reading this and the police haven't discovered who killed me, you need to talk to Jake Solomon. If he's alive. He's the one person who understands what's going on. He's also the one person you can trust absolutely with anything on this earth. And he's the person the killer will target next. Here's his phone number and address."

"That's the main number at Compass Points. It's on the card I gave you." Jake stared straight ahead.

He seemed to be operating on autopilot, having as difficult time as she was dealing with Randy's letter.

"Tell Jake I said to steer a straight course and keep his eyes on the horizon. And when he finds the motherfucker who killed me, not to bother with restraint.

"All my love always,

Uncle Randy"

Taylor held the last page to her chest. "My love back."

A muscle in Jake's jaw worked. "No restraint, buddy. None at all."

CHAPTER 28

Taylor stood up to return the pages to the envelope and put everything back into the ammo can. Jake stared at the door, looking at a past she couldn't see. It was her turn to offer comfort. She turned to him, bringing his head to her shoulder. His arms went around her waist, and she rocked him with the barest of motion.

Peace filled her. Randy had trusted this man—as it turned out, with his life. They gambled, and Randy lost. But he hadn't lost his trust. She ran her fingers through Jake's hair. Her own was coarse and curly. His, silky and straight. She closed her eyes, enjoying the pleasure he brought.

Maybe she was attracted to him because he was safe—by twenty years or so. Not that age was an issue. The man was a hunk. And that was before she looked deeper. She liked the part of him that had nothing to do with how he looked.

Or maybe her attraction was because his voice reminded her of Mark. Jake's was deeper but held the same accent. Beyond that, they weren't too much alike. Mark had been impatient with himself and everyone else. Jake's patience went on and on. Physically, they weren't alike at all. Mark had been shorter, swarthy, muscled. Jake's lean frame had plenty of muscles, but they weren't as obvious as Mark's had been.

She'd decided her attraction had nothing to do with either of those things. Quite simply, she liked Jake as a woman likes a man. She enjoyed him. She wanted to spend time with him. To be with him.

The scent of his shampoo filled her senses. Sandalwood. As she savored his scent, Jake shifted in the chair and pulled her to his lap.

His hands cupped her face. "You're the most beautiful woman I've ever known."

"I—"

"No backtalk." He bent his head and kissed her.

Heat exploded. No, nothing like Mark. All Jake. She kissed him back and reveled when his arms tightened. He tasted of the sea and of strength.

He shifted again, moving one hand to cup her breast. She tangled her hands in his hair to get closer, but he wasn't close enough.

"Hang on." She pushed off his lap and drew her Happy shirt over her head.

Jake pulled her down and unhooked her bra. His lips followed his fingers moving a strap down her arm and left a smoldering trail in their wake.

She shrugged her bra to the floor. Jake's shirt followed.

Without his shirt to cover them, his muscles were distinct. The man worked out. A long scar ran from beneath the right side of his collarbone to the area underneath his right arm.

She traced it. "What happened?"

"I lived. Despite the machete." He cupped her breasts. "I like these better."

Every light in the room was on, but she didn't care. A shiver ran up her spine.

"You're cold." He pulled the bedspread down. "Get in bed."

Her shiver had nothing to do with being cold. After pulling off her shoes and socks, she slid in, not needing him to ask her twice.

He turned off the light by her head, the overhead light, and the one on the other nightstand before toeing off his shoes and joining her. The lights in the vanity area and bathroom still shone and created twilight on this side of the room.

Jake slid down and took her left breast in his mouth. His warm breath burned as much as his tongue on her nipple. Flames erupted where his fingers slid over her skin.

She hadn't been with a man in a long time. And never on fire like this. Not even with Mark. Jake left her breast and returned his lips to her mouth. She ran her hands over his body. Hard, muscled flesh met her fingers. She reached for his belt, loosened it, and moved her hands to the button on his shorts.

His hand covered hers. "Not yet." He kissed her again.

Her mind spun. In her experience, no man had ever said *not yet*.

He moved his hand, splaying it over her stomach. "You're so tiny. I don't want to hurt you."

She almost didn't believe what she heard. "You're not going to hurt me. I want you."

Jake's gentle kiss rocked her world. He brought his head up and looked at her. "God help me, I want you, too."

The primal growl of his words pulsed deep inside her. She pushed his shoulder, tilting him to his back, and straddled his stomach. When she bent to kiss him, her nipples brushed his chest.

His quick intake of breath matched her own as an electric charge passed through her. She worked her way down his belly guided by her tongue. His skin, hot and smooth, covered taut muscles. He was as well-toned as men half his age. Better than most. Her fingers slipped under his waistband, freed the button—she needed skin-to-skin contact, top to bottom—and reached for the zipper.

Jake grabbed her wrist. "Wait."

Taylor traced the outline of his belly button with a fingernail.

He pulled out his wallet and produced a condom. "You want to do the honors?"

She opened the black foil and slipped the condom over Jake's very erect penis.

Jake put the wrapper on the nightstand with his wallet before turning her on her back and pulling the covers over them. He took over with her where she left off with him, unbuttoning her jeans and working them down and off her legs. His shorts brushed her feet when he removed them. The jingle of keys or change created a muted melody.

His hands slid under her ass, kneading, as he kissed his way up. His breath came hot and heavy on her thighs and her back arched.

"Oh, God, Jake. If you don't hurry up, I'm gonna die here."

"Savor the moment." His tongue moved to the top of her bikinis while his fingers stayed on her thighs.

She couldn't stay still.

Her panties slid past her knees, slipping over one foot, then the other.

Like he did when he removed her jeans, he kissed his way back up, this time moving on top of her. She moaned at finally getting the full body contact she craved. Her arms circled his neck, bringing his lips to hers.

His deep kiss brought her to a peak, and she pressed against him. Impossibly, his kiss went deeper. The world around her ceased to exist. All she knew was Jake. He surrounded her. She spread her legs wider, and he pushed inside.

Exquisite. She moved. Slowly. Never wanting this pleasure to end. Then Jake moved. And their motions became one.

Holy. God. In. Heaven.

Her mind spun out of control. Flashes of color. Vivid red. Neon green. Sparkling blue. She wanted them all. A noise.

What was that sound? Thunder. No . . . her. Or Jake. Or both.

Without warning, her world exploded. And kept exploding. She held onto Jake, not wanting even a whisper of air to come between them.

His body grew rigid. She could barely breathe, but that was all right. Her fingers curved and her nails sunk into his flesh.

"Taylor...Taylor." He drew out the last syllable as he came.

They clung to each other, two shipwrecked sailors hanging onto life on a sea of sweaty sheets. Their ragged breathing overpowered the constant swoosh of the air conditioner.

Jake gathered her to him and rolled to his side. She lay snuggled in the crook of his arm, protected. From here she could rule the world if need be. Her eyelashes fluttered against her cheeks.

And Mark Vitulli's face flashed in her mind, his cocky grin and smiling eyes. He gave her a thumbs-up. Her eyes flew open.

Jake rubbed her shoulder. "What?"

In that way Jake and Mark were alike—neither would let her slide. She might as well get it over with. "I need to tell you something."

"Shoot. As long as it's not in the family of *this-has-been-good-but.*"

She snuggled closer. "Not in that family."

Jake kissed her hair.

"One of my classmates at the Academy was Mark Vitulli. He majored in engineering. Very smart. Everyone liked him."

"You included."

"Myself included. Junior year, our friendship changed. We became more than friends. More than friends with benefits. We fell in love. Mark grew up in Brooklyn."

Jake raised up on his elbow and searched her face. "That's how you recognized my accent."

"Funny how the ear remembers the little things. Anyway, I told you Mark was smart—number three in our class. I wasn't in his league in the brains department."

"I like your brain just fine." He brought her hand to his lips and kissed her palm.

She pushed it against his face. "Good. It's the only one I have. Anyway, our class had one hundred sixty-eight cadets. My number was eighteen."

"Not a slouch, but you missed the top ten percent."

Since Jake understood the top ten part, the next part came easier. "Not long before graduation, Mark went windsurfing. A freak accident—a strong gust from an approaching storm—caught the sail and flipped him. The shallow water didn't give him enough room to maneuver. The fall broke his neck. By the time those on shore reached him, he was dead."

As she spoke, Jake's face went from interest to . . . nothing. He might have been staring at a wall by the time she finished.

He leaned back just a little too much. "I'm sorry you lost him."

"It was a hard time." Her mind churned trying to comprehend what had caused Jake's shift. "I'm not in love with him, or anything like that, but he'll always be a part of me."

"I understand." But instead of looking at her, he focused on picking at the sheet he'd pulled up almost to his armpits.

Surely he wasn't upset she'd once been in love with another man. Taylor lifted her head. When she finished what she had to say, she'd ask what had turned him off. "I wanted to tell you the story because I want you to know who I am. A couple of weeks later, the dean told me my official class ranking had moved up to number seventeen. I became one of the privileged few, but only because Mark died."

"A series of trade-offs." He glanced up and back down.

She had to get all of this out. "I busted my ass because I owed him. I still do. Mark lost everything. I could never forgive myself if I screwed up."

"Everybody screws up at one time or another. Even Mark." Jake turned to the side of the bed and reached to the foot for his clothes.

She touched his back. "What's the matter?"

"Nothing." He pulled on his briefs and stood to put on his shorts. "Go on. Finish."

She frowned at Jake's dressing. "Mark died. As a result, I received prime duty assignments. I got my pick of graduate schools.

High-profile cutters. Sure I screwed up early on. But I feel his weight on my shoulders every day. If I mess up, it means he died in vain and I've wasted the benefits I gained from his death. It means I'm not worthy of everything he lost. It means my actions dishonor the Coast Guard. And Mark. I couldn't handle that."

Jake sat on the edge of the bed. Another quarter inch, and his butt would've landed on the floor. *Nothing, my ass.*

His stiff back leaned forward while he put on his shoes. "Mark's death had nothing to do with the Coast Guard, Taylor. He put himself at risk by not knowing the depth of the water, or respecting an approaching storm. He should have checked on both before he got on his board. He knew the dangers."

"No."

"If you hadn't performed well, you wouldn't be looking at captain. You'd be counting the days until you could put in your retirement letter. So don't give me any crap about it being about Mark Vitulli."

His words stung. Taylor wasn't sure what to say. She stared at her hands. When she looked up, Jake was buttoning his shirt. She couldn't be angry at him. What he said was true, only she just now realized it.

"I never thought about it in that way. It did start out being about Mark. I kept telling myself it continued because of him. I tried to be perfect because then I didn't have to think about anything but Coast Guard. I still screw up, but I try to fix it when I do. If Mark had lived, I wouldn't be in the position I am. Nor would I be the same Taylor. Like you wouldn't be the same Jake without your experiences."

Jake stayed silent. A muscle in his jaw jumped around.

She pulled the sheet loose, wrapping it around her as she stood. Enough was enough. "What's the matter? Why are you pulling away?"

Instead of sparkling green eyes, deep green sad ones looked back at her. "I'm not the man you think I am, Taylor."

Her brows pulled together. "I don't understand."

"I know you don't."

"Are you going to tell me more?"

He marched to the bathroom. "I'm going to show you."

He wasn't gone for five seconds. When he came out, he carried a chair to the vanity, stood on it, and reached to the corner of the ceiling.

"What the hell is wrong with you?"

Anger rolled off him in waves as he passed her. His energy became a physical presence. He moved the table out from in front of the door and stood on the chair he'd sat in earlier. He removed two things from the damn smoke detector he'd stared at all night and came back to her.

"This is what's wrong. Hold out your hand." He dropped four tiny objects into it.

"What are these?"

"Cameras." His jaw clenched. "They're cameras, Taylor. I planted them Monday afternoon."

She stepped back and heat filled her face. "What? You planned this?" Her voice wavered, and her words came out through clenched teeth. "You wanted a record of fucking me?"

"No."

Taylor shook so hard one of the cameras fell to the carpet. "Do you keep score? You sick—"

"No! I put them in here to know if anyone broke in."

"You've been watching me all this time? And you didn't tell me? In the *bathroom*?"

"No, Taylor. The cameras don't work like—"

"Get out. Now." She couldn't think. This couldn't be happening.

Jake turned toward the door.

Something else occurred to her. "Wait."

He stopped.

"How could Randy trust someone like you?"

He didn't turn to her when he spoke. "He didn't. He trusted my father."

And then he was gone.

CHAPTER 29

Jake closed the door of Taylor's room and sank back against it. He was a heartless bastard. A soulless, arrogant, in-your-face piece of sun-dried cow dung who just sealed his fate in the inner circle of hell.

Taylor hadn't turned the deadbolt yet. He'd give her another minute.

What was he supposed to do? He hadn't meant to have sex with her, but he hadn't been able to resist the temptation. To resist her. He turned off the lights and used the sheets and comforter so she wouldn't see his body couldn't be that of a man in his sixties.

Then the sex turned into more. They were making love. Even then he never intended to reveal his identity. He rationalized he would tell her later. Maybe here in Rock Harbor, maybe after she returned to Charleston. After they got to know one another better, see if the attraction grew.

If she hadn't told him about Mark Vitulli, that's how it would've played out. But Vitulli was like all the other men in Taylor's life. Gone. Accidentally, for sure—the man hadn't intended to die. Either he'd been negligent or the arrogance of youth sold him on invincibility. The result had been the same.

And suddenly he had hated himself for not being up-front with her. For leading her down the wrong path. Taylor would never admit fragility, but he saw the vulnerability in her determination to find Randy's killer. Her story confirmed it. The important men in her life all left. Her dad included. Taylor never mentioned him. According to his dad, Randy said she didn't have one.

Jake couldn't put her through that kind of loss again.

The only way he knew to be less of a son of a bitch was to tell her the truth. Yet when he'd attempted that, everything fell apart. He foundered. For a man who always had a plan, the feeling was new. He didn't like it.

Taylor still hadn't set the deadbolt. He knocked, waited. No answer. He knocked harder.

"Who is it?"

"Me, Taylor. Lock the door."

The bolt snapped into place.

"Thank you. Good night."

He walked diagonally across the hall to his room and let himself inside. Tomorrow Taylor and Will would go sailing. He'd already scouted places with unobstructed views of the bay and easy access to a boat he could steal, if necessary. His job was to keep an eye on her. He would do his job. But he wouldn't tell his dad about this part of the night. Man to man his dad might understand, but Jake's mistake was one his dad would never have made.

Taylor finished putting the items back in the ammo can—*slamming* would be more accurate. Thinking about the personal effects Randy left behind did no more good now than when she and Jake had opened the can. Less, because now all she could think of was Jake.

What a fool. Well, never again. How could she have fallen for a man who would stoop to such depths? *Because he has dancing green eyes and a magic touch, that's how. You know better.* Maybe she was doomed to never have a permanent man in her life. The ones she loved never stayed.

Jake consumed her. Or whoever he was consumed her.

Had he told her the truth about the cameras? She thought so, but she couldn't be sure. It explained why he'd kept staring at the smoke detector.

Someone knocked on her door. She tucked the sheet in at her breast and it trailed behind her like a bridal train. *Get that thought out of your head, Taylor. A bridal train plays no role in your future.*

The knock came again.

"Who is it?" No one should be knocking on her door at this hour.

"Me, Taylor. Lock the door."

Son of a bitch. She snapped the bolt into place and flipped over the safety latch.

"Thank you. Good night."

She stepped back and tripped over the sheet, almost falling to the floor. Had he been waiting out there this whole time? To hear her lock the door against him?

Taylor ripped off the sheet and pulled her shirt back on. Happy. Ha. She should have worn Dopey today. She slumped into the chair Jake used to remove the camera from the smoke alarm. Nothing made sense. The man she made love with less than an hour before wasn't the man she thought he was. He was that man's son. But he still attracted her like nobody's business and broke through the barriers she'd erected to keep from becoming involved with anyone. He was the man who was here to protect her and, perhaps, help her find Randy's killer.

She jumped up, dug her jeans out from the foot of the bed, and pulled her phone from the pocket. She punched in 411 and waited for a real person.

"I need a number for Jacob Solomon in New York City."

"One moment. Manhattan or Brooklyn?"

"Brooklyn. Number only, please—don't connect me."

She needed some sleep in order to enjoy her boat ride. In the morning, she would call the Brooklyn number and see if it connected her to the Jake Solomon who knew Randy Rankin. If it did, she'd find out once and for all what was going on.

CHAPTER 30

Taylor zipped the PFD Will had handed her. "What can I do?"

"Nothing. I invited you, remember? Besides, you could re-injure your hand. If a summer squall stirs up, I may yell for help. Otherwise, enjoy. We'll be out a couple of hours." He helped her aboard the *Red Witch*, which was tied up at the end of the quay.

She smothered a smile. If she couldn't climb aboard a boat on her own, she might as well resign her commission. She knew enough about Will to understand he meant no disrespect. Her Coast Guard career didn't matter to him. He was all about chivalry.

A couple of hours was a good run. And she would be home in plenty of time to rest and get ready for Dan's party. She leaned over the hull and ran her hand along the edge of a patch. "This catamaran is a beauty. You do good work."

"Thanks. The owner treats her like a mangy alley cat."

Nate Brady. She'd asked Dan about him, but no one else. Aside from Brady having scant respect for boats and people, that's all she knew about him.

"When is he coming back?"

"A couple of weeks. Gives me time to repair anything that doesn't check out today, then sit back and watch the paint dry."

"You don't act like the watching-paint-dry type. Does Nate Brady have friends here?"

Will shrugged. "He and Zia were so-so for a while. I don't run in his crowd. From what I can tell, they come here to party out of the view of people in their hometowns."

"Did Randy know him?" Taylor could still see Brady's pig eyes.

"Everybody in any part of the boat business knows him."

"Some people never learn to take care of their toys. They usually don't have respect for anyone else's belongings either."

"Truer words and all. Find yourself a spot."

Taylor crossed the trampoline to give Will room. He cast off and pushed away from the quay. She made a mental note about Nate Brady. Not that she expected to do anything with the knowledge. If the police couldn't tell Randy's death was a murder, how could she expect to locate her uncle's killer? She couldn't remember if Brady had the scar Jake described or if he wore a bracelet. She should have told Jake about Brady's eyes. Maybe they matched the eyes of the man he—no, his father—suspected.

Will raised the mainsail and the jib and caught the wind, tacking into the bay eastward toward St. Joseph's Island. The day couldn't have been more gorgeous. Hot as hell, but the steady southeast breeze kept her cool. The bay could be choppy, but today the swells were less than a foot and evenly spaced. The few puffy clouds made perfect accents in the bright blue sky. They crossed the Intracoastal Waterway, Will keeping the *Red Witch* on a straight and steady course.

Taylor let her thoughts wander. Before she left her hotel room, she had called the number she received for Jacob Solomon.

A woman answered on the first ring. "Compass Points."

Whatever. She thought the number was his home. "Jacob Solomon, please."

"Mr. Solomon isn't in. We're having difficulty with our voicemail. I'll be happy to take a brief message."

So even a high-flying security company had voicemail problems. Taylor smiled. Maybe Jake wasn't as smart as he thought he was. She had left her name and number for Jacob Solomon to call her. Who knew if he would or when it would be. Probably while she was out here on the bay and her phone back on land. She wouldn't chance it going overboard.

She took a deep breath and pointed toward the island. "Are we going there?"

Will shook his head and tacked north, just off the wind.

Salt spray slapped her across the face, and she laughed out loud. "I love this!"

He gave her a thumbs-up, sheeted the jib, and they really took off. To her right, a group of fishermen waved as they rocketed past. She waved back.

Taylor closed her eyes, enjoying the sun and salt spray and wind in her hair. This was the first time in years she'd been on the water without any responsibility. She could take pleasure in everything she'd first fallen in love with. The shushing of the sea against the hull. The tang of salt on her lips. After several minutes, she opened her eyes.

Jake came immediately to mind. She blinked to make his face go away. Today she would enjoy the water and the time with Dan and A.J. later. Tonight would be soon enough to think through the Jake puzzle.

The Rock Harbor marina lay ahead, and Will flew with the wind until he drew alongside the entrance. Then he furled the jib, slowing the catamaran, and sailed into a small cove created by the outer dock of the marina on the west and a fishing jetty on the east. No other boats were around.

On shore big tents spotted the area, and loud Texas music bounced over the water. People roamed everywhere. "What's happening?"

"The First Annual Rock Harbor Redfish Romp." He headed the cat into the wind, dropped anchor, and lowered the mainsail. "How's this?"

"Perfect. What a ride. I'm glad we get to do it again."

"When we go home, we'll give her a workout to make sure she's good for Brady to tear her up again. If you want to go to the festival, we can come back later. I can't leave the Stiletto unattended."

"I've been to plenty of festivals. Don't need another one today. I'm having too much fun being on the water."

Will scooted to the cooler and pulled out several items. "I love being out here. Hope you're hungry."

She pulled on her *Susquehanna* ball cap. With only a slight breeze, the heat exploded, and sweat gathered around her bra.

"Here, have some water." He held out a bottle. "I have chicken and sides, more than enough of everything, so eat up."

Taylor poured a long swallow down her throat.

The boat bobbed up and down on the tiny swells almost in time with the music. She loaded a plate with cold salads and fried chicken strips and leaned against the mast to enjoy the music and food.

"This is really good."

"Best the deli had to offer."

Waves lapped against the hulls and seagulls laughed while they hovered for goodies in the cloudless sky. They didn't get anything from her. She wiped her mouth. "That's the best meal I've had since I've been here. Or at least tied for best. I had barbeque for lunch one day, and Lulu's."

"Damn Lulu. She made you a burger, I'll bet."

She grinned. "Yep. Texas food is different from that on the East Coast. I'd almost forgotten how it tasted. Like that Texas country playing over there."

"I've only lived here, but I've traveled some. The other places told me Texas is home."

"I'm the opposite. I don't want to miss out on anything, so I want to visit everywhere."

"Randy once told me that's why he liked watching the water. It had been every place in the world and shared all its secrets."

If she hadn't known about Solomon's Compass, she would've thought that statement was romantic. "He's told me pretty much the same thing. He liked it here."

The mast shook.

"What the hell?" Will jumped up.

It shook again.

"Get down, Taylor! Make yourself flat. We've got two bullet holes in the mast."

A good twenty feet up in one of the live oaks in front of Rankin's house, shielded from the brutal sun and anyone passing by, Jake found the perfect spot to police the red sails on the catamaran. His military binoculars gave him distance and bearing in the lens. Will sailed almost three miles into the bay before turning west-northwest and picking up speed. Taylor leaned back and let the wind blow through her hair.

Jake ached to kiss the smile on her face, but that would never happen again.

It couldn't matter. His job was more important.

He scanned the area. Two miles up the coast, a point of land jutted out. Will slowed and turned north. In the background, the Rock Harbor marina came into view. Will took the catamaran into the outer harbor between a marina and a short stretch of beach. Off the beach and wrapped around one side of the marina, several white tents had been set up and hundreds of people roamed around. Another security nightmare. His dad would've stroked out.

Jake brought the binoculars back to the catamaran and watched Will pull food out of a large cooler. While Will and Taylor ate, Jake kept the binoculars in motion. People on shore, people on boats in the marina, more boats passing in the bay as well as coming and going from the marina. And him in a tree more than two miles away.

It was what it was.

The cat, the people, the cat, the boats, the cat, the bay. And back again.

At one point, he removed the binoculars and wiped them and his face with the tail of his shirt to get rid of the sweat. He checked again. Nothing had changed.

The cat, the people, the cat, the boats, the cat—what the hell?

Taylor lay spread-eagled across the trampoline. His heart launched into his throat before training took over.

Will crouched with his head lower than his ass. Nothing looked amiss. Maybe a hungry gull had swooped—and then the mast trembled.

"Fuck!" Jake looked up and saw two holes in the sail. He followed the mast downward. It shook again, but remained intact. The cables remained taut. Taylor and Will were talking, and there was no blood. He released a pent-up breath and worked his shoulders.

He swung the binoculars to the shore. Only one thing could have caused the holes. Bullets. No one at the fair or on the beach appeared frightened. No sign of anyone with a gun.

Marina traffic consisted of a single lazy shrimper coming in. No one stood on the far shore on the other side of the channel. Nothing at the marina.

Jake returned his attention to the cat. The port hull rode lower in the water. Taylor and Will were already moving out. As long as they were dealing, he was okay. Taylor was much more than competent.

The bullets had to have come from one of the boats in the bay. He pulled the notebook from his pocket. One by one he followed each boat until he saw a name or registration number. When he finished, he had a list of fifteen boats and a basic description of people he saw aboard. And one boxer puppy. Anyone who would fire toward hundreds of people had to be an expert shooter or be a couple of beers short of a six-pack. Or both.

Jake wiped his face again. Before he brought the binoculars up, loud metal-on-metal clanging sounded from below and startled him. He would have fallen if he hadn't grabbed a branch and braced with both feet. He couldn't see anything through the bushy branches until he adjusted his position.

Someone had jumped the gate at the boatyard and was pounding the shit out of Will's truck with a sledgehammer. By the force of the blows, Jake judged the person to be male, but he couldn't be sure. The vandal's attire consisted of a ball cap, coveralls, and work boots. Jake observed and resisted pulling out his phone. He didn't want to get hung up with the PD—he may need to take action. If the guy went for Will's business or headed this way for Taylor's car—or Jake's—he would step in. Otherwise, a watchful eye would do.

This man wasn't the shooter. From this distance he would have needed a high-powered rifle and a tripod to inflict the sort of damage Jake saw. High-powered rifles didn't come cheap, especially for a street hood, and neither rifle nor tripod was in sight.

The steady pounding and clanging became part of the background. A minute or two from the sound of the first blow, Jake pulled the binoculars back to his eyes and found the wounded catamaran. They'd just passed the entrance to the marina channel. Taylor worked the tiller and Will had control of the sails. Or that's what it looked like. And it looked like they were heading home. Jake wasn't a sailor. He liked boats, but only when they had big motors.

The shrimper had tied up in a row of a dozen or more. They all looked alike to Jake.

The pounding stopped. Across the road the vandal, his ball cap in his back pocket—male, slender, Hispanic—climbed over the gate and strutted toward the main road carrying the hammer over his shoulder. At Church Street, he turned right.

The truck smashing had been ongoing for a good five minutes, but loud noises at a boatyard weren't out of the ordinary. Jake would be surprised if anyone called 911.

If Taylor had been at Rankin's place—and with two cars in the driveway that would be anyone's logical assumption—she would have heard the noise, seen what was happening, and called the police. The vandal had known she was gone. In Jake's book, that indicated the shooter and the truck hammerer were connected.

He watched the Hispanic man. "Come on, pick 'em up and put 'em down. We gotta move it outta here." Jake's words didn't make those skinny feet and legs move any faster. The man strutted to his own drumbeat and stopped half a block later at a beat-to-hell blue pickup.

Jake wrote down the plate number and made certain the man drove away. Another check on Taylor showed the cat was less than half a mile out. Plenty of time.

Will was having some trouble with the sails, but they were making progress. Taylor glowed with confidence—a sailor enjoying a challenge. A smile formed on Jake's face.

Commander Snow White. And Jake was damn proud of her.

CHAPTER 31

Taylor and Will didn't talk much until they cleared the marina no-wake zone. They had lain flat on the tramp for about two minutes. When no more shots came, they decided to head home before the shooter could turn around and come after them again. They agreed it was better to take their chances moving.

She hadn't piloted a catamaran in years, and then only Hobie 16s—without bullet holes in the hulls and mainsail. Like not forgetting how to ride a bike, she hadn't forgotten the principles or the feel of the tiller.

"You sure you're okay?" From the front of the tarp, Will's voice carried over the music and the wind noise.

"Yeah."

"Stay about fifty feet outboard of the piers. If we have a problem, we'll have room to correct."

Having room could be a life saver. Mark had known that. He had been careless. But it took Jake to point it out to her. Yesterday, Mark's memories might have consumed her in this situation. Today, they didn't. She might not have been his equal in the classroom, but she was better on the water. Where it counted. Recognition of her ability gave her strength.

Will turned his attention to the boom. "Both the jib and mainsail are tight. No holes in the jib. In the mainsail, the hole nearest the bottom is ripping. I'm going to stay out here in case we have to take it down."

"Good."

He inspected all ten feet of the boom before turning back toward the front.

"Will! You're bleeding."

"What?"

"Come here."

He moved aft toward her.

"Turn around. The back of your arm is bleeding."

"I must have scraped it on something."

"Turn around. Let me see."

"Aye, aye, Captain."

"Better. Either a bad scrape or a minor bullet graze. You didn't feel it?"

Will shook his head. "Adrenaline. I'll tend to it when we're ashore." He turned back to his inspection duties.

Ever so slowly she inched them down the coast toward the boatyard. She rubbed the knotted cords of her neck to ward off a tension headache.

"Taylor!"

Startled, she turned her head. "What?"

"I asked if you thought someone mistook us for Nate Brady and guest. Do you?"

Will's face held about as much hope as she felt. "Not unless the two of you look alike." Which she knew they didn't.

"No. But he plays fast, hard, and loose. Anyone might recognize his boat without knowing what he looks like."

"Maybe he's messing with somebody's wife, and the guy decided to get even."

"Brady's messed with so many wives I'm surprised he recognizes his own." Will's head sagged. "I think someone told me his wife died a while back."

"Considering the phone calls, I don't think the shots were for Brady." She wished she thought otherwise.

"I was afraid you'd say that."

She scanned the bay. Anything was possible, but she knew the shots came from someone intending to frighten her. To make her leave Rock Harbor. *Not happening, you sorry bastard.*

"Will, did you tell anyone we would be sailing today? Or be near the harbor?"

"Trinh. Zia. A.J."

And Jake. She'd scanned the bay when the shots occurred, but a dozen or more boats ran or anchored within range. On land, the same results. Hundreds of people, but no gun in sight. They decided a slow run back to the boatyard was their best option. Both hulls had been hit, the port one probably more than once beneath the waterline. They'd been lucky.

The cat was beating against the wind, and she had to concentrate to keep the mainsail sheeted in tight. With the leeward pontoon taking on water, a small gust could flip them. Will said both hulls had positive flotation, so they wouldn't sink. Even if they submerged, they were never too far out to swim to shore.

They bounced over wavelets toward the boatyard. A tug pushing a string of barges moved toward them in the ICW. She yelled to Will, and he scooted back. "Tug in the Ditch. I think we'll be inside your jetties before the wake. If not, in the water and swim away from the sails at the first sign of trouble. Don't be a hero."

Will gave her two thumbs up and moved back forward.

The more the distance closed between them and the lead barge, the sweatier her hands got. A thousand yards shrunk fast. Finally they sailed close enough for her to eyeball the jetty opening. It lay about a hundred yards ahead and three times that into shore. "Let's head in here so we can make a gentle turn."

"No. We're too far out. Wait until we're almost close enough to reach out and touch it. Then swing out like you're parking in a tight spot. Lots of rocks on the bottom."

Before she started the turn, she flexed her fingers and backed the jib to help push them through the wind. The change in direction went smoothly. Safe inside the jetties, she wiped her palms on her shorts. "Actually, this is the first time I've sailed a cat this large, but the technique is the same. I wish I could've raced her."

"I watched you earlier, and now working the tiller. You were meant to be out here."

"One day I'll get my own boat."

They limped into the boatyard basin. Will dropped the main, and they bobbled close enough for him to pull them quayside. After he secured the lines, they both sank to the trampoline.

Will lifted his sunglasses. "Water?"

"Please. I'm parched."

He pulled two bottles from the cooler. She downed half her water in one long draw.

"I have a hard time believing someone shot at us." Will removed his sunglasses and wiped his face. "But we're sitting on the proof."

"I'm sorry I've gotten you involved. Let me see your arm again."

He slid his glasses back into place and turned for her to examine his arm. "Don't be. I want the bastard stopped. Especially after this incident. Threatening phone calls are one thing, but this is my livelihood. The insurance issue alone will be a nightmare, not to mention Brady if the cat's not back in shape in time for his race."

"Go to the clinic and get this gouge cleaned out. It's nasty. Lots of ugly stuff lives in this water we love. If they give you antibiotics, take them—all of them." She finished her water and pushed to her feet. "My phone's locked in my car. I'm going to call Glen."

"Use mine."

A waterproof, floatable case sheathed his phone. When she traded up to a smartphone, she was going to get one of those, too. She punched in Glen's number, hoping she remembered it correctly.

He answered on the first ring.

"It's Taylor."

He didn't let her continue. "Are you all right?"

"Yes, but—"

"Where are you?"

What was going on? Did he know about the shots? "At Will's. We just docked."

Taylor had heard worse than the string of foul words that flew from Will's mouth, but Glen winced.

The beautiful truck with the fancy wheels was heading to an early grave in a junkyard. Dents in every panel, including the roof. All the glass busted. Headlights, taillights gone. Dashboard smashed. Even the WILL U plate sported a few dings.

Will's fists clenched, and his chest heaved with every breath. If he didn't calm down, he'd explode. He paced around his truck and kicked the back tire. Not once, but twice. Then he circled the truck again.

"The insurance company will total her. I just made the final payment two months ago."

Glen draped his arm over Will's shoulder. "That's the way it works, didn't you get the memo?" He squeezed Will's bicep, jostling him a bit. "In all seriousness . . . you gonna be okay?"

"Yeah. This isn't the only thing that happened today. Taylor and I—"

"I know about someone shooting at you."

Will stepped out from Glen's arm. "How the hell do you know about that?"

A car pulled up outside the gate.

"Someone called it in. I drove over to Water Street, found you, and kept an eye peeled. Recognized you through binoculars. When I came here to wait, I found your truck."

Jake got out of the car. He was how Glen knew—she didn't doubt it for one second. Jake scaled the locked gate and approached with long strides. God help her, but he turned her on like nobody's business.

He reached them. "What happened?"

A blood vessel stood out on Will's forehead as he rounded on Jake. "The new street look. What the hell you think happened? Somebody beat the shit out of my truck. I don't suppose it was you?"

Jake's lips thinned into a straight line. "I don't suppose it was." His posture was loose and relaxed, his feet apart—a fighting stance. If Will made a move, Jake would have him on the ground before he finished taking the first step.

Glen stepped between them. "Settle down, you two. Will, you know Jake Solomon?"

Will nodded.

"He's all right. Let it go." Glen turned to Jake. "Someone used Will and Taylor for target practice while his truck was being tortured."

"What?" Jake took a step back, surprise on his face.

His expression appeared genuine, but she could tell he was acting. How did she know him so well in such a short time? "Glen, who phoned you? Was the voice like my caller?"

"No. A man. For sure. Show me the catamaran. What were you doing with Nate Brady's boat?" He touched Will's elbow and walked him toward the quay.

She rounded on Jake, hands on her hips. He shrugged and followed the others. Men. She hurried to catch up.

"—out for a trial. I asked Taylor along because I thought she'd enjoy it."

"Did you tell anyone you were going out?"

"Taylor asked me that. I told Trinh. Zia at the deli this morning. And A.J. He was in Lulu's when I stopped in yesterday—all kinds of people in there."

"So anyone could've known."

"Yeah." Will's shoulders drooped.

Glen turned to her. "How about you?"

She hung her thumb at Jake. "Him. Yesterday when Will came over about the call, he mentioned about going out today. I filled Jake in later."

"One happy family." Glen scratched his head. "You were the only boat. The shooter wasn't aiming at something else."

"Right."

"Neither of you figured out where the shots came from?"

"No. We started out of the harbor within minutes and headed back without any more trouble."

They reached the catamaran. Glen whistled. "Brady's gonna let the bullshit fly over this one."

Beside her, Jake snickered. "Who's this Brady?"

"He and the department have a long history. The man's a bigger pain than a stingray caught in the shallows. When I leave here, I'm gonna drive by his house. See if he's around. Make sure his other boat's secure. Despite how it looks, I wouldn't be surprised if he concocted a scheme to get a chunk of insurance money. Come open the gate for me, Will. I'm not as young as I used to be. Climbing it once was enough."

They left her alone with Jake.

He cupped her shoulder. "I'm glad you're all right."

She was happy her sunglasses hid her eyes. He couldn't tell how his touch excited her. "Me, too."

"You knew I was the one who called Upchurch." He dropped his hand.

It wasn't a question. "Please. Who else could it have been?"

"It could have been the trigger puller. Or someone other than me who saw what went down and didn't want to be involved. Glen and I have talked in broad terms. Have you met Brady?"

Broad terms? Were they feeling each other out or what? Men. "Brady's a pig."

"Hey, you two." Will motioned them toward the road. "Come on. I'm going to lock up. Glen's dropping me at the car rental place. I have to pick up one of my men and get that cat out of the water."

CHAPTER 32

After Will turned away, Taylor pulled her fingers through Jake's hair and brought her palm back.

"What are you doing?" Jake's eyes grew wary.

She held out a live oak leaf. "You missed one."

"Crap."

"No one else noticed. They only saw you from the front. The tiny points catch on the least little thing." Even his silky hair. "You were up in one of Randy's trees."

"You're observant."

She shrugged. "You must have powerful binoculars." Like those on the *Susquehanna*.

"Yeah."

Silence followed. She wanted to ask him about his father. She wanted to tell him to go bungee jumping without a cord. Hell, she didn't know what she wanted. He studied his shoes and didn't look at her. She studied him. Every once in a while he opened his mouth, apparently thought better of what he'd been about to say, and closed it. This went on for an eternity—or at least thirty seconds—before Will yelled at them again to hurry up.

"Look, Taylor. I'm sorry for last night." He still didn't look at her.

Was she supposed to forgive him with nothing more than *I'm sorry*? What happened to the Act of Contrition and scrubbing floors at the convent? Not that she'd ever experienced those. Not that she would tell.

He looked at her then, and she went weak at the knees.

"We need to talk, Taylor, but I have things to do right now. I don't know how long it will take. Will you meet me for breakfast in the morning?"

"I'm meeting Dan out here at six." Let Jake adjust his timing.

"I'll be here at five-thirty."

At least he had a plan. Jake didn't know how much he'd tell Taylor, but he could figure that out before five-thirty in the morning. If not, he'd wing it. Wouldn't be the first time.

Upchurch and Knox were already gone. He turned around in Rankin's driveway and waited while Taylor backed out. She took her usual route toward the hotel. He followed for two blocks before turning left on a street that went to the highway and stopping at a convenience store on the corner.

He called Kelly from the lot. "How's Dad?"

"His fever is gone. The doctors are less concerned today—one of them actually smiled. You caught me at home for once instead of at the hospital. Taylor Campbell called Dad this morning."

Jake wasn't surprised. Taylor believed in direct access.

"Why would she do that when she thinks you're him?"

Why indeed. Jake didn't say anything.

Kelly gave him five seconds. "She knows. How did she find out?"

"Not important. Does Dad know?"

"Hell no. His strength is returning. He might have killed the messenger."

Jake breathed easier. "Fill me in."

"Commander Campbell called on Dad's only publicly listed number. Those calls download to a black hole voice mail, and the number is only associated with my phone. Every day or so, I run the calls through a program that gives me a mini-bio of the caller. Or tells me the number is a pay phone or throwaway. I always have to listen to more calls than I want, usually crazies or people looking for a handout. Dad only hears about the threats. He makes the decision to call the appropriate authorities or handle it in-house."

"You always say he doesn't trust you, Kel, but from this, I'd say he trusts you plenty. I had no idea about the number."

"Whatever. Then I clear the box. Only I hadn't remembered to do that since the hospital turned me into a zombie. The box saturated. This morning as I was leaving the hospital, I noticed missed calls for that number on my cell and realized what had happened. Before I could delete them, a call came through from the Rock Harbor area code."

"Ambulance coming. Siren is blaring. Hold on." The siren grew in intensity for a few seconds until the ambulance blew past heading toward Corpus Christi. "Okay. So the call was from Taylor?"

"As it turned out. I gave her a line about a voicemail glitch and asked if she wanted to leave a message."

"Did she?"

"Only her name and number for Dad to call. What happened? Do I need to pass her call on to Dad when he's better?"

"I wasn't careful enough. We talked this afternoon. No need to worry Dad." He hoped to hell Kelly listened.

"I figured something like that. If the job had blown to shit you would've found me right away—one way or another. How is everything else?"

Blown to shit. Even so, Jake's blood warmed a few degrees. "Moving along. I'll fill in details later. Do you have time for some tracking?"

"Sure. As long as it isn't too involved."

"Find out who owns this truck." He gave her the plate number. "Name, address, phone, rap sheet, anything available."

"Five minutes. What's next?"

"Nate Brady's working himself up the list. Might be Nathan or Nathaniel. Main address is in north Texas someplace, but I need Rock Harbor info." Even Upchurch had indicated the possibility of insurance fraud.

"Got it."

"Same thing on him as on the truck owner. Get me the truck owner first. I'll call you back sometime later today to get Brady's."

"Okay. Anything else?"

"I need to know who owns each one of these boats. It's a long list of registration numbers, mostly Texas. I'll indicate otherwise."

"Go ahead."

He read them off. "That's all. Truck first, then Brady, then the boats. Oh, and a shrimp boat in Rock Harbor named *Ladybug*. One word. I don't have any numbers on her."

"Okay, bro. I'm on it."

"Say hi to Mom and Dad for me."

Jake hung up, went inside for a bottle of water, and returned to his car to wait. He didn't have to wait long.

"The truck is a 1977 Ford F100. Blue. Registered to Jose Martinez." Kelly gave him Martinez's Rock Harbor address and phone.

Jake copied the information and read it back.

"I'll give you more on Martinez if you want, but he reported the truck stolen yesterday morning."

Damn it to hell. "If I need more I'll call you back. Don't lose it."

"It's saved. By the way, I found a few extra seconds to link my phone to my computer through Compass Points security layers, so I can do simple jobs from the hospital. Some places I have to turn it off, but for the most part, I think we'll be good to go."

"Good. What does Mr. Martinez do?"

"Old guy. Retired. In his line of work, I think that means cash only now. He's a handyman."

"More power to him."

Jake hung up and used his map to find Martinez's address—he hated the damned condescending voice on the GPS. A manicured lawn with mounds of multi-colored flowers surrounded the small, well-kept house. In the rear, the open door of the garage revealed a new model hybrid and a van, both blue. He rang the doorbell.

The woman who opened the inner door was Taylor's size with white hair and bright brown eyes.

Jake placed his card against the storm door glass for her to read. "I'm not with the police, and you don't have to tell me anything. My name is Jake Solomon. I understand someone stole your husband's truck, and I came to talk about it."

"Let me get Joe for you. I was in Austin and only got home a few minutes ago." She turned around. "Joe! A man about your truck."

"Okay," carried from somewhere in the house.

"Would you like to come in?"

Jake shook his head. "It's dangerous to invite strangers into your home, ma'am. I'm in security."

"This is Rock Harbor. We hardly ever lock the door."

"Maybe you should. Someone stole your truck, remember."

"Isn't that the strangest thing? I mean, who would even want it? Joe keeps it clean, but it's an eyesore. And falling apart besides. He keeps her together with baling wire and a prayer."

A man in plaid shorts and a purple T-shirt appeared behind her, and she pointed to Jake's card. "Are you talking about Matilda?" The man's eyes twinkled behind wire rimmed glasses.

"I'll leave you two alone." Joe's wife left the way Joe had arrived.

Streaks of silver highlighted the man's black hair. He glanced at Jake's card. "Joe Martinez. Mr. Solomon?"

"Right. If Matilda's your truck, she's the one I came to talk to you about."

Joe laughed and stepped onto the porch. The sweet aroma of apple pie floated out the open door.

"I brought my kids home from the hospital in Matilda. And she went to work with me every day. Had to call her something. If I chose a"—he moved his hands to illustrate the shape of a woman—"name, Eva would've gone to war."

Jake smiled. "You reported Matilda stolen yesterday?"

"Got up, and she wasn't in the driveway. We were going fishing, so I had to use the van. I called it in. Kids like the old trucks now, but poor old Matilda is wrinkled and gray, and her heart's about to give out. I love her, but she won't be with us long, I'm afraid." He made the sign of the cross. Then he winked.

"Any ideas about who might've taken her?"

He shrugged. "People in town know me. I probably did jobs for most of them, one time or another. My son has the business now—a whole fleet of new Matildas. Well, two. Rock Harbor's small. Nobody I know would've taken her. Cops keep a close watch on some gang types living a few blocks over. Matilda's not much to look at, but I hope someone finds her. How did you find out she was gone?"

"I met with a detective about another matter. In passing he mentioned your truck. It might be a lead on my case, so I decided to check into it." Sometimes a lie worked better than the truth. Jake thought of Taylor. Sometimes not. "Thanks for your time, Mr. Martinez."

Joe had waved his arm in a general northwesterly direction when he talked about the gang types. When Jake left, he drove around the area. Three blocks from the Martinez house, the neighborhood deteriorated as clearly as if someone had strung yellow crime scene tape across the intersection to mark the dividing line.

He drove slowly up and down the streets and blocks, but not slowly enough for anyone to think he came to score in any way. He didn't spy Matilda, but he did spot a man who could've been the thug he watched destroy Will's truck.

The man wore the same type of coveralls, boots, and ball cap as the hammer-wielding punk. He walked with the same swagger, and his profile matched—the same nose and jaw line.

Jake cut him off and lowered the passenger window four inches. "Get in." The man moved so slowly, Jake wasn't too worried about him sitting in the passenger seat.

"Fuck you."

"Get in or I'll have every cop in the county here—the first patrol car in under two. I saw what you did." He held up his phone. "All I do is press send. Now get in."

The man glanced around and kept walking, going into a growth of weeds to get around Jake's bumper. Jake let the vandal get five feet ahead of his bumper—at the point he probably thought he could break away down one of the many driveways that were coming up—then gunned the engine and cut him off again. The passenger mirror came within inches of the man's midsection.

"Try it again. Next time, I'll run you down. In the car or on foot. Doesn't matter to me. If that's the way it plays out, your homies won't recognize you. Your choice."

The man searched the area again before reaching for the handle. "Open up, dude."

Jake raised the window and clicked the locks open. Before the man's ass touched the seat, Jake grabbed his wrist and pulled him the rest of the way inside. Sweat beads popped out on the man's smooth forehead, and with them, the stench of fear.

Jake applied a slight amount of pressure to the man's wrist. "Close the door."

The man's eyes went wild, but he pulled the door closed with his right hand.

Jake locked it but didn't release the man's wrist. "Place your right hand on the dashboard."

The man didn't comply.

Jake shook his head and added pressure to his grip while bending the man's hand back. "You're either too fucking stupid to join the gene pool or too son-bitching stubborn to admit when something's for your own damn good."

The man scowled and squirmed in his seat.

"Hear this. I learned a hell of a lot in sniper school. And survival school. Oh, and in hand-to-hand combat. Plus some other places I can't talk about. I practice a lot, and I'm damned fast. If you're carrying, don't think about trying anything. You'll lose." He released his grip. "Fasten your seatbelt and place both hands on the dash."

After the man did as he was told, Jake drove to the Martinez home. His passenger kept asking where they were going, but Jake said nothing until he put the car in park and scanned the area for anyone who might be outside. "Where's this man's truck?"

"You're talking shit."

"You stole this man's truck. Where is it?" Jake spoke slowly so there would be no misunderstanding.

"I ain't stole nothing."

"Where'd you get the sledge?"

Silence.

"I asked you a question. Did you steal it, too?"

"Dude, you keep accusing me of shit—"

Jake took his hands off the wheel, turned them over, studied his nails. Then raised an eyebrow. "Where's the truck?"

"What the fu—"

Jake grabbed the man's seatbelt with his right hand and yanked it across his throat and around his neck, leaving him barely room to take shallow breaths.

"The truck?"

The man waved his arms and shook his head. Jake tightened the belt.

"I'm going to stop being nice in a minute if you don't tell me where the truck is." He tightened it a little more.

The man's eyes grew round, and he made a spewing sound.

"Ready yet?" He pulled it again.

The man tried to slip his fingers under the belt. He looked like a fish on a boat deck, his mouth gaping wide, eyes round and wild. Jake figured he had ten seconds before the goon passed out, and he counted to himself.

At eight, the man nodded.

"Sure?"

The nod did double time, and the man's wide eyes pleaded.

Jake released the pressure but didn't move the belt. The man took several deep breaths.

"Careful, you'll hyperventilate. I don't have a paper bag."

"You're fucking *crazy*, dude!"

Jake gave him a big scary grin. "You ready to take me to this man's truck?"

"Motherfucker got two good cars. What he want with that piece-a-shit truck anyway?"

"Don't go tough on me. I'm holding the seatbelt." Not too stubborn. Definitely stupid.

The man started sliding down in the seat, but the belt caught his chin and he pushed himself up. "Okay, dude. Turn right at the corner and go to the highway."

Jake let go of the seatbelt and patted the man's shoulder. "Hands on the dash. Don't move them. You do, I consider it a threat."

The man put his hands above the glove compartment and nodded.

"Remember, I'm fast. The seatbelt was nothing."

The man's Adam's apple bounced up and down.

Another crazy grin spread across Jake's face as he put the car in gear.

Five minutes later, on a snaky back road, the pickup came into view. Several feet behind it, Jake applied the brakes. "Hand me your wallet, then put your hands back. Don't try anything."

The man handed Jake a worn black nylon wallet. "Rafael Barrera. It's your photo. Maybe your name. What are the odds you really live in Midland? Or ever lived there? I'm guessing pretty long. Put your wallet away, and return your hands to the dash."

Again, the man did as told.

"I'm going to ask you one more question then I'm going to drive you back to the neighborhood. If you don't give me the answer I want, I hope you told your mama you loved her. Understand?"

Rafael nodded.

"Who hired you to bash the truck at the boatyard?"

CHAPTER 33

Taylor needed time alone to give her nerves a chance to calm down. Not only from being shot at, but from seeing Jake again. Any more stress-filled situations and she might float around the bend screaming and yelling before she sank to the bottom.

So she drove around Rock Harbor trying to find the library, thinking they would have information on the fishing tournament advertised on the shirt in Randy's treasure can. If they did, she would get an early start on figuring out the clue. She drove up one block and down the next for about five minutes before spotting the library sign. They were closed. She should've guessed. Even in Charleston, just the main branch was open on Sunday—and only for a few hours in the afternoon.

In the car, Taylor stared through the windshield, not seeing anything except the fishing shirt in her mind. She'd memorized the tournament info on the back, paid attention to the sponsors. Nothing pointed to anyone she knew. Nothing had appeared to inspire Jake either.

Maybe Randy was right. Maybe someone left the shirt hanging on his door, a discarded garment that held no significance. But the shirt and the belt buckles from Denver were the best clues she had.

Taylor returned to the hotel. In the lobby, the desk clerk motioned to her. "You're Commander Campbell?"

"Yes."

"This was delivered for you by a local messenger. Have a nice evening, ma'am."

"Thank you." A message from Jake?

The elevator dinged, and Taylor punched the button for her floor before opening the envelope, careful of the edges. She didn't want to cut her healing hand or fingers. A single sheet of paper was inside. The words had been cut and pasted from a newspaper—*Next time I won't miss.*

Jake dropped off the truck thief and put in another call to Kelly from under a big tree in Lulu's parking lot.

"What's up, boss man? Did you find Martinez?"

He smiled. "Of course. Found his truck, too."

"Saint Jake of Brooklyn."

He envisioned her blessing the phone. "You been getting a drip in that hospital or what?"

"It's called ready-to-collapse."

"I'll treat you to a spa day after this is finished. Just be there for Dad."

"You'd be here, too, if you could. Mom said to tell you not to forget to eat your spinach."

He laughed. Telling him to eat his spinach had long been her shorthand for reminding him to prepare and be ready for whatever came up. "Tell her I had a can this morning."

"She's the strongest one in our little clan. Most of the nurses are afraid of her."

"Not surprised. Before I forget—I intend to run into a man named Bill Abbott around nine tomorrow morning."

"Important because . . ."

"He may know who's been killing the Compass Points."

A car door slammed nearby. Jake pinpointed which car when the engine growled to life.

"Wonderful! Is it him?"

"Doubtful, from what I hear. I have to convince him to tell me what he knows." *And not send someone after me.* "Any news yet on Nate Brady?"

"Funny about Mr. Brady."

Jake sat straighter and flipped open his pad. "How funny?"

"In a lot of ways funny. His wife died a few years ago. Official cause of death was suicide. Note in her handwriting. She'd been getting treatment for depression for a year or so, ever since she found Nate Baby in bed with a local horse trainer of the female variety. The sheriff's office didn't have enough evidence to build a case, but they liked Nate for it. The case is officially closed, but it gets talked about on occasion."

"Interesting." He chewed on his cheek. "Brady still involved with the horse trainer?"

"She moved on to greener pastures. Pardon the pun."

"Left Nate holding an empty feed bag?" Food. Jake's stomach growled again.

"Yeah, except it wasn't empty. Among other things, the guy owns a ranch with more acres than Manhattan. Cattle. Oil."

"A money ranch. So what's wrong with him?"

"Besides being a possible murderer?"

"Yeah. Besides that."

"He likes rough sex and compliant women, if you get my drift. Hot tempered. Small things set him off. He likes to gamble and doesn't like to lose. When he does, he pays up and refills his coffers by running drugs for a side-shoot of one of the Mexican cartels. Last year he vowed to stay away from the tables and from private poker games."

"Something must've spooked him." Jake frowned. "How do you know he vowed? Did you make that up?"

"I don't need to. I don't even need to speculate. Everything you need to know about everything is out there if you know where to search and how to get in and out without leaving a trail."

"Orwell had it wrong."

"What? Big Brother? He's been here for a while."

"No. He should have named it Little Sister. What happened to spook Brady?"

"I haven't ventured farther down that road, but I will. Probably tomorrow, though. I have to grab a few minutes of sleep every once in a while. I wanted to give you an overview. As I was saying, lots of funny things. The wife. The gambling. Flies his own plane, but so far the plane appears normal. Has two boats in Rock Harbor. One is a catamaran. The other is a sportfisher. The registration number of Brady's sportfisher matches one on your list."

Jake zoomed to full alert. "Where is Brady now?"

"Don't know. Let me back up. So far I've found bare bones on Brady. When I found the matching TX number, I stayed and looked up the rest of them, except for the shrimp boat. It's on my to-do list. I had to come back to the hospital before I could plug into Brady again."

"No sweat." Kelly would get the answers to him as soon as she could.

"Let me give you the other owners and their info. Then I need to go back in with Dad."

"Dad comes first. Keep remembering." He wrote down the information Kelly gave him. None of the new names jumped out. "Thanks, Kel. I mean that."

"I know. I love you, too."

"One more thing."

"No problem."

He gave her a list of names, including the current players in Taylor's life, and asked her to check on any connection to Denver or to the fishing contest in Rock Harbor. "Include Brady on the list, too."

"Okay. I'll be in touch." She hung up.

Kelly was a genius, not a magician. Jake doubted she'd be in touch until tomorrow. He put the car in gear and drove back to the Martinez home. No one was home. He wrote directions to Matilda on the back of his card and left it in the door.

On the drive to Lulu's, his mind strayed to the truck smasher. Chances were he'd spilled the truth, but if Abbott turned out to be a set-up, Jake would handle it and move on. That's one of the things that made the game exciting—being the first to discover the hole in the maze.

Dan and A.J.'s house was as easy to find as he'd said. Taylor parked at the curb behind Zia's car. *Damn.* She'd hoped to be the first to arrive so she could ask Dan about the names of his shop and gallery and the others. She'd totally forgotten yesterday after he told her about the wedding. Taylor sighed. Tomorrow she'd ask about the signs. For sure.

The small white house with black Bahama shutters sat back from the street amid a garden filled with tropical plants. Taylor followed a winding gravel path from the street to the red front door, smiling the entire time.

A.J. answered the bell. "Welcome."

"Your yard and house are lovely. If I ever stop renting, I'm calling you."

"Dan had the overall idea. I supplied the details. We worked together to make it happen. Come on in."

"Wow." The feeling of welcome carried over into the modern open space inside. Hardwood floors, large windows. The piquant aroma of crab boil made her mouth water. Not a ruffle or length of fringe in sight, but lived-in and comfortable instead of photo-perfect like the exterior. The Dan she thought she knew would never live in a house like this. "Inside is as great as out."

The living room gave way to a wide kitchen workspace separated by the biggest island she'd ever seen. Zia sat on a bar stool in front of it with a glass of red wine in her hand.

Dan waved from behind it. "Come on in."

"Sure. Hi, Zia."

Zia raised her glass in greeting, her face pouty. Her baby-blue mini consisted of three tiers of long ruffles that matched her eyes and the blue sandals on the floor. Taylor was glad Dan had told her Zia might be out of sorts. And she was glad she decided to wear her travel clothes instead of a clean dwarf.

"Dan, I told A.J. how much I love your home. In a million years I wouldn't have guessed you liked sleek living spaces."

"I told you I get my chintz fix at work. That's business. I relax here."

He looked relaxed, too, stacking peeled boiled shrimp around the edge of a square black plate instead of running around powered by fresh batteries. Her mouth watered when he set a white bowl filled with cocktail sauce in the center.

Dan looked up as he set the plate aside. "I hope you brought an appetite."

"I'm always hungry." Dan and A.J. owned all the toys—wine cooler, espresso maker, pot filler, you name it. "I can't get over you living here. No antiques."

"You and I are kindred spirits, Taylor. Zia, here, likes lots of stuff. And lots of color."

"I have limits." Zia sipped her wine. "I still think you should add some red in here. Or orange."

A.J. patted Zia's shoulder. "Red front door. It's good luck, too."

Taylor dropped her keys in her bag. "Speaking of red, my mother gave me a small red Chinese chest that sits at the foot of my bed."

"Means you're a hussy." Dan grinned and winked at her.

Everyone laughed, but Dan might be right. Especially after last night.

A.J. touched her arm. "What can I get you to drink?"

"White wine, if you have it."

"Coming up." A.J. headed to the wine cooler.

"Let's go on the patio and party." Dan carried the plate and opened French doors onto paradise.

"I keep thinking your home couldn't get any better, but it just did. Screened and ceiling fans. If this is a dream, don't wake me."

A.J. handed her a glass of wine, and she settled in a chair. Dan placed the shrimp on a low table covered with more plates filled with fruit, cheese, olives, and crackers. They continued to talk and laugh through the food and another round of drinks. Dusk settled in, and tiny white lights came on in the yard.

"It's romantic and whimsical at the same time." *And would be even more romantic if Jake were here. The jerk.* "Thank you so much for inviting me."

"You're the guest of honor. How could we not?" Dan bent and pulled up a package from under the table. "Open."

The brown paper fell away to reveal one of A.J.'s paintings, small enough for her to put in her carry-on. The background was red. *Omigod! The red hussy chest.* A bolt of yellow splashed in an upper corner. Zia's hair. Two vertical black stripes anchored the bottom. Boots? Some squiggles of purple and orange in the center.

"I love this! How many times have I said those words tonight? It's not a recording, I promise." She jumped up and hugged A.J. first, then Dan, then Zia. "It goes with my red Chinese chest."

Dan touched her arm. "Remember at the opening I told you we picked one that reminded us of you?"

She nodded, still looking at the painting. "Oh, Zia, you signed, too. Thank you."

"You're welcome." They were the first words Zia had spoken directly to her, and she hadn't made eye contact. Even now.

Dan went on as if no one had spoken. "We chose this one because of the red. The color shows the passion hidden underneath your all-business exterior. A.J. and I both see it. Learn to trust it, Taylor. You won't be sorry."

She blinked back the tears that stung her eyes. She'd let her passion flow last night, and where had it gotten her? Absolutely nowhere.

A.J. refilled their glasses and raised his. "A toast."

They held their glasses above the table, smiling.

"To passion. To life."

Everyone repeated the toast, clinked glasses, and drank.

Zia's fingers touched hers. "Sometimes we keep our true selves hidden behind what we allow the world to see. We even hide the truth from ourselves. Maybe this will help you find the real Taylor." She patted Taylor's fingers and smiled before turning away and downing her wine.

Taylor was marooned on a patio with an army of free-thinking mavericks, each one different from the people she normally associated with, yet she felt right at home. She shook her head and took another sip. People still surprised her. She took another sip of wine. Why did the new friends she'd met in Rock Harbor think she didn't honor her passion? The Coast Guard was her true passion. She held command of a United States Coast Guard cutter. She was in line for captain. Everything she'd always wanted. She *was* happy. Damn it.

CHAPTER 34

J ake shot a few games of pool at Lulu's and lost like a gentleman. Locals didn't take kindly to strangers taking their money, even if the payoff came in the form of a beer. While he downed his favorite burger in the world, he watched the Mets wallop the Astros. He was the only one watching who didn't piss and moan at the outcome, so he kept his fist pumping to himself.

When he left, purple twilight had taken the place of bright sunshine. The outdoor lights were on at Knox's boatyard, so Jake drove over and honked at the locked gate.

A few seconds later Knox rounded the corner, his right hand on the butt of a Glock holstered at his waist.

Jake waved. He hoped Knox was a good shot and didn't have the gun only for show. Bravado would get him killed. "How's the boat?"

Knox was already jogging to the gate. Reaching it, he stooped to pull a vine away from the gate post. "Not nearly as bad as I thought. The tramp is sound. No damage to the centerboards. I've already ordered a new mast and mainsail. The hulls have been patched so many times a few more won't matter. The mainsail's the only real problem."

"Why? You don't have to do anything with that except hook it up."

"The color is special order. But I've used the supplier before, so I hope they can put it on rush. I'll find out in the morning.

Worst case, I'll give Brady a white one from the store at no charge if the other one isn't here in time for his race. He'll be a true bastard about it, but too fucking bad."

Security work was easy compared to dealing with this kind of detail. "What happened to your arm?"

"One of those bullets grazed it. A nurse I know cleaned it for me. Hurt like a sonofabitch. Told me to see a doc." The tone of Will's voice said that suggestion was going nowhere.

"I saw your lights and came by to pick your brain."

"Good luck. Not much of it left."

Jake gave him a quick practiced grin. "Do you know a place called Cecil's?"

"Everybody knows it. Why?" Will took a step back.

"Tell me about it."

"It's a beer joint on the other side of the freeway. Mosquitoes, not ever much of a breeze. Old and falling down. Cecil sold us beer when we were in high school. Mostly geezers now." He pulled down the brim of his ball cap. "No offense."

Jake gave him the same grin. He was beginning to feel old. "None taken. When does it open?"

"Cecil lives in the back. He opens up in the mornings and serves coffee until noon. Like I said, mostly old farts. They stop for coffee and come back for beer. Somebody recommend it?"

"Something like that."

Jake left and followed Will's directions, finding Cecil's without a hitch. Clouds had begun to form over the Gulf, but it would be a while before they moved in, if at all.

Cecil's looked like a four-car garage with all the doors raised. Inside, beer signs glowed from the walls and lights hung from large ceiling fans. Older pickups stood in a line across the lot—two side by side, a space, three more, two spaces, and a lone truck at the other end, as if each customer had an assigned slot. Maybe they did.

Jake lowered his window. "Rock Around the Clock" floated in the air along with a fine haze of cigarette smoke. He drove on a couple of miles until the road veered to the right. Nothing except flat land and high grass. A few fishing shacks and mobile homes here and there. In the morning, he'd arrive early and make the same trek with the thermal imaging binoculars Compass Points International was field testing.

He'd followed Taylor's progress to Dan's earlier on his phone. On his way back from Cecil's, he tracked her back to the hotel, and pulled up in time to catch her sliding out from behind the steering wheel. What a mess he'd made last night. Then today. He should've prevented her from going out on the cat with Will, but he thought he had everything covered.

His dad trusted him to protect her. Jake failed all the way around plus made her so angry she would barely look at him, and he didn't blame her. Not one bit. He was damned pissed at himself.

Don't tell her you're not me. Don't tell anyone you're not me. No matter what. No one must know. How many times had his dad said those words? Jake had lost count. Since he'd already failed, this seemed like a good time to tell Taylor the whole truth. She was smart and made good decisions. He trusted she would understand his dad's position. Or she might hate him more than she had last night because he couldn't keep his mouth shut. He had to take the chance.

On the short distance from Dan's to the motel, Taylor kept glancing at the rewrapped painting in the passenger seat. Would she ever become as free-spirited as Zia? Probably not. But she might loosen up. Spending a day or two a week with friends and adding some zest to her life would be the perfect reward for making captain.

The hotel came into view, and she reined in her thoughts. The wine had helped her to relax. A car pulled into the space next to hers as she turned around to beep the lock. Jake. She wasn't surprised and kept walking, but he caught up with her outside the lobby. A light mist had begun to fall, and she cradled the painting against her chest.

He reached to open the door for her but kept it closed. "We need to talk. Your room or mine?"

Part of her wanted to see him dangle by his balls, but the other part had decidedly different ideas about that part of his anatomy. And the mist had turned to drizzle. Lightning flashed. "What the hell. Mine."

He pulled open the door. "After you."

Taylor could only imagine what he had to say. He probably wanted to grill her about what happened this afternoon.

They entered the elevator, and she pulled out her room key.

"You should have your key ready before you step into the elevator."

She glared at him. "Why? I have you."

One corner of his mouth twitched. "I deserved that."

"Yes, you did."

The elevator dinged as it reached her floor. Jake made her stand back while he stepped out first.

"Okay, clear."

An eerie sense of déjà vu followed her as she walked to her room and opened the door, but there would be no repeat of last night. She wouldn't allow herself to be dragged down that road again.

Jake locked the door. "What's in the package?"

She forced a smile. "I had dinner with Dan and A.J. and Zia tonight. A.J. gave me one of his paintings."

"May I look?"

She unfolded the brown paper.

"I like this. A.J.'s work is dynamic."

"He and Dan said this reminded them of me."

Jake studied the painting for only a moment. "I agree."

"You do?" She'd expected a flippant remark.

"Sure. I realize A.J. painted this as an interpretation of Zia, but it fits you in a different way. Black at the bottom, your practical self, your anchor. The orange and purple, your intellect and intuition, vivid and intense but almost hidden by the bright flash at the top, the show you put on for others to keep them away from the real you."

"I don't put on a show. I'm always the *real me*." Jake hadn't said anything about the red. Dan was full of crap.

"Yes you do. You don't mind if someone looks around the yellow flash and finds the black or the orange and purple. You don't encourage it, but you don't shut them out, though you'd prefer all anyone saw was the bright splash of yellow to blind them from the real you—the red that fills the entire space."

Taylor ground her teeth. "And?"

"The red shows how passionate you are."

Damn it. "No."

"Not just sexy passionate." Jake smiled. "Although there's plenty of that, your energy and interest overflows for everything that touches you. Your passion for life and living was the first trait I noticed about you. You have an intense interest in everything and everyone. You have emotional passion, too—I've seen it—but you hold it so close the yellow keeps it hidden."

"Did Dan pay you to say that?"

Jake laid the painting on top of the brown paper. "No. I haven't talked to Dan. Or A.J. It's the truth. Let me guess—Dan said much the same, and you thought he was spouting garbage."

"Pretty much."

His hands rested on her arms. "It's true, Taylor. You're the only one who doesn't recognize who you are."

What did they know? Jake's hands moved to cup her face, and she sighed. Her traitorous body was a slut. All it wanted was to lean against him and enjoy his never-ending touch. Despite last night. Her mother would be proud.

Taylor moved away and rewrapped the painting before turning back to him. "You wanted to talk?" She sat at the table.

He didn't join her. Instead he paced in silence. She waited. Jake wasn't shy; he would tell her in his own way, in his own time, what he wanted her to know.

After four or five trips across the room and back, he sat across from her and took her hand. "I'm going to give you a lot of information that will fill in some blanks. It won't take but a few minutes, and I'll leave."

His hand was strong and lean, warm. Hers looked tiny in comparison. She pulled it away before it became too snug.

"Everything I told you about my dad and your uncle, and the entire story about Vietnam, Bangkok, the murders—everything—was the truth except for one detail." He took her hand back, trapping it between both of his.

"You aren't Jake." She searched his solemn eyes, and he looked away.

"Make that two details, both tied together. I am Jake—Jacob *Paul* Solomon. The Jake your uncle knew—Jacob *Daniel* Solomon—is my dad." He licked his lips. "In telling you the story, I told you I married several years later, but the marriage didn't last."

Taylor focused on the table. Here it came. He was married with a wife, three kids, and a dog at home. The real reason he'd felt like a slimeball last night. She studied the floor.

His thumb massaged the top of her hand, leaving tingles where skin met skin. "I told you Dad's story. From his point of view. Except for one detail. In truth, I have never been married. And in truth, my mom and dad married while he was in sniper school."

Nothing about the table was remarkable, but Taylor studied the flat top, afraid to move from its safety. "How romantic." He didn't have a wife! Or three kids. She didn't know about a dog.

"Actually, yes. He and mom had been high school sweethearts—he tells this story much better than I do, with all the details. The down-and-dirty version is when he realized what he'd gotten into, he went AWOL one weekend and asked Mom to meet him in Maryland. They got married. He got into trouble. She got pregnant. Neither thought they'd ever be together again."

Taylor's fingers curled around Jake's, and she finally looked up. Jake squeezed her hand.

"Nine months later, I came along. Mom got letters, but Dad never came home until he came home for good and went to school. While he was gone, she went to school. I don't remember that. I just remember she was a teacher. My sister was born while Dad was in graduate school."

"What about your parents?" Taylor kept eyeing at him. Since meeting Jake in the barbeque restaurant, her hormones had run amok, even believing him more Randy's age than hers. It hadn't mattered. Now that she knew he was her age, the magnet pulling her toward him switched to power surge. Despite all he had told her, all he had done.

"Mom and Dad are still married. Still in love." A smile spread across Jake's face.

"It must have been wonderful to grow up in a home like that. Mother is never happy with anyone, even herself. I never knew my dad. Randy was my rock."

Jake shrugged, but his thumb played with her fingers. "It wasn't an easy time. Dad had a lot of adjusting to do. Mom, too. It took a while, but they loved each other. And me. I sensed it, even as a kid, and never doubted it. They finally worked their problems out. After Dad finished school, he was gone most of the time building the business. That was hard, too. I went to school, got accepted for Annapolis, and became a SEAL."

She released his hand and sat up straight. "That's how you pulled it off. You're authentic."

"When I left the Navy, I went to work for Dad. I guess I trained for the family business."

She stood and walked around. This man totally charmed her, and she couldn't let him. "Why are you here? Why isn't your dad?"

"Dad put the pieces together and warned Randy, but he didn't tell anyone at CPI about the danger he was in. He didn't confide in me, either." Jake ran his hands over his head. "I didn't know about the incident in Bangkok or the truth about the remainder of his service until six months ago. The only reason he told me was because he was diagnosed with prostate cancer and has been undergoing treatment. He wouldn't take the chance you would come here when he couldn't protect you."

She stopped pacing. "How is he?"

"Right now he's in the hospital—he's been running a fever. Overall, we're hopeful. The last reports were good."

"I'm glad. For all of you." Taylor paced again. It was the only way to keep her thoughts away from Jake.

"Dad rehearsed me for hours on end. 'Treat it like a mission.' He repeated those words a million times. And wasn't convinced until I could perform every part perfectly in his eyes." Jake's looked away for a moment. "Like I said yesterday, your uncle asked Dad to watch over you, and that's become my mission. Dad takes his promises seriously. So do I. We'd like to identify the killer, but this is all about keeping you safe. Dad would run my ass up and down the beach for a few hours if he even thought I'd spilled his backstory. Or revealed my true identity."

Taylor touched Jake's hair. "You share a strong resemblance. I recognized you right away from the old photo in the ammo can."

Jake shrugged. "That's why Dad thought I could pull off the impersonation. That and my SEAL training. He believed I would be in more danger as myself."

"I agree. You'd be a free target for the killer. Like I am. Only the killer would save you for later." Taylor felt safe enough to sit and returned to her chair. How bizarre that she felt safe—she just acknowledged that she was in the killer's crosshairs.

"Or the killer would use me as a pawn against Dad. Against you, too. Dad also feared you wouldn't believe me as myself, but you would believe him."

How could someone she'd never met understand her so well? "He's right."

She wanted to tell Jake so much. She would try to be freer. Have a life outside the Coast Guard. Take a vacation. But the words wouldn't come. Her head hurt. "Jake . . . the past few days . . . I've learned so much. I want to say—"

Jake smiled. "You just have to learn to live, Taylor. That old up-close-and-personal thing. Your passion needs an outlet. Life's short."

"I'll try. But next week I'll be back at sea."

He moved behind her and kneaded her shoulders. "It will come. We were talking about how much Dad and I look alike. Mom said when they got married, his hair was black. When he came home, it was the same color mine is now. The same change happened to me. Late twenties, over a period of a few months. I'm taller than Dad—not much. He's a little leaner. His face is more lined and leathery now. Craggier. Our eyes are the same. We sound alike, but both his voice and word choice are usually rougher."

His voice soothed her. His magic touch was melting the knots.

"I think I'd like your parents." Her chin rested on her chest muffling her words. Jake's hands kept moving, prodding, digging into her muscles. She could sit here until morning as long as he never stopped.

"They'd like you. God, Taylor, do you ever relax?"

"I am relaxed."

"No you're not."

His hands moved from her shoulders and pulled her to her feet. He tilted her chin so she was forced to look at him. Her breath hitched at the mix of tenderness and pain in those amazing green eyes.

"I'm sorry for keeping you in the dark. I booted myself in the butt all day for placing the cameras. No, that's not correct. I still would have placed the cameras to avert a possible disaster. I need to put up new ones. And you need to know I secured a tracking device to your car so I know your whereabouts. It will stay in place."

"That's how you followed me so easily."

He shrugged. "I haven't forgiven myself for not having enough control to keep my hands off you when I knew the cameras were in place. I couldn't help myself. You have that much power over me, Taylor. Can you forgive me for being such an ass?"

She had power over him? His expression had turned despondent. Probably because his dad would run him up and down the beach. *I have power over him!*

She stood on tiptoe and kissed his chin. "I couldn't restrain myself either. It takes two. I forgive you, if you forgive me."

Jake kissed her.

Nothing had changed between them, despite all the changes. The fire in Taylor's belly burned twice as hot. He wore a tee, and she lifted it up and over his head. His lips left hers only for the half-second it took for the shirt to go over his head. The rest of their clothes flew off in record time. She wasn't certain who removed what or when they moved to the bed. Somewhere along the way, Jake had put on a condom.

She wanted him, plain and simple. She kissed her way down his body, to his feet, and back up again, heady at his musky scent. Her fingers smoothed the strip of dark hair that ran up to his belly button, enjoying its silkiness. His chest, back, arms, and legs were hard muscle, but his belly was softer and moved with her touch. She liked his reaction and continued to smooth his tummy with her hands.

His fingers tightened in her hair, and he ground out a moan. She moved up, stopping at his chest to feel his heartbeat throbbing beneath her touch. She continued upward and tasted the skin at the hollow of his neck, salty from the sea air, the skin rough.

"You taste like a sailor."

Jake's soft laughter rumbled in his throat.

The hoppy taste of beer joined the salt when she moved her lips to his mouth. His tongue played with hers while his hands explored her body, seemingly every place at once, freeing any inhibitions she might have held.

Taylor soared. At the moment her entire world existed only here, with Jake. He rolled her over, kissing her face, her neck, her lips. She raised her hips, and he lowered himself into her. They moved slowly together for a long time, his breathing the melody to the drumbeat of her heart. Her legs tightened around him, and their tempo increased.

She couldn't hold on another beat.

"Let go, Taylor."

She nodded, afraid if she spoke, she would scream.

They connected on so many levels Taylor could hardly believe she hadn't known Jake forever. His warmth filled her, and combined with hers, left her sated. She couldn't move a muscle. He moved enough to the side to not lie directly on top of her.

Taylor studied his face, the way his eyelashes lay against his cheek. His breathing relaxed and became heavy. Her own sleep would come with the next breath or two. She kept watch over him, smiling, as her eyes closed and she drifted in limbo between consciousness and dreams.

Her eyes popped open. The answer had come in a flash. She knew how to draw out Randy's killer and expose him for the son of a bitch he really was.

CHAPTER 35

The note lay on Jake's pillow. Taylor picked it up and rolled to her back.

Taylor –
You're always beautiful, but especially when you sleep. I couldn't disturb you. This morning I'm meeting with someone who should provide a lead about who fired on you and Will yesterday. I want to arrive early enough to scout the area and be in place long before he arrives. I'll be in touch. Stay safe.
Jake

She couldn't believe she hadn't noticed when he got out of bed, or heard the door when he left. Her fingers traced the words he'd written. His handwriting, the same as the list he'd made of the ammo can contents, consisted of strong, bold, no-nonsense strokes. Closed *a*'s and *o*'s. He could keep a secret. As if she needed his handwriting to tell her that.

A smile spread over her face, and she rolled over to laze where he had slept. The bed was warm. The click of the door as he closed it might have been what wakened her. She glanced at the clock—four-thirty. Snuggling down under the covers and holding Jake's note, she closed her eyes.

"Oh, crap!" She'd almost forgotten her plan. It required an early start, too. And she needed coffee.

An hour later, she opened the door to Randy's salvage shop. After turning on the lights, she returned to the car for her coffee and the ammo can. If this didn't work, she was pulling up anchor and leaving the solving of Randy's homicide to Detective Upchurch—if he reopened the case—or to Jake and his dad. She and Dan had a day or two remaining to work, and that would leave her a day or two to enjoy Rock Harbor, find out all the area had to offer. A day or two to enjoy Jake.

After a few sips of coffee, she shoved the watch Randy made up past her elbow and rearranged items on the short countertop just inside the door to give her about a foot of clear space. She opened the ammo can and took out what remained of Randy's belt, the shirt, and the old peanut container. She took the buckles out of the container and put them back in the ammo can. The killer had kept the buckles as souvenirs. Those were what he wanted, but he would recognize the peanut container, too, especially if it held significance for him.

Taylor couldn't figure out why the killer had sent the buckles and later the shirt to Randy before killing him. Perhaps he grew tired of Randy's presumed inability to focus. She believed the buckles were meant to tell Randy that one person had killed the other Compass Points and was coming for him next. And the shirt was a do-I-have-to-show-you-everything move.

The reality could be entirely different.

She guessed the killer planned to retrieve his souvenirs and Randy's belt and buckle after he was dead. But Uncle Randy had the last laugh. Good for him.

Randy's buckle was the only one the killer hadn't possessed. He would really want it now, after a year's time had passed. She removed the buckle from what remained of his belt and closed it inside the peanut container. The belt went back in the ammo can.

The peanut container, but no buckles inside except for Randy's. No stone in the buckle. No belt. That should fry the killer's balls.

Next she unrolled the shirt and shook it. With any luck, she'd find out this morning if the shirt provided a significant clue. If it did, she could abandon her plan and tell Glen what she learned. If not, the shirt would be simply another item on display.

She closed the ammo can and took it back to the trunk of the car. The sun had come up, but the light was still gray. Back inside, she decided to prop Randy's buckle on top of the peanut container—the killer wouldn't miss that. She set the container in the center of the countertop.

Making an artful display wasn't in her job description. She messed with the shirt—folding, unfolding. Draping it across the counter. Nothing looked right. She glanced at the time on her phone. Dan would arrive in a few minutes. She needed to finish.

Standing back, she eyed the countertop from the door then picked up the shirt, folded it so only the top half of the back with the tournament logo showed, and laid it on the countertop at an angle, one sleeve hanging off. She set the peanut can and buckle on top and near the back before rearranging the items she'd pushed to the side. The layout would do. To anyone but the killer, it would be another shelf of junk. But the killer should react in some way.

Tires crunched on the driveway. She grabbed her coffee and plopped down on an old camp stool. Dan was her first test subject.

A minute later the door opened. "You'll never believe my morning so far."

Ha. He'd never believe hers either. "Try me."

He closed the door. A white paper bag dangled from the hand holding his coffee. "Take this first. I brought bagels."

"What about your cholesterol?"

"I'll worry about that tomorrow. Our electric went out at home. A.J. said it's something to do with the breaker panel. I'm so glad I listened to him about having a gas water heater. Even though it's summer, I don't enjoy cold showers." He shivered.

She pulled out a bagel and handed the bag back. "Thanks."

"If that wasn't enough, cats held an orgy outside our bedroom in the wee hours. A.J. can sleep through anything. Not me.

Wake me up if you discover me crashed over a pile of unforgettables."

She laughed. "Nothing in here is unforgettable."

He pulled out the remaining bagel and crushed the bag into a ball. "I was in no mood for oatmeal. Oooh, what's that on your *arm!*"

She held it out. "I worked in here on Saturday and found this. I know it's junk, but I fell in love with it."

He moved closer. "I'm not an expert on gems, but I think this is lapis lazuli. Have it appraised when you get back to Charleston. The watch will need repair. Looks like a makeshift band."

"The whole watch looks like something a teenager would make. It's a little off the wall, but I love it."

He popped the last bite of his bagel and walked past her without one comment on the countertop. Her handiwork passed the Dan test. It was good to go.

"No sleep makes me hungry. Wow! You really did work back here."

"All I did was clear trash from a couple of rows of tables."

"I'm serious, Taylor. If you'll continue with clearing trash, I think we can finish today. If not today, with only a few hours tomorrow."

Taylor pulled a box of rusty, ragged lures from under a table and called Dan over.

"These are mine. Decorators pay top dollar for these. Mark my words. They'll all be gone in thirty days, and I'll get a minimum of ten dollars each for the worst ones. Much more for the others."

The door opened and A.J. walked in. "I brought coffee."

Dan rushed to the front. "You're wonderful. Thank you."

A.J. beamed. "I know how cranky you are when you don't get enough sleep. I felt sorry for Taylor." He held hers out.

"Thanks."

"Besides, I'm tired from looking like an artist all weekend. I'm going fishing."

"Catch dinner. Or stop by the fish market if nothing's biting."

"It's early enough, maybe I can round up a redfish out of Laguna del Sol. If I head out in the boat, I'll call and let you know where I'm going and when I'll be back."

"I'll walk you out."

Neither of them paid attention to her or her catch-the-killer display. Now that she knew the display didn't draw unwarranted attention, Taylor planned to tell the few people she knew here that they could come out and have anything they wanted for free—provided Dan didn't want their choices. Word would get around town. If the killer was here, he would find an excuse to show up and look for the items he coveted.

She would call Glen and Zia, but she could walk across the street right now while she drank her coffee and tell Will and Trinh. The last person she would tell would be Lulu, because she wouldn't get over there until lunch or after Dan left.

She touched Dan's shoulder as she passed. "I'm going to talk to Trinh and Will. If anyone wants items from in here, I'd like them to have them at no cost. People have been good to me, and I want to return the favor. You already have yours. A.J., you can look now or come back when you have time and look around."

A smile spread over A.J.'s face. "I did spot a couple of items. Thanks."

Trinh looked up from the floor. Her lap brimmed with pre-packaged aluminum cleats.

"Inventory time?"

Trinh's eyes rolled and she shook her head. "I only wish. Customer with a kid. I hate kids. They're always in here making a mess. Four, maybe five years old. Dumped out everything on this end cap. I had to smile and tell daddy how cute he was." She made a gagging face. "Now I have to sort and put them back in the right bins. Did I say I hate kids?"

Taylor chuckled. "Yeah, you did. I came over to tell you Dan and I are close to finishing across the street."

"So soon? I shouldn't be surprised. Dan Blair is a never-ending speed demon when he gets wound up. How long are you staying here? Will told me about your adventures yesterday."

"I'm going back Thursday, so just a few more days. Anyway, I'd like you to come over and scout around. We moved everything from the house to the shop or the trash bin. Dan is taking a few items, but the rest will be sold as one lot. So come over and see if there's anything you want. It's yours. No charge."

Trinh continued to put cleats in piles as she talked. "Thanks. My cousin is an artist and makes all kinds of things from junk. I'll find out what she needs."

"Bring her. Free for her, too, unless she needs a truck to haul it off. Then I'll give her a good deal."

"Got it. How about Will?"

"I was going to tell him, too, if he's here."

Trinh emptied her lap and bounced up. "He went into Corpus. You want me to tell him?"

"Please. Tell him there's a lot of junk but a lot of marine items, too. Those we can talk about."

CHAPTER 36

L eaving Taylor's bed tore Jake in two. The note he left told her bare minimum, but enough. He hoped.

After stopping for coffee and Krispy Kreme at a convenience store, he drove past Cecil's at ten past five and continued on to the bend in the road. He turned around, drove a short distance, and pulled as far as he could onto the meager shoulder, mosquitoes swarming in his high beams. He cut his lights, put the car in park, and got his sugar and caffeine fix while the eastern sky lightened from charcoal to gray.

No headlights had appeared from either direction. The punk who bashed Will's truck told him he would find Bill Abbott here around nine any morning of the week. His gut told him the thug wasn't above informing Abbott someone was looking for him. He'd been itching to try the thermal imaging binoculars, and the timing, going from night to day, was perfect.

For more than an hour he kept the binoculars trained on the areas surrounding Cecil's. They worked as well in the light as in the darkness. He'd write a good report on them when he got back to New York. He drove ahead holding the binoculars, and by the time he reached Cecil's, one of the doors was raised. No one lay hidden in the grass.

He grabbed a zippered notebook from the backseat. His cover.

The place stank of stale beer and cigarettes, mold and piss. A wizened old elf sat in a tall chair behind a stainless bar watching a morning news show on a television near the door. From his perch, the hoary relic could see both the television and the door. He glanced up and returned his attention to the cute blonde anchorwoman wearing lots of makeup.

Jake walked past and placed his notebook on the bar. "You Cecil?"

"Now just who the hell else would I be?"

Crotchety old coot. "My name's Jake. I'm working on a piece for a magazine about older Texans. Regular folks, not fancy ones or news-makers. I'm traveling around, stopping in small towns. Woman at the hotel told me I might find what I'm looking for out here. You have time to talk for a bit?"

Cecil looked at him again. Squinted his eyes, cocked his head. Hair stood out all around. "Wait 'til the commercial." He grinned. Cecil didn't have any teeth.

While Cecil lusted after the blonde, Jake unzipped his notebook, took out a cheap recorder and a pencil. A few minutes passed before a commercial break. Cecil turned around.

Jake punched a button on the recorder, gave his name and date, and asked Cecil for his name. Cecil told his life story in three- and four-minute sound bites during commercials, except for one to make change and one to make fresh coffee. In the interim, Jake talked to others who came in. None matched the description of Bill Abbott, and none stayed around after finishing their coffees.

At a quarter to nine, he started wrapping up with Cecil. "I really appreciate your talking to me. If it's all right, I'll stay around a bit, talk to a few others before I go on to my next stop."

Cecil nodded, his focus back on the television. Jake kept his same spot. At eight fifty-five a tan pickup rolled into the lot— the same color truck he was told Abbott drove. The man who got out matched Abbott's description—Anglo, sixties, medium height and build, balding, fat nose. And a tattoo of a blue shark on his forearm. Like the other customers, he walked around the bar, poured a mug of coffee, and left a dollar on the counter.

Jake introduced himself. "I've been talking to Cecil, and I spoke briefly with a few others. If you have time while you drink your coffee, I'd like to ask you a few questions, too."

"Why not. Cecil's not much of a talker while the television's on."

"Let's go sit over here." Jake led the way to a table in the center of the room. "What's your name?"

"Bill Abbott."

"Retired?"

"I still work here and there."

Jake scribbled. "I met someone who knows you."

Abbott reached for his mug, but Jake grabbed his wrist. "Will Knox. Ring a bell?"

The unscrupulous lowlife was cool on the outside, but Jake didn't miss the half-second of fear that flashed in his eyes.

"Nah."

Jake added a little pressure to his wrist. "I understand you know who wanted Mr. Knox's truck bashed."

Abbott clenched his teeth and shook his head.

"I can make it look as if you attacked me, and I acted in self-defense."

Abbott half-stood and reached for him with his free hand. Jake added pressure to his wrist, and the fear returned to Abbott's eyes.

"You're going to tell me who wanted Knox's truck trashed. If you don't, first I'll break your wrist. Then I'll set you up to take the fall for assault. I'm going to count to three. You won't be able to do much to defend yourself in jail with a broken wrist. Who knows if they'll set it correctly. One."

"Motherfucker."

"Two. Th—"

"Okay. Okay. Brady ordered it. Nate Brady."

Jake released his wrist. "Drink up. You're coming with me."

"My truck."

"Will stay here. Tell Cecil you're going to show me something and you'll pick it up later."

He loaded Abbott inside his rental and had him buckle up with hands on the dash, the same as with yesterday's goon. Inspiring obedience was about showing the other guy he meant business straight from the start. And not letting up on the attitude.

When they were rolling, Jake called Upchurch. "It's Jake Solomon."

"What's up?"

Jake gave him the location of the convenience store he'd stopped at this morning. "Meet me in five minutes."

Jake took the freeway and arrived in three. He'd just parked when Upchurch turned in and stopped behind him. The detective got out and walked to Jake's lowered window.

"Morning. What are you doing with that sleaze?" He inclined his chin toward Abbott, who mumbled something Jake didn't catch, but probably fit his standard scumbag vocabulary.

Jake turned to Abbott. "Tell him what you told me."

"Fuck off."

"Watch your mouth, Abbott. You know what happens when I get pissed off."

Upchurch backed away a couple of steps. "I don't want to hear this."

Jake lowered his voice. "If you don't tell the detective what you told me, I'll find Brady myself and tell him you're the snitch. You want him to come after you? I'll give him enough time before I tell the detective where to find him. And you. It's your choice. Don't make me count to three again. Oh, and you can walk back to your truck, too. Think you can make it before I can find Brady?"

"You're—"

"Yeah, yeah. What's your decision?"

This time Jake understood the mumbled *all right*.

Abbott gave Upchurch the information about Nate Brady.

Upchurch nodded and looked at Jake. "Pick me up at the station for lunch. We need to talk."

Jake dropped Abbott at Cecil's and headed for Rankin's.

CHAPTER 37

Taylor stuffed another armload of paper into a trash bag. She'd talked to Zia and left a message for Glen, so now the waiting game began. Only a few more tables and she would be finished. The work was easier since learning Randy's dementia had been an act and he had wrecked the house and salvage shop for a reason.

A car pulled up outside.

Dan raised his head. "Incoming."

The door opened and Jake walked through.

She waved. "Over here."

He grinned. "Is it safe in here?"

Dan sneezed. "Just barely, but we'll get there."

Jake's smile vanished. He'd seen her display. Taylor hustled to the front.

He hooked his thumb toward the peanut can. "Are you crazy?" His voice was a whisper.

"I'm setting a trap to draw out the killer." Her voice matched his. "Word will get out, and he'll show up to find his trophies."

"This is foolish. We're dealing with a killer. You don't have any way to protect yourself."

"I have my phone . . . and Glen on speed dial."

"A killer, Taylor. And you have the watch on your arm. This isn't a Coast Guard rescue."

"So what do you suggest I do? Hide in a corner with a .357 propped on a stack of crab traps?"

"What are you two whispering about?" Dan came up the aisle between tables.

Jake draped an arm over her shoulder but didn't say anything. The tips of his fingers played with Randy's watch at her elbow. Bastard.

"I was telling him—"

Jake kissed the top of her head.

"Ahh!" Dan clapped his hands. "I should have seen this coming."

He actually did a Snoopy dance, and Jake laughed. She plastered on a smile backed by fury.

"Congratulations. Both of you. Taylor, you should have told me. No wonder you're wearing a glow today." He sneezed again. "I'm going outside to get some of the dust out of my nose."

Jake hugged her closer. She wanted to kick him in the kneecaps except she couldn't turn her body. As soon as the door closed behind Dan, he released her.

"How *dare* you make disparaging remarks about the Coast Guard."

"I'm not disparaging anyone. The work you do is important. You save lives. But you don't deal with killers every day, people who pull the trigger for money or jollies."

"Excuse me. We do save lives. But we also carry live rounds. We perform armed boardings. We participate in joint operations with every other military service. Illegal trawlers, drug runners, migrant boaters—they all believe they make their own laws at sea. It's our job to show them a different scenario. Don't you *dare* tell me I don't put my life on the line every single day."

"I meant no disrespect. It's different when it's one on one. That's my job. I'm here to protect you, and I can't do that if you go around setting traps. The killer will scoff at your display, Taylor."

He was making her madder by the minute. "Scoff? Randy's murderer is not going to scoff when he sees this buckle. Or this shirt. Oh shit!" She flung her hand in the general direction of the counter before covering her mouth with it.

"What?" Concern flooded Jake's face.

"I've been so busy here, I haven't called about the shirt."

The door opened and Zia entered, followed by Dan. "I think I got the sneezing out of my system, and I found Zia the Beautiful. She said you called her about looking at our assemblage of items no one should live without."

Everyone laughed, Taylor included, although she kept her attention on Zia. "I did. Only I didn't expect you here so soon. Make yourself at home. Look around. Except for the two tables right behind this counter, the rest is clear of trash and broken items. Grab anything you want for free now or pay top dollar in an antique store later."

"Except Echoes. Zia and I have a pact." Dan placed a hand on Zia's shoulder.

Echoes. The code. After Zia left, Taylor would ask Dan about it.

Zia ignored Dan's hand and moved closer to Jake. "Are you looking for items for that condo I showed you?"

He smiled. "Still thinking."

She patted his cheek. "Don't think too much."

Taylor wanted to slap Zia's hand away. But Zia had no way of knowing about Taylor's new relationship with Jake. Not that it would've mattered. Zia was Zia. Jake winked at her as Zia swept toward the back of the shop without a glance at the display.

Dan stood wide-eyed through the whole exchange. He turned to Taylor. "Girlfriend, you are the poster girl for restraint. Kudos." His voice was soft. He favored her with a deep nod.

"I had a moment before I remembered it was Zia."

"She even flirts with A.J." Dan sighed. "Back to work."

Jake took Taylor's hand for the few steps to the door. "I'll check into the shirt if you want and let you know what I learn. Upchurch asked me to meet him for lunch, or I'd hang around."

"Good. Tell Glen what you know. Is it about your meeting this morning? About Randy?"

Jake leaned his head toward the back of the shop. "We'll talk later."

He walked out, and she got as far as her display when her phone rang with a private number. She stiffened. "Hello?"

"It's Jake. I just pulled out of your driveway. Walk outside to talk."

"One second." She moved into Dan's field of vision and raised her voice. "I have to take this call. I'll be right back."

Neither he nor Zia looked up. He waved her out.

"Okay, I'm outside, walking toward the driveway."

"Keep looking toward Will's, and walk about halfway down your driveway before you turn around. By then I'll be out of your range of vision. The fewer people who know about us, the better for you."

She understood what Jake meant. If no one realized they were involved, no one could use one as an emotional or real hostage against the other. Maybe her subconscious had guided her non-response to Zia's flirting. The only reason Jake had opened up with Dan was to distract him and keep her from telling him about the shirt and buckle. She understood that, too.

"Got it. You have news?"

"Yes, but it's only a lead. I'll learn more when I talk to Glen."

"So tell me."

"You have the right to know. But you need to play your cards close. Can you do that?"

"Jake. Pay attention. Did we not just have this conversation? True, I'm not a SEAL. But I com—"

"Jesus H., Taylor. This has nothing to do with your life in the Coast Guard."

"You're wrong. It has everything to do with my life in the Coast Guard. I hold a command position and have for years. Years, Jake. It's who I am. I'm not some bimbo who's going to hang on your every word and do exactly what you say just because you say it. I have a brain, and I use it to draw my own conclusions and make my own decisions. I respect your input, and I expect you to respect mine."

"You—"

"I'm not finished. I'm responsible for the actions and safety of one hundred men and women both in port and at sea. For a cutter, a helo, and small boats. Most of our missions are drug interdiction or Homeland Security related. All are classified. Did you get that, Jake? So to answer your question, yes, I think I can play my cards close to my chest. And I can also make quick decisions. I've been making those for years, too."

Sweet mother of God. Taylor rubbed her forehead. How the hell had she fallen head over heels for such a jerk?

"I apologize, Taylor. You're right."

She raised her head. Had Jake really said she was right? His tone hadn't been condescending, either.

"I'm accustomed to telling people with no training how to protect themselves. I can't tell them about what's going on behind the scenes because either they don't want to know or they don't understand that what I tell them is confidential and, if heard by the wrong person, could get them killed. I know you aren't like either of those examples."

"Thank you."

"But you're a woman. A very desirable woman. As a man, I want to protect you. It's what men do—hardwired in our DNA. When that section of my brain fires up, the rest of me tends to forget you're a capable military officer who will outrank me as soon as you add that fourth stripe."

Jake's words made Taylor feel special. She hadn't felt special in a long time.

"Can you forgive me for questioning your abilities?" He sounded honest and sincere.

Taylor smiled. "I forgive you. I may have overreacted a bit."

"We're just getting to know each other." Jake's voice perked up. "I haven't gotten over seeing your killer bait. It took me by surprise."

"Good. I want my display to startle the killer, too."

"I understand."

"Let's start over. Tell me your news."

"The lead I got points toward Nate Brady."

"I *knew* it. Those mean little pig eyes."

"Excuse me?"

"Of course we don't know. It's a lead. But Brady has mean little pig eyes. He looks like he could kill." *Shut up, Taylor. He'll think you're one of the bimbos you said you weren't.*

"It always pays to trust your instincts."

Yes!

"Promise me you won't be at the shop alone. I'm not saying you're not capable. I would ask that of anyone who presented himself as a target."

"I promise. When Dan leaves, I'll go back to the hotel. But I can't tell him about my plan. He would be too nervous. And tell someone."

"Agreed. We'll get through this, Taylor. Stay alert."

"I will."

"By the way, I know why you chose Sleepy today." His voice dropped in pitch, and became a seductive growl in Taylor's ear.

Warmth flowed through her, and she matched her tone to his. "Three hours' sleep isn't very much. But I wouldn't trade it for eight."

"Neither would I."

If she were a cat, she'd stretch and purr. They'd had their first meeting of minds without a huge blow-up argument. And make-up phone cuddling. "I'm turning around now."

"If I find out more about Nate, I'll let you know. Keep in touch with me."

"Okay. I'm going back inside."

The shop door opened and Zia came out.

"Hey, Zia. Find anything?" Taylor pressed her phone off and returned it to her pocket.

"No. I'm a fan of estate sales, though, because you never know what you'll find. I was hoping something would reach out and hug me, but the only one that did was a table Dan already has dibs on."

"I gave him first shot. If he hadn't been here to help, I would have thrown up my hands in frustration the first day. He's a godsend."

Zia hugged her. "Thanks for asking me."

Back inside, Taylor went into full speed cleanup mode and finished the first table. "One more to go, Dan, and the trash will be history."

"Let's go celebrate. I want to take you to my sister's restaurant for lunch."

"I'm not dressed to go anyplace."

"You and Sleepy are fine. Trust me. This is Rock Harbor, and Julie is my sister. When we come back, we'll finish."

Dan washed up first so the air conditioner could begin cooling his car. She grabbed her bag and locked up.

"Where are we going?"

"Juliet's Tango."

"By your gallery?"

He nodded, looking over his shoulder as he backed out of the drive.

"Dan, can I ask you something?"

"Sure."

"It's about the names of your gallery and shop. Bravo. Echoes. Your sister's tearoom."

"Juliet's Tango. Her husband owns Mike's Golf."

"Thank God!"

"What?"

"I was imagining some sort of weird conspiracy."

Dan laughed so hard he shook all over.

"Hey, watch the road."

"We wanted a gimmick to tie our businesses together in some way when we moved to the new spaces a couple of years ago."

She combed her fingers through her hair, happy to have learned the answer to the riddle.

Dan turned onto Church Street. "You're Coast Guard. Of course you'd notice. Before we moved to Zia's block, Julie was in town, but in another location, as Julie's Tearoom. Mike was in a strip center up near the airport. He's always been Mike's Golf Shop, so that's what gave us the idea. My gallery-slash-chintz shop was called Dan's Designs, and it was in a different strip center."

"You're so funny. Especially since I've seen how you live."

He flashed a grin. "Every once in a while, someone asks one of us about the names. Or the flags. Not often."

"Thanks for telling me."

"You can ask me anything, Taylor. I told you, we're kindred spirits."

She was coming to believe him.

A few minutes later, Taylor stepped into a contemporary version of a tea room. Small tables covered with white tablecloths were set with cobalt chargers and white luncheon plates topped with starched yellow napkins. Hung on the lemon wall facing the entrance was a large Juliet flag—wide blue bars at top and bottom, white in the center. A vessel traveling with a raised Juliet flag meant it was on fire and carrying dangerous cargo.

The hostess settled them at a table by a window. Dan leaned across. "What do you think?"

"Lovely. Much better than tea cozies and ribbon."

He laughed. "Julie will be pleased. She's not the ruffles and bows type either. I'd introduce you, but she's at the dentist."

"Another time." Taylor looked at the menu. The selections echoed the Juliet flag—*on fire and dangerous cargo*. Among the choices were Shrimp Salad Diablo and Buffalo Chicken Salad. "I love it."

"All Julie's customers do. Everything comes mild, spicy, or with a sexy firefighter. Even the PB&J sandwich. Julie makes her own jalapeño jelly."

The waitress came to take their order, and Taylor chose the shrimp salad, spicy version. Dan ordered Cayenne Rubbed Ribeye.

"Doesn't that scorch your throat?"

"I'll give you a bite—four ounces of rare ribeye, sliced extra thin, and served over arugula with her special chipotle vinaigrette. To. Die. For."

"Yummy. I'll trade you a shrimp. When I get back to Charleston, I may try making the steak myself."

"You won't be sorry. She won't say what she puts in the rub besides cayenne. Maybe you can tell by the taste."

"If I were her I wouldn't reveal the ingredients either. You're not the best at keeping secrets. You'd tell me, and then her secret wouldn't be special anymore."

"You're right about that. She's smarter than I am."

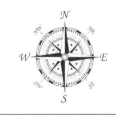

CHAPTER 38

J ake's phone rang as soon as he hung up with Taylor.

"Hey, Kelly. Got good news for me?"

"Yes, for once. Dad is out of ICU and will probably go home tomorrow. Mom said the doctors were hopeful about his latest MRI. I won't be able to access the reports until tomorrow after the hospital uploads overnight."

"All right! He's a fighter."

"So is Mom. They had a mini love-fest for a few minutes in his room. I could feel the positive energy flowing between them. It was that strong."

"I believe it."

"Then Dad called food services and asked for enough food to feed the floor."

"Life is good, Kelly Jane. Dad's back in charge."

"That's what Mom said. And don't call me Kelly Jane."

Jake wished he'd been there to share in their happy moment, but if he had, he would've missed out on meeting Taylor. Kelly could handle things back in New York just fine.

"Oh, in the excitement, I almost forgot. You asked me to check the names for Denver connections."

"Who hit?"

"Nate Brady. Some kind of cattlemen's convention last spring. He was registered, and he paid for his room with his

American Express card. I also found him on security camera archives. So far I haven't found anyone else connected to Denver or the convention, but I'm still searching. Brady's quacking like a duck."

"Waddles like one, too. See if you can find any link between him and Dad."

"I'm on it." She hung up.

Jake continued to the police department. Upchurch waited out front and wasted no time climbing in out of the heat. "Hot enough for you out there?"

The detective snorted as he buckled up.

"Lulu's work for you?"

Upchurch patted his stomach. "Can't you tell?"

Lulu greeted them when they walked through the door, and they moved to a back booth. The television was tuned to a news channel with captions, and *Carmen* played in the background. A fair amount of customers filled the booths and tables, but it wasn't packed.

After Lulu took their orders, Upchurch got down to business. "You know I don't condone your methods."

Jake shrugged one shoulder. "I'm not a peace officer."

"The man still has rights."

This was why his dad didn't like dealing with law enforcement any more than necessary. He laced his fingers on the table and leaned forward. "Taylor Campbell? Will Knox? What about their rights?"

Upchurch rubbed his cheek with his knuckles. "I have to toe the line. That still goes if Abbott files a complaint against you."

"Nothing I did violated his rights in any way." Except being a hair away from breaking his wrist. "He chose to believe my words. Putting the fear of God into a suspect is part of my job description."

"No matter the consequences?"

"My obligation is to our client. I'm damned good at my job, by the way."

"I don't doubt that for a moment. Like I told you yesterday, your firm has a sterling reputation. Otherwise I wouldn't be here with you. All the same, I have my rules the same as you have yours."

Lulu arrived with their drinks. Jake opened his beer.

Upchurch raised his brow and held up his glass. "Truce?"

"Truce." After a quick swallow, Jake spoke first. "What did you find out about Brady?"

"I went out to his place yesterday. No one was home. I walked out to the dock and checked the boat. It was locked down. No spent casings. No way to tell if it had been out."

Jake hadn't expected any different. The boat had been in the area, but he wouldn't share the knowledge with Upchurch until Kelly learned if there was a connection between Brady and their dad. "Had the neighbors seen him?"

"I talked with three. One had, one hadn't, and one wasn't sure if he saw him Saturday or Sunday."

Jake stayed silent and picked at the Bud label.

"No one I talked to knew if he took the boat out, but they wouldn't unless they were outside and watching. Zia Markham was showing a house next door. She said a red truck had been in the driveway when she arrived, but she was busy opening the property and making sure everything was in order. Her clients confirmed the truck was there when they arrived. The wife said she noticed it because it was bright red."

"Let me guess. You never made contact with Brady."

"No. He flies his own plane here. It's at the airport. We're looking for him—"

"Person of interest?"

"Not yet. Possible witness. We don't want to spook him."

It would do for a start.

Returning from lunch, Taylor flinched at the sight of the peanut can, buckle, and shirt on the counter—even though she knew they were there. Jake hadn't called her and Dan was still outside chatting with A.J.

She would make the call about the shirt. It wouldn't hurt, even if she duplicated Jake's efforts. The woman at the Chamber of Commerce gave her the name and phone number of the man who organized the tournament, but she had to leave a voicemail. Story of her life these days.

Dan rushed through the door. "Okay, I'm ready to finish this."

"I hear you. I'm looking forward to a bit of tourist time."

For several minutes, they worked in silence.

"Hey, Taylor." Dan's muffled voice came from under the next table where he pulled on a small trawl net. "This net is caught under here."

"I'll lift a corner of the table."

"Won't work. The net's knotted up in the middle, not near a leg. I thought I could free it, but I need to move gear out until I find what's holding it." He shoved a Coleman stove into the aisle, followed by a life ring and a box of romance novels.

"That get it?" Taylor pushed the items down the row.

"No."

"I'll work from the other side."

"Found it."

A heavy object scraped the floor, and the sounds Dan made could've come from a bull elephant.

"What the hell is it?"

"I don't know. You tell me."

Dan reappeared feet first, pulling the item across the floor.

"A brass bitt." She dropped to her knees and helped him pull. "This is old. They don't make them like this anymore. Newer ones are more angular and less massive."

The bitt could be a hundred years old, but probably not. More likely it came off a World War II-era ship. She hadn't seen one in years, except in books. Five equally spaced bolt holes cut through the ten-inch circular base. The bollard was five inches in diameter and stood a foot tall. Two arms extended outward at a one-eighty for eighteen inches across the top. The solid brass was in dire need of polishing, but she couldn't keep her hands off the mottled patina.

"Does it go on a pier?" Dan ran a finger along the top surface, scowled, and turned his finger over to see if the green came off.

"No. On a ship, bolted to the deck. Whatever ship it belonged to was scrapped a long time ago. This is mine." A smile spread across her face.

"What on earth will you use it for?"

She shrugged.

"You're smiling, Taylor. Give."

"Decoration. Or on my patio to prop my feet on. Will you help me move it inside the house? Who knows . . . maybe it came from an old Coast Guard cutter."

"Of course I'll help you." He dusted it with the edge of the trawl net.

Less than two hours later, they deposited the last of the trash in the bin and walked back to the salvage shop. Taylor gave a whoop, her waving arm sending a kayak paddle clunking into a metal lamp base. "Can you believe we're finally finished?"

"I'll admit it's been a project. But worth every drop of sweat and every blister."

She rubbed the smooth leather of the watchband at her elbow. "I agree."

"Come over here. I want to tell you a story, and sitting sounds really good."

They plopped down on two canvas camp stools.

"Remember way back on Tuesday when I kept insisting you let me help you?"

Taylor snickered. "All the way back to last week? I seem to recall you begging."

"I wanted to help you because I understood what you were going through. How you feel losing your uncle. How it is going through his things. His life. But I also wanted to help myself. So it worked out for both of us."

Taylor covered Dan's hand with hers. He must have recently lost one of his parents. "Losing someone you love is hard. I don't think people know how hard it is until it happens to them. I'm so happy you convinced me to let you help. I would still be working in Randy's house."

Dan chuckled. "I can be pushy."

"It all worked out."

"Yes, it did. What I want to tell you is I learned how hard death is in high school."

Taylor frowned. Dan was fidgeting and gnawing at his lower lip.

"Julie and I grew up in Houston. We had an older brother, Stewart. I was in high school, Julie in junior high. Stewart had been to college and dropped out to work construction. To make some money before he went back. Housing was booming."

Dan paused. His eyes looked far away and pain filled his face. His lips trembled. Finally he sighed and went on. "I walked in after school and Stewart stood in the middle of the living room holding Dad's gun."

"Oh, no." Taylor's fingers tightened on Dan's hand. His brother must have killed himself.

"I asked Stewart what was going on. He said he and a new guy got into a fight on the job site."

"What happened? I can't imagine anyone related to you getting into a fight."

"Stewart could handle himself, but he wasn't an instigator. The guy accused him of stealing his tools. Stewart wasn't a thief."

A knot formed in Taylor's stomach. "I'm getting a bad feeling."

"Stewart had a black eye and bruised knuckles. We didn't hear the full story until later. Mom and Dad were both at work. Stewart told me to leave. Actually he pushed me out the door and locked it. I ran to find Julie so she wouldn't go home."

Taylor couldn't imagine dealing with such a horrible experience in high school. "I hope you found her."

"Two blocks away. We went to a neighbor's and called Dad."

"Good."

"When I hung up, Mrs. Light, our neighbor, called the police. While she was on the phone, a tricked-out car pulled up and three men got out. The shots came while she was on the phone."

"No." The betrayal and anger Taylor had felt at Randy's death returned as if they'd never left. She shook her head.

Dan took a deep breath. "Julie got the plate number when they drove off. Dad and the police arrived about the same time. She gave the number to the police, and they stopped the car before the men ever got out of town."

"I don't know what to say."

He patted her hand. "One man was killed in prison, one died in a jailbreak, and the third was wanted for two murders in Arizona. Last I heard he's in prison there. Life with no parole."

"I'm so sorry, Dan. How awful!"

Dan gave her a clipped nod. "Stewart died right away. His boss said the guy was bragging about getting rid of Stewart, and he recommended one of his buddies to take his place. The boss fired him on the spot. That's when they came looking for Stewart. We never knew who told them where we lived. Stewart's boss got there about the same time the police did. Stewart never fired Dad's gun."

Dan had tears in his eyes, and Taylor fought against the burning in hers. She wrapped her arms around him.

After a couple of minutes Taylor straightened. "You'll always be my friend. We are kindred spirits."

More than he knew.

CHAPTER 39

J ake drove Upchurch back to the police station. Among other things, he learned he wouldn't want to face Upchurch on the other end of a gun. Or across a poker table.

"Make the block around the building." Upchurch pulled at his ear.

"Reconnoitering?"

"Old habit."

Jake laughed. "Right. You know what they say about old habits."

"Yeah. They're worn by old nuns. My name's Upchurch. I get away with telling jokes like that."

"Someone should have put a stop to that a long time ago. Old habits will get you killed."

The detective's sunglasses hid his eyes, but it was Jake's best guess they hadn't flashed a smile. Except for the slight side-to-side motion of his head, Upchurch didn't move. A man on the hunt. At some point in his career, Upchurch had been surprised or ambushed right at his own nest, and he didn't intend for it to happen again.

On the sidewalk in front of the station, Upchurch lowered his sunglasses and gave Jake a hard stare. "You didn't hear this from me."

Jake barely inclined his head in acknowledgment. Upchurch had decided to trust him.

"Brady and Ms. Markham had a lot of extracurricular activity going on between them once upon a time."

Jake forced himself to copy Upchurch's deadpan face to not give away he already had the knowledge. He counted through his breathing, thankful his mouth hadn't fallen open of its own accord. No law enforcement officer had ever shared case-related material with him before.

"A couple years ago, word got around they were kaput. I don't know if they still are or not."

—*four, five, exhale.*

"I didn't press her on Brady. Timing wasn't appropriate with her clients present. You might find her approachable for more, under different circumstances." He stood up. "Have a good day, now."

"Thanks." Approachable. Jake liked the word.

It was Upchurch's turn to nod. He closed the door and entered the building.

Jake pulled away from the curb and drove to Zia's office while his mind wove random thoughts into a plan.

The receptionist looked up from a magazine. "May I help you?"

"Zia Markham please."

"I'm sorry. She's out for the rest of the afternoon. Do you want to leave a message?"

Jake handed her a card from his wallet. "I'll try to reach her, but if I'm not successful, please tell her I'd like to talk about the condo space she showed me last week."

Back in his car, he sat for a minute or two staring at nothing. Then he pulled out his phone and called Kelly.

"I was ninety seconds from calling you."

Jake grabbed his pad and pencil. "Shoot."

"Remember those Navy flags in town?"

"The signal flags."

"Right. I gave you the owners of those four places."

"Yes."

"Dan Blair and Julie Quitman are siblings."

"Ah, a family marker. The flags are probably their own insider code." When he talked with Taylor, he'd give her the news so she could cross that mystery off her list.

"I found out who owns Elements." Jake watched a seagull swoop in for a scrap of ice cream cone on the sidewalk.

"You told me it was a Delaware corporation. Did you uncover the principals?"

"The corporation is called B-J-Q. That's the letters B for boy, a dash, J for joy, a dash, and Q for—"

"Quitman."

"You always gotta spoil it."

"I'm guessing B for Blair and J for Janacek, too."

"August Janacek, Mr. Smarty Pants."

"I've met these people. My gut tells me nothing sinister is going on, but information is power if I need it. Most likely they want to be in a good place to franchise Elements if the business is a hit."

"I get it."

"How's Denver coming?"

"No new hits. Still searching."

"What about the other things?"

"Iffy. I don't want you acting on hearsay I can't confirm because you find yourself in an either/or situation. Soon as I clear it up, you'll be the first to know. And if that's not enough, the black hats hacked into several state vital records servers over the weekend. I'm waiting on a couple of those. They're starting to come back up, one by one."

"Make it happen."

Even with Kelly on the job, fact-finding took time. No wonder his dad had come up empty all those years.

Taylor and Dan got back to work. He started at the rear of the shop making a list of top items on a yellow legal pad. She worked at the front carrying a laundry basket and tossing in loops of steering cable. The mess irritated her. The least she could do was put like items together. Her phone rang, and a couple of loops flipped out of the basket when she set it on the floor.

"Hi. I'm returning your call about the fishing tournament." The male voice was the same as on the voicemail greeting.

"Thanks for calling. Hang on a second." She walked over to Dan. "I'm going to step outside and take this."

"I'll be right here." He shooed her out with the pad.

As she closed the door, she put the phone to her ear. "Thanks for holding, and for returning my call so quickly." She headed down the driveway again, toward the boatyard.

"How can I help you?"

"I have a question about the tournament five years ago."

"Okay. I'll make some notes."

"You still have the records?" She crossed her fingers.

"Since day one."

"Wonderful. I hoped you would."

"We retain everything. I volunteered to keep them because I have what my wife calls a man cave out back. We have two file cabinets filled with older records. More recent tournament information is scanned and stored online."

A string of brown pelicans flew along the shore toward the marina, and she paused to watch. The birds fascinated her. Always had.

"Ma'am? Hello?"

"Oh, sorry. Distracted. Would it be possible for me to look at the records?"

"Umm . . ."

She wouldn't let him blow her off. "You can stay to make sure I don't destroy or take anything. I don't know exactly what I need. I'm trying to solve a family puzzle. I might start with looking for one thing but end by asking for something different after I have the information I wanted originally. You know how that goes."

"Sounds like my day job. Well . . . I guess I can do that."

"What time?" Her implication was for today so this wouldn't drag out longer than necessary.

"After five-thirty. I work in Corpus and get off at four-thirty. Never can tell about traffic."

"How about seven?" That would give enough time for Trinh and her cousin to poke through the shop. Trinh could lock up if they stayed longer.

"Works for me."

The directions he gave her were easy to understand—he lived only a block off Church Street. Walking back to the shop, she looked around. The stuffed trash bin would go tomorrow. The place was in fair shape and would hold until she returned next summer. She'd hire a handyman to tackle her growing list of fix-its. Dan, Zia, and Will would help her compile a list of reputable people. Plus she had some remodeling ideas to discuss. A weekend trip or two shouldn't be a problem, if necessary.

"Wait up!" Will's footsteps pounded behind her. "Trinh just told me you'll deal on Rankin's inventory."

"Below-market price for you on marine parts. No charge for anything else."

"Fair enough. I'll get an overview and come back in the morning for a more thorough look. I'd do it now, but I'm up to the top of my noggin in headaches."

They went inside. "Go ahead. I'll sit up here and rest for a bit."

Will looked around, stopped at items here and there. Near the back, he stopped and talked to Dan, borrowed Dan's pen, and wrote on his hand. A minute later, he joined her near the door.

"I jotted down a few items." He flashed his palm at her. "I'll get back to you with what I think is a fair price. We can start there."

"Sounds good."

The door opened before Will could leave, and Glen entered. After half a minute of small talk, Will left and Glen turned to her. "I got your message."

"Thanks for coming by. I got a message yesterday afternoon at the hotel."

"Another call?"

"No. A note." She relayed the message and what the clerk told her about a delivery.

"You have it?"

"It's safe." Locked in the bag that held her worthless piece-of-crap laptop.

"Good. I doubt the sender left prints, but I'll pick it up from you later. I'll also have a chat with the desk clerk about the messenger." Glen took a peppermint from a tin and popped it in his mouth. "Want one?"

"No thanks."

He returned the tin to his pocket. "I have some news for you, too. Or non-news. The report on your uncle has been sent to the state archives. It will be a week or more before I receive it. But the wheels are in motion."

Taylor sighed. "We'll be at sea by the time it gets here. You have my cell number and email. You can let me know." She pushed aside her disappointment. Government time never got in a hurry.

"I will."

She wouldn't let Randy's murder—and she was now as convinced as Jake that Randy was murdered—go uninvestigated. If Glen wasn't able to get the case reopened, she would explore alternatives. When she got back to Charleston, she'd call someone at District Legal to find out what those alternatives were. She had a plan. She turned her thoughts back to Glen.

"The other reason I called you is Dan and I are done in here. I thought you might like a better look. If you find anything you want, take it. The rest will go to an as-is buyer, so a few items won't make any difference."

Glen reached for the fishing shirt. If he took it, half her display would disappear. His fingers touched the placket, turned it a few different ways, and checked the collar before putting it back. "Too small. I need an extra large. I remember that tournament."

"You do?" The words escaped before she could stop them.

"It was only five years ago."

"You fish all the time. How do you remember one tournament?"

"Nate Brady won. I still think he cheated."

Nate Brady. Every lead kept coming back to that pig-eyed, egotistical wannabe sailor. If Glen hadn't been standing in front of her, she would've pumped her fist and shouted *Yes!* She had to tell Jake.

CHAPTER 40

Glen gathered a few items, including two boat fenders. As soon as he left, Taylor called Jake, excited to tell him the news about Nate Brady. He picked up on the first ring.

"I know who won the grand prize in the fishing tournament."

"Who?"

"Nate Brady."

"How did you find out?" His voice sounded tight.

"Glen stopped in to look around. He told me."

"I told you I'd call."

"Did you?" She could accuse as easily as he did.

"I've been busy."

She huffed and threw up her free hand. "So have I. Don't get ticked at me because I gave you a name. See what else you can find out. I have to go." She hung up before he said anything else.

Taylor went back to work, more to expend energy than to accomplish anything. Men. Always difficult. She ended up sorting through a lot and finding baskets and boxes and other containers for several like items. Enough to fill an entire table.

Dan interrupted her search for gears and pulleys. "That's it, Taylor. Stop sorting. Potential buyers won't care. We can stick a fork in it—*we're done.*"

She surveyed the massive space. Where Randy had artfully crafted confusion and chaos, now most items could be partially seen and pathways defined the area. Randy had wanted her to do this. "Thank you again."

Dan waved off her thanks. "You'll net more for what's here than you would have for everything, including the items I'm taking, if you'd tried to sell in the original condition with all the trash and debris."

"I'm glad we don't have to take inventory. Can you imagine?"

He chose random items and listed them on an imaginary slate. "Two white pottery coffee mugs. One kayak paddle, however many inches. Five stainless cleats."

Taylor laughed. "We'd be here a month."

"For not much more money. I compiled a general category listing. Bulk buyers like a bullet list of what they're buying."

Paraphernalia of all kinds still stuffed the space, but Rankin's Marine Salvage was nothing like the junk heap it had been.

"Tonight I'll figure out a price for what I'm taking. I've been keeping a running total, but I want to recalculate."

She touched his arm. "Don't worry. I'm serious. Your help was priceless. I'm giving things to others for free, and to you, too. You helped above and beyond the call of duty."

"No, I can't—"

"You helped me and will continue to help me by finding a buyer for the rest. Consider your treasures a gift from me and from Randy. Believe me, you earned whatever they're worth. I don't care if you picked an antique worth a million dollars."

"Absolutely not." He pursed his lips and shook his head.

Her phone rang. "We'll finish talking about this in a bit."

"I'll start loading the pieces that will fit in my car. Tomorrow I'll bring A.J.'s truck for the rest." He picked up a box filled with old metal toys as she answered.

"Taylor Campbell."

"Boy, I'm glad I caught you. I have to work overtime, and I won't be able to meet you today to go through those tournament records."

Her spirits fell. She was sure the answer hinged on the shirt. Nate Brady won the tournament, but other names might provide additional clues or elevate Nate Brady's importance. His name might or might not be the one she needed.

"My replacement had an appointment and is running late. I keep saying I'm going to find a job outside of refinery work, but the money's too good."

"Not your fault. How about tomorrow?"

"Tomorrow works. Do you have any idea what you need? I might know the answer without looking at the file."

"I'm looking for names, but I don't know which ones. Someone who would've had a patch from that tournament. Or a shirt with the logo on the back."

"That could be anyone who paid the entry fee. In both cases."

"Or names of the winners. Or a booby prize winner. Something distinctive."

"I'll work in that direction when I get home. My wife will be home in a bit. I'll call and leave her a message."

Dan came back in.

"Thanks. I appreciate your help." She hung up.

Dan leaned against the door and smiled. "I understand you mean well, and you want to repay me for helping you. But, really, I love wallowing in chintz."

She laughed.

"And I loved getting to know you. Our time together was good therapy. If you hadn't let me help, I would've been hurt."

"I would've thrown everything into about ten Bixby bins. You realize that."

"What a shame that would've been." He his sad eyes brightened. "Ooh, an idea!"

"What?"

"I'll pay you a fair price for my items. That means about a third of what they're worth on the market. A little better than you'd get from a pawn shop on things they'd take."

She shook her head.

"Hear me out." He held up his hands. "In return you can pay me a finder's fee for locating someone to buy the rest of these treasures."

"Fifteen percent."

He laughed. "Five."

"Ten." She glared at him with her hands on her hips.

But he didn't give in. "Five."

She lifted her hand with her pointer finger raised. "And a beer. Or two." She raised the next finger to join the first.

"Deal."

Five minutes later, they walked into an energy-filled Lulu's.

Glen sat at the bar with a man she didn't recognize. She waved as she followed Dan to the back near the patio. Two servers worked the booths and tables. Lulu stayed behind the bar.

They slid into a booth and Taylor ordered beers and chips and salsa for both of them. "I finally feel myself relaxing. We accomplished a lot." She stretched.

"You deserve an award for being willing to tackle the mess. Most people I know would've run away. Speaking of which . . . you're leaving Thursday?"

"Right. If I hit a delay, it gives me enough time to check in on Friday. I need the weekend to catch up with what's happened on the *Susquehanna* while I've been here. Monday we get underway for Savannah to stand guard at the Tall Ships Festival, then on to patrol."

"How long do you stay at sea?"

"Patrols are various lengths, but usually in the neighborhood of thirty days." Often patrols were extended for one reason or another, but rarely cut short. "We're scheduled to be back in port the first week of August."

Dan's phone rang. Taylor patted her phone pocket out of habit. Empty. She checked both pockets. Then looked in her chair, on the floor, and in her bag.

"Okay. Thanks for letting me know. Bye." Dan turned to Taylor. "Julie. My youngest niece sprained her ankle. Uncle Dan will take her a feel-better gift on the way home. Our custom."

"That's sweet. I can't find my phone. Either it slipped out of my pocket in the car or back at the shop. I have to track it down—don't let anyone steal my beer."

Jake pulled into Lulu's lot. Searching for a place to park, he spied Taylor's car sitting among the pickups and SUVs and smiled. She'd been so feisty this afternoon, and he wanted to discover where all that energy led. Damn! He hadn't found out about the shirt. He'd spent the day looking for Nate Brady and come up empty. But he had a list of places to keep looking, and he'd make another pass or two before calling it a day. A pickup backed out ahead of him and he didn't let the spot get cold.

His phone rang before he put the car in park, so he fished it out and kept his foot on the brake. Taylor hurried out of Lulu's a few cars away from him and darted toward her car.

"Hang on, Kel." He put the car in park, unbuckled the seatbelt, and swiveled around to keep an eye on Taylor.

She moved her hands over the driver's seat, next to the console, and looked on the floor both front and back before climbing in and speeding out of the lot. He and fifty million others had made the same moves. She'd lost something—probably her phone—and would be heading back to the shop. He'd follow as soon as he talked to Kelly, in case he needed to write.

"Okay. Whatcha got?"

CHAPTER 41

Taylor opened the shop door less than two minutes after she left Lulu's and went straight to where she and Dan had been standing. After ending the call about the fishing tournament, she had slipped the phone into her pocket. Her pocket didn't have a hole, so she must have missed and dropped the phone on the floor. Taylor got on all fours to search.

Ah! There—under a small grill stashed beneath a table. What a klutz. As she stood, she pressed the flashing voicemail button. The computer voice said she had one new message.

The door opened. She looked up. Zia stood backlit by the bright outdoor light. "On the phone. Come on in. I'll just be a minute."

Taylor missed the beginning of the message and pressed the button to start over, turning toward the wall as she did.

The message started again. "Hello, Ms. Campbell. I have the basic information you asked for. Turns out my wife was already home, and she looked up the names you asked for."

As she listened to the man ramble on and on, Taylor watched Zia saunter to the far end of the shop, looking at some things, ignoring others. Still searching for a treasure to reach out and hug her, Taylor guessed.

"I don't know why I didn't remember this before when we talked, but as soon as my wife read the winners off, that tournament came back crystal clear."

Zia turned and started toward her. She wore a necklace with six chunks of lapis lazuli held in place by narrow bands of silver. Holy Mother of God. The lapis matched the quality of the stones on Taylor's watchband and in Jake's belt buckle—free of calcite, and touched with streaks of gold pyrite—but smaller. The nuggets had been cut, like the pieces on the watchband.

Taylor tried to smile, but it wouldn't come. Instead, she covered her other ear with her hand, as if to hear the message better.

"The grand prize winner was Nate Brady. Besides Brady, the winners for other species were Adam Ballinger, Jeff Malek, and Cesar Vargas."

Zia twisted the silver strands of her necklace around her finger, her vacant eyes staring straight ahead.

Taylor's quaking insides could measure nine-point-five on the Richter scale. What should she do? Listen to the message until she thought of something?

"The big news that year was the blowup between Nate Brady and ol' Ross Markham's baby brother, Hunter."

Markham and Brady?

"They got into a fistfight at the scale."

Sweat popped out on Taylor's palms. As it was, they shook so much the phone bounced against her ear. Her breath caught in her throat.

"Hunter Markham accused Nate Brady of stuffing sinkers in the fish, but turned out the win was clean. Brady's fish won by one ounce and half an inch. So I'd think the name you're looking for would be either Markham or Brady."

Zia fingered several of the items on the nearest table, turning over a neon green tackle box as if looking for a price.

"Hunter Markham, though, he died the next year. Damndest thing, too. Out at the golf course drunker'n a skunk. Golf ball hit him in the head, and he fell into a water hazard. They pulled him out, but he was a goner."

Taylor wondered who hit the ball. Zia moved to the next table, bent to look at something on the floor.

"Well, that's it. I mean there's more, but this should start you out. You call me now you need any more help. Pleasure talking to you."

The room started to spin. Taylor's hands shook, but she kept the phone to her ear as if she were listening. She backed toward the door. If she called 9-1-1 and kept the phone in her pocket, the police should send an officer to investigate the open line even if the dispatcher couldn't hear her conversation with Zia.

She took the phone from her ear to press the numbers.

Zia stood, a big black semiautomatic in her hand, and walked toward her. "Give me your phone."

"No. I need it for the Coast Guard to contact me if I'm needed back." Taylor pressed the numbers.

"I don't give a good, long, satisfying fuck what it's for." Zia wrested the phone from Taylor's hand and tossed it to the back of the room. Taylor's last means of communication lay on the floor between two tables, shattered into a hundred pieces.

Taylor had vanished from Jake's view for several seconds before parking in Rankin's drive and going back in the shop.

"I'll spare you the boring details, big bro. But I needed data from two different state servers. Finally, *finally* the first one came up. While I searched that one, the other server popped back. If I had four hands, I could have done this half a minute quicker."

"I love you, Kelly Ja—"

"Don't. Say. It."

He laughed. "You have my word."

Zia's car pulled into Taylor's driveway, all the way up directly behind her car. His hackles rose. Zia got out and went inside. Hustle time. The only reason someone parked so close to another car, barring a space issue, was to keep them from having room to leave. He refastened his seatbelt. If he needed to write, Kelly would have to call back.

"So I finally got the information on Nate Brady."

Taylor backed up half a step to keep from appearing confrontational. "Zia—"

"Don't *Zia* me." Fire flashed in Zia's eyes. "I'm looking for Jake, but I'll find the bastard when I've finished with you."

"Put the gun down." Taylor exercised every bit of control she could scare up to keep her voice low-pitched and her words clear. She wanted to scream and run away, but those actions would accomplish nothing except getting her wounded or killed.

"Not happening." Zia shook her head. "Tell me what Randy told you."

It would only take a flick of Zia's thumb, but right now the safety was on. Maybe—a huge maybe—the extra half-second would give Taylor enough time to grab the gun, but action would be her last resort. She was better with words.

"Randy didn't tell me anything. I was in the middle of the Atlantic when he died." She chose those words carefully, spoke in a soft voice, and purposely didn't say *when you killed him.* This was the wrong time to reveal what she suspected. Antagonizing someone holding a loaded gun wasn't smart. "I couldn't come for his funeral. It's been a year, and this is the first chance I've had."

"He left you all his fucking property. How could he not have told you anything?"

"My cutter was part of a cadet cruise to Scandinavia and the Mediterranean. I didn't know I inherited until Randy's attorney contacted me." *Holy crap, this is hard. Don't tell her you know Randy was murdered, Taylor.* "He sent a registered letter I had to sign for, and we didn't return until late August."

"Poor little girl. That's what everyone thinks, isn't it? Poor Taylor this. Poor Taylor that. You're tiny and cute. People like you and do things for you."

"Is that what you think?" Taylor made herself breathe normally. In. Out.

"You can't say it's not true. Jake licking your ass and drooling over you. Dan helping you day in and day out in this junk-filled dungeon. Then he and A.J. had the audacity to give you one of my paintings—*in front of me*, of all things. And A.J. even asked me to sign it."

Zia was losing it. *Think, Taylor.* Her mind just kept saying *gun, gun.* Her mouth was so dry she could barely swallow. Jake was right—it was different one on one. "That's not at all the case. I can't control what others do."

How was Nate Brady involved? Somehow he had to be.

Zia's arm jerked out from her side and swept the peanut can, buckle, and shirt to the floor. "What were you trying to do with these? You couldn't have thought I'd actually acknowledge them."

Jake had been right again. Taylor had been naïve.

Zia held out her hand. "Give me the watch."

"No."

"I'll rip it off your arm if you don't give it to me. It's mine."

"It's not yours."

Zia picked up the buckle and shirt and placed them back on the counter, all the while keeping her blue stare and her gun locked on Taylor. "These are mine, too. Where are the other buckles?"

Maybe Zia had talked Brady into doing her dirty work. "I don't know what you're talking about."

Zia stepped forward and slapped her, the *smack* vibrating in the silence.

Tears sprang to Taylor's eyes, but her jaw clenched. The gun frightened her. But the slap made her angry and steeled her resolve. Taylor would spare no mercy. Nobody touched her. Nobody.

She needed to convince Zia to leave the shop. Once they were outside, she had a better chance of surviving anything Zia might try.

"Stop lying. You know about the buckles because I put them in the fucking peanut can myself. Now I want all the buckles and Randy's belt."

Taylor's cheek throbbed, and the coppery taste of blood oozed into her mouth from where a tooth had bitten into her flesh, but she squared her chin. Zia was the murderer. "No."

"Did Randy or Jake tell you about my daddy?"

"Who is your father, Zia?" This must be the man Jake's dad thought was the killer.

"Don't play Little Miss I-Don't-Know with me."

"Did Randy figure out you killed his friends?"

Zia's lips pursed, and she breathed loudly through her nose. "Randy knew he was next. I wanted him to know it was me. I wanted all of them to understand they would die because they killed my daddy."

Should she ask Zia again about her father? Before Taylor had time to think further, Zia continued.

"No matter what I did, Randy didn't get it. I sent him the buckles. I left the shirt so he would know Nate and I were a team and would come after him. Bastard was too far gone to figure it out. Finally I came out here and drove him to my house. I took him upstairs. We had a few drinks and a good fuck. He might've been crazy, but he hadn't forgotten how to please a woman."

Taylor didn't want to hear those things about Randy, though she realized Zia was deliberately seeking to rattle her cage. But poor Randy. He hadn't been able to resist Zia when she poured on the charm and the liquor. She wanted to claw out Zia's eyes. But Zia held the gun.

"Afterward, Randy saw the belts. He ripped them off the wall and ran out. Finally he put everything together, but he violated my home. Those belts were mine! I let him go—it was still daylight."

Taylor scrunched up enough courage to speak. "So what happened then, Zia? Did you lurk in the dark like a coward?"

Zia shook her hair back. "I'm far from a coward. I've killed three men, and the stupid daughter of one of them. The bitch thought she could outwit *me*."

Jake's dad was right.

Zia licked her lips. "You can't imagine the high. Better than any fuck. Even Randy."

Randy hadn't stood a chance. Taylor imagined the others hadn't either. Would Jake have fallen for Zia's act, too? Taylor didn't know.

"When your crazy motherfucking uncle left, I called Nate and told him to get Randy out in his boat however he had to do it."

"Nate Brady?"

"Of course Nate Brady. I told him to get Randy drunk and to stay on the bay until I called. I had to get my belts back."

"You found them?"

"Lying on his kitchen table. What a shithole. But no buckles. No shirt. Even out on the boat when he knew he was dead, the cocksucker wouldn't tell me where they were."

Good for you, Uncle Randy.

"I've looked dozens of times in the house and out here for them."

"What happened to Randy on the boat?" Taylor didn't want to hear how Randy died, but she had to know. Like knowing not to bite down on a sore tooth.

"Nate anchored by that old pier. Randy was too drunk to talk, but he dove off and started swimming. I followed him to shore. Cocky bastard waited for me. Told me I wouldn't get away with it."

"How did you make him lay there when the tide came in? There were no marks, no bruises on his body."

"I'm smart. Smarter than Randy. Smarter than the police. A hell of a lot smarter than those stupid doctors. And smarter than you. I talked to him. Let him try to convince me not to kill him. Told him how sleepy he was, let him put his head in my lap. He was asleep in about two minutes. The tide was coming in. I moved so his head was on the sand. When the water reached his face, I lay between him and the bay. Kissed him awake. Aroused him. As soon as the water was high enough, I stopped playing with his hair and held his head under. He fought some, but he was too drunk. I'm strong."

Poor Randy. Any bruising would have been hidden beneath his hair.

"I'm going to kill you, too." Zia rocked from one foot to the other. "Where did you find the buckles?"

Her last words came fast and without emotion. Taylor had to strain to make sense of them because the sounds all ran together.

"I said *where did you find them?*" Zia screamed the words.

Taylor shook her head and tried to smile. "Not telling." She concentrated on the gun. The safety was still on.

Zia took a deep breath. And another. Then she brushed her hair back with her free hand and smiled. "So where are my buckles?" Her voice sounded normal.

A chill ran up Taylor's spine, and her ears rang. "I don't know where the buckles are, Zia."

Zia's maniacal laughter bounced off the walls. "Oh, you're good. Really good. Better than those fucking doctors. I'll tell you what I whispered in Randy's ear while he was dying. My daddy was Hamblen Norberg. The sons of bitches of Solomon's Compass killed him. Every last one of them. On Jake Solomon's orders. I'm paying them back."

CHAPTER 42

"What about Brady?" Jake slammed the gear lever into reverse, but two pickups were stopped behind him waiting on traffic.

"He's half of your puzzle. The other half is Zia Grant Markham."

And Zia was with Taylor. One truck pulled into the street giving him room to back out.

"Zia accompanied Brady to Denver last year. She told everyone she was going to Aruba."

"The affair was still on."

"Right. Long-term. Currently widow and widower. So why the secrecy? I figured it couldn't be good."

"Exactly."

"I got confirmation of a rumor right before I called. Zia Grant was born Lucia Catherine Norberg. She's Hamblen Norberg's daughter."

"Son of a bitch." The damned truck wouldn't move. His wrist jerked on the steering wheel—two clicks up, one down. Like his dad's. "So Dad had it wrong. Fallon isn't involved."

"Looks that way. I find no connection. After Ham committed suicide, his wife petitioned the court for a name change. Her sister was a nun, an uncle a priest. She didn't want to bear shame on them. Blah, blah. It's a long document. The judge sanctioned the name change and sealed the records."

"Un-fucking-believable. I kept telling Dad to call you in."

"Don't dwell on it, bro. Best I can tell, she started going by Zia at Ohio State. This followed a few years in therapy, including a brief in-patient stint right after Daddy did himself in. Mommy died several years later. Sibs scattered. Once I had her name, tracking her wasn't a problem. She lived in Chicago and Nashville before moving to Atlanta, where she met and married Ross Markham and they moved to Rock Harbor."

He had a lot of questions, but they'd keep. Right now he had to get to Rankin's.

"No more now, Kelly. Tell me later. I gotta go."

He keyed in 9-1-1, told the dispatcher someone broke into Rankin's store and was inside, and said he'd already passed by so they wouldn't keep his line open. The second truck pulled out, but by the time he got to the street, he had to wait on a string of semis lumbering past. He called Upchurch and pounded the steering wheel. "Come on, you slow bastards."

The call rolled to voicemail. "Get over to Rankin's. It's going down."

The last semi passed, and Jake bolted out of the lot. In all his scenarios, he hadn't ruled out Zia, but nothing had sent her to the top of his list.

"Fuck!" The leather tiebacks in Zia's bedroom. They were the Solomon's Compass belts, most likely the ones belonging to Ed and Kyle. Her father's belt would be in an honored location, brought out only for celebration and worship.

"What do you mean all of them killed him? Your father committed suicide, Zia. Let's sit over here and talk." The two camp stools she and Dan had used earlier were still open.

"No." Zia shook her head. "Not sitting. Daddy hanged himself, but they forced him."

Taylor didn't have the right training for this situation, but if she kept Zia talking, she might latch onto something she could use to calm her. As long as Zia kept the safety on, the gun wouldn't fire.

"How did they force him, Zia? Were they there?" Ideas for Zia to think about.

Zia tried scrunching her face, but it barely moved. Botox—had to be.

"No, they weren't there. Daddy would've told me they were coming." Zia licked her lips. "Vietnam. He couldn't live with what happened. I was born after he got back. He was always sick. No one would help him. Daddy loved those men as if they were his own flesh and blood brothers. He wore that damned belt every day, but when he reached out to them, no one would help him. No one."

"You're wrong, Zia."

Jake!

Both Taylor and Zia turned toward the door. With her attention focused on Zia, Taylor hadn't heard the door open or even noticed more light in the space.

Zia took a step toward him. "You! I couldn't believe you came to me that night on the sidewalk. You're the worst one. Daddy went with you to Bangkok. If you hadn't gone on leave, Daddy would still be alive. That's why I saved you until last. So you could realize the others were dead because of you, and you would have to live with their blood on your hands until I killed you."

Jake didn't move from the doorway. "What did Ham tell you happened in Bangkok?"

"The truth. I don't care what you say."

"He killed two men, Zia."

"For you. They were trying to kill you. He killed them to keep them from killing you."

Zia's voice became louder and more strident with each word. Taylor slid a short distance toward the kayak paddle to see if Zia paid attention. She didn't, so Taylor took another step.

"Not true, Zia. I was with him, yes, but he was drunk. We both were. His quick temper and the booze produced a bad combination. He went off on those men with a length of pipe."

"No. He did everything for you, because you asked, you fucking lying bastard."

From her vantage point, Taylor saw Zia's thumb flip off the safety. Jake couldn't have seen it. Her heart already beat in double-time, but it sped up.

"I told you the truth, Zia. Believe me. I'm sorry you lost your dad. I'm sorry I lost a friend. Four friends. I don't understand why you thought Kyle, Ed, and Randy had to die."

Taylor moved her hand to the kayak paddle and brought it slowly to her side. For too brief a moment, her gaze collided with Jake's.

"Why? Are you that stupid? Because they took your precious belts. And they wore them. Like Daddy. Like you. You think you're so smart. You don't even know I killed Lorna Easley."

Jake's face hardened. Zia was sick, but she'd killed four innocent people. Taylor wouldn't allow her to kill more.

"Zia—" Jake took a step forward.

Taylor gripped the paddle with both hands—

"*Stop Zia-ing me!*" She screamed the words at Jake and extended her arms in a shooter's stance.

—and swung at Zia's neck.

The gun went off at the same time the edge of the paddle made contact with the back of Zia's head.

Zia fired again and turned toward Taylor. This time the kayak blade sliced into the bridge of her nose.

Zia screeched. Blood flew everywhere. She swiped at her face with her free hand, smearing blood into her eyes.

Taylor bent and swung at Zia's midsection. Glass shattered behind Taylor from a third bullet.

She backed up and swung at Zia's gun hand.

The gun hit the floor.

Taylor cringed.

It slid down and across the aisle but didn't fire.

Zia's nose still bled, and she cradled her right wrist with her left hand. Taylor reached for the gun, but two arms wrapped themselves around her and pulled her close. Thank God Jake was safe.

"Taylor, I almost had a heart attack. You're okay?"

Dan!

"The gun. I have to get the gun." She shoved at his arms.

Zia was rushing for it.

Dan released her, and she charged for the gun. Zia grabbed it. She pointed it toward Taylor with her good left hand and glared. "You sneaking, sly, two-faced, fucking bitch."

"Put the gun down, Zia." Another male voice.

Taylor thought the voice belonged to Glen, but she kept her focus locked on the gun. She could barely hear over the roaring in her ears. Where was Jake?

Sirens sounded.

"Put the gun down." Glen's voice sounded closer. "You don't want any more trouble."

"Like hell. You don't know what I want. Jake Solomon was the last fucking one. Now he's dead, too. My job is done, except for this bitch."

Jake couldn't be dead. With the gun leveled at her midsection, Taylor shivered and risked a quick glance toward the door. Jake lay in a pool of blood. One paramedic knelt at his side. Another ran up with the trauma box.

"What about me?" Taylor stepped toward the table and hoped Dan had the sense to get out. Zia followed her, turning her back on the door. She seemed to forget about Dan and about Glen.

Taylor pitched her voice low and, she hoped, loud enough for Glen to hear. "You want a taste of what Randy told me? How badly do you want to know, Zia? Do you want to know what he thought of you? What he told me about you? What he did to get under your skin? Is that what you're craving? What you need to understand?"

"Shut up."

"Do you want to know what he planned to do? What he did with the buckles you sent? I know where Randy's belt is, too. If you kill me, all the answers are lost to you. Lost. Gone."

"I said *shut up!*"

"You're losing control, Zia. Listen to yourself. You're scream-ing. You remember what happens when you lose control."

Zia straightened, took a breath, and pushed her hair out of her face. "I'm not screaming." Her voice sounded calmer.

"Good cover, Zia, but doctors won't tumble to your act again."

She shook her head again. "No doctors. I'm not going back."

Glen and two uniformed officers moved slowly forward.

"What did the doctors tell you? Did they say you were de-lusional?"

The officers inched closer.

"Those dumb pricks didn't have any idea about me. At first they thought I killed him. My own daddy. Put me on a suicide watch. Drugged me."

"They wanted to be sure you were all right."

"Stop! Not true. They tried to make me believe the cover-up, that he had PTSD and wouldn't take his meds. Nothing was wrong with my daddy except that fucking load of Solomon's Com-pass crap. I loved him. Dumb-shit bastard doctors with their talk and their drugs. Nobody cared about Daddy or anything I said. I got tired of fighting them and finally said what they wanted to hear. But I never believed them. They were wrong. I never forgot—"

Two uniformed officers grabbed Zia's arms. After a brief struggle, she slumped. The officers held her upright by her elbows. Glen slid the pistol from her fingers. "It's over, Zia." He nodded to one of the officers who cuffed her hands behind her back.

Dan hugged her again. "Why did you keep talking? Zia got angrier by the second."

"And focused on me, not on you or Glen or the officers moving toward her."

"She could've killed you."

"But she didn't. Jake drew her attention from me in the same way I drew it away from Glen and the officers. I acted as a dis-traction, that's all."

Jake. He had to stay alive. He couldn't die. He was too strong. She willed him to fight, to live, as she watched the paramedics tending to him.

"How did you know about the doctors?"

"She mentioned them earlier. I took a guess because of her behavior. If she'd have said I needed my head examined or some other behavior indicated she didn't have a mental problem, I would've riffed off her words. Always have a Plan B, Dan. Always have a Plan B."

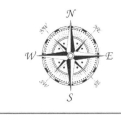

CHAPTER 43

A s soon as the officers led Zia outside, Taylor hurried to the doorway with Dan beside her. The paramedics were sliding a backboard under Jake to lift him to the gurney. He grimaced and told them to take it easy.

"How is he?"

The paramedic at Jake's side smiled. "He lost some blood—two entrance wounds—but we stopped the flow. One bullet made a clean exit. Not sure about the other. Docs will stitch him up, and he'll be good as new."

She swallowed. "Okay. Where are you taking him?"

"Halo Flight is three minutes from touchdown. They're probably taking him to Memorial in Corpus. I'll find out."

He turned to use the radio on his collar.

She grasped Jake's hand. The iciness made her shiver. With her other hand, she smoothed his hair away from his face. The silky feel between her fingers calmed her. "You're going to be all right. They're finding out where the helicopter will take you, and I'll ask Dan to drive me. You'll be in surgery by the time we arrive, but I'll be there. I'll see you as soon as they let me."

He smiled. "Good."

"Can I do anything for you? Anyone you want me to call?"

"Phone . . . in pocket. Call Kelly."

"Kelly." She repeated the name to make sure she understood.

"Right." He grimaced. His breaths were shallow, and his lips had thinned to a narrow line as he dealt with pain.

"I'll call as soon as I get your phone. You hang on."

He nodded. "Not . . . first . . . rodeo."

"You're a fine cowboy. Being from Brooklyn and all."

He tried to smile.

The paramedic returned. "Christus Spohn Memorial. Off the Crosstown between Morgan and Buford."

Dan nodded.

She touched the paramedic's arm. "Will you find his phone for me?"

The paramedic patted Jake down and pulled the phone from his pants pocket.

"Thanks." She looked back at Jake. "I have your phone. Hear the helo? It's dropping down now."

He nodded again, not opening his eyes.

Fear lashed her heart and left huge gaping wounds, much worse than when she faced Zia's gun. Then it had been only her. This was Jake, and she'd only just found him. She bent to his ear. "Listen to me, Jake Solomon. You're fit and you're smart and you've survived a hell of a lot worse than this. Don't you dare die on me. I'm just getting to know you, and I need lots of time to do the job right. You understand?"

His lips twitched in what she thought was a smile.

She kissed his cheek, not wanting to let go. "The Airedales are coming. I'll see you in a few hours." She backed away to allow the flight crew to do their work.

Dan draped his arm across her shoulders, and she leaned against him, thankful he stood beside her. Tears ran down her cheeks. After the helo took off, she turned and hugged him. That's when the sobs came.

He held her and sheltered her while she cried. All the emotion of the past two weeks gushed out. Uncle Randy. Jake. Will. Trinh. A.J. Dan. Nate. Zia. All the fear and love, hurt and sadness poured from deep within, from a place she hadn't realized existed.

Waves of sorrow crashed over her. She couldn't breathe. Time stopped, and she indulged herself in her own miserable pit of despair, drowning in feelings that were completely new. She wanted to scream at the pain to go away, leave her alone, but it took over and crushed her.

Even when she returned to the *Susquehanna* and her old life, she would never be the same. Her life would be forever different because she hadn't had a real life before. Now she knew love, and with love came the passion Dan and A.J. had talked about. She ached—her body, her heart, her soul—to touch and to be touched, to love and to be loved by the most fabulous man in the world. Whose body had just been pierced by two bullets.

Jake had to live or her heart would die. She prayed for Jake's life and mourned for what might have been. For all of them. For all the Compass Points, but for that fateful night in Bangkok.

Time vanished until nothing remained but emptiness. Dan rubbed her back, and she snuffled. He'd steadied her through all this, even now as she pulled herself together piece by piece, and he held out a handkerchief.

"Thanks." Only it came out sounding more like *hrnkx*. She blew her nose and tried again. "Thanks."

His usually lively face was pale and filled with concern. "Are you okay?"

She nodded while dabbing at her eyes. "Thank you for being here. For holding on to me. For not letting me fall. For the handkerchief. I'll wash it and mail it back."

Some of the concern vanished, but he didn't release her. "Don't be silly. I buy them by the dozen."

Her fingers still clutched Jake's phone. "Jake wants me to call someone named Kelly."

Dan loosened his arms, and she stepped out of their protectiveness. She found several calls to and from Kelly Wetmore, so she steeled herself and pressed the number.

Kelly answered on the first ring. "What's up, Jake, my man?" Her voice sounded strong and sassy.

"Jake asked me to call you. My name is Taylor Campbell."

"Is he all right?"

"There's not an easy way to say this." Why was this so different from similar calls she'd made in an official Coast Guard capacity? "He's been shot."

"Is he alive?"

"Yes."

"Thank God."

"They're Halo Flighting him to Corpus Christi. Memorial Hospital, I think." She rubbed her forehead. "It has a name in front of Memorial, but I don't remember what. A lot was going on."

"No worries. I'll be there as soon as possible, however long it takes. At least three or four hours flight time. I'm in New York. If he wakes up before I arrive, tell him not to die before I get there or I'll kick his ass."

Taylor laughed, but Kelly had already hung up. Who was Kelly Wetmore? And how did she figure in Jake's life?

Officers milled around everywhere, and a small crowd had gathered. Will and Trinh stood in the driveway. She hadn't seen anyone before, but they had to have been standing there while she talked to Kelly. It must've been a mix of shock and adrenaline that caused her to notice things in increments.

She faced Dan. "Whoever Kelly is, she sounds as tough as Jake. She's flying in from New York."

"Good. Having someone he knows at his side will help him recover quicker."

Her heart sank. Someone he knew. How well? Well enough he wanted her here. Taylor's shoulders drooped.

Glen walked up. "Better?"

The shock had abated, and she lifted her chin. "Yes."

"You'll need to come to the station and give a statement."

"Not now. I promised Jake I'd be at the hospital."

"Stop by in the morning. Be prepared to stay a few hours. We'll do a video statement, ask any questions needed for clarification, and have you sign an affidavit."

"I leave Thursday morning."

He nodded. "Not a problem. Eight o'clock. By the way, when you talk to Jake, tell him we picked up Nate Brady. His lawyer's already working a plea deal for him rolling on Zia. Claims Brady was a victim."

Dan covered Taylor's hand with his. "How are you holding up?"

"Okay."

He drove her car. A.J. would meet them at the hospital. When she'd seen Jake lying in his own blood, everything she felt for him slammed home. She kept playing those few moments over and over. Much like Ham Norberg must have done with the events that happened in Bangkok.

"He'll be all right." Dan patted her knee. "Can I ask you something?"

"Sure."

"Are you bothered that he's older?"

She hadn't fully understood the necessity of the charade until she saw Zia in action. Jake's dad was right. She would have killed Jake without a backward glance and then gone after his father.

Taylor sighed. She couldn't share with Dan that Jake wasn't older. "What I feel for Jake goes beyond any emotion I've ever experienced. If we're together for one day, it's better than never being together at all. I'll be happy for whatever we have. Nothing in life is guaranteed."

"I'm happy for you. It's exactly how I feel about A.J."

They rode in silence the rest of the way. Dan dropped her at the emergency room and said he'd meet her inside. The triage nurse told her Jake had already gone to surgery and gave her directions to the waiting room. Ten minutes later, Dan and A.J. walked in carrying three large containers of coffee.

"You're a godsend. Both of you."

A.J. handed her a container. "Friends help friends."

A small group of people waited at the other end of the room. A.J. plugged in earbuds and picked up a magazine. Taylor and Dan sat in silence.

Several minutes passed before a woman in blue scrubs, her surgical mask hanging down, stopped in the doorway. The last rays of sunshine spotlighted her fuchsia Crocs. "Solomon? Campbell?"

Taylor jumped up. "Here. Taylor Campbell."

The woman met them halfway. "Mr. Solomon is in surgery. He made sure to inform us that we could tell you what was going on. He insisted on it, in fact."

Taylor smiled. "He's like that."

"They'll be a while, but everything looks good. One bullet nicked a vein, and he lost a bit of blood. They patched it first and transfused him, now they're working on the rest of the damage. The vein was the big concern, and it's back in service. He's stable. I don't have more details for you yet."

"When will we be able to see him?"

"Sometime after midnight."

CHAPTER 44

Where was he? Jake heard voices. Far away. Padded footsteps. His nose twitched. Ah, hospital. Antiseptic. All the memories flooded back.

He was alive. What else? Jake moved his toes, fingers. Things were looking up. He cranked open an eyelid. Tubes ran from everywhere, but none down his throat. The bullet must have missed his lung.

"There you are. Welcome back to the living, Mr. Solomon." He smelled flowers.

He turned his head to the other side. A nurse with red hair and a smile beamed down at him.

"You gave them a wee scare in the OR, but our docs are good. You got no more worries. They patched you up better than new, and it all works. Would you like some ice?"

He nodded. His throat burned, and his cracked lips stung.

"Got it for you right here. You're hooked up to our auto-vitals system, so I don't even have to make you wait while I take your temp. Here you go."

He sucked on half a spoon of crushed ice. Nothing had ever tasted so good.

"You're in recovery. You'll be mine for a while then I gotta send you on your way. Those wicked bitches in SICU got the winning ticket, so they'll get their way with you for a day or so. Think you can handle them?"

He thought he smiled, but couldn't be sure.

"I'm going to be about six feet away, propping up my feet and wishing for a tequila shot. But I'm keeping my good eye on you. You'll probably drift in and out for a while. Enjoy those sweet dreams. I'm here to keep the zombies away. You need me and I'm not right here, just breathe hard. All the alarms will sound."

Jake liked her. She liked her job.

"More ice?"

He'd dozed. "Yeah." It came out a croak.

"You're perking right up. I may have to give you over to those evil Jezebels before I'm ready to lose your smiling face, you keep up this progress." An alarm sounded. "Be right back."

He remembered everything. Zia. Ham Bone's daughter. Taylor, fighting for him, coming to him after Zia walked past and spit on him. Taylor's fingers in his hair. Her kiss on his cheek.

"You're a regular sleepyhead, but your naps are getting shorter. Have some more ice. All your vitals are strong. I'll be waving bye to you before long."

Jake closed his eyes and thought about Taylor.

"Taylor Campbell?"

Taylor looked up. In the doorway stood a woman her age or a little younger. Reddish hair framed her face. Tall and slim, straight nose, wide mouth, and a beautiful creamy complexion. Deep blue eyes, the color of the sky at dusk. She wore orange capris dotted with green dragonflies, an orange knit top, and chartreuse sandals.

"I'm Taylor. Kelly?" She stood up, feeling like the eighth dwarf.

"That's me." Kelly joined them, pulling her bag. "Love your shirt. Do you have the whole set? I've almost worn mine out. Simon loves them."

Taylor liked her—whoever she was. She introduced everyone, and Dan and A.J. went to find more coffee.

Kelly dropped into the adjoining chair. "I'm pooped, and I'm sick to death of hospitals. How's Jake?"

Did he make a habit of landing in hospitals? "In recovery. He's having a hard time coming out of the anesthesia, but his vitals are strong. They won't let us see him until they move him to SICU. The nurse said he'll be there for at least twenty-four hours. Two bullets. One did some damage, but they repaired everything. He lost quite a bit of blood."

"But he's going to be okay, right?"

"Yes. They said recovery will be slow—"

"A crock of shit. They don't know Jake. He'll be jogging in two weeks. Mark my word. Three max."

Taylor smiled. "He is amazing. If I'd been half a second faster, Zia wouldn't have shot him."

"I'll tell you what Jake would, and that's don't guilt yourself out. Things happen. Sometimes even when we *are* half a second faster." Her eyes took on a faraway expression.

"I know. It's hard not to blame ourselves when something goes wrong." Taylor rubbed her forehead.

Kelly came back to the present and really looked at her for the first time. "So . . . you and Jake, huh?"

She didn't know how to respond. Might as well get it out there. "Yeah. At least I think so."

Kelly grinned. "Good. He thinks so, too, or he wouldn't have risked so much for you. Dad will go berserk when he hears, but only because Jake spilled the big secret. And Jake will, too, when he learns I knew before he told me."

Taylor hadn't followed all of that. "Dad? Secret?"

"Yeah. We're a competitive bunch. He would've come down, too, except—oh, shit." She grabbed Taylor's arms. "You don't know who I am. I'm Jake's sister."

Taylor's head fell back, the weight of uncertainty gone. "In his phone, it said Kelly Wetmore. Jake just said to call Kelly."

Kelly nodded through the whole time Taylor talked. "Men. What are you gonna do? Simon's the same way. Simon Wetmore—my husband. But I'm in the family business, so I've been working with Jake, but from New York, because Dad's in the hospital. Dad's going home tomorrow."

Kelly bounced from thought to thought so fast her words couldn't quite keep up. Taylor smiled and found her voice. "Jake told me he had a sister, but I never knew your name."

Kelly laughed. "That's Jake. I'm the family geek. What I do is mostly legal. I'll share my data—my legal data—with the police in the morning. Dad and Jake know that. It's how we operate."

Dan and A.J. delivered more coffee and said goodnight right after Taylor told them Kelly was Jake's sister. At one-thirty the following morning, the doctors allowed them into SICU. Taylor's over-caffeinated nerves wanted to jump out of her skin.

A nurse walked them back. "Mr. Solomon lost more than two pints of blood, but he hung on. His heart and his spirit are strong. His vitals are good. Not strong yet, but on the way. The next twelve, twenty-four hours will be crucial. If he doesn't crash, he should pull through fine, but he'll be weak for a bit."

"He'll be up and strong before you think he will." Kelly's comment earned her a look of reproach from the nurse, and Kelly responded with a sweet smile. Taylor liked her even more.

"You might be right about him being up soon. He's quite feisty."

Kelly let out a belly laugh and clapped her hand over her mouth. "Sorry."

Taylor couldn't stop smiling.

The nurse led them to a bed across from a bank of monitors and several rolling chairs. The three of them moved to Jake's side.

Taylor touched his shoulder. "It's me, Jake. I told you I'd be here."

He smiled and mumbled so softly she couldn't understand. She bent down. "Tell me again."

"I love you. I got you down to my level on purpose."

She smiled and touched his face. "I love you, too."

"Can you stay?"

"No. They'll be kicking us out in a few minutes. In the morning, I have to give a statement to the police, but I'll be here tomorrow afternoon."

"I'll be sitting up by then. After I get out of here, a long R&R in Charleston would do me good."

"Come for Coast Guard Day. I'll be back from patrol. I'll take leave . . . for some up close and personal time."

Jake smiled. "Good."

"Kelly's here. Want to talk to her?"

He nodded. "Stay."

"I will." She motioned for Kelly.

Kelly went to the other side of the bed. "Hey, Slick. You told me you were going to stay out of trouble."

"I lied. This was my plan to introduce you to Taylor. Whatcha think?"

Taylor and Kelly both laughed.

Kelly touched his cheek, gave it a soft pat. "You did good, bro."

"Thanks, Kelly Jane."

"How many times do I have to tell you not to call me that? Don't you ever listen?"

"No."

Kelly glanced at Taylor and shook her head. "He's like that."

Taylor smiled at Jake. "I'm getting an evil glare from the nurse. I think it's time to go." She kissed his lips.

He kissed her back. "I'm the luckiest man in the universe." His words were a low growl, meant only for her.

THE END

Acknowledgments

The *Point Whitebanks* mentioned in *Solomon's Compass* is fictional, but the 82-foot U.S. Coast Guard Point Class boats that served in Vietnam were real—all twenty-six of them. The boats were grouped into three divisions that comprised Squadron One, in country from 1965-1970. The *Point Whitebanks* is an amalgamation of all the Point boats in the campaign, a combination of the names of two of the actual boats—the *Point White* and the *Point Banks*. You can learn more about the Point Class boats here:

- *The official U.S. Coast Guard site, with much information:* http://www.uscg.mil/history/uscghist/VietnamPhotoIndex_A.asp
- http://www.warboats.org/wpb.htm
- http://en.wikipedia.org/wiki/Point_class_cutter

Learning about the Point boats was only the beginning. The entire writing of *Solomon's Compass* was a unique experience that included dealing with a cast of rebellious characters. And Jake Solomon was the worst of all. He is one insistent man!

Despite the complications, Taylor and Jake's story finally came together, but not without the help of others. I owe each of the following people a huge thank you.

First to Capt. Anne T. Ewalt, USCG, Retired, for her frank answers to my questions about women in the Coast Guard, their concerns, and the problems they face. Taylor Campbell is not Captain Ewalt, unless we share a cosmic connection I know nothing about. But because of Captain Ewalt's help, Taylor became the woman and Coast Guard officer she is.

I owe another thanks to Captain Ewalt for introducing me to Bob Hurst, a retired Coast Guard officer and lifelong sailor. I've never sailed a catamaran, and when I yelled for help, Bob stepped up. Anything I got wrong is all on me. Thank you, Bob, for being the best technical advisor ever!

Thanks to my critique partners, Jan Christensen and Rita Toews, who love making me work. And to Alison Dasho, editor extraordinaire . . . thank you for *everything*. I learned so much.

Thanks also go to Christine LePorte for her copy editing and proofing skills—and especially for helping me solve a last-minute dilemma. To Lisa DeSpain for making it possible for you to read this on your e-reader or in a paperback by making it look good and work properly. And to Derek Murphy for another outstanding cover.

Saving the best for last, thanks to my own special Coast Guard husband. He's my lighthouse, my compass, and my hero. I love him more than words can express. He is *Semper Paratus* personified . . . and he grills a mean steak.

Author Bio

Carol Kilgore is the wife of a now-retired U.S. Coast Guard officer. They've lived in many locations up and down the East Coast, on the Gulf Coast, on a river in the Heartland, and even the mountains of New Mexico. Don't ask. She won't tell.

She's now back in her native Texas, and lives with her hero and two herding dogs in a suburb of San Antonio. She spends her days writing and playing dodge dog. Evenings are a different story.

Solomon's Compass is Carol's second novel. Her first, *In Name Only*, is also set on the Texas Gulf Coast and is available at Amazon. She is a member of Romance Writers of America, Mystery Writers of America, and Sisters in Crime. Learn more about her and follow her here:

Blog: http://www.underthetikihut.blogspot.com

Website: http://www.carolkilgore.net

Facebook: http://www.facebook.com/carolkilgore.author

Twitter: http://www.twitter.com/#!/carol_kilgore

Goodreads:
http://www.goodreads.com/author/show/6094110.Carol_Kilgore

Amazon Author Page:
https://www.amazon.com/author/ckilgore

Excerpt from

IN NAME ONLY

by

Carol Kilgore

CHAPTER I

S ummer Newcombe's nose twitched. Smoke. Nasty smoke, not the tantalizing kind from some south-of-the-border concoction in the Pink Tortilla's kitchen. The acrid tang that made her eyes water meant fire. She took stock of the customers as she balanced the chips and salsa tray, and none appeared to notice. She sniffed again. Definitely smoke. Something was burning, and she had no intention of getting her fanny scorched in a run-down Texas beach dive.

As she slapped two menus in front of a young couple, a woman's scream tore through the happy Friday night sounds. Summer turned. A narrow lick of flame teased the creaky floorboards at the rear corner. A second flame erupted.

People jammed the small Upper Padre Island eatery, all eager to get an early start on the weekend. Fifty, at least, plus staff. The twenty or so in her section crowded toward the exit. Screams and shouts of "Hurry!" and "Get out!" drowned the shuffle of feet on the wooden floor.

For a couple of seconds she couldn't move, as if someone had nailed her feet to the floor. Then real time slammed into her, and she jumped on a chair. Across the central bar area, people fled from a second dining area.

Fire had consumed the entire back corner and danced outward, twenty feet away at most. Its heat warmed her body, and smoke clotted in her throat. "Everybody, don't panic. Two by two through the archway into the main room. That's it. I'll be the last out. Don't leave me flopping on the floor if I fall off this chair. Go!" She hopped down but kept directing them.

Summer stole a glance behind her. Flames, hungry for more fuel, burned inches from the chair she'd stood on. Damn. She fought the urge to push everyone out of the way and rush to the exit. "Move it, people. No time to chitchat."

Her throat burned. In the bar area, the air immediately cooled, but not enough. Sweat rolled down her back, and smoke curled along the ceiling in long, black ringlets searching for a way out.

On her left, a woman tugged on the tray of a high chair while the toddler in the seat banged a spoon on the top. A little girl cried and clung to the woman's leg.

Summer moved the woman aside. "Here, let me." The new high chairs had arrived just that morning. Charlie Duran, the restaurant owner, had demonstrated how they worked. The tray slid off on her first try.

The woman hugged her. "Gracias." She scooped her baby into her arms, then pried her daughter's arms from her leg and grabbed her hand.

The lights blinked off. Screams tore through the blackness. The emergency beacons flicked on, and with them Summer's hackles rose. The glow reminded her the smoke alarms hadn't gone off.

She turned her attention to the others at the table, a man handing his little boy to a woman in a wheelchair. Tears stained the woman's face, and rosary beads dangled from one of her hands.

Summer directed her words to the father. "Push the wheel-chair. I'll hold your son's hand."

The little boy clambered down and took her hand.

"Okay, everybody, let's boogie."

Her eyes burned more than her throat. The emergency lights became distant moons shrouded in heavy fog. She ushered her charges out the front door and returned the little boy to his parents.

A server rushed by, and she grabbed his arm. "Is everyone out?"

"I think so." A dazed expression filled his face.

A string of coughs racked her body, and for a second she couldn't catch her breath. Her eyes watered. After the last cough, she inhaled without a problem. Salt air filled her lungs.

She had time to go back and retrieve the cash register. Charlie had been good to her. Hired her for his eatery sight unseen. He must have wondered about her story, but he'd never asked. This was her chance to return the favor. It would take five seconds. But Charlie wasn't the only reason she went back.

Her ring was inside. The stone had come loose in the setting, and Charlie had placed it in the cash register for safekeeping. She wasn't leaving it. Her dad had given it to her, and it was all she had left of him. While sirens screamed nearby, she retraced her steps.

Inside, smoke, thicker than when she left, ravaged her eyes and throat. Another tongue of flame caressed one of the pillars at the end of the bar. Fire whooshed and sighed. Mixed with its breathing, crackles of burning wood became bursts of mad laughter.

She tore her gaze from the flame and grabbed a bar cloth to protect her hands. The cash register stood on the counter. It weighed only a few pounds, but she had to yank the cord to free the plug. She collected the lockbox Charlie kept on the shelf beneath the counter, too, setting it atop the register keys.

The fire's breath kissed her skin with a fevered touch. A shadow moved by the kitchen, but she blinked it away as nonsense. No one else could be inside. If she was seeing things, it was past time to get out.

The room spun. Too much smoke had entered her lungs even though she'd taken shallow breaths. She crouched, set the cash register in front of her on the wood floor, and dropped to her hands and knees.

Greedy for space, swirls of smoke reached in every direction, dipping into cracks, filling her nose, her mouth, her eyes. She pushed the register ahead of her and crawled toward the door, a million miles away.

It was too far. She'd never make it. Don't go there. This fire wouldn't beat her. She wouldn't die in here. She wouldn't. The bastard who killed her parents hadn't killed her, and neither would this damn fire. Shove the register. Crawl. Again.

The room grew darker, but she reached the entrance. One last shove. The register tumbled through the opening, and the lockbox toppled off the keys and landed upside down. A beam crashed to the floor in slow motion and landed two feet from her head. Flying embers waved at her until fingers of darkness closed over her eyes.

Something covered Summer's face, but she couldn't push it away. Her eyes wouldn't open either. She coughed. The more she coughed, the harder it was to breathe.

Firm hands grabbed her wrists. "Glad to see you back with us, ma'am. My name's Ana. You're all right."

She needed to tell her she couldn't breathe, but when she tried, she broke into another coughing fit.

"Don't talk. You have a little smoke in your lungs. But your color's good, and the last mucus you coughed up was clear. Give the oxygen a few more minutes. We washed your eyes to get the smoke out. I'm taking the gauze pads off now, but your eyes still need to rest. Leave them closed while the oxygen works."

Her words and confident manner gave Summer comfort. She nodded to show she understood and concentrated on breathing. In. Out. *Whoosh. Sigh.* Like the fire. Panic jangled her nerves. But she breathed through it, and the fire in her mind faded.

Ana's footsteps moved away, and Summer's hands found her fanny pack. The outer compartment held her tip money and a tube of lipstick. The section next to her body held the important things. She opened the zipper and felt inside. Driver's license, keys, cell phone. All there. Along with her Beretta Tomcat.

Her ring! Memory flooded back. When she noticed the loose stone, she slipped the ring into her fanny pack. The second time she unzipped the outer pocket to add a tip, her ring almost went to the floor. The other section was out of the running. She'd fashioned a slit in the seam large enough for her finger to slide through and hook around the Beretta's trigger. So she took her ring straight to Charlie, who put it in the bottom of the cash register for her.

Shouts from firefighters rose above the deep rumble of fire engines. She had done all she could. The pros were here now, and the fire was their baby. She turned her head in the direction of the loudest noise and opened her eyes enough to peer through her lashes. Christ, she was lying in the middle of the parking lot. She might as well have a target painted on her chest. As soon as Ana untethered her from the oxygen supply she was out of here.

A pair of firefighter boots stepped from behind her head and blocked her view. They continued past and stopped in front of Ana. Summer's gaze traveled up from the boots and fixed on the back of a helmet. Ana's lips moved, but she spoke too softly for her to hear. Infuriating.

A mosquito buzzed her ear, and she brushed it away. Someone else could be its dinner. For now, no one paid her much attention, at least not from this direction. Flames lit the sky, joined by knotty fingers of black smoke against the royal blue of early night. Firefighters worked everywhere pulling yellow hoses that slithered across the parking lot.

She hadn't coughed in at least a full minute, so Ana should remove the oxygen mask before long. Soot covered her arms. Probably her face, too. What a mess. The black soot had covered her eyes and lungs. She tasted it in her throat. Too bad the firemen couldn't hose her down, inside and out.

The familiar apathy returned. She hated it, wanted to kick it away, drown it in the sea. But no matter what she tried, it remained. Short-lived panic jumped up from time to time, but fear, love, anger—she hadn't felt any of them since she killed the man who murdered her father.

She wanted nothing more than to feel again. Really feel. Anything. To care beyond surface sensibilities and sexual desire. To lose herself in emotion, have it wash over her and carry her away. Instead, a black hole sucked at her humanity and left her an empty shell.

Ana broke away from the fireman and walked toward her. "Let's see how you do." She bent and removed the mask.

Summer inhaled smoke-tinged air.

"If you're all right in about five minutes, you're good to go. If the cough returns or you get hoarse or have shortness of breath, see your doctor. Same if you notice any headache or confusion, or if your eyes go haywire."

She sat up. "Got it." Her voice sounded almost normal, just a little rough around the edges. Better to sit and see than lie flat and be exposed.

"Here. Scoot back. Lean against this old palm for a few minutes. You'll be fine."

The tree at her back was even better. No news crews had arrived yet, but they would. At least the goo provided a little camouflage. While Ana packed her gear, the other firefighter crouched in front of Summer.

Good God! What a hunk. Better than the photos on the firefighter calendar one of her girlfriends had given her, back when she still had a real life. His face was all planes and angles, with a straight nose and the sexiest brown eyes she'd ever seen.

"Ms. Newcombe, I understand you're the hero of the day. I'm Captain Duran."

"Duran? Like Charlie?" The name couldn't be a coincidence.

Ana stood. "See you back at the station, Cap."

The firefighter nodded. "Charlie Duran's my father. I'd like to talk to you about tonight, if you feel up to it."

She would talk to him any day. "Hero might be a little out there. More like fool. I thought I had time to retrieve Charlie's cash register."

A gust of wind blew smoke over them, and she coughed.

"Are you all right?" He lifted her chin to check her face, concern for her evident in his eyes.

She cleared her throat. "Fine. I'd wrestle a shark for water." His fingers lingered on her chin.

He yelled to Ana and mimicked a drinking motion. His hand was muscled and lean. Ana nodded, and the fire captain turned back to her.

"No need to wrestle a shark. And Charlie would've rescued his receipts himself if he thought they were important enough. I haven't talked to him yet, but Ana said she had to hold him back to keep him from going in after you. It was a foolish attempt." The smile in his eyes belied his harsh words.

The smile spread to his lips. Laugh lines at the corners of his eyes deepened to give extra dimension to his face. "You more than made up for any foolishness, though, by saving six lives first. Whatever possessed you to go back inside?"

"Why not? Charlie's been wonderful to me. I wanted to do something for him. It only took seconds to grab the register. But the heat and smoke . . . I didn't realize it could happen so fast." She couldn't tell anyone how much the ring meant.

"Always get out. Never go back."

A shiver passed along her spine. He might have been talking about the past five years of her life. She'd become expert in getting out because she could never go back.

Ana arrived with the water.

"Thanks for still taking care of me." She couldn't unscrew the top quick enough. While she drank, Ana waved goodbye. Summer emptied the bottle and turned to Charlie Duran's son. "And thank you, too. I feel better already. What did you want to ask?"

He nudged his helmet back from his forehead with his thumb. "Tell me about the few minutes before you noticed the fire. Did you see or hear anything suspicious?"

A Corpus Christi patrol car pulled to a stop a few feet away, reminding her that this section of the island was part of the city. The officer jumped out, flung on a fluorescent green traffic vest, and grabbed a Maglite. As he trotted back to the highway, the steady *whup-whup-whup* of a helicopter grew in intensity. She glanced up expecting to see the familiar white and blue Halo Flight chopper, but at the sight of the call sign of a local television station, she ducked her head.

Keeping her face lowered, Summer looked toward the highway. "Traffic out there must be horrible."

"I'm sure. Back to my question. Anything strike you as odd before the blaze erupted?"

She closed her eyes a moment to make sure of what she recalled. "No, nothing unusual. I'd been to the kitchen for chips and salsa. On the way back, a smell—like nail polish remover. Someone must have spilled a bottle in the ladies room, but I never got to check."

He rubbed his jaw. "What else?"

She had a thing for hands, and his turned her on. She'd tried not to notice when he tilted her chin and pushed his helmet back. He was the first man since Joe O'Brien who roused more than a physical attraction in her. Even here in the open she felt safer with him at her side.

"Ms. Newcombe? Are you all right?"

She forced her gaze from his hands. "Sorry. I was lost in thought. What did you ask?"

"If anything struck you odd immediately prior to the fire. You told me about the nail polish remover and not having time to check it out."

"The closer I got to the dining area, smoke replaced the polish remover. But it wasn't mouth-watering, like from fajitas."

"Can you describe the odor?"

"Repulsive. Like a bad experiment in chemistry lab."

He laughed and pulled out a black notebook before frown lines formed on his forehead.

She hadn't known Charlie Duran long, but he'd never spoken about a son. Now that she knew he had one, why he hadn't talked about his family piqued her interest. But not as much as his son did. The son who called his father Charlie instead of Dad.

"How long did it take for the smoke alarms to go off?"

She slapped at a mosquito on her arm. For a moment, she returned to the fire. She would never forget how it breathed. "They never went off."

"You're sure? Think back."

She closed her eyes again and replayed those few minutes. "No alarms, not even after the place filled with smoke. They're loud. The emergency lights worked, though."

He spoke while writing in the notebook again. "The lights are battery operated. They work anytime the power goes out. Is Charlie still a perfectionist?"

"I've only been here a week, but I do see him every day. Some of the time he's a little obsessive. He likes to look after people. And he wants things to be perfect for them."

Captain Duran's face looked puzzled, as if he just realized she was there. "You got all that in a few days?"

"Impressions. You know how that is." She'd formed instant opinions about people all her life. Over the past five years her intuition had become more accurate. "You don't live on this earth for thirty years and not pick up a few tidbits."

The strange look lingered on his face. "Anything out of the ordinary today?"

"I was waiting when he got here this morning, so we came in together. He turned off the security system and punched the button on the smoke alarm above the register before he put his keys back in his pocket. The alarms blared. Why didn't they work when it counted?"

"The breaker box was near the point of origin. It's possible flames burned through the electric supply line before smoke reached the closest alarm."

He was lying. She knew by the way his gaze skittered from her own.

Still crouched in front of her, he shifted position and stared at her for a few seconds. She probably looked like an overdone cookie with frizzy frosting. He, on the other hand, was no mere firefighter of the month. He was one hundred percent pure cover material. Sheer force of willpower kept her from touching his stubbled cheek.

A coughing fit jerked her back to reality.

He rubbed her back. "Do you need anything? More water?"

She cleared her throat. "I'm good. Charlie's going to be upset those smoke detectors didn't work."

A muscle in his jaw tightened, but he made no comment, confirming her suspicion that there must be a reason they didn't work. Like someone cut the line. Or flipped off the breaker.

"Did you have reason to go outside any time after six?"

He was asking if she'd had the opportunity. Good. He was smart and didn't take things at face value. "No. Happy Hour starts at five. We're busy from then till close."

Another gust of wind blew the stench of burned plastic and electrical components into her face. She twitched her nose, trying to rid it of the odor.

He lifted his helmet long enough to run his fingers through short dark hair that was as wet as if he'd just stepped from a shower. Then he was all business again. "Any customer exhibit overt nervousness or inappropriate behavior?"

"No."

"How about a disgruntled customer or employee?"

"My tables were good. I didn't hear any complaints. Best I could tell, people were happy. Customers and staff. Lots of laughing. Is it all right if I stand up?"

He stood and offered his hand. "Sure, but hold on to me for a minute in case you get dizzy."

His hand was as strong and muscular as it looked. She didn't let go. Standing, the top of her head stopped just beneath his chin. He wore boots; she, sandals. If this were a romance novel—and she'd read a lot of them—she'd think about how her heart beat faster at the touch of his skin, the roughness of his coat, the rise and fall of his chest with each breath. And how her belly quivered at his nearness. But she couldn't let herself be carried away. Romance could never enter her life. Even if the firefighter was the God of Fire in the flesh.

At the sound of a horn, they both looked toward the highway. Two blondes in bikinis straddled a black Harley and waved at the crowd. When a firefighter several yards away waved, Captain Duran shook his head. "I need to talk to that rookie before he gets hurt."

"Friends of yours?" Summer asked, a half smile playing on her face.

"Not my type."

"Let me guess . . . wife and kiddies at home."

"Just me. And a firehouse cat."

"So what is your type?"

"Blondes whose hands fit perfectly in mine."

She glanced at their clasped hands before looking at him. "I see. Tall, dark, and strong has always worked for me."

"It's okay to hold on for a while. For support, of course."

"Of course." She made no effort to remove her hand from his. "The world was spinning for a minute, but it's stopped."

"Good. Think you can walk? A family over there wants to say thank you."

"Sure." She took a step. Two. Her knees buckled.

He stepped in front of her and grabbed her other arm. "Whoa. Stand still a little longer. Give your body a bit more time to equalize. I'll hold on to you."

She leaned against him. He was as strong as the old oak she'd climbed as a girl. She rested her hands at his waist and closed her eyes. Despite his earlier denial, he probably had a sexy girlfriend who'd be more than a little upset to see them standing together as they were. At the thought, her eyes popped open.

Firefighters tended to hoses that appeared stretched in every direction possible. From somewhere out of her view, a male voice shouted for someone to start checking for hot spots. Hot spots. That was a good one. That's how she felt snuggled against this man—like a hot spot waiting to break into flame. She had to stop this line of thought because nothing could ever happen between them.

The helicopter hovered aft of the ruins. At any moment, the camera person would decide they had enough aerial footage, the pilot would land, and she'd be news. Not something the Federal Witness Security Program encouraged. She had to leave.

"Let's try this again. Never had such a time getting my sea legs before." She smiled when she completed her circle around him.

"Smoke and heat take a lot out of you."

"I think I'm fine this time." She ran her fingers along the name patch on the front of his coat. "I don't even know your name. Besides Captain, I mean."

"Gabriel. Everyone calls me Gabe."

Her knees almost buckled again from the force of the smile he turned on her. Holy God in Heaven. How would she have the strength to resist this man? She pulled some strands of composure out of the air and held onto them for dear life. "Nice to meet you, Gabe."

Another firefighter jogged up. "'Scuse me, Cap. Broussard wants you at the back."

"He say why?"

"Said he found the point of ignition. And you weren't going to like it."

Gabe's mouth narrowed to a straight line and his eyes hardened. "Tell him I'll be right there."

Perfect timing for her getaway.

He turned back to her. "Are you going to be all right?"

She nodded. "I'm going home. And I'm going to try to get clean."

"Don't forget the family who wants to talk to you. Go see Ana before you leave. She'll be happy to know you're good. Tell her I said to give you a plastic bag to use over your car seat so you don't get soot all over it."

What the hell. She stood on tiptoe and kissed his cheek. "Thank you."

"Watch out!" Gabe pulled her to him.

She looked where she'd stood. A lime-green Volkswagen was backing in their direction, trying to turn around in the tight space.

Gabe slapped his palm hard on the VW's trunk, and the driver slammed on the brakes.

"Sorry!" The man waved a hand out his window, inched forward, and maneuvered around the police car.

Summer pulled her nerves back inside and smiled. "Thanks for not letting him run over me."

Before he could answer, something tore through the fronds of the palm and bounced off the top of the patrol car. A small black box hit the pavement and rolled end over end for several yards. It must have come from the news chopper because the sound from above was a godawful banging roar.

She looked up in time to see the tail rotor fly off like a crazed Frisbee. The next thing she knew, she was on the ground and Gabe was on top of her.

Books by Carol Kilgore

Solomon's Compass

In Name Only

Available at Amazon

in Paperback and Kindle

3478937R00206

Made in the USA
San Bernardino, CA
09 August 2013